THE SEVEN HILLS OF PARADISE

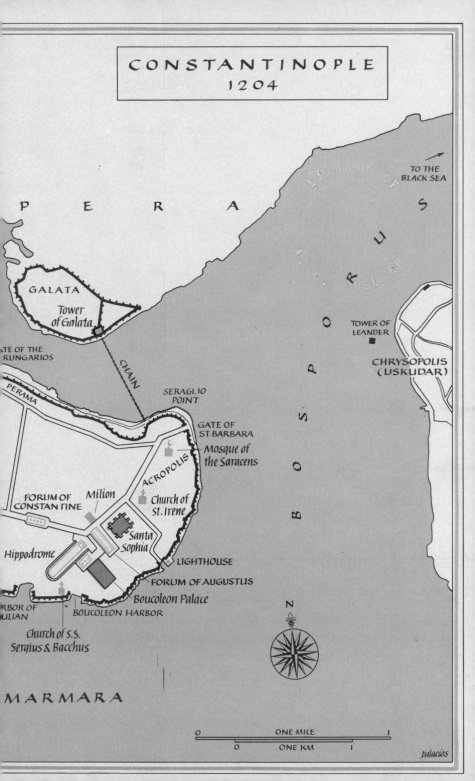

CONSTANTINOPLE
1204

TO THE
BLACK SEA

PERA

GALATA

Tower
of Galata

ATE OF THE
RUNGARIOS

CHAIN

PERAMA

SERAGLIO
POINT

GATE OF
ST. BARBARA

Mosque of
the Saracens

ACROPOLIS

FORUM OF
CONSTANTINE

Milion

Church of
St. Irene

Santa
Sophia

Hippodrome

LIGHTHOUSE

FORUM OF AUGUSTUS

Boucoleon Palace

RBOR OF
ULIAN

BOUCOLEON HARBOR

Church of S.S.
Sergius & Bacchus

MARMARA

BOSPORUS

TOWER OF
LEANDER

CHRYSOPOLIS
(USKUDAR)

N

0 — ONE MILE — 1
0 — ONE KM — 1

palacios

THE
SEVEN
HILLS
OF
PARADISE

Rosemary Simpson

DOUBLEDAY & COMPANY, INC.
GARDEN CITY, NEW YORK
1980

Library of Congress Cataloging in Publication Data

Simpson, Rosemary, 1942–
The seven hills of paradise.

1. Crusades—Fourth, 1202–1204—Fiction.
I. Title.
PZ4.S61463Se [PS3569.I516]   813'.54
ISBN 0-385-15775-4
Library of Congress Catalog Card Number 79–8439

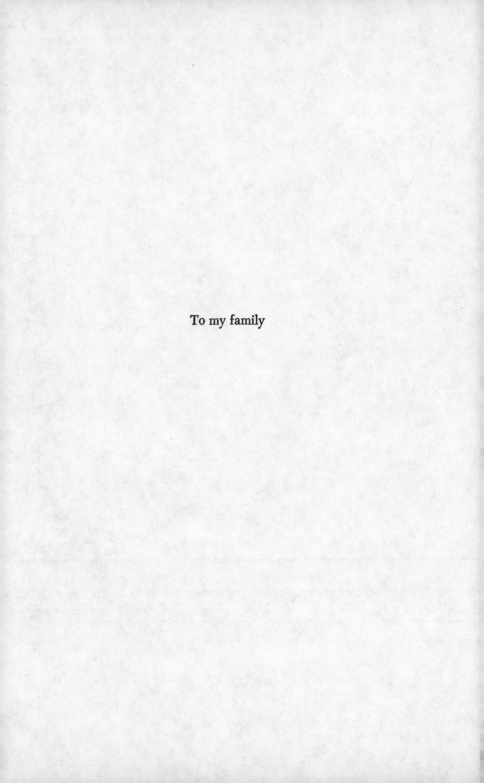

To my family

THE SEVEN HILLS OF PARADISE

PROLOGUE

"Know that eleven hundred and ninety-seven years after the In-
carnation of Our Lord Jesus Christ, in the time of Innocent,
Pope of Rome, and Philip, King of France, and Richard, King of
England, there was a holy man in France whose name was Fulk
of Neuilly . . . And this Fulk of whom I tell you began to speak
of God throughout France . . . and Our Lord performed many
miracles through him. The fame of this holy man spread to
Rome and Innocent commanded him to preach the cross by his
authority . . . All who would take the cross and serve God for a
year in the host would be absolved of all the sins they had committed and confessed to. And because this indulgence was so
great, many hearts were moved, and many took the cross.

"One year after the worthy Fulk began to preach, there was a
tournament held in Champagne, at a castle named Ecri; and by
the grace of God Thibaut, Count of Champagne and Brie, took
the cross, and also Count Louis of Blois and Chartres, and this
was at the beginning of Advent. Know that this Count Thibaut
was a young man, not more than twenty-two years of age; Count
Louis was not more than twenty-seven . . . With these two
counts also took the cross many noble barons of France . . . At
the beginning of Lent, on Ash Wednesday, Count Baldwin of
Flanders and Hainault took the cross at Bruges, and also the
Countess Mary, his wife, who was the sister of Count Thibaut of
Champagne . . .

"Afterward the barons met in parliament at Soissons to decide
when they would depart and where they would go . . . Many
opinions were given and heard; but the end result of the council
was the decision to send out envoys, the best that could be
found, with full powers to negotiate, as if they were the lords
themselves . . . The envoys of Count Thibaut were Geoffrey of
Villehardouin, the Marshal of Champagne, and Miles the Brabant; the envoys of Count Baldwin were Conon of Béthune and

Alard Maquereau; the envoys of Count Louis were John of Friaise and Walter of Gaudonville. To these six the affair was committed, to such a degree that they gave them sealed charters attesting that they would hold firm to all the agreements that these six would make in all seaports, wherever they might go. Thus were the six envoys sent, as you have heard, and they counseled together; and their counsel was that in Venice they thought to find a greater number of vessels than in any other port. And they rode daily until they arrived there in the first week of Lent."

La Conquête de Constantinople
by Geoffroy de Villehardouin
(AUTHOR'S TRANSLATION)

PART
I

January, 1201–June, 1202

Let he who would not live disgraced
Come forward joyously to die for God.
For the death which conquers Paradise
Is exquisitely sweet.
Not one of these souls will truly die;
All will live in Glory Everlasting.
And he who returns, he who does not die,
Will be forever wed to Honor.

—Chanson de croisade
Conon of Béthune

I

January, 1201

So much snow had fallen that winter that by the Feast of the
Three Kings the roads were nearly obliterated and the hills and
valleys around Nanteuil had become as softly contoured as
cloud banks. The midday sun shone blindingly bright, but the
air was too coldly sharp to breathe without pain and the drifts
had been piled so high by the recent storm that a man or
woman on foot would have found them impassable.

Tiny wisps of gray smoke hung above the huts of those bound
to the land; the fires within were being fed one stick or twig at a
time. What fuel there was could not be wasted on heat; it had to
be hoarded for the desperate business of coaxing a handful of
grain to swell and soften in the pots filled with melted snow. Old
and young, male and female, they huddled together beneath
ragged blankets, the dirt on their bodies, the coarse woolen
clothing that barely hid their nakedness and the straw in which
they lay their only defense against the freezing cold. Many
would die before spring; their bellies were emptier than those of
the deer who stripped the bark from the trees, their hovels neither as warm nor as secure as the burrows into which the small
furry creatures of the forest had scurried when the first heavy
flakes began to fall.

The cold was piercing even in the stone tower that guarded
the roadway and the bend in the river. Ice had formed in every
mortared joint of the walls, it lay in dangerously slippery
patches in the exact center of each of the hundred steps that spi-
raled upward to the flat, circular roof on which the watch was

posted, it had made a layer two inches deep in the only well on
the hill, and in the niche that served as chapel the vial of Jordan
water was frozen solid.

There was no shortage of food or wine in the tower, however.
There they were better provisioned against the winter than at
any time in the past thirty years, and small mountains of logs
and kindling wood were stacked in the deep pit that was both
foundation, storeroom, prison cell and a terrible place to die no
matter what the season. Aboveground, a fire burned night and
day in the single large room that was hall, kitchen, living and
sleeping quarters for the lord and his family, and another,
smaller fire hissed and crackled in the chamber just under the
roof. The sentry paused for a few moments each time he crossed
the spot, welcoming a feeble warmth from below that momentarily softened the stiff leather of his shoes and set his chil-
blained toes to tingling. For days nothing had moved through the
whiteness that made an island of the tower, no animal or human
life had dared approach the wooden palisade, and though
wolves occasionally howled in the distance and would eventually be driven from the forest by the force of their hunger, the
villeins would choose to die quietly in their huts rather than beg
a boon from the lord of Nanteuil.

The deep snow muffled sound. It swallowed up the neigh of a
horse feeling cold steel rammed between its teeth, deepened the
treble of the voice that coaxed and commanded, sent only the
faintest echo of prancing hooves against the base of the tower
and reduced the creak of the palisade gate to the merest suggestion of movement. When the rider burst through the gate and
came into the sentry's line of sight he crossed himself, thankful
that the successful assault had been made from within. And then,
since only the young Lady Anne rode a horse that was as black
as her hair, he crossed himself again. No one else loved the Lady
Marie enough to try to reach the priest; only her full-blood sister
would defy their half brother and risk valuable horseflesh in the
attempt.

Because he was a practical man, the sentry quickly said a
prayer for his own death. He prayed that it would come in
spring or summer or early autumn; he had no family that he
could remember and certainly none of the women with whom he

bedded would do more than close his eyes and rifle through his pouch when he was gone. He watched as the stableboy came running to relatch the gate, signed to him to return to the heat of his beasts and then walked back to where the snow had melted. He had no orders to stop the Lady Anne; it was sufficient to have taken notice of her leaving and to keep warm and alert enough to warn of her return.

Halfway down the sloping base of the hill, Anne slowed her horse to a walk. The animal was precious to her, the last feast-day gift she had received from her dead father, and Marie, though she had been spitting blood and was too weak to raise her head, had nevertheless promised to live until Father Antoine brought the viaticum. Her sister had assured her that there was no pain at all to this manner of dying, nor was there any great reason for haste.

"It may be days yet before it's over," Marie had said, "yet I would feel comforted to confess soon. I drift into sleep so often, and each time I find it harder to awaken."

Thierri, their brother, had ignored the quiet plea. Still sodden with last night's drinking, he had already commanded another cask to be tapped. So many of his waking hours had been spent like that for so many years that Anne had long ago ceased to feel anything but disgust for him. Marie had never felt his fist crashing against her jaw, had never known that his fingers could twist and pinch soft flesh until it turned blue, had never, because she had been ill for a very long time, felt his eyes hating the strength and agility of legs that could mount a horse when his could not. Marie, pious and weak, still pitied and loved the man who was more than twenty years older than she and shared only half her blood. Anne, because she was healthy and had grown into beauty, was also his chosen victim, and she knew that Thierri was crippled in more than body. His soul was like the bread dough she had once left too long on the board; it had rotted where it should have risen, turned in upon itself to consume the few bubblings of hope that faith might have nourished, soured finally until the self-hatred became abuse of all those unable to protest or resist.

Once, long ago, there had been a winter nearly as bad as this one, but none of Nanteuil's people had died of either hunger or the cold. The old lord, Anne's father, had placed her on the saddle in front of him and instructed her in duty and charity as he rode from hut to hut in the village, urging his peasants not to lose heart, promising that a family in dire need had only to come to the tower to be given a measure of food and all the wood a husband or father could carry away in his arms. Anne remembered seeing them climb the hill, dozens of men and women struggling weakly through the snow. Whether they were truly grateful for what they received she did not know; no one could read a villein's closed face, least of all the master who owned him.

Thierri had been openly scornful of their father's gesture. "They breed like hares anyway," he had said. "What good does it do us to save the weak?" And this winter, the first truly severe one since the old lord's death, he was making no effort to do so. If anything he rejoiced in having read the signs aright, congratulated himself on his foresight and cared not a whit that he had forced all who labored for him to remain so long in his fields that the harvest from their own small plots was far too meager to sustain them. He was determined that they would get no help from the tower, and after eight long years of his rule they knew him well enough to expect none. It was a sad state of affairs, but not an uncommon one. There were many lords far crueler than Anne's brother.

Father Antoine stood waiting for her on the porch of his church, the oils for the anointing of the dying wrapped in a piece of thick wool to keep them liquid. He had used them once today already, on a child who had died suckling its mother's empty breast. The woman had been too stolid to grieve for her loss; she had gnawed hungrily on the crust of bread that was all the priest could spare from his own depleted larder, gulping it down noisily while he prayed for the dead infant and the other children in the hut stared at what their mother would not share with them.

Hard times brought out the worst in most people; their faith was shallow at best and many poor souls possessed it not at all. The Lady Marie was different. Her death would be a peaceful one, an exemplary Christian rendering up of life. Sitting beside

her as she left this world would do much to soothe his own soul;
even old priests needed to be reminded from time to time that
there was true joy in going home to God.

"I was on my way to return these to the sacristy when I recognized your horse," Father Antoine said. There was no need to
ask why she had come for him. "Will he carry double weight?
My mule disappeared five days ago."

"Are the people that hungry?"

"The beast was more hair and bone than meat, but yes, they
are that hungry."

"And you, Father?"

He shrugged his thin shoulders and smiled at the youthful
earnestness of the question. "It's not good for a priest to get as
fat as a monk," he said simply, "and when you're as old as I am
you find fasting not nearly as difficult as it once was." He understood the clouded look that came into Anne's eyes and knew she
was thinking of Marie, who would never grow any older. "If you
bring the horse over beside that low wall I'll be able to get up
behind you," he added softly, "though I think that even then
you'll have to give me a hand."

Father Antoine, at well past fifty, weighed less than eighteen-
year-old Anne. Her strong arm pulled him up as easily as if he
were a child, and the horse, its nose turned homeward, cantered
eagerly along the narrow track it had beaten down through the
snow.

"She's on her way back, Thierri, and the priest is with her."

His wife's heavily pregnant body blocked the heat of the fire
and he snarled at her to move away. She wrapped the cape of
rabbit skins more tightly around herself and did as she was told.
Jeanne was clubfooted and disfigured by a large red birthmark
that covered half her face; the lord of Nanteuil was the only
husband her father had been able to procure for her. She spent
her days trying to please him, hiding her hatred under cringing
servility, for at night she was obliged to share the bed in which
he had lain for nearly all his adult years, and though his legs
were paralyzed and withered, his arms and shoulders were as
strong as any normal man's. There were things he could force
her to do that were too obscene for word or thought; the silent

struggle sometimes lasted for hours. He would not be denied the exercise of the last vestige of manhood that remained to him, and even in her hard-gotten pregnancy he did not spare her. In the two years since she had become his wife she had learned more about pain and humiliation than in all the terrible years of her childhood.

For decency's sake Jeanne dipped a cloth in the bucket of drinking water and washed the blood from Marie's lips. Her sister-in-law's pallet was in the coldest corner of the room, at so great a distance from the fire that there were droplets of ice on the wall beside it. While there had been some hope that she might live and while Father Antoine had been a frequent visitor Thierri had allowed Marie to lie close beside him, but when the coughing suddenly grew so deep and rattling that the noise of it kept him awake in spite of his wine, he had ordered her placed as far away as was possible.

Father Antoine would have some very bitter things to say about this new proof of the lord of Nanteuil's callousness. His love for Marie was almost as deep as his love of Christ, and far more vulnerable. He had baptized her, consented to the vow by which her father had consecrated her to the service of the Holy Mother and been largely responsible for the nurturing of her soul and her vocation. Had Thierri not refused to release the remainder of Marie's dowry the priest would have escorted her to the convent at Soissons years ago, before the illness had eaten its way into her lungs. But as soon as the old lord died, his son had found better uses for the money.

It cost more to marry a girl off than to make a nun of her, so Thierri had allowed the matter to slide from year to year, periodically writing the Abbess that he would soon be ready to honor his father's promise to God and her house. The Abbess had pointedly informed him that the younger the girl the easier she was to train for the religious life, but she had not offered to return the half of the dowry that had already been paid.

Jeanne had been considered too worthless to be educated in reading and writing, but she was clever, and now that the term of her pregnancy was nearly over, she had planned a future from which Thierri and Anne were both to be excluded. She herself had been so eager to escape from the father who

blamed her for having been born deformed that she had consented to marry a man no other woman would have. Anne, bereft
of her fragile confidante and only source of affection, would be
even more desperate to leave the home that was in many ways
worse than a prison. Experience had taught Jeanne that once
given, it was harder to wrest money back from the Church than
from a Lombard banker; far better to complete the transaction
and send Anne to Soissons in her sister's place.

It would not be difficult. Jeanne believed she had only to
point out to her husband that the cruelest thing he could do to a
girl who found her greatest pleasure in riding the hills would be
to shut her up for life behind walls from which there was no
possible escape. Thierri's own flesh gave him no peace. She
would suggest to him how gratifying he would find it to know
that Anne's would never be satisfied, that the full breasts she
had grown these past few years would be tortured by a tight-
fitting shirt of hair, that the long, perfect legs that flashed
whitely whenever she leaped bareback onto her horse would
soon become rheumatic and deformed from hours of kneeling on
stone floors. He would consent and he would even pay the
dowry.

Her sister-in-law was not certain why it was so important to
be rid of Anne in this way rather than by marriage, but she had
begun to suspect that any man who came to know her intimately
would eventually find himself in willing thralldom to her body.
When the time came that Jeanne was strong enough to relegate
Thierri to the corner in which Marie now lay, or to his grave,
she wanted no interference, no stranger to push his wife's claim
to Nanteuil on the entirely believable grounds that a paralyzed
man could not possibly have sired children. Her sworn oath that
she had come virgin to her husband's bed and conceived no
child that was not his would carry no weight at all in any
bishop's court. God often afflicted His creatures with infirmities
that were nearly unbearable, but the Devil also marked his own.
When it was a woman who was deformed or blemished the men
who judged her remembered that the first woman to betray a
man had succumbed all too easily to the lure of the Unholy One.
Never having known justice, Jeanne expected none.

There was not a single human being under Thierri's thumb

who would not welcome the day on which the lady of Nanteuil
wrested control of the region from him in the name of her son.
She had never given them reason to suspect that she might be as
harsh and unyielding a mistress as he was a master. Pray God
the babe leaping in her womb was a boy. But if she had to, if all
the candles she had lit and the coins she had parted with failed,
if this child were a girl, she would find it a wet nurse in the village and as soon as the birth bleeding ceased climb back into
her husband's bed and see that new seed was quickly planted.

He had come to this tower hundreds of times since Thierri's
accident, but Father Antoine had never gotten used to the sight
of the person the once handsome young knight had become. Because he was a priest it was his duty to pray for Thierri's soul,
and because he understood that the decay of that soul had
begun with the injuries to the body that housed it, he also
prayed daily for the miracle of a cure. His petition had changed
very little in all the twenty years that he had been making it, except that after the old lord's death he had begun to plead that
the miracle be granted for the sake of three immortal souls. The
mercy of God was unfathomable; Marie would return to Him as
spotless and innocent as at the moment of her baptism, but the
priest knew that for Anne he would double both his hours of
prayer and the penances and mortifications with which he
sought to make them more efficacious. In all the world that child
who was already a woman would soon have no living friend but
him.

"They moved her pallet three days ago. She's lying nearly
under the staircase now."

It was the first time Anne had spoken since leaving the
church. She had helped Father Antoine dismount and followed
him across the yard to the tower door before being able to
force the words out, not wanting him to see her face when she
told him. The venom in her voice was proof of a greater sin than
any curse she could have uttered.

Before he could trust himself to say either a prayer or an oath,
she had brushed swiftly past him and opened the door. It was
like a scene from hell; only the dancing, fork-tailed devils were
absent.

The windowless tower had been built to withstand attack; its lower story was lit only by the bright red and yellow flames of the two logs burning in the fire pit. At one end of the shallow hole a caldron had been suspended over a bed of glowing coals and beside it a piece of meat hung from a spit. The heavy odor of old venison was strong, but stronger still were the smells of unwashed flesh and the unemptied waste pot left in plain sight at the foot of Thierri's bed.

It was always a shock to find that article of furniture in the very center of the common hall. In other manor towers, even smaller and more crowded with life than this one, the lord and his lady slept and made love in a curtained alcove where the sight of what they did together was hidden though the sound of it could not be. But Thierri, when he came into his inheritance, had had the bed in which he and his two half sisters had been conceived pulled from its place of relative privacy, the hangings taken down and burned, the tall posts onto which they had been fastened chopped off and the mutilated object he had made more Roman couch than properly Christian retreat set up again where no one, asleep or awake, could possibly be unaware of it. He would no longer lie on a pallet like a child or a servant, nor would he allow himself to be tied into a cushioned chair.

He began to rule Nanteuil as he intended to go on governing it, making himself and the couch on which he lay the center of all tower life and the court before which his villeins stood with bowed heads and trembling lips, looking only when commanded to do so at the often unshaven, often drunk, always frightfully scarred and implacably cruel face of the man who judged and punished them. When Jeanne came to live with the devil and share his bed they named her the devil's lady and they pitied her, but they also made the sign against the evil eye when he filled her belly.

She was very near the time to give birth, Father Antoine judged, her habitual clumsiness grotesquely accentuated by the swollen breasts rolling and shifting above the hard mound that had dropped considerably lower since the last time he had seen her. He had known many cases in which sound and even handsome children issued from the wombs of diseased or ugly women, and because he had been a good priest for so long that charity of thought was now an intrinsic part of his nature, he prayed that it might be so with her.

He had lost sight of Anne in the room that was a dark circle with flame at its center, but now, looking toward the spot where the stone steps began their upward climb, he saw her white, stricken face, so bleached and lifeless that it might have been a pale oval moon at which he gazed.

"Marie is dead," Anne said dully. "She has ice on her lips."

Only Father Antoine moved. Only he of the four people in the hall made the sign of the cross. Jeanne remained bent over the haunch of venison, turning the spit with mechanical precision; Thierri merely grunted and continued to stare into the fire.

Neither of them is surprised, the priest thought as he hurried to anoint the body in which the soul might still be lingering. Neither of them cares. He knelt beside Marie and placed his hand over her empty blue eyes. The last tears she had shed were frozen to her eyelashes. Tears of anguish that he had not reached her in time? They melted under his fingers and the lids came down.

He had said the prayers for the dead so often that he no longer needed to think about them. He wept as he warmed the vials of blessed oil in his hands, but he was weeping alone. Anne had moved one step away from the priest and her sister's stiffening corpse. She was standing quite still, hands clenched at her sides, breathing in quick, shallow gasps like one who has come to the end of a race, the blue eyes that were so like Marie's fixed like stone or ice on the relaxed, reclining figure of her brother.

Three weeks later Father Antoine returned to the tower to baptize Jeanne's child. The snow was still too deep to risk carrying a fourteen-day-old infant to the church, and although the boy was as likely to live as any other bit of animal life born at the wrong season, the saints would be slow to respond to the prayers said on his behalf until he was made a Christian. There would be no feast to complete the ceremony, no largess of wine and meat distributed to the villeins of Nanteuil, nothing in fact but the sprinkling of water on his head and the single Latin sentence to miraculously transform him into a child of God. The priest knew that only the sacrament itself mattered, but he sighed neverthe-

prayers they mouthed. She would bungle the job if he chose to be obstinate, pour the water at the wrong moment, produce a gabble of syllables that might mean anything or nothing, and he could not be certain that her heart's intention would be pure enough to make such a parody of ritual valid.

He cleansed his mind of Anne, emptied his soul of all but priestly concentration on this most important of the sacraments and purified another soul as solemnly as if the child were being held over a cathedral font. The unfocused eyes flew open when cold water dripped onto his forehead, and a loud wail proclaimed that the devil within him had fled. Jeanne suckled him briefly, then tucked him back into his cradle and busied herself pouring wine into three pewter cups.

They drank the infant's health, Father Antoine sipping cautiously because he had eaten nothing since the day before, Thierri gulping the wine down as if it were no stronger than the milk his child had been given. Jeanne refilled his cup and placed two stools beside his bed.

The warmth from the fire melted the cold of the priest's bones, and for a few moments he was content to sit there with hands held out to the flames, at rest and at peace because it seemed just possible that the birth of a son might be the miracle he had prayed for. Perhaps now Thierri might begin to mellow, might accept his paralysis and bear it resignedly because of the gift of a babe who would, please God, grow as straight and tall as he himself had once been.

Father Antoine had a weakness for children, his favorite and most frequent meditation being contemplation of the innocent face of the Divine Child before He grew to manhood and approached the Cross. It pained him to remember that many children were more often abused and unloved than cherished, but his lonely and dedicated old heart had already given itself to this new babe, and he would somehow, without neglecting the other souls to whom he ministered, find time every week in all the years to come to be with the boy and teach him to grow in grace while others taught him the arts of war.

He didn't remember having drunk all his wine, but Jeanne was lifting the pitcher from the floor and pouring more of the deep purple liquid into his cup. He should ask for a mouthful of bread or a piece of cheese to accompany it; there was no shame in admitting hunger. So as not to upset the balance of his lord's temper by seeming to reproach him, he could mention a private fast. His mind was muddled by the fumes rising from his belly; he could not recall the feast today nor whether its importance in the liturgical calendar demanded abstinence.

"My father discharged many half-forgotten debts when I was born," Thierri was saying. "It beggared him for a few years to do so all at once, but at the coming of an heir a knight must not count his coins as closely as a miser."

"Your people will bless you for relieving their misery," Father Antoine said, one hand already rising of its own accord to make the sign. "So many are near death that I must labor night and day over their souls. They are ignorant and tempted to despair."

"I doubt that a villein has a soul," Thierri answered sharply, "or that if he has it is worth saving."

"My lord is speaking of the person who claims to be his half sister," Jeanne said. It had been an inspired thought to couple bastardy with cupidity, to play on Thierri's touchy pride and to hint that all along he had hated Anne because she was no blood of his. Now he had forgotten in whose brain the lovely doubt had been born. "Drink your wine, Father. The animals are restless in their stalls. We'll have more snow by morning."

Thierri addressed the priest again. "She's a proud and haughty bitch, more like her mother than my father. He was old when he married for the second time; I've often wondered who really sired those girls. You've seen that my son's hair is as light as mine, and I am as blond as my late lord. I remember a certain black-haired bailiff who was hanged for thievery as I recall. And there were no more children, not even suspicion of a pregnancy after that."

Father Antoine was on his feet, his whole body trembling, his mind struggling for clear thought. "I was your father's confessor. He loved his daughters, but he loved his son even more. Would you insult his memory by this slander?" He had meant to shout, to frighten them with the truth of the confessional, but his voice had come out cracked and hollow. Jeanne's strong arm pulled him down onto the stool again. She calmly refilled the cup he

had overturned and held it for him. "Their lady mother was
black-haired," he finished lamely.

"She was. But Jeanne too is dark, yet her true-born son resem-
bles his father."

"Darkness is often stronger than light." He was not certain he
had spoken the words aloud; they were the thoughts of a priest,
not the observations of a midwife.

"So be it. If you can persuade Anne to be obedient to my will
I shall speak no more of bastardy. If she continues to refuse the
life I have chosen for her she will be repudiated. In spite of the
dishonor it will bring to my father's name I will declare her to
be the get of a thief and a whore." The lord of Nanteuil's face
was flushed; his eyes glittered with a malicious delight. "Shall I
turn her out onto the roads or allow her to remain here to service my men and empty the slops?"

The fight went out of the priest. Horror and a terrible sense of
helplessness took its place. There was no doubt in his mind that
Thierri would relish reducing his sister to the most degrading
form of slavery that could be forced on a woman. It was an
abomination, the man himself was an unnatural monster, and
the new mother who sat by his side saying nothing was as vile as
he.

"What life have you chosen for her?"

"I am prepared to allow her dignity, even sanctity, in spite of
her unworthiness," Thierri said pompously. "I have decided that
she shall go to Soissons to be made a nun."

"It's a strict house, one that seldom gives the bishop cause for
concern," Jeanne added complacently. "Her blood being what
we suspect it to be, neither my lord husband nor I could consent
to her marrying. This is as great an act of charity as can be performed under the circumstances."

"The Abbess will see that she is beaten into submission if she
hesitates to be vowed." Thierri licked the spittle from his lips;
one hand was fumbling under the fur robes that covered him,
the other held the cup of wine so tightly that the knuckles whit-
ened.

Father Antoine closed his eyes. He wanted nothing more than
to sleep and dream away this nightmare, but the pressure of
Jeanne's hand on his shoulder was too insistent. To spend one's

years in the service of God was not so bleak a life; he himself
had never imagined he would be a priest until the decision had
been made for him. Why else did the Church allow mothers and
fathers to dispose of their children as they wished, if not to
honor the commandment to obey one's parents? He remembered
now that he had often wept during the period of his training,
but in the end he had found his vocation and his God. Anne's
path would be smoothed by his prayers on her behalf, and
surely Marie, who had earned her heaven hard, would not abandon her sister. He would help Anne to do as he knew she must.

"Where is she?" The place on his shoulder where Jeanne's
hand had lain was as hot as though touched by fire.

"In the pit," Thierri said. "For the past eight days."

Anne had been roused from her cold-induced sleep by the
shrill baptismal wail of her nephew, but the sound registered
only as something other than silent blackness. The stones above
her head were those of the hall floor, so carefully laid that not
even a footstep penetrated to where she lay. There had been a
line of firelight around the wooden trapdoor at first, but someone, probably Jeanne, had thrown a rug or heaps of straw over
it. She had had no way of counting the days and nights, but for
a very long time there had been nothing.

She had bitten her nails to the quick and chewed her lips until
they bled to keep from screaming, but she had neither gone insane nor starved to death, either of which she knew would have
pleased Thierri as much as surrender. Jeanne had set a pitcher
of water and two loaves of bread on the floor, then stood like a
sentinel over her defiant sister-in-law while Thierri's men carried
all the barrels and baskets of stored food up the ladder to the
hall. The casks of wine were too heavy to be moved, but no tool
was left in the pit with which she could have opened them.

"You'll get nothing else until you make up your mind to obey,"
Jeanne had said. Her body was strong and triumphant; childbirth had weakened her no more than it did an ox. Anne had
given her one hard, remembering look and then turned away.
Every pore on the woman's face was impressed on her memory;
she could conjure it up at will in the blackness and cursing it
would sustain her.

"Untie her. She'll need the use of her hands to fight off the rats."

She had shuddered then, but only for a few seconds. Thierri's mocking laugh echoed down into the pit. It was he who had reminded Jeanne to mention the rats, and he had been waiting, as sharp-eared as they, for the sound of the word. The feel of little needle teeth nibbling at toes and fingers and the horrible brush of silky fur against the sensitive skin of the face were always mentioned by prisoners. They did more to inspire fear than the promise of death.

The man who loosed the rope that bound her had fumbled with the knot and bent his head the better to undo it. "Behind the casks," he had whispered. "Salted fish." He jerked the rope sharply. She cried out and then deliberately spat in his face. The sentry whose vigils she had often shared had moved away quickly, his eyes alight at her spirit and skill in playacting, his face screwed up in what passed for anger and disgust.

As soon as her eyes adjusted to the darkness she had crawled along the wall, hands reaching out for the fish he had left her. When she found them, hidden under a scrap of old hide, she had carefully gone back the way she had come, knowing instinctively that if she stood up or ventured out into the center of the pit she would lose all sense of direction and might never, in the panic that was sure to follow, find the water and the bread again. She wrapped the food securely in the old hide, her fingers testing for small open places a rat might smell out. Only then had she allowed herself to lean back against the stone wall and think about what had been done to her.

The flame of the candle in Father Antoine's hand hurt her eyes more than the sudden flood of dimmer light from the open square above. She held up her hand against it, blinking away the dry pain of seeing again, knowing, when the trapdoor fell back into place, that she and the priest were alone.

He dripped wax onto the floor a few paces away from where she sat and fixed the candle into it. One part of his brain was entirely numb, that part which he must force to reason and convince her that to be a nun was better than to be branded a bastard and made a whore of. The other part, where the senses interpreted stimuli as sight and smell, touch, taste and hearing, was preposterously alert. He smelled feces, and he saw that she had relieved herself as a cat does, away from its lair, all in one spot, the stinking mound covered over with straw. The pitcher was protected against thirsty rats by a torn piece of her skirt; a very few drops of water remained in the bottom. There was no evidence of any food left uneaten.

"I knew they would send you to me eventually," Anne said. "Look at me, Father. I've survived very well."

Her lips were scabbed and blue with cold beneath the sores, her face pinched by hunger and paler than Marie's had been in death, her hands as mutilated as her mouth. But the eyes that bore into his soul, the pupils larger and darker than he had ever seen them, were as fiery and alive as the old lord's had been when he talked of battles he had fought and won. In the space of eight days she had grown far older than he, not in body or years, but in spirit, in knowledge of the ways in which life could be distorted or destroyed. The eyes hooded over from within; they were blank now, and impossibly ancient.

"Did they provide you with new arguments to use against me, some lie more inventive than claiming I am not my father's daughter? Perhaps my brother tires of his clubfooted wife and would prefer a sister in his bed."

"Anne, you must not."

"Don't touch me, Father. I'm not a child who can be held and comforted out of its troubles with tears and promises of sweet-meats. Did you know that rats' eyes gleam as red as hot coals even in total darkness? Have you ever had to eat salted fish and then lick the ice from a stone wall to assuage your thirst? Do you know, Father, that to escape from a place like this a person will consent to any crime, embrace any degeneracy, choose even the devil over Christ and believe the exchange a fortunate one?"

"Soissons is not far away. It's strength of will that makes a good nun."

"I know that. I know also that strength of will can accomplish greater things. It can beat back dying even when both the body and the heart yearn for it. It can defeat any man. In this world it is one of the only two weapons a woman has. The other is her body."

She was past caring if she shocked or wounded him, and un-concerned that he might guess her intentions. Father Antoine had ceased trying to change his world or the people who ruled it. He brought his fears and pitiful pleas to the altar, left them there and believed that they were noticed by a God who valued sacrifice and rewarded constancy. He meant well, but he was timid and a fool.

Out of all the memories that had tormented her in darkness she had found not a single one to contradict a very hard truth. Every man she had ever known had betrayed her, even the fa-ther who had loved his vicious son too much to place his daugh-ters in the hands of a kinder guardian. Her sex had made her powerless since the day of her birth. But no longer. She would allow no man to abuse her into death or poison her mind and filthily use her body. All capacity to love, all trust and gentleness had begun to die in her with Marie, but the half of her soul that was her sister had fought fiercely to live. Now that portion of her was dead, as cold as yesterday's ashes. Thierri and the pit had seen to that, and she was glad the battle was over. Her deci-sion had been made days ago, but to have given in then would have been an admission of weakness, something she had excised from her soul as cleanly as a surgeon lances a boil.

"Tell them I consent, that I will leave here today, and that you alone must take me. Soldiers don't matter. He can send as many as he thinks necessary to ensure his commands are carried out. But not Jeanne. I will speak to neither of them ever again."

She was going to Soissons to put on the habit of religion, even take the vows if the months stretched into years. But she would not remain. She would not live and die a victim or a nun. Some-day she would break free.

In the city of Amiens, in Picardy, Aleaumes of Clari requested an interview with his bishop.

"The messenger arrived last night," he said. "My father is on the point of death and I am bidden to his side."

"Then you must go, my son." The bishop was a man of consid-erable years and weight, so grossly fat that his fingers were white and near to bursting, the features of his face all squashed together. His eyes shone out like the plump black raisins of a boiled pudding, but they were shrewd eyes. The crusader's cross was blindingly white against his clerk's black robe.

"Stay at Clari only until your father is laid away, Aleaumes," he said. "When you return we will discuss your future. Every man must undergo a period of trial, and yours, I think, is nearly ended. The writing desks of this chancery have taught you the hard lessons of patience and obedience. Holy Mother Church rewards her faithful sons in this life as well as in the next. There is a stream of upward movement in life into which a man must slip when the current breaks to admit him. The man who has negotiated the flow and ridden it to the prominence of a high bank looks back and sees the eddies, the whirls, the tiny open spaces. He sees the debris that floats on the surface, and he sees too the specks of life which dance and leap and surge along more quickly than the others. Only he can reach out to remove an obstacle, to break the downward round which pulls at a fragment of bark, to lift a twig and put it ahead of its fellows." He paused, loving the sound of his own voice and the image he had conjured up. Years of preaching had made him a master of the art. "I am that man," he said finally, sketching the dismissal blessing over Aleaumes' head. "Go in peace and return in hope."

The road to Clari was a pleasant one that followed the river Somme, and in spite of the urgency and the sadness of his errand, Aleaumes rode it with pleasure. The feel of a good strong horse between his legs set his loins to tingling. His powerful shoulder muscles rippled with holding back the beast who knew that fresh hay and cool water lay at the end of the journey, and the broad uncalloused palms of his hands welcomed the chafing of the reins.

He was twenty-three years old, the younger son of two, a clerk vowed to Christ and celibacy, proficient in Latin and the rituals of the Church, one of many such attached to the cathedral of Amiens, a drone among drones, a restless, unsatisfied man who slept badly, dreamed dreams of fleshly delights and the hard service of knighthood, woke to pace the cloisters and fight back the lure of those dreams, sleep and wake again, a fighter without much heart for the fight in which he was engaged, but a fighter, nonetheless, who would persist until the battle was won. Yet he was worldly enough to know that a day might come when he would gladly accept defeat and see it as a victory.

He hadn't much faith in the bishop's promises, and the carefully constructed image of the river of life had gone out of his head as soon as he had ridden from the cathedral yard. It was skillfully done, he admitted, but the bishop himself was such a venal, disappointing old man that Aleaumes was no longer blinded by hints of expectations that might never be realized. He would promise anything to keep a skilled, well-trained clerk in his chancery. And a clerk whose family was too poor to buy him a living could render devoted, cheap service for years to come.

The bishop had not been pleased when Aleaumes took the cross, and had intimated more than once that he would consent to dispensing him from his obligation. But though he had expressed his gratitude to his superior, Aleaumes had not asked for the dispensation, preferring to wait, as were so many others, for news from Champagne. No one knew exactly when the envoys sent to Venice had set out on their journey; no one knew precisely when they would return. All that was generally agreed upon was that great and powerful lords had received the Count of Champagne's mandate to find a fleet of ships for the army everyone thought of as his. How long it would take to build, equip and supply the vessels was anyone's guess. Only knights who had made the last great voyage to the Holy Land suspected that it could be a year or more before the first of them would sail. Aleaumes, young, impatient, never having seen open waters in his life, scoffed at such pessimism. His good friend Thomas, chanoine of the cathedral, agreed with him.

What Thomas's motives were for taking the cross Aleaumes did not know. But knowing as he did that his own were such a complex tangle of hidden discontents and wantings that it would verge on blasphemy to give them voice, he answered casual inquiries from his fellows with the sign of the cross and the time-honored, time-accepted formula, "To avenge the shame of Christ."

The obligation every Christian felt to liberate the holy places was indeed one of the factors that had influenced his decision. He was honest and sincere in his faith, as honest as he could bear to be about the rest of his life. The accident of being second born had made him an obvious candidate for the priesthood, and while he often envied his elder brother, Robert—the heir, the knight, recently the husband—he could not hate him merely for having preceded him in their mother's womb. He was often hugely amused, however, at the trick that fate and blood had played on both of them.

The brothers were alike in coloring, brown-haired, brown-eyed, somewhat olive of skin, and in the shape of high-bridged nose, sensual mouth and squared-off chin they resembled one another as closely as twins. Even their facial expressions were similar, and both shrugged their shoulders with the same measure of insouciance, an offhand, indifferent-seeming gesture that women found immensely attractive. But to look at them standing side by side or striding along deep in conversation one could only wonder what mischievous patron saint had persuaded the good Lord God to give the one a body so obviously suited to the other.

The knight was tall and slender, well formed in shoulder and hip, a man of sleeping maleness, one felt. Yet, and this one very quickly added, not seeming the type inclined to that particular sin. He was strong and lithe in every part of his body, but the bones of his hands were delicate and fine, and he brooded in an almost gentle, abstract manner wholly unlike the deep, fierce, animal broodings of other knights. At other times his face was so appealing in its withdrawal that one could easily imagine him on his knees before an altar. He was slow to anger, not from an excess of forbearance, but because he did not seem to care to arouse himself, yet when his temper did finally break, he did not redden and shout in the explosively normal way of men bred to war. His dark skin paled, the lips one yearned to kiss were drawn so tautly thin they disappeared, the snap of eyes was black and cold, and the reprimand, the caustic retort, the challenge to defend oneself, was so icily cold and impersonal that one shivered with fear in spite of knowing that he was just a man, and a rather puny-looking one at that. Robert of Clari was twenty-five years old. Women often thought him younger. Most men, his brother among them, found his personality an exasperating blend of ordinary sensuality, occasional naïveté, periods of lassitude and indifference, moments of passionate concern and unpredictable, inexplicable outbursts of cold temper. Robert himself never thought about it at all.

Aleaumes was the one whose body was sculpted for the wearing of armor, the carrying of sword and ax, the hard ram of the lance. A head taller than Robert, he was almost twice as broad in the shoulders, his hands were absurdly large for the handling of a quill or altar vessel, and he pounded along, you could not call it a walk or a stroll, on legs as tough and thick around as the trunks of young pine trees. He had about him all the aura of barely leashed power, the suppressed, bubbling fury, the frightening, titillating cruelty that marked a very few, very famous knights. One wondered for what great sin this warrior was doing penance dressed in a priest's robe. And then the tonsure was seen for what it was, not the thinning out of hair rubbed to the roots by a too-tight helmet, but the deliberate shaving that marked God's own.

The face that turned to meet a curious gaze was handsome, only the spaces between the fine features, the high planes of cheek and forehead making it so different from his brother's. A good-looking face, a face more often animated with the zest of life than not, but in the eyes that did not snap and burn as did Robert's you read deep disappointment, resignation, a devil and an angel warring, the knowledge that here was a man who, whatever it cost him, would be what he must be. He was a clerk, a priest. He should have been a knight. He would be both somehow.

But times were changing. The calls for clerical reform were becoming more and more frequent, were more and more often being answered. A princely bishop, a noble cardinal, could still wear both his vestments and his sword, and most did, for the Church to them was less a vocation than a career. But a misplaced clerk of merely adequate family lineage and no wealth at all could not doff his robes that easily. He could not don armor, carry a sword, ride side by side with men far less physically suited to war than he. There were so many things he was forbidden to do.

He was, however, able to act as chaplain and leech to an army, welcome there for the confessions he would hear, the wills and letters he would write, the wounds he would bind up, the comfort he would bring to departing souls. And if at some perilous moment on campaign in the Holy Land he snatched up a sword or ax and dispatched a Saracen or two, such an act would be almost a prayer in motion.

Aleaumes did not want the regimentation, the awesome discipline and lack of privacy that were the basis of the rule of martial religious orders such as the Templars. He wanted to be away from Amiens and its fat bishop, but honorably and independently so, still a clerk, yes, because he could not betray the vows he had taken of his own free will, but as something more than a clerk, more than a rustling, long-skirted presence in sandals. With all the vagueness of his yearnings gnawing at him, with all the sleepless nights and sweat-soaked dreams disturbing him, with all the unworthy occasional jealousy of his brother increasing his guilt, with some hope for being different, somewhere, anywhere, he took the cross and vowed himself to Jerusalem. He wanted to be free. Decently free. In another land, another world, a place where a war was still being fought that had begun more than a hundred years ago, where things had not changed, where time had virtually stood still.

Some of this he had explained to Robert five months ago, when his brother had married Aelis. It was an odd conversation to be having only four days after the ceremony, odder still that Robert had introduced the subject of the crusade himself.

"For father's sake I held back from taking the cross when my lord Peter did," Robert said quietly. "The interdict imposed by the Pope because of King Philip's divorce made it impossible to marry, and I could not leave until an heir was sired. But now . . ."

"You will come with us?" asked Aleaumes.

"I'll ride back to Amiens with you, and then on to Vignacourt to pledge myself. The marriage is both a fact and a failure."

Aleaumes did not question the statement. Pale little Aelis had never promised much more than her inheritance, and though she had been betrothed to Robert since babyhood, she had never spoken more than a dozen words to him until their wedding day. But because the lands that would be hers on her majority ad-

joined those Robert would inherit, the marriage had been avidly
sought after by Clari's slowly dying master, the knight Gilo.

Several months before the wedding there had been some
quickly disavowed rumors of an attempted withdrawal into a
nearby convent, but as neither Gilo nor his wife, Lady Agatha,
had ever discussed it with him, Aleaumes did not know how
much truth there was to the story. Something about Aelis's having run away in the night, about an abbess who took her in,
calmed her with reassuring promises and a sleeping potion, then
sent for her mother. He had heard servants gossiping about the
beating Lady Maud gave her daughter, and about the bread and
water the girl had lived on for months in a locked tower room
until her will was broken, a room she never left until the day she
rode in a litter to Clari. She could not have been more than fourteen at the time, an hysterical, too-often-indulged only child, he
judged, one of those maidens who swoons at the sight of what a
man carries between his legs. But what a pity for Robert that it
should be so.

"She won't change," Robert said, "not that one. It's best that I
get her with child as quickly as possible. The sooner she is pregnant the sooner we can avoid one another's company. And the
child should be born before we leave."

"Do you think it likely . . . ?"

"In three nights? No, the moon was not right, nor was my lady
properly cooperative. Have you heard men boast about the bed-
ding of their brides, Aleaumes?"

"A few. Those who enjoyed it mightily and those who needed
to hear the story told aloud so as to reassure themselves. Most
make a separation in their minds between their lady and their
whores. For a year or two, at least."

"I fit into neither category then." Robert was silent for so long
that Aleaumes glanced inquiringly at him, the same look which
had often prompted embarrassed sinners to pick up their tales of
wrongdoing and spin them out to the end.

"She fought me at first. The marks of her nails are on my chest
and back. I tried to woo her honestly. I whispered love words, I
was gentle and slow. But while I called her 'sweeting' and 'dove'
and kissed her throat and wound her hair around my fingers, she
held herself stiffly away from me and mumbled Aves in my ear.

I had her pinned beneath me and I held her hands behind her back. What else could I do? She would have clawed my eyes out. That stubbornness angered me, Aleaumes, and the sound of the Aves in my ear was like a call to murder. I slapped her face to silence her, I beat her nearly senseless, and then I mounted her. Our wedding night, the night after and last night too. And if she persists, I'll repeat the performance blow for blow until the day she can tell me she's with child."

It was so like a confession that out of habit Aleaumes crossed himself.

"And I don't repent, brother priest," Robert said firmly. "She won't change, she'll never be decent bed sport, but in time she'll learn to do her duty with good grace, and that's all I want of her. A woman who inherits must expect to marry where her property is most valued. Father and I have helped Lady Maud in her widowhood for years. We've dealt with her villeins and guarded her holdings as securely as our own. The girl and her lands were to be our reward. Well, we have the property now, and I the female part of it. I judge the bargain to be about equal."

Robert of Clari was a hard young man, but no harder nor more bitterly realistic than Aleaumes, and neither as sternly unyielding as the father who lay dying.

Aleaumes' horse had been spotted by the tower guard and he himself recognized, so that as he clattered over the drawbridge that spanned the narrow moat, he saw Robert waiting for him. His brother looked lean and fit, not overly relaxed and slightly paunchy as even younger men were apt to get in the first year of a happy, lust-filled marriage. So the situation had not changed. Impolite though it might be, he decided not to ask immediately about Aelis. If she were pregnant, Robert would tell him soon enough. If not, silence would be more discreet.

"Father seems to have rallied since we sent the messenger to you," Robert said, leading Aleaumes into the hall. "The priest said it was the Sacrament that stopped the bloody flux, but our lady mother claims it was the herbs she got from the witch woman who lives in the cave by the river. Whatever it was, his suffering has eased, and this morning he lay on a pallet in the sunshine for a while. When the fever is not on him he trembles with cold and must have a fire burning hotly beside him."

"In March?" exclaimed Aleaumes. The hall was stiflingly hot, and his dark robes already clung clammily to his back. He paused just inside the door, adjusting his eyes to the gloom.

Gilo lay on a pallet near the central hearth fire, furs and rugs heaped over his thin body. He raised a skeletal white hand to greet his son, then fumbled for the cup that stood on the floor beside him.

"Mother is purifying the sleeping chambers today," explained Robert as he held the cup to Gilo's mouth. "She has all the maids scrubbing and laying fresh rushes and the linen draped over every bush in the garden."

"Damn fool nonsense," said Gilo irritably. "The time to purify is after I'm dead."

"As long as you have the strength to complain you're far from dead, Father," Aleaumes said. Gilo already looked more like a corpse than a living man, but both his sons had seen him like this before. Ever since his return from the Holy Land he had suffered periodically from the bowel sickness contracted at Acre. He had battled it for nine years now, but each bout of illness left him a little thinner, a little weaker than before.

"What news do you bring from Amiens?" Gilo asked, unable to bear the pitying look in Aleaumes' eyes.

"Nothing yet," answered Aleaumes, settling himself comfortably on the floor as far away from the fire as he could get. "My lord Peter sent messengers to St. Pol last week. The Count is as ignorant of what's been decided as the rest of us. There is a rumor, though, that Thibaut of Champagne is ill. A few fools have him dead and laid away already. They're even making wagers on who will succeed him."

"Coeur-de-Lion nearly died a dozen or more times in the Holy Land. I shared the same trench with him more than once when both of us had bowels that were running blood and water. Richard wouldn't let himself die of some womanish sickness and neither will the Count of Champagne. The men who spread stories about the poor state of their commander's health are usually the same men who are as anxious to remove the cross as they were to put it on." Gilo smiled ruefully at the two sons who never minded listening to him reminisce. "It takes years for the bloody flux to kill a strong man."

"I doubt that I'll be fortunate or cursed enough to squat beside Thibaut or any other stricken count or baron," Aleaumes said. "All the clerics are expected to be conspicuously absent once the enemy is engaged, though my lord Peter says that regulation is always the first one broken."

"We're both so low in rank that the greatest lord we shall ever have speech with is Peter, bowels or no bowels."

"War changes things," said Gilo angrily. "Even rank takes on a different meaning in the field. And for a poor man war brings opportunities undreamed of in peacetime. I am ambitious for both my sons. I have little else but my dreams to keep me going now."

"What do you see for us, Father?" asked Aleaumes. He knew that the sick were often soothed by the recounting of the visions that came to them in the delirium of fever. He wondered if Gilo's dreams could possibly match his own.

"Only greatness, Aleaumes." Gilo sank back into his cushions and his voice became stronger as he found the words to describe the images that danced through his brain these days. "For you I dream of a bishopric in the Holy Land. No, don't laugh. Hear me out. You're not boys any longer, and if you've grown to be half the men I think you are you'll see the truth in what I say. The infidels will continue to threaten the Church long after all of us are dead. More than ever the Holy Land will need churchmen who are as at home in armor and on horseback as before their altars. You are such a man, my son, else you would not have taken the cross in the first place. Were your ambition a small and puny thing you had only to remain securely attached to the cathedral, waiting patiently for death to open a place for you higher up in the Church's ranks. But you did not, and so I say that my dream is yours as well."

Aleaumes did not laugh. He had scrupulously hidden his unhappiness from the man who had ordered him to be what he was, yet Gilo had somehow pierced to the secret place of his son's heart where discontent and ambition twisted and twined one about the other so that the load he carried grew daily heavier and more difficult to bear. His vows denied him advancement through marriage; the secular world was closed to him. But within the Church herself a man could aim high. It was true what Gilo said. In spirit he was a warrior-bishop out of the past, and in size and strength of body a match for any knight he had ever met. Often at night when his body hungered for the flesh of a woman, he subdued it, not with the knotted cords of the discipline, but with the very dream his father had given voice to.

Gilo opened his eyes, saw the glazed expression on Aleaumes' face, and raised himself to point a trembling finger at Robert. "For you there will be a more difficult choice. This Clari we hold is poor and will always remain a tiny, obscure fief, but the name it has given you may shine more brightly in a faraway land. There will be castles to hold after the conquest, lonely outposts that look out over Saracen-held lands, high hilltop places that have known many names and many lords over the centuries. If you perform your knight's service well, such a place may be given to you, and with it the rank to command and rule it. Many in the Holy Land have named their castles after places they will never see again. And begotten heirs of the women of that country."

"I have a wife."

"There lies the choice. If Aelis quickens before you leave and bears you a son to inherit this Clari, her only duty in this world will have been done. In her heart she will always be the nun her mother would not permit her to be, and if you choose to let her go, she will take the vows that will free you in the sight of God and man. Whether to live your life in the Holy Land, never seeing the son who will succeed you here, or return and find peace in obscurity will be a decision only you can make."

"If you could influence that decision, Father, what would you say to me?"

Gilo shrugged, falling wearily back on his pillows. "I would say only that the bones of father, grandfather and great-grandfather lie here, but that they too were men bred to war, soldiers who were accustomed to expecting little and demanding nothing."

He closed his eyes, utterly exhausted, while the two brothers stared at one another. He had stirred the flame of Aleaumes' ambition, but made Robert more coldly angry and viciously uncertain than he had ever been before. With one breath the old man scorned Clari, with the next he seemed to be pleading with his elder son to continue the line unbroken on the lands from which it had sprung. Yet only a few moments before he had envisioned a new Clari, and seemed to take it for granted that Robert would want to found a second, more brilliant dynasty off an unnamed woman who might not even exist. His mind has begun to wander, Aleaumes' eyes were saying. Sickness and age have broken him as they will some day break all of us.

Lady Agatha bustled into the hall, Aelis following behind like a pale shadow. She kissed Aleaumes briskly on both cheeks, held him close for a moment, then turned her attention to her husband.

"My lord, your chamber is as fresh and sweet-smelling as a newly mown field," she said lightly. "You will rest more comfortably in your own bed. Robert and Aleaumes will carry you there and I will send a servant with more wine."

Gilo grumbled bitterly at being disturbed, but Lady Agatha paid no mind to his protests. She had nursed him successfully through so many bouts of this heathen illness that she had absolute confidence in her time-proven remedies. A clean chamber to lie in, fresh air to sweeten the body's foulness, herbal brews to bind the bowels, others to induce sleep. As soon as he was stronger she would send for a competent leech to bleed him and restore the body's humors to their proper balance. In the meantime the good red wine he drank to ease the pain in his lower parts kept him as manageable as a child.

As Robert and Aleaumes together lifted the pallet on which Gilo lay, one of the fur rugs fell to the floor. Aelis darted forward to retrieve it, flushing as she felt Aleaumes' appraising glance linger on her flat belly and tiny breasts. She replaced the rug, murmured a shy greeting to her brother-in-law, then melted back behind Lady Agatha's substantial body. She felt safely hidden there, for not even her redoubtable mother-in-law had eyes in the back of her head, and for hours at a stretch seemed not to notice the shadow at her skirts. Spring was a task-filled season on the manor, and Lady Agatha had lately been inclined to ignore her daughter-in-law's barrenness in return for the girl's servant-like devotion and willing, clever hands. Now she sent her off to the kitchens to inform the cook that Master Aleaumes was at home. This son had an enormous appetite. At least two more hares would have to be slaughtered for the evening meal and more spices measured out from their meager supply.

Aelis went willingly from the hall, eager to escape from her husband's family. They would talk about her, she was certain, but as long as she did not hear the talk she did not care. This morning she had awakened with the familiar cramps that always preceded her moon flow, and though later she would weep when obliged to confess to her husband that once more his hopes were not to be fulfilled, secretly she was glad not to bear a child.

Most women would rather have died than admit to barrenness, but she rejoiced in it. Soon Robert would be leaving Clari, perhaps forever. He must get him an heir before he went. If she did not quicken by summer they would begin to talk of dissolving the marriage, and willingly, oh how willingly, she would agree to it.

She submitted her body almost nightly to Robert's will, having learned the wisdom of passive acceptance, but in her heart and mind she remained untouched. She longed to be shut up away from the world, to sleep alone even though the bed be hard, to know her days and all the years of her life would be regulated by the sound of bells and the sweet singing of the Holy Office. If the convent she chose were strict enough in its observance of the Rule, she would not even be obliged to see her mother more than once or twice a year. And that, she thought, would be comparable to the bliss of heaven.

II

Geoffrey of Villehardouin flexed the painfully stiff fingers of his right hand, cursing under his breath at the swollen joints and inflamed knuckles. Last night's stay in the damp, chill monastery atop the pass of Mont Cenis had brought on another attack of what he called his Venetian illness. Tossing and turning in the hard guesthouse bed until long past Matins, he had managed barely a few hours of uninterrupted sleep. This morning every bone in his body ached and he was uncharacteristically short of temper.

His horse moved restively beneath him, eager to crop the soft new April grass growing in ragged clumps by the roadside. He reined the beast in sharply, flinching as another wave of pain throbbed upward to his shoulders. High above him someone waved an arm in a slow, graceful arc. Ignoring both his pain and the grating sound of bone adhering to socket, he returned the signal. The road ahead lay empty of fellow travelers and thieves.

He relaxed in the saddle, loosened his feet in the stirrups and sat at ease, watching the pack animals of the train he commanded snake their way down the slope he had just descended. Heavily laden and skittish, they were herded on by men who had been warned that early spring was avalanche season in these mountains. The crust of each high-piled bank was thin, Father Abbot had reminded them, and beneath it the snow was beginning to melt and shift. Any loud noise, a man's shout, the bray of a donkey, even honest laughter, could dislodge it and send it tumbling down on them. So they maneuvered the descent in unbroken silence, muscles taut, faces gleaming with the sweat of their fear.

My face, too, looked like that a few minutes ago, Villehar-douin thought disgustedly. He turned away from the sight of men crouched over in their saddles, shrunken by their own fear to the size of children. Alard Maquereau, phlegmatically calm and capable, would see them safely down. In this at least a younger man led better than an old one.

Geoffrey gave in gratefully to his fatigue, letting the reins slide through his fingers so that the horse lowered its head and began to graze contentedly. Here below the air was not as thin as on the peaks. It was easier to breathe, softer, fragrant with the scent of fragile wildflowers. The ground was almost free of snow, bare brown earth with here and there a burst of color that foretold the carpet of life soon to cover it.

He closed his eyes, red-rimmed and smarting. Long-forgotten memories of youth had danced in his brain all morning, surging up to mingle confusedly with other, more recent images, faces and places passing before his mind's eye in dizzying rapidity. He felt an urgent need to put some order to them, to examine them quickly, marshal them to their proper ranks, then put them from his conscious thought. Finding no logical reason for the strange mood that had overtaken him, he blamed it on the mountains. They towered above and on all sides, blotting out the sky, bearing down on the spirit, inducing a melancholy that threatened to overwhelm a naturally introspective nature. A few more hours and he would be out of them, but in the meantime . . .

He let himself drift into the kind of disciplined half sleep the monks called meditation. The pious avowed that it led the soul to truer knowledge of God; Geoffrey sought only deeper knowledge of the self he was and had become, and perhaps a moment's respite from the bouts of pain and fever that had begun so unexpectedly to wrack his body and depress his soul.

He remembered that in childhood he had been robustly healthy, a boy who never sickened with summer's fevers or the deadly winter disease that closed the throat and filled the lungs with thick yellow mucus. Seemingly immune to the illnesses that carried off so many of his contemporaries, he had grown up high-spirited, energetic, quick at his lessons, his body muscular and well formed, his temperament a mixture of easygoing tolerance, sound common sense and pride in his rank and person.

He had served his time as page and squire, received his knighthood, married, fathered children, outlived one wife, taken another. Strange how the events of the domestic side of his life kaleidoscoped themselves into patterns pleasant to view but oddly remote. The birth of his eldest son, the softness of his first wife's young flesh, the order and comfort brought into his days by his able second lady, the land itself, fertile and rolling, tall stands of golden wheat awaiting the harvest, vineyards heavy with the scent of wine-producing grapes, pastures in which his fine horses grazed and kicked up their heels, woodlands through which to ride and hunt on a fine autumn morning. All were mere backdrops for the active life he had chosen, for during the past fifteen years he had served Champagne as Marshal, an arduous, honorable charge that set his character firmly in a mold few men could fit.

He had taught himself to be moderate at table, the better to guard his tongue and keep his wits about him on missions of diplomacy. He watered his wine and ate sparingly of the heavily sauced dishes that thickened most nobles of his age, bloating their bodies and exacerbating their naturally choleric temperaments. Scorning a litter or a well-tamed horse when he traveled, he preferred an animal whose energies forced him to a level of physical exertion usually enjoyed only by younger men. And on those journeys, visiting courts and cities throughout France, riding into Burgundy, Flanders, Hainault, Provence, wherever the interests of Champagne called him, he formed the habit of seeking out the company of scholars, men who were masters of law, science, mathematics and theology, conversing with them more and more as an equal as the years went on.

He believed himself to be at his peak now, his mind alert, well informed yet still curious, his physical passions controlled but not denied, his opinions based on fact but hardly ever viewed even by himself as unalterable, his tongue practiced in the art of flattery and the ability to seem to concede all while gaining what was most important, this world and the next well ordered, intelligible, secure. And finally, he allowed his heart, and indeed all his being, to rest freely and devotedly in the service of the Count he served and the lands he loved.

Many men nearing their fiftieth year rose up each morning

a little less eager for life than the day before. Wives grew rake-thin and quarrelsome or florid-faced and heavy with fat, sons rebelled, wondering aloud why God saw fit to delay the hour of their inheriting, daughters bitterly reproached the parents who had married them well but unhappily, and grandchildren, when they lived, were noisy, demanding, ill-mannered pups who disrupted the peace of the hall and were better left in the care of servants. Life lost its savor and its tang when you got old.

Or so some would have him believe, in those unguarded moments when the fire burned low, the wine flowed freely and the memories of youth and lusty young manhood overlaid the present with the black depression of unfulfilled ambition and oft-discarded hopes. Had he been less analytical or more inclined to view the passage of time as a series of unconnected events with neither cause nor effect to bind them together, he might have shared their opinion, but neither his mind nor, until a few weeks ago, his body, had become rigid with age.

Fog so thick that it was very nearly rain had shrouded Venice's canals throughout his six-week stay, burned off by a feeble sun for only a few hours a day. All the envoys had complained of it, but only he had actually fallen ill. Perhaps if he had been able to keep to his bed he might have shaken it off, but under the circumstances that had been impossible.

After their credentials had been accepted and the nature of their mission revealed, the emissaries had had little time to themselves. When not actually in attendance at the Doge's court they had been obliged to endure with good grace dozens of official and unofficial banquets and entertainments mounted for their benefit. Wealthy Venice was lavish in its hospitality, its nobles and rich merchants, in spite of the Lenten season, determined that every moment of the ambassadors' visit be a memorable one. The activity had very effectively kept them from lingering in the anterooms of the Doge's palace, a practice which Villehardouin knew from long experience enabled one to pick up tidbits of gossip and rumor which usually proved invaluable at the negotiating table.

Including their one official visit to the Arsenal, the most famous shipbuilding yard in Europe, they had seen only what the city's ruler wished them to see, heard only what he wished them to hear. And there was no doubt about it, they had been mightily impressed.

They had witnessed Venice's supreme achievement, a long, sleek war galley that grew from ribbed skeleton to completed vessel in one afternoon, slipped that same day into the harbor, only one of many others exactly alike. And concealing their amazement so as not to seem too eager, they had peered over the shoulders of the Director of the Arsenal while he sketched with charcoal on a thin piece of wood the type of troopship he proposed to build for them, a vessel with specially constructed sides that could be let down in a matter of minutes, the sides becoming bridges over which mounted knights could stream ashore, wave after unconquerable wave of them. He sketched the outlines and interiors of other ships too, each one modified according to the cargo it would carry, broad-bellied vessels, their holds transformed into vast bins for grain or layered with sleeping niches for the common soldiers. It was an undreamed-of guarantee he offered them; hardly a man or a horse would sicken in too-cramped quarters, not a handful of grain spoil or a cask of wine split, no matter how rough the sea.

"Even your civilian pilgrims will travel in comfort and safety," he promised. "The priests among them will have nothing to complain of."

The waiting had been harder to bear after that.

"Patience, my lords. The Doge is meeting again with the Council of Six," they had been told. "Today it is the Council of Forty which assembles to consider your request." Later it had been groups reputed to number one hundred, two hundred, a thousand, two thousand.

"When does he meet with the beggars and the whores?" Miles the Brabant had demanded irritably.

"Patience, Miles, and hold your tongue." Even in the seclusion of their private quarters Villehardouin was conscious that spying eyes watched and servants seemed unnaturally alert. "The Doge only plays at indecision. In the end he will consent to supply us with the ships we need, but for form's sake he must appear to hesitate."

The Brabant had tossed down his wine and paced the chamber restlessly. Night after night he had marched back and forth in that narrow space, the steady drumming of his heavy footsteps an irritant that had gradually driven the ambassadors to renewal of an old quarrel. Why Venice? Why not Genoa or Pisa? Why Italy at all? Flanders could not match the Arsenal's galleys, but her troop and merchant vessels were as fine as any that plied the seas.

"Venice can put a hundred or more ships in the water in a year's time," Alard Maquereau had told them in his quiet voice. And in the silence his statement produced he added flatly, "We cannot match that number even by half. Nor can Genoa or Pisa, however much they boast of their abilities. It must be Venice or nowhere."

In the end even Miles the Brabant had consented to the ploy devised by Villehardouin and the poet, Conon of Béthune. "We have appealed to their piety and their purses," Conon explained. "When the Mass is concluded we shall play upon their emotions."

Ten thousand Venetians had crowded the church of St. Mark, spilling out onto the porch and the grassy square in front of the cathedral, staring expectantly at the foreign envoys they had come to hear. Rumors of the new crusade and of the success with which it was being preached in France had reached them over a year before. Those committed to the cross already number in the thousands, they told one another complacently. And when they had heard that the army was swelling into the tens of thousands, they had begun to count the months off on their fingers, knowing it was just a matter of time before ambassadors would be sent to them.

The Mass being celebrated that day in St. Mark's was dedicated to the Holy Ghost. Villehardouin prayed for the gift of wisdom and the power to inspire the congregation with the same flame of resolution that had caused a new army of crusaders to be born in faraway France. "For only if all my people consent can I commit them to what you ask of me," the Doge had told him bluntly.

He would have to address them through an interpreter, a prospect that initially dismayed him. Should the man's inflection be flat, his voice devoid of either enthusiasm or supplication, the Venetians were apt to respond apathetically if at all. But when he mounted the pulpit just inside the altar rail the Doge had nodded reassuringly at him and he knew that the interpreter had received his instructions.

He had spoken slowly at first, testing the measure of the interpreter's skill, describing the tournment field at Ecri, the meadow on which had bloomed the tents of the participants, the bevy of regally clad noble ladies in the loges, the stands crowded with the common folk of the neighborhood, the pages and squires darting through the throng on urgent last-minute errands, the destriers pawing the ground, whinnying to one another as saddle girths were tightened, the fully armored knights striding toward their mounts, forming their ranks on either end of the field, the hush that fell when Blanche, Countess of Champagne, rose to her feet to command the running of the first course.

He had paused then to allow the scene to take hold of their imaginations. He was planning to tell a deliberate lie, to present as fact a version of subsequent events that had gained great popularity throughout Europe, a tale which more than any other betrayed the people's avid wish for the perfection of romance. "What difference will it make?" Conon of Béthune had demanded. "No one believes me now when I tell them Fulk was not at the tournament. I'm even beginning to believe he was there myself."

"Before the Countess could give the signal," Villehardouin had told the Venetians, his voice rising and falling dramatically in the drawn-out cadences favored by professional storytellers, "a priest appeared, no one could say from where, and strode to the very center of the field. It was as if God held us all in the palm of His Hand, for not a voice was raised to question or protest, not a hand stretched out to impede his passage. He was recognized, and even before he began to speak we knew why he had come. A thousand lips formed the name, Fulk of Neuilly, but not even a whisper escaped them. He raised his arms to heaven and preached the shame of Christ, reminding us that infidels profaned the land His Feet had trod, that pilgrims journeyed to Jerusalem in peril of their lives, that the saints and angels hid their faces for shame because Christian knights blunted swords and lances in sport when those very weapons were so sorely needed in the Holy Land. Tears streamed down his face. We could see them glittering like diamonds in the cold November sunshine. 'Will you take the cross?' he asked us, and before the echo of his plea died away Count Thibaut of Champagne had fallen to his knees at the preacher's feet. Fulk blessed him, cried out to Heaven that here at least was one knight willing to become God's champion, raised the Count up and gave him the kiss of peace. Louis, Count of Blois and Chartres, took his cousin's place, and by nightfall every knight, every squire, every man-at-arms, had also knelt and made his vow. Soon after, Count Baldwin of Flanders and his lady, the Countess Mary, took the cross in Bruges, then Hugh, Count of St. Pol, and so many others that it would take days to tell you all their names. There is but one thing lacking to God's army, and that only Venice can provide. We must have ships to cross the sea, a fleet larger than any the world has ever seen, vessels that will speed us safely to the relief of the Holy Sepulcher as God has ordained from the beginning of time."

This was the signal phrase he and Conon had agreed upon, the words at which John of Friaise, Walter of Gaudonville, Miles the Brabant and Alard Maquereau were to leave their seats of honor at the side of the altar and advance toward the congregation with arms outstretched in supplication while Villehardouin continued to praise Venice's resources and entreat the citizens' cooperation from the pulpit. But the envoys had been eclipsed by no less a figure than the Doge himself.

Somehow Villehardouin was hustled from his place. He found himself just one among the group of kneeling foreigners, his view of the congregation cut off by the shimmering skirts of Enrico Dandolo. And he heard the Doge raise his voice and plead with his people to succor the noble representatives of the crusade.

"Look with love and pity on these men kneeling before you," he commanded them. "See how they weep to do their duty. Their enterprise is noble, and their lords the greatest in Christendom. Shall we dishonor ourselves by sending them from us without the ships they ask for? Will we bring upon ourselves the condemnation of heaven and earth? Or shall we join ourselves to their cause as brothers in Christ? Will you consent, citizens of Venice, will you consent?"

A heartbeat's silence followed. Not a priest, not a server, not a single one of the thousands of Venetians moved. But as the Doge lifted both arms as if he himself hung bleeding from the Cross, a sound like thunder filled the church. "We consent, we consent." Over and over they chanted the words, shouted them, whispered them to one another, spoke them in laughter and in tears.

"What happened?" Conon asked later.

"I'm not sure," Villehardouin replied. "But it seems apparent that our instinct was as sure as Dandolo's. The only difference is that he outmaneuvered us. He honored us, but at the same time he made it appear that our entire army waited breathlessly and somewhat ill-prepared for Venice to take it in hand and give it direction. He cast us in a secondary role and raised himself to the place of prominence."

"Let him enjoy it for as long as he will," Conon said carelessly. "Whatever airs he may choose to give himself and his Republic, he is, after all, nothing but a shipbuilder. Once we have reached the Holy Land no one will remember his name."

But that was before they came to the signing of the Treaty of Nolis.

Alard Maquereau herded the last pack animals in among the others, watching them fan out to graze. He spoke briefly to the sergeant, who nodded his head respectfully, waited while the men-at-arms positioned themselves in a semicircle around the small herd, then walked his horse to where Villehardouin waited, a little apart from the others as befitted his rank. The animals carried rich gifts from the Doge to the noble counts of Champagne, Flanders and Blois, and though the most dangerous part of the journey was over, it would be foolhardy to relax their vigilance. Bands of robbers and unemployed soldiers watched all the roads, preying on merchant caravans and any traveler foolish enough to venture out unprotected by a strongly armed escort. There was little chance that thieves would risk an encounter with a force of professional fighting men such as theirs, but it was always when one least expected it that trouble came.

"Shall we rest the animals here awhile and break our fast,

Geoffrey? It seems a likely spot, still high and open enough to give us ample warning of unwanted company."

Villehardouin hesitated, gazing down the winding road, mentally ticking off the leagues still to be ridden before nightfall. Were it not for the pack animals he could cover the distance in a quarter of the time. He himself was rested enough to continue immediately, but Alard's horse still breathed heavily and sweat glistened on its flanks.

"I suppose we'll make better time this afternoon if we do," he said reluctantly. "All right, Alard, but tell the sergeant that three men are to remain mounted and on guard, and to be sure that all the animals are well hobbled."

Villehardouin stayed mounted until his orders had been carried out and a squire had come to hold his horse's bridle. The men-at-arms were hungrily choking down bread and cold meats before he eased himself from the saddle, managing to do so with apparent ease although all his muscles were tight with the effort.

Alard discreetly turned his head away. Any man stiffened after long hours on horseback; he himself was so saddle weary that he groaned openly as he dismounted. But the Marshal was deriving a grim sort of pleasure by denying even the most natural of bodily discomfort, for his pride had been challenged during those long weeks in Venice.

He had never once referred to his malady, thinking he kept the secret well, but Alard had an observant eye. Day after day he had watched Villehardouin bend the knee and bow gracefully throughout the tedious ceremonial of the Court, a sudden whiteness that came and went across his face the only sign that he was often feverish and in pain. And because his bedchamber was next to Villehardouin's he had heard the discreet footsteps of the servants who nightly brought basins of heated water and hot stones wrapped in soft wool to the Marshal's room.

The worst of the illness, whatever it was, seemed to be over now. It had not left Villehardouin precisely an old man, but certainly there were lines engraved on his face that had not been there at the outset of their journey.

"It's good to feel the sun again," Alard remarked conversationally as they walked together toward a grassy little knoll.

"I'll never understand what possessed us to spend Lent in Venice, why we didn't wait until spring. I don't think the clouds broke more than once or twice during the whole six weeks we were there. What was the phrase Conon of Béthune used to describe the fogs over the canals?"

"He called them heavy, gray gauze draperies veiling rottenness and decay from honest eyes. Twice-daily phantoms rising from the devil's deep miasmic pit." Villehardouin shrugged his shoulders and shook his head. "I suppose a poet finds inspiration wherever he can, but when Conon stops writing of love and talks of phantoms in the fog he's hard pressed indeed."

"I found him often moody and unpredictable," said Alard thoughtfully, "but likeable nonetheless. I wonder if he lingered in Genoa as he talked of doing. The others seemed determined to hurry on to Pisa before news of the treaty becomes common knowledge."

"Wasted effort," said Villehardouin sharply. "They'd all have done better to return home immediately." He waited until the two squires serving them had poured wine and laid out cheese, bread and meat on thick white napkins spread on the grass, then waved them off to rejoin the others. "Neither Genoa nor Pisa will supply a single ship now that we have entered into a formal pact with Venice. Their rivalry is of too long standing. Conon will accomplish nothing by chasing all over Italy, and he knows it. His fame as a poet makes him welcome anywhere, of course, but the others are laying themselves open to ridicule, and, what is worse, implying by their actions that they are dissatisfied with what was arranged in Venice."

. "I think it is more a point of pride, Geoffrey," said Alard gently. "After all, it was you and I who favored Venice most strongly. Don't you remember how we talked and argued a whole night through before deciding to approach the Venetians first?"

"I remember. One foolish, ill-considered argument after another. At the time you were the only one of the six of us who had ever even visited a shipyard, yet to hear us talk anyone would have believed we had spent half our lives at sea."

"There's no harm in men talking. It's a way of clearing the air. And if I remember correctly we were all short-tempered that night. Count Thibaut was particularly uneasy. He said he had the eerie feeling that it was all just words, that unless we made a binding contract somewhere, anywhere, the army would dissolve and slip away through our fingers. He favored Venice also."

"It was important to move swiftly."

"We did, and with happy results, I believe. When John of Friaise and Walter of Gaudonville report back to Count Louis they will declare that by the witness of their own eyes neither Genoa nor Pisa can even begin to match the ships of Venice. Conon will have found new ladies to sigh after and inspiration aplenty for his poetry, and Miles the Brabant an even deeper scorn for all things Italian. One visit to the Arsenal was enough to satisfy them at the time the convenant was sworn to, but having explored other possibilities as well, it will be easier for them to admit that I knew what I was talking about all along."

"You make a good diplomat, Alard," Villehardouin said, laughing softly to himself at the thought of an aging poet, a thick-headed soldier and Count Louis's two obstinate knights roaming northern Italy merely to salve their wounded pride.

"It's not the profession of my choice, Geoffrey. I know ships and I know men, but I haven't the gift of fine words nor the patience to play a diplomat's games. Count Baldwin picked me for this mission because he trusted me to spy out any defects in the Arsenal's building methods, just as he sent Conon because he expected him to charm the Doge with his honeyed tongue. I don't discount Conon's powers, but I was glad, nevertheless, when you were chosen spokesman."

"The Doge is not the kind of man who values poetry. I judge him indifferent to everything except profit, but he places great importance on appearances. He expected to be petitioned by the Marshal of Champagne and would have been insulted had anyone else addressed him. If Conon had insisted on making a long, flowery speech he would have raised his price to make up for the time wasted listening to him."

"Then thank God and His Holy Mother he gave way gracefully. The price was high enough as it was."

Both men fell silent, sipping reflectively at their wine. Eighty-five thousand silver marks was an enormous sum, and they had had to borrow five thousand from the Venetian moneylenders to ensure that work on the fleet would be begun at once. The interest on that amount alone was staggering.

But they had over a full year in which to raise the money, and already a sizable amount was deposited with the monks at Cîteaux from the donations Fulk of Neuilly had been given and the collections taken up by the various bishops. Those collections would continue, and once the army had assembled in Venice each man's passage price would be taken up in a general levy, many of the wealthier barons providing for their landless household knights, who seldom had any funds of their own. Weighing all the possibilities carefully, Alard could imagine an endless stream of coins pouring into the army's coffers. This time it seemed that Christendom would hold nothing back; no sacrifice would be too great. It was a relief to know that lack of funds, at least, would not be one of their problems.

"My lords, there is a party of riders approaching."

Villehardouin and Alard Maquereau stared for a moment at the soldier who stood before them, then exchanged quick, worried looks.

"Robbers? This close to Lyons?"

"No, my lord. It's a large party of knights and men-at-arms. We cannot make out their blazon yet, but they closed ranks and slowed their horses to a walk as soon as they spotted us."

"My horse," commanded Villehardouin, rising to his feet and shading his eyes against the sun. He cursed himself for having left the precious treaty in his saddlebag. His squire was hauling frantically at the horse's bridle, but the animal plunged and reared, excited by the smell of danger and the men running past him to their own mounts. If it bolted . . .

Then, abruptly, he relaxed. The standard carried at the head of the long line of armed men now drawing more rapidly near proclaimed the leader to be Walter, Count of Brienne, an old friend and one of those who had taken the cross at Ecri.

"I still cannot make it out clearly," marveled Alard minutes after Villehardouin had sent a messenger galloping down the road to inform the Count that the Marshal of Champagne awaited his pleasure.

"That's one of the advantages of growing older, my friend," replied Villehardouin in good humor. "The near sight grows somewhat dim, but objects seen at a distance are as clear and sharp as though one held them at arm's length." The frenzied activity of the past few minutes had ceased, but the men-at-arms stood alert and expectant beside their horses. They had almost been taken unawares, and the sergeant covered his shame-facedness by sitting sword straight in his saddle, ready to execute whatever command Villehardouin might give. "It's overlarge for an escort party, yet it could be nothing else. Count Thibaut honors us."

Villehardouin was deeply touched that his liege lord had thought to send so magnificent an escort to bring them back to Troyes. He had an enormous pride in the House of Champagne and a fatherly affection for the young Count, whom he had watched grow from rather sickly child to handsome, strong knight, judging him far worthier of the title he bore than had been the brother from whom he had inherited it.

Poor Henry had been rather easily led, the reluctant third husband of Queen Isabella of Jerusalem, and the victim of a ludicrous accident which had resulted in his death. Thibaut was far bolder, much more daring than his brother had ever been, the type of man who scoffed at danger and hungered for great adventure. It was almost a foregone conclusion that he would be elected supreme commander of the army in spite of his youth and relative lack of experience. With wise old heads to guide him in matters of strategy, men at his side who were veterans of past campaigns in the Holy Land, he would acquit himself honorably and well. He possessed the rare, special gift of inspiring a fierce personal loyalty in the men who served him, so that wherever he led they would follow without hesitation, bound one to the other by ties even stronger than the formal vows they had proclaimed on the altars of religion. The court poets named him golden, handsome young manhood that could not be defeated, a shining, unblemished knight, the sight of whom ennobled and strengthened even common soldiers far back in the ranks. It might be mere dream or myth, but that hardly mattered if Christ and Champagne be well served.

Walter of Brienne's troop met and mingled with Villehardouin's soldiers, calling out familiarly to old comrades, men and horses milling about on the roadside while the horseboys unpacked provisions and squires ran to fetch food and drink for the Count and his knights. Walter himself was talking quietly to three men clustered closely around him, men who seemed to be holding themselves unnaturally tight, as though they sought to steel themselves to meet some difficult ordeal. Abruptly they turned and walked toward the knoll where Villehardouin and Alard stood waiting to greet them. One was the Count's nephew, Robert of Joinville, the two others, Walter of Montbéliard and Eustace of Conflans, were knights Villehardouin had known for years.

"I did not expect to see you until I reached Troyes, Walter," Villehardouin said, clasping the Count's outstretched hand firmly, smiling warmly and nodding to the others. "What brings you this far from Champagne?"

"It is a tale best told over a cup of wine, Geoffrey," the Count replied, settling himself comfortably on the cloak his squire hurriedly spread on the ground. "We've been in the saddle since dawn and have not yet broken our fast." He stretched his legs out before him, kneading the knotted muscles of his calves, his eyes following the squire who had run off to fetch food and wine for his lord.

"What news from Troyes, Walter?"

"Count Thibaut is lying abed of some fever." Brienne frowned worriedly. "It came upon him some weeks ago, a form of the sweating sickness, the physicians say. They bleed and purge him, and claim that he is much improved, but he cannot even rise from his bed for the weakness in his legs. The Countess is greatly concerned and has Masses said every morning for his recovery. The physicians will not let her enter his chamber for fear the babe she carries will come before its time should she too sicken. She is very near to her lying-in, poor lady, and between praying for a son and besieging heaven for her lord's good health, spends most of each day in the chapel on her knees. The court has become a gloomy place, Geoffrey, yet if the news you bring is good, it will do more to hasten Thibaut's cure than all the physicians' remedies. When I took my leave of him he commanded that should I have the good fortune to meet you on the road I was to urge you to hasten quickly back to Troyes."

"But you will not be returning there with us, Walter?" Villehardouin asked softly. Beside him Alard Maquereau stiffened and the others too sat frozen in attentive silence.

"No, my lord." Walter of Brienne's words and tone of voice were unexpectedly formal. He gulped down his wine and held the cup out to be refilled, then dismissed his squire. Servants' listening ears were usually ignored, but the Count was obviously taking pains to ensure that this conversation would remain beyond the reach of gossip.

Completely unattended, the six knights sat far enough away from their men so that only by shouting could they attract their attention. Curious and mystified, Villehardouin looked inquiringly at Robert of Joinville, but the latter sat with head averted, gazing up at the pass of Mont Cenis. Below them on the road Villehardouin could see that the men of his train were glancing covertly at the solemn group of knights. They knew the Count's destination and the nature of his mission, had learned it almost immediately from Brienne's men-at-arms. They were watching for the Marshal's reaction.

"Time is short, Walter," said Villehardouin, prodding delicately, "and you said you had a tale to tell."

The Count raised his head from his wine cup, his eyes drawn like Joinville's toward the pass that led to Italy. He sighed once, deeply, then turned to Villehardouin, his expression at once defiant and subtly pleading.

"My companions and I go to conquer Lecce and Apulia, Geoffrey. At the Pope's request and with Count Thibaut's blessing."

"Lecce and Apulia are lands belonging to the kingdom of Sicily," exclaimed Villehardouin in surprise. "What have men vowed to the Holy Land to do with Sicily?"

"Slowly, Geoffrey, slowly." Walter of Brienne was keeping a tight rein on himself. The Marshal's quick reply had been near to a slur on his honor and Brienne was hot-tempered. He had not looked forward to this meeting, had dreaded it all the long ride from Troyes. Now that the moment had come, he must find the words to convince Villehardouin, as he himself was convinced, that he was not deserting the crusade, only going on before the rest of the army. "I know what you are thinking, both of you," he said, quick to notice that Alard Maquereau's face was flushed and set, "and your thoughts do me and my loyal knights great disservice."

Alard Maquereau stared pointedly at the cross stitched to Walter of Brienne's shoulder, but said nothing.

"When the Pope commands, he must be obeyed, as the Voice of Christ Himself," said Villehardouin soothingly. "Yet you still wear the cross . . ." His voice trailed off invitingly.

"We have sought no dispensation from our vows, nor will we. We are men careful for our honor and for the shame of Christ. When the army is ready to sail we will rejoin it at the appointed place and time."

"Fifteen months from now, on the feast of Saints Peter and Paul, we set sail from the port of Venice."

"That is good news indeed, my lord," exclaimed Robert of Joinville, a genuine excitement in his voice momentarily breaking the reserve in which he had held himself. He grinned delightedly at the Count. "We'll have Lecce and Apulia subdued and obedient to my lord's rule in less than six months."

"Four with any luck," put in Eustace of Conflans.

"Where is Miles the Brabant?" asked Walter of Montbéliard, as if noticing for the first time that of the six envoys sent to Venice, only two were returning. "And Conon of Béthune? Did you leave him behind in the clutches of some dark-eyed Italian lady?"

"They decided to visit Genoa and Pisa in company with John of Friaise and Walter of Gaudonville," Villehardouin answered carefully.

"I don't understand, Geoffrey. Does that mean there is no firm treaty with Venice?" demanded Walter of Brienne.

"There is," replied Villehardouin. "But we thought it best to leave no possibility unexplored. No one knows for certain how large this army will grow." He had spoken offhandedly, as if the matter were of no consequence, but he watched the faces of his listeners with great attentiveness. If doubt about the treaty or the worth of the fleet were to surface, it would do so as soon as it became widely known that four of the envoys had seen fit to look elsewhere for ships. Wealthy barons like the Count of Brienne might then be tempted to raise fleets of their own, and that at all costs must be prevented. He was relieved to see that his explanation had apparently been accepted, for all looked satisfied, nodding approvingly at the extra measure of caution.

"I have seen the war galleys Venice builds," said Walter of Brienne, "and its merchant ships, also. They are the finest vessels afloat. We'll have few losses at sea."

At the mention of war galleys Alard Maquereau glanced briefly at Villehardouin, his eyebrows raised in silent question. The Marshal almost imperceptibly shook his head and Alard steered the conversation to a different track.

"I mean no disrespect, my lord," he said, "but I am curious to know why the Pope's commission fell to you. Was His Holiness unaware that you had taken the cross?"

"The situation in Sicily is very delicate," replied Brienne, choosing to ignore Alard's last question. "There are two factions intriguing for possession of the boy-king Frederick, the German lords installed by his late father who seek to return the kingdom to the Empire, and his own native Sicilian barons who despise the Hohenstaufen rule and have vowed to preserve their independence at all costs. The child was made a ward of the Pope by Queen Constance's will, but both parties are hostile to the papacy. If Innocent is not to be forgotten in the fray he must have his own party at court."

"He fears the Hohenstaufen claims in Italy," corrected Villehardouin, openly admiring the shrewd tactics of the lawyer who now occupied the Throne of Peter. "When the German barons refused to accept the rule of a minor and elected Philip of Swabia Emperor, as is their right, they stirred up sleeping ambitions elsewhere. Otto of Brunswick disputes the election, and his uncle, King John, has promised him an army of English soldiers to help him to the throne. No man of any sense puts his faith in Lackland's promises, but Innocent also favors Otto. He wants a weakling at the helm of the Empire, and if that weakling is also in his debt, so much the better. Philip of Swabia may be a pious man, but he remains a Hohenstaufen. Once rid of Otto he would immediately turn his attention to Italy, and Innocent would very quickly find himself once more the temporal ruler of a few tiny papal states completely encircled by the Empire."

The Count barely managed to conceal his annoyance. Villehardouin had made it sound as though he, proud Walter of

Brienne, were a mere pawn on some vast chessboard, moved impersonally around to serve everyone's interests but his own. He immediately moved to correct that false impression.

"My lady wife, as you know, is the Princess Albiria, eldest daughter of the late King Tancred. She is heiress to the counties of Lecce and Apulia, some say rightful Queen of Sicily, since her brother William was most foully murdered at the Emperor's command."

"There is a story going round that the boy still lives, that Henry had him castrated and made a monk," interrupted Villehardouin.

"Queen Sibylla is certain that her son is dead. So are the princesses. A man sympathetic to their misfortune risked his life to bring the news to them while they were still under close guard in Alsace. There will be false pretenders, no doubt, but no one to support their claims. As there is no man of their own blood still living, it has fallen to me to avenge the wrongs done to the Queen and her daughters."

"Henry is dead and his Empire in jeopardy. It would seem that God Himself has avenged them."

"My lady wife has legitimate right to Lecce and Apulia. In her name I will conquer and rule them. She has renounced all claims to the crown itself so that with a clear conscience we can ensure that Frederick grows to be a worthy king and an obedient son of the Church."

"A noble gesture worthy of a noble princess." Also eminently practical, Villehardouin decided. There was no hope whatever that Albiria would become Queen of Sicily, but by the simple act of renouncing a meaningless claim she had secured for herself and her husband titles, lands, power behind the throne and the Pope's considerable support. Innocent had probably insisted on it before ever publicly inviting Brienne to drive the Germans out of southern Italy for him. That would be a simple enough task for as formidable a fighter as the Count had on numerous occasions proved himself to be. The real test would come in the intrigue-filled, murder-prone court at Palermo.

"My lady's life has been one of great tragedy, Geoffrey," the Count continued earnestly. "She yearns for quiet, peaceful years in which to recover from the many atrocities she was forced to

witness when the Hohenstaufen first came to Sicily. Henry was
fond of mass public executions, and often the princesses were
forced to watch while relatives and loyal supporters of their
house were put to death. He even went so far as to have the
bodies of King Tancred and his eldest son dragged from their
tombs and beheaded at the palace gates. My duty to my lady
wife as husband and knight is clear, yet she herself has urged
me to remember my greater duty to serve Christ and the cross I
wear. There are still men in Sicily who will honor and support
Tancred's daughter. Once the fighting is over I can safely leave
her to govern her lands with the advice and assistance of these
loyal, much-persecuted men."

"And the court at Palermo? Will you be able to leave that
also?"

"The Pope knows that I am determined on the Holy Land. All
he asks is that I open the way to Frederick for him. When that is
done he will install his own loyal men in Palermo."

Villehardouin would have continued the discussion, but
Brienne threw aside his wine cup and rose gracefully to his feet,
the signal his impatiently waiting men had been watching for.
The serving boys and squires cleared away the remains of the
meal and the long train of men-at-arms quickly re-formed its
ranks, a well-disciplined fighting machine eager to get on with
the profitable business of conquest.

"This is only the vanguard of the army I have raised," Walter
said proudly. "The rest are to follow in a few weeks."

Villehardouin said nothing, though Alard Maquereau managed an appropriately admiring comment.

"There will be criticism of what I am doing, Geoffrey. Indeed,
I have already heard a few remarks by rash men who did not
trouble to lower their voices." The Count's face hardened for a
moment. "Your good opinion is precious to me, my friend, as
precious as my honor. I will not fail you in Venice, nor leave
behind me any man who wears the cross. I do not give my word
lightly, but I pledge it to you as Christ is my witness." The
Count touched first the cross on his shoulder, then the hilt of his
sword.

"I wish you speedy success, Walter, and the joy of opponents
worthy of your skill." Villehardouin held out his hand, his lack

of any reference to meeting again in Venice unnoticed in the small confusion of leavetaking.

"Do you think he really believes what he said?" Alard asked scornfully. The Count had become a small faraway figure at the head of the long procession winding its way up to the pass which would admit them, finally, to Italy.

"Every word of it," replied Villehardouin, feeling last night's weariness creep over him again. "Whatever his faults, Brienne is a man of great and honorable reputation and he did not come by it unearned. But he will not be in Venice next summer, and neither will any of those who ride with him. The Pope will dispense them when the time comes, and they will be anxious to forget they ever took the cross. What we are watching, Alard, is the first mass defection from our army, a loss I estimate at several thousand good men who will not be easily replaced. I pray God the lure of quick profit does not entice other thousands to Apulia."

"Can it really matter so much how many end up in Sicily instead of Venice, Geoffrey? Even if only half the number committed to the Holy Land keep to their vows there will not be enough ships to carry all of them. We've already agreed that many will have to remain behind or sail on their own from other ports."

"One desertion breeds another," Villehardouin answered worriedly. "It's like a contagion that lingers in the air, infecting even strong and healthy bodies. And as it spreads it breeds fear and uncertainty everywhere." He hesitated a moment before continuing. "Did you mark how many Champenois traveled with Brienne? They could not have enlisted without Count Thibaut's approval. There is not a man anywhere more bound to the Holy Land than is my lord, yet someone has persuaded him to what I fear is a grave error in judgment."

"But if he is ill, Geoffrey . . ."

"I should have been with him, and if we had not dawdled at Montferrat's court I would have been."

"Not even you could have stopped Brienne."

"No, but I could perhaps have insisted that he allow no man vowed to the cross to join his army. Even in Champagne there are many knights and thousands of common soldiers who have held back. It is those men who should go to Apulia."

"Walter may surprise us yet," said Alard, sensitive to the personal humiliation engraved in every line of Villehardouin's face.

"If I were a few years younger, Alard, I would clutch eagerly at that hope. But age and experience have made a realist of me. It's not a comfortable way of thinking, but at least I am less often surprised or shocked at human failings. And there is another factor to consider. A man like Brienne begets heirs almost without thinking of it. Yet once he has a son the Count will find he cares greatly for the dynasty he has founded. He will be loath to leave his hard-won lands in the hands of a woman and a babe. And make no mistake about it, he will feel duty bound to get him an heir before leaving Sicily. You heard him speak of factions in Palermo. He will have enemies on all sides in that court, men whose characters are so hardened by old hatreds that he will not dare turn his back on them for even an instant. He will call for more French knights to increase his strength, and they will flock to his side. For every German turned out of his fief there will be a dozen land-hungry younger sons of France clamoring for the honor of holding castle, town or manor in liege service to Brienne or that boy-king everyone is so anxious to influence. Accept it, Alard. I have, though not without dismay and even pain. And when you make your report to Count Baldwin, as you must, give him my personal assurance that this is the last mass desertion Thibaut will permit."

"Desertion is a strong word, Geoffrey."

"Desertion it is and so I name it. There are other strong words I could use as well, but for the sake of unity and harmony among us I will hold my tongue. Brienne's decision was made before he had knowledge of the treaty. Let that be his excuse. He was impatient, bored with the peace we are enjoying, honor bound to avenge his lady wife and perhaps doubtful that a fleet could be raised for many years yet. The situation has changed now, did change the moment we set our seals to the Doge's proposal, though only we knew of it. As soon as we reach Troyes the treaty must be made public. We will have copies sent to every important court in the land, and proclamations read aloud on the church porches. Every man who has taken the cross or will take it must know that he is pledged to sail from Venice in fifteen months' time, and that no one will be permitted to jeopardize that sailing in any way. The Venetians will hold us to the letter of the contract, and if by some misadventure we are unable to honor it all Christendom will condemn us."

The Marshal turned sharply on his heel and began to stride angrily toward the waiting horses, his back stiff and rigid.

"Geoffrey, wait," called Alard, running to overtake him. "One thing more before we go. Why, when the Count spoke of Venetian war galleys, did you not tell him of the Doge's gift? It was generously done and will strengthen the fleet immeasurably."

"I don't know why I held back, Alard," Villehardouin answered honestly. "It was a feeling I had, a premonition perhaps that we may have to pay too dearly for those extra ships. And I did not want to have to answer Brienne's questions."

"Others will ask. It is too ostentatious a gesture to go unremarked."

"Venice is a city of merchants and traders," began Villehardouin, reasoning aloud as if the sound of his own voice would help him thread his way through a difficult maze. "Profit, power and the accumulation of wealth are the only voices which are heard there. Yet the Doge, with no prompting from us, has bound himself to supply fifty of his finest war galleys to our fleet. He will man and supply them at his own expense for one full year from the date of our sailing. Why, Alard? I cannot find the key to his self-interest. There is little profit to be made in the Holy Land."

"One half of all the lands we conquer during that year will go to Venice. That means Egypt and all the ports between there and the Holy Land. The Doge will turn the Mediterranean into a Venetian sea."

"Venice already enjoys many trading privileges among the infidels. There is some other reason, some hidden expectation they are counting on that I have not the cunning to ferret out." His own words to Conon of Béthune came back to him. "He has outmaneuvered us." He remembered the Doge's face as he had last seen it, enormous hooked nose jutting out over pallid lips, sunken cheeks out of which all breath of laughter had been sucked, eyes too black and expressionless to fathom. Only one other man he had ever seen had eyes like that. He shuddered, wondering why he had not noticed the similarity before. The Marquis of Montferrat, perfect host, urbane conversationalist, powerful subject of the Holy Roman Empire, had studied both the treaty and his guests with the same catlike secrecy and non-chalance. Villehardouin had spent almost a week in close daily contact with Montferrat, but until this moment he had not realized that the Marquis made him acutely uncomfortable. What was Alard saying?

"Perhaps we have misjudged the Doge. A man of his advanced age must live each day in the shadow of his own death, knowing that every breath he draws may be his last. Isn't it possible that he has determined on one final, magnificent gesture for his soul's salvation?"

Was there a link between Dandolo and Montferrat? Resolutely pushing the thought aside until he could examine the possibility with reason and calm, Villehardouin closed his mind to everything but the Doge and what he guessed to be the man's true inner feelings.

"No," he said. "You know as well as I do that Enrico Dandolo fears neither death nor what must come after. Venice is his heaven and her service the only one he acknowledges. I begin to think he has it in mind to use us for his own purposes, and he is a patient man. We are bound together in law and honor more tightly than any of us could have foreseen, yet if each side fulfills its obligations to the other Christ will be nobly served."

"And if not?"

"The Count of Brienne is a wealthy man who has pledged a generous sum to the army's treasury. Do you think that we shall see a single coin of it now? Apulia will be the richer and Christ the poorer. Eighty-five thousand silver marks, Alard. The Doge does not bargain, he demands. Think what a position we would be in if we cannot meet that demand."

"That is preposterous and impossible, Geoffrey."

"No, just think about it for a moment," Villehardouin insisted.

"The Pope would make up the deficit."

"Would he? I think not, even if the funds were available to him. Innocent has an overriding ambition which motivates his every action. He would leave temporal affairs to the kings, he says, but in matters of religion he would be absolute master over them. Can you separate the temporal from the spiritual? Is not every action we perform subject to a moral judgment? The subjects of a king under a ban of excommunication are no longer morally bound to serve him. Kings are mortal men with souls to save just like the rest of us, and they can be weakened and brought low. Innocent's purse is a slender one. Not a coin will be spent that does not further his grand design. We have his blessing on what we do, but that costs him nothing. If we are in default to the Venetians he will declare it a problem lying in the realm of temporal affairs and leave us to solve it as best we can."

"You are seeing Conon's phantoms in dark, empty air, Geoffrey. I tell you it will not happen."

For the first time in his adult life Villehardouin rebelled against the iron control he maintained over his temper, savoring the unaccustomed pleasure of raw sarcasm, not even caring that he inflicted pain on one who, of all men, deserved it least.

"Do you read the stars then, Alard? Did they tell you Thibaut would sicken? Will we reach Troyes only to kneel in vigil around a deathbed? All things are possible."

III

But Thibaut was not dead when they reached Troyes after several days' forced march with few stops and little rest for anyone. The court was subdued, quiet and anxious, but neither the physicians nor the astrologers had yet given up hope. By day the Countess Blanche smiled cheerfully, but her ladies whispered of stifled sobs and sounds of anguished weeping in the night.

Geoffrey of Joinville, Seneschal of Champagne, had come to the mounting yard to greet Villehardouin and escort him to Thibaut's bedchamber.

"He is very anxious to see you, Geoffrey, and to learn from your own lips everything that was said and done in Venice. He would have come himself had he been able. Even so, I had to promise to bring you straight to his side to calm his excitement."

"Tell me truly how he does, my friend," Villehardouin asked as they mounted the steps to the Great Hall. "Brienne told me only that the physicians feel he is mending though there is still no strength in his legs."

"He has had many good days since the illness began, but the fever always returns and his limbs become weak and feeble as an infant's. His legs will not support him; they tremble and crumple under his weight, and sometimes the trembling passes to his arms so that his squire must hold the cup to his lips. He has been given every potion known to medicine, for the doctors have not been able to agree among themselves on a common diagnosis, much less a treatment."

The Seneschal stopped and drew Villehardouin into a tiny alcove. Below them the knights of Thibaut's court clustered eagerly around Alard Maquereau, demanding to know the result of the embassy. "On the feast of Saints Peter and Paul," they heard him say. Deafening cheers and shouts echoed up the staircase to where the two Geoffreys stood. Joinville crossed himself reverently, then laid a pleading hand on Villehardouin's shoulder.

"Count Thibaut's arms and legs are so scarred from the bleedings that the physicians must open old wounds to let out fresh blood. Sometimes, after he is purged, his face is so white and drawn that it looks like the face of a man already dead. A man can be bled to death on a bed as well as on a battlefield, Geoffrey, and these meeching, sour-faced doctors will surely kill him if it goes on much longer. I have pleaded with the Lady Blanche to order them off, but she will not hear of it. She is convinced that only her prayers and their ministrations will cure him. She has a high regard for you, Geoffrey, and has always listened courteously to your advice. Go to her, reason with her, convince her that they only weaken him further. He needs rest and sleep, but night and day they badger him and he gets neither."

It was dim in the alcove, so dark that Villehardouin could hardly make out the features of Joinville's face. But the Seneschal's voice revealed a compassionate love for the young Count that was possibly even greater than Villehardouin's own.

"I will do what I can, Geoffrey," Villehardouin promised, "but I must see him first."

The Count's bedchamber was stuffy and foul-smelling, the odors of sickness thickly overlaid with the acrid fumes of burning herbs. The windows were tightly shuttered against the air and the light, and two thick night candles burned on either side of the bed, eating up what little breathable air had filtered into the room.

Villehardouin choked and was seized with a fit of coughing. The physician in attendance hurried to his side, urging him to control the convulsive hacking that sounded doubly loud in that silent place, but Villehardouin angrily pushed him aside, ripped down the heavy tapestry that had been nailed over the largest window and flung wide the shutters. Sunlight and fresh air streamed into the room, spilling over the bed and the figure of

the man who stirred feebly under a fur rug and several
thicknesses of blankets.

The physician stood as if struck dumb, swelling visibly with
indignation, his fat red jowls puffed out like a toad's, the bonnet
of his profession knocked absurdly askew in the brief struggle.

"Get out," ordered Villehardouin sharply, opening the chamber's other window. "And don't come back until you are summoned."

"My lady Blanche will hear of this," the physician muttered
ominously.

Villehardouin picked up the heavy wooden box that contained
the instruments for bloodletting, the leeches, the cupping bowls,
the dried herbs and bits and pieces of shriveled animal organs,
and thrust it into the man's hands. He propelled him roughly
through the door, then shut and bolted it behind him.

He heard weak hiccups of laughter from the great bed, and
turning, saw that the Count was attempting to sit up.

"My lord, let me help you," he begged, holding the Count
cradled in his arms while he propped pillows up behind him.
Thibaut was hot to the touch and frighteningly light, his hair
close cropped and his eyes enormous above deeply sunken
cheeks.

When he had made him comfortable he drew a chair close to
the bed and laid the treaty in Thibaut's hands. The thin fingers
plucked restlessly at the seals, then smoothed the parchment out
flat, caressing it as lovingly and gently as if it were a woman's
body.

"Wine," whispered Thibaut, and as Villehardouin reached for
water to dilute it, he added, "Full strength. They treat me like a
woman or a child, but with this covenant between my fingers I
feel my manhood returning." He smiled feebly. "Tell me everything."

Villehardouin described their arrival in Venice, the numerous
audiences with the Doge, the visit to the Arsenal, the long wait
while the Doge conferred with his councils, the petty bickering
and small jealousies to which the impatient, worried ambassadors had all fallen prey. Thibaut nodded and smiled, and as
Villehardouin interrupted himself to hold the wine cup to the

Count's lips, he felt the fever heat cool and saw that a flush of color had returned to the sick man's cheeks.

"I feel better now," Thibaut said in a stronger voice. "Had it not been for my lady's entreaties, I would have kicked that pompous fool of a doctor out long ago."

"She meant well, my lord," Villehardouin said soothingly, "but physicians consider it their duty to thoroughly frighten their patients' loved ones. He'll be back, of course, but I'll see to it that his hands are tied."

He picked up the parchment and began to read the treaty aloud, pausing after each article to glance at the Count. Thibaut approved it all, though he frowned at the mention of the sum the Venetians demanded and seemed perplexed at the addition of the unasked-for war galleys.

"Read that part again," he demanded, leaning back more deeply into his pillows and closing his eyes the better to concentrate.

As Villehardouin finished the second reading Thibaut snorted, then opened his eyes and laughed as if greatly amused.

"The crafty old bastard is so certain we shall succeed that he cannot bear to be left out of the victory," he declared.

"So it would seem, my lord." Whatever doubts he might have begun to feel about Venice's motives during the past few days Villehardouin would keep to himself, at least for the moment. Geoffrey of Joinville had spoken of weakness, pallor and death, but until he had seen Thibaut with his own eyes Villehardouin had thought it all exaggeration. Now he knew that it was not, and he fervently thanked God for sending the Count of Brienne to speed his return. A few more days, and who knew what might have happened.

"My lord, if you will agree to it, I will send for my lady wife to nurse you. She is greatly skilled in these matters and brought my eldest son back to health when the doctors had given up all hope for him. She can be here by nightfall."

"Chane de Lezinnes is a gracious lady, Geoffrey, and does honor to your name. I would gladly place myself in her hands."

"She will have you well in ten days' time, my lord," promised Villehardouin, hoping that it was not too late for even Chane's formidable skill in healing. He had once called her a worker of miracles, though she herself, being of a supremely practical mind, scoffed at such an idea. She was the despair of orthodox physicians, for she held that a strong man's body would often heal itself if left in peace to do so. And she never troubled to keep her opinions to herself.

He held the cup to Thibaut's lips again, and laid the treaty back upon the bed where the Count's straying fingers promptly felt and rested on it. Thibaut's eyes closed, his breathing, though light and shallow, was regular and as effortless as a child's. Within a few moments he was asleep.

Thibaut slept for three nights and two days, awakened at regular intervals by the lady of Villehardouin, who forced him to swallow rich broths of fowl and then beef even though he protested that he had no appetite. The cooks in the kitchen muttered rebelliously, for the lady demanded that the healthy, delicious fat be skimmed from the surface of the soups, and had gone so far as to intrude into their jealously guarded domain to show them how to do it properly. But Villehardouin's lady had her way, on the Countess's orders and in spite of the dire predictions of the physicians. On the morning of the third day the Count was able to eat several small bits of the tenderest of boiled fowl and morsels of fresh white bread soaked in wine. That evening he ate almost hungrily and Chane pronounced him well out of danger.

The Countess ordered a Mass of Thanksgiving to be said for his miraculous recovery while the doctors announced that they had at last succeeded in interpreting the astrological signs that had all along signified health and good fortune for Champagne. Without being actually rude they managed to ostentatiously ignore the presence of an amateur healer in their midst, providing the court fool with a heaven-sent opportunity to mock them behind their dignified backs.

But Chane de Lezinnes would not stay in Troyes to enjoy the well-deserved praise heaped on her, even though the Countess herself begged her to remain with them.

"My lady, you have only to see that the diet I have prescribed be rigidly followed, that there is no more bleeding or purging, and that the Count be left alone to sleep as much as he will," she declared. "Above all he must not overly exert himself, though he may begin to walk about as soon as he is able. But if he tires he is to take to his bed again immediately."

Villehardouin respected his second wife immensely, knowing that once she made up her mind, there was no changing it. She was a tiny, handsome woman, with a will of iron and a deep-rooted dislike of court life. Her world began and ended seven leagues east of Troyes, where she ruled their estates so well and so efficiently that Villehardouin was happy to leave all such matters in her capable hands. He was a little in awe of such strength of character, though as he helped her mount her horse he kissed her fondly and promised to steal some time from court as soon as he was able.

"Count Thibaut is young and strong," she told him, "but there is always the possibility of a relapse. Send for me at once if his fever returns. And if you could manage to banish his chief physician from court you would be doing the one thing that will guarantee his complete recovery."

"My love, you amaze me." Geoffrey patted the little hand which held the reins so competently.

She smiled affectionately at him, bright and birdlike in the sunshine, but he could tell by the absentminded way she let her hand rest in his that she was already half absorbed in thoughts of home. Her parting admonition proved it.

"Don't come upon us unannounced as you did last time," she chided him. "The castle needs freshening and all the linens a good washing. You don't want to find yourself without a dry bed to sleep in."

"Or a wife too busy to pleasure her lord."

They had been married for more years than either of them cared to think about, but she blushed girlishly at his remark, clicking her tongue against her teeth to hide her pleasure at the knowledge that even after all this time he still found her desirable.

Day by day the Count grew stronger. First for an hour, then two, then three, he was able to leave his bed and meet informally with his council in the small retiring room just off his bedchamber. There was an enormous amount of work to be done, for the always complex business of ruling Champagne had almost ground to a halt during the worst weeks of his illness. And now in addition there were letters to dictate to Louis of Blois and Baldwin of Flanders, Hugh of St. Pol, Geoffrey of Perche and many of the lesser barons who had taken the cross. In the strongest possible language they were enjoined to hold fast to the terms of the treaty negotiated by Villehardouin and to ready themselves and their liege men for the overland march to Venice, which must be begun immediately after Pentecost next.

Alard Maquereau stayed in Troyes only long enough to see that Thibaut was mending rapidly, and then departed for Flanders, bearing a copy of the treaty, letters to Baldwin from his cousin of Champagne and the many fine gifts by which the Doge expressed his esteem for the ruler of Flanders and Hainault. Villehardouin was sorry to see him go, this close companion of a long and difficult mission, the only man to whom he could talk freely of his still simmering anger against the Count of Brienne, and the one person to whom he had ever spoken of his troubling suspicions of their Venetian allies. Alard, so practical, so matter of fact, with his great knowledge of the sea and his absolute confidence in the worth of the vessels Venice would build them, was a comfortable, reassuring person to have around. But Flanders and his duties there could not be ignored, and in early May he set out for Bruges.

The weather grew warmer each day as spring took firm hold and promised a glorious summer. Thibaut dressed and attended Mass each morning, and the danger of contagion being long past, spent many idle hours in the pleasure garden at his lady's side, amused by the minstrels who competed vainly with the songbirds for their entertainment. Her babe was due at the end of the month, so that Blanche, in the last, heavy days of her pregnancy, was content to sit in the cool shade and dream of the fine, healthy boy child she would soon be giving to Champagne.

As placid day followed placid day, Thibaut grew restless, pacing the shaved paths of the garden until he had worn through the tender grass, coming to an abrupt halt whenever the hunting horns sounded and the baying of hounds rang through the air. The buzzing of the bees began to annoy him intensely, and the sight of busy gardeners going about their tasks with sharp knives and trowels was an embarrassing reminder of his convalescent state. He was denied the sport of the exercise yard and its swordplay, the challenge of the quintain, even the pleasure of putting his great war-horse through its paces in the cool of the morning. Someone else led the hunt, and when the fresh meat of noble deer and dangerous wild hog appeared on the tables of the Great Hall he choked on it. A man, a knight, a warrior, ought to get his own meat. Yet they expected him to relish what had come from other hands, and to listen to the recounting of each kill as intently as though he himself had flung the lance that brought the beast down.

One unbearably beautiful morning toward the end of May he declared himself wholly cured and as fit as ever.

"We have had no feast magnificent enough to do justice to the treaty our lord Marshal brought back to us from Venice," he told his council at the conclusion of that day's brief meeting. "We shame Jerusalem and the cross we wear with our long faces and solemnity. Heaven rejoices at what is to come and wonders that we soldiers of Christ do not share our Master's happiness."

"You were near to death, my lord," interrupted Villehardouin.

"All the more reason then to celebrate what God in His Mercy has vouchsafed us. Life, health, the honor of His Service, the babe who will soon be among us." All the councillors wore a single, horrified look, but Thibaut ignored them. "I shall lead the hunt today, as is my right and place, and tonight we shall feast on the fruits of our pleasure. I want to hear gay music and laughter again and to partner my lady in the dance. We shall banish the smell of sickness from this place. God's Blood, I've had enough of it." He frowned warningly and rose to tower over them. "I'll brook no arguments in this, my lords, and tolerate no opposition."

He strode from the council chamber, calling to his squires and body servants to attend him. It was the old, vigorous Thibaut, the lord of that place, giving orders again and expecting to be instantly obeyed. Some of the councillors smiled to hear his voice, the sound of his footsteps and the scurryings as his attendants ran to keep up with him.

"I rejoice to see this day," said Geoffrey of Joinville, forgetting that only a few moments before he had feared Thibaut's new mood of recklessness, "and I thank God Who has restored our Count to us."

"It is too soon," muttered Villehardouin. "I must speak to the Countess. The lady will find the words to restrain him from his folly." Leaving his papers all jumbled together on the table, he ran quickly from the room.

But no one could stop Thibaut, not even the lady Blanche, who sent word to the stables that she felt her pains beginning. The shamefaced midwife, hastily summoned and dragged unwillingly to the mounting yard, could not meet the Count's eyes. Standing up to her ankles in mud while the horses and hounds milled about, she confessed in a halting voice that my lady was perhaps mistaken, though it was true enough that it could be any day now. The Count laughed and sent a private, loving message to the wife who had employed so feminine a stratagem to keep him by her side, promising that in her honor he would personally bring down the biggest buck of the day.

They hunted for what remained of the morning and throughout the afternoon, the Count urging them on with frenetic energy. Carts heavily laden with slaughtered game were driven back to the castle to be unloaded by the sweating kitchen boys. Then, relieved of their load, blood dripping over their wheels into the dust, they rolled back out to rejoin the hunt.

The kitchens were noisy with quarreling, competing cooks and their squealing helpers, urged to bestir themselves and be useful with cracks over the head and frantic arm pullings. The maids carried in armloads of fresh herbs and violets to strew in the rushes of the Great Hall, set the tables with snowy linen cloths, highly polished silver bowls containing salt and the jewel-encrusted goblets of purest gold from which the Count and his lady would drink. New torches and fresh candles were placed in all the wall sconces and the minstrels tuned their instruments and practiced their songs, their pure voices rising occasionally over the din. In the chapel, where the noise of all these preparations could not penetrate, the lady Blanche knelt and prayed.

By sunset two red spots burned in Thibaut's cheeks, but the faces of all the returning riders were bathed in evening's red glow, and tired and exhilarated as the men were, no one remarked on their unnatural brightness. Thibaut laughed to see the Countess Blanche, the chaplain and his much despised physician standing anxiously on the steps of the Great Hall as the hunting party rode in.

"You see, my lady," he called out, "I have kept my promise to you." He flung out an arm toward the heavily antlered deer tied securely across the back of his squire's horse, but the gesture seemed to unbalance him. Very slowly he swayed in his saddle, crumpled, then slid to the ground, one foot still caught in a stirrup.

They carried him back to his bed unconscious, his skin so hot to the touch that it burned their fingers through his clothing. In the absence of Chane de Lezinnes the physician bled him in two places. By morning it was obvious that he was dying.

On May 25 the Bishop of Troyes heard Thibaut's last confession and administered the sacrament. Then a strange procession began to pass through the death chamber. One by one Champagne's vassal knights and barons, those who had taken the cross at Ecri and afterward, came to kneel by the Count's bed and repeat their vows to the Holy Land. To each man he gave a portion of his treasury so that after his death no one could seek dispensation from his solemn oath on grounds of poverty. Another, larger sum would go into the common coffers of the army, and still another he willed to whichever great lord would take his place.

When all was done, when the last knight had gone to join the group in the antechamber, when his seal had been affixed to his will and the weeping Countess led from the chamber by her frightened women and anxious midwife, Thibaut extracted one last promise from his Marshal.

"The army must have a single commander," he said, his voice so low and feeble that Villehardouin had to bend over the bed to catch the words. "Though there be a council to advise him, one man alone must hold the reins of decision. You know that it must be so, Geoffrey. To you and to no other do I entrust the task of finding a man strong enough to hold this army together. We are both practical men. The sum I have left in my will may help to attract candidates. But it must not be too hungry a lord. Choose, if you can, a man accustomed to power, one who has a

care for his name and his house. Swear to me that you will not
fail in this."

"I swear, my lord."

"Then I am content to die."

The bishop stepped from the shadows and folded Thibaut's
arms across his chest. "Jerusalem," the Count whispered, his eyes
straining to see the cross on Garnier's splendid vestments. A mist
enveloped him, cool and comforting after the fever. Moments
later the bishop traced the sign of the cross on Thibaut's forehead and gently drew the lids down over his staring, empty
eyes.

Although he escorted the body of the Count to its last resting
place in the Church of St. Stephen, and later joined in the tear-
ful rejoicing with which the new Count was ushered into the
world five days after his father's death, emotionally Geoffrey
held himself aloof from the daily life of the suddenly bereft and
uncertain court. He could not yet allow himself the luxury of a
mourning which weakened the will and confused the mind.
Later, he promised the dead man, later I will weep for you and
spend hours on my knees in prayer for your soul, but for now I
must accomplish the task you set me.

Others shared his concern, knowing of the charge with which
Thibaut had entrusted him, and as soon as decently possible,
Villehardouin called them together to plan the future: Matthew
of Montmorency, Simon of Montfort and the Seneschal, Geoffrey
of Joinville.

"This haste is unseemly," complained Simon of Montfort, who
was a stickler for proper observance of the forms dictated by
custom. "Montmorency will be the military commander of
Champagne's battalions. Why can't we simply announce this fact
to Blois and Flanders and let it go at that?"

"I have not the rank for such a command," said Matthew of
Montmorency simply.

"Rank!" exploded Montfort angrily. "Experience is what will
be needed in the Holy Land, and of that you have more than
most men. How many others can claim as much?"

Montmorency shifted uncomfortably under his kinsman's hot
passion. "Explain it to him, Geoffrey," he said.

"Matthew is not being slighted in this, nor any other who served Count Thibaut," began Villehardouin slowly. It was a delicate, time-consuming task to have to explain shades of gray to a soldier who saw only blacks and whites. "But we must consider the effect the Count's death will have on those who are not as single-minded in their purpose as we. Thibaut himself was aware of it. That is why he forced each of his vassals to renew his vow individually."

"And thereby hastened his own death," said Montfort acidly, seeing in his mind's eye the long line of men who had passed through the death chamber, each one draining a tiny bit of strength from the mortally ill man who had summoned them.

"Perhaps," conceded Geoffrey of Joinville. "But when death is certain, the manner of one's dying becomes of supreme importance. Thibaut willingly sacrificed a few short hours of the life that remained to him, knowing that humankind is frail and fearful. What is unseemly is that we should quarrel over the dead."

"Consider this, Simon," continued Villehardouin patiently. "Men take the cross after hearing Fulk of Neuilly preach, many because of the sense of shame his sermons arouse in them, but most for reasons which are a tenuous balance of religious fervor and the yearning for adventure. But once they have sewn the cross to their garments, what is it that keeps them faithful? Not the praise of their comrades, for that is too quickly given and forgotten in the dull, hard lives most soldiers live. And remember, we are speaking of the mass of men, those who will make up the bulk of the army, the common soldiers and the poorer knights whom we expect to follow us. No," he said, refusing to allow Montfort to interrupt him, "these are not to be despised. As a commander yourself, you know I speak the truth." Montfort subsided reluctantly. "What do the minstrels sing about? What songs are asked for over and over again? The old tales, the stories of kings and champions who rode gloriously into battle and met death with hymns on their lips and joy in their hearts. Duty is not enough. It is fame, glory and the immortality of legend that alone satisfy men's souls."

"Roland was a fool," said Montfort, unable to contain himself any longer. "And Olivier an even greater one."

"Not even a handful of men would agree with you," said

Matthew of Montmorency crisply, amazed that Simon of Montfort would speak so disparagingly of two of the most precious
figures of chivalry. "Not even you yourself believe it, in your
heart of hearts. I know you too well, Simon."

Villehardouin and Geoffrey of Joinville exchanged exasperated
looks. If Montfort and Montmorency once got locked in a fierce
debate over two long-dead heroes of Charlemagne the important
point of the whole conversation would never be made.

"The fact is that three of the most nobly born counts of
France took the cross and thereby inspired an army to rise from
out of nowhere." Villehardouin clipped his words off sharply,
forcing back Montfort's wandering attention. "Now one of those
counts is dead. Before Blois or Flanders can waver, before whispers and rumor can hint that the men of Champagne have already begun to defect, before anyone can say that God called
Thibaut before his time as a sign that the army should disband,
another noble lord of equal rank must seem to step forward
spontaneously to fill the void."

"Seem to step forward spontaneously?" questioned Montfort,
all his senses alert now. "Will that not happen as a matter of
course, Geoffrey?"

"I fear not," answered Villehardouin. "The Count of St. Pol
was the last great lord to take the cross, and that was over a
year ago. There has been no one else since."

"Think about that for a while," said Geoffrey of Joinville
softly.

"Shall we go a-begging then, to men who have already
shunned their duty?" asked Montfort scornfully.

"Beggars in Christ's name," said Montmorency. "I have already fought once in the Holy Land. There is no humiliation I
would not willingly endure for the privilege of fighting there
again."

Simon of Montfort stared incredulously at him. Coming from
any other man such a statement would have been met with a
snort of disgust. But Montmorency was sincere, and he choked
back a hot reply. Going as Christ's ambassadors, they would be
honorably received in any court in Christendom, and if they met
with no success, the blame and shame of it would not lie on
their heads but on the reputations of those who valued comfort

and security more than a chance to fight the infidel and save their immortal souls. Villehardouin was right. The entire crusade teetered on the brink of ignominious defeat before a single blow had been struck. Inaction could push it over the edge, and who knew when the call would come again? There could be no turning back. Characteristically, his decision quickly made, he was at once the most determined of the four.

"Where do we go first?" he asked.

"Burgundy," said Villehardouin. "The present Duke's father fought at Acre and died later at Tyre. We have only to remind him that the late Duke is still unavenged and his pride will do the rest. He will not refuse us."

But, unbelievably, he did, immune to the appeal for vengeance and indifferent to the promise that if he would only take the cross all of Thibaut's treasure should be his. Burgundy's ruler might be poor at the moment, but he had not forgotten the painful lesson Philip Augustus had taught his father fifteen years before. The French king had forced the old Duke to abandon his family's custom of systematically and at regular intervals plundering the rich abbeys of the duchy and had seen to it that Hugh made restitution to his victims. From that moment on Burgundy had been a faithful vassal of France, and soon, Odo believed, he would begin to reap the rewards of loyal service. King John of England had stolen away the intended bride of the Count of La Marche. Soon, very soon, the outraged Count would appeal to Philip Augustus for justice. And Burgundy knew that when the King of France decided that the moment had come to crush John Lackland once and for all, those loyal vassals who had not gone chasing a will-o'-the-wisp in the Holy Land would earn the King's good favor and share in the lands the English king could not hope to hold. Burgundy, not too regretfully, declined the honor.

Villehardouin knew himself in check. He tried one more move, sending Geoffrey of Joinville to the court of Thibaut, Count of Bar-le-Duc. The Count mourned his cousin of Champagne as sincerely as he had wept for his elder brother who had died at Acre. But here too the answer was no. Checkmate.

At the end of June the barons met at Soissons, Count Baldwin of Flanders and Hainault, Count Louis of Blois and Chartres, Count Hugh of St. Pol, Count Geoffrey of Perche, many of their most important vassals and, of course, Villehardouin.

"I have one more name to propose to the assembly," Villehardouin told Geoffrey of Joinville. "I am certain that this lord will not refuse us, yet though we badly need his leadership I am reluctant to name him."

"We are desperate, Geoffrey," said Joinville bitterly. He still smarted painfully from the abrupt manner in which Bar-le-Duc had dealt with him. "Baldwin of Flanders is here to attend the parliament, but rumor has it that he would be only too glad to see it fail. Were it not for the Countess Mary he would long since have sought a dispensation from his vow."

"Thank God for our noble ladies," breathed Villehardouin sincerely. Not once had the Countess Blanche reproached him for doing all in his power since her husband's death to ensure that she would be left virtually alone in Champagne. Daughter to one King of Navarre, sister to another, she had been imbued with a sense of duty since earliest childhood, so that when Villehardouin had asked for an audience with her to explain where he felt his first duty lay, she had greeted him from her lying-in bed with the words: "My lord Marshal, I had not thought to find you still about Champagne's business. You have my permission, indeed my command, to go about the Lord's." It meant the end of Champagne's proud independence, for Blanche would have to make humble submission to Philip Augustus to guarantee the safety of her infant son's inheritance, but peace and honor were never cheaply bought.

And now Mary of Flanders, a proud daughter of Champagne, sister to the dead Thibaut, was all that held Baldwin fast to his duty. If the Duke of Burgundy counted on a war between France and England to make his fortune, how much more eagerly Baldwin must yearn for one. Flanders was a vassal state of the Holy Roman Empire although the Count was a liege subject of the French king, and from England Baldwin and his nobles regularly received large sums of money, yearly pensions to ensure neutrality if not outright allegiance to King John. Philip Augustus had been obliged to invade Flanders a few years ago, so endangering his own person that on more than one occasion he had almost been captured by the Flemings. An uneasy truce now existed between the two men, for Baldwin had turned indecisive at the last moment, unwilling or unable to follow up his obvious advantage. With an ally like John Lackland, no man ever knew just where he stood. But to Villehardouin's way of thinking that indecisiveness was a serious flaw in the Count's character. Never, under any circumstances, could he be allowed a position of supreme authority over the army of crusaders.

The only man the Marshal was absolutely certain would never waver, never hesitate, never abandon an advantage was the Marquis of Montferrat, the man whom very soon he would persuade the parliament to send for.

To Geoffrey of Joinville he now confided the details of his brief visit to Montferrat in April, hiding nothing, neither the Marquis's deep skepticism nor the impression of carefully concealed ambition he had sensed. Joinville listened patiently, even when Villehardouin, usually so adept and polished in his speech, hesitated and repeated himself, searching for exactly the right words to describe the peculiar look that had come into Montferrat's eyes during his reading of the treaty.

"Naturally he would be surprised, even shocked by the size of the sum the Doge has demanded. We all were at first," Joinville declared. "But in my opinion that weighs more in his favor than had he blithely dismissed it. We want a man of caution, Geoffrey, but also one of great determination. I will support you in this and speak out for Montferrat myself if more persuasion is necessary. We must have more than one check on Baldwin. The others too will fall under the Marquis's spell as they would not that of a younger, less experienced man. Montferrat is a respected name in the Holy Land, and the present Marquis is a man to whom family pride means much. Thibaut would have applauded your choice."

The French knights vowed to the cross were hard men, practical men, their boyhoods long behind them and best forgotten. Although a man did not truly become a man until he was knighted at twenty-one or thereabouts, he ceased to be a child on the day he was sent to do his page's service in a faraway

household where every face turned to him was set in lines of
unremitting criticism and stern rebuke.

For nine years, first as page, then as squire, he nourished himself on scraps from his lord's table, slept where and when he
could, polished sword, shield and armor until his fingers ran
blood, learned the care and currying of horses, practiced the arts
of war and single combat until his body toughened, his bones
knit tight and hard, and bruise on top of bruise permanently
darkened his skin. He learned to satisfy his body's dark cravings
with other boys and serving girls, paid lip service to the beauty
and purity of his lord's wife and daughters, picked up a song or
two to sing in polite company, confessed himself regularly to a
priest, performed the same penances for the same old sins, forgot the fear of hell and sinned again. But most of all, he
dreamed of knighthood, of wearing gold or silver spurs, of striding into strange halls with the proud clank of sword against hip,
of hearing himself addressed as "sir knight," of freedom, of leaving the ranks of the oppressed, of acquiring the right and the
power to send mottle-faced page boys and worshipful squires
scurrying off to do *his* bidding.

And by the time that day came, when he felt the touch of
sword on shoulder and the hard slap across his face, when he
leaped from ground to saddle without touching the stirrup,
when he ran successfully at the quintain, balanced a lance with
ease and precision and swung his heavy sword so quickly
through the air that it hissed and glittered like a dangerous un-
coiled serpent, by the time that day came he had lost all his illu-
sions, he had come to grips with life and bested it, he had survived the tests and mock battles, and the pattern of his life had
been set. To fight and survive were his goals, to fight and win, to
fight and make light of broken bones and deep wounds, to fight,
and eventually, though the future stretched out so far before
him that it was dreamlike and unreal, to die fighting.

When Thibaut of Champagne died, many knights felt that the
prospect of the most glorious fight of all died with him. Some
made plans to go to Apulia, others reluctantly resheathed their
swords and counseled patience, a not inconsiderable number
looked around for other wars to fight and prudently began to

speak of seeking dispensations from their vows. All were uncertain. All felt cheated.

Aleaumes' bishop complained that his clerk spent more time at Clari that spring and summer than he did in the chancery. By late June his patience was at an end.

"This is the last visit I will sanction," he thundered, "the very last one. If your father will not die and cannot mend, at least let him have the grace to do his lingering in Amiens."

"I'll tell him of Your Grace's concern." Aleaumes' spirits were high. At Clari he was fed to bursting by his mother and made much of by everyone else for the news he brought. The wine was far better than a clerk's ration and his cup was never empty. "Shall I inform him that he is invited to die in the episcopal palace?"

"Get out," bellowed the bishop. "You have three days, not a second longer."

It made a good story to be told and laughed over when the board had been cleared and the women were occupied with their everlasting spinning. Lady Agatha kept one ear open for what her husband and sons were discussing, but Aelis heard none of it. She was living more and more of her life in dreams. It annoyed the older woman and disturbed her more than she cared to admit. The cause the boys were vowed to was a holy one, as holy as Gilo's had been, and just as dangerous. In the empty years that would begin soon enough a wife's only companion was the memory of talk, her only consolation the knowledge that the commanders were skilled men who made the chances of living or dying about even.

"My lord Peter has left to join St. Pol at Soissons," Aleaumes announced. "To attend the parliament assembling there."

"And talk and talk and accomplish nothing," said Robert. By now every crusader knew that Burgundy and Bar-le-Duc had refused to join the army.

"According to the letter brought by St. Pol's messenger, the Marshal of Champagne has been assuring the barons, privately of course, that he has approached another great lord who seems willing to take Thibaut's place. But the Marshal will not name him until all the barons are present at the parliament."

"Is there a reason for such secrecy?" questioned Robert.

Aleaumes shrugged his shoulders, but Gilo, a knowing gleam in his eye, struggled to prop himself on one elbow. "The Marshal is shrewd," he said, "a man who reads the thoughts and sees into the hearts of other men. By withholding the name of his candidate until the last moment he forestalls opposition and can force an immediate vote. The barons will have already talked amongst themselves. They will be anxious and uncertain, willing to accept any worthy lord of suitable rank. Villehardouin counts on this."

"Surely they will not accept just anyone?"

"No, of course not. Yet Villehardouin must feel that some amongst them would oppose his choice were they given more time to consider it."

"But this parliament is not called to elect a single commander for the entire army, Father. St. Pol's letter said nothing of that. I know that my lord Peter had the impression that he would vote merely on the matter of who should take Thibaut's place on the inner council and receive the monies the Count left to whoever was chosen to be his successor."

"I am sure that Peter honestly believed what he told you, Aleaumes," said Gilo condescendingly. "But an old soldier like me has a sixth sense about command, and my bones tell me that more will come out of this parliament than anyone expects. While Count Thibaut lived who heard the name Villehardouin? He was a loyal servant of Champagne, a man entrusted with his master's commissions and the making of treaties, but always a figure half hidden in the background. Now he calls a parliament, men of higher rank than he defer to his judgment, and we all know his name. He would have made the Count of Champagne commander-in-chief, but as that is no longer possible he looks elsewhere. The man is setting himself up to be a kingmaker. Villehardouin has already promised supreme command to someone. He plays a dangerous game, one that could end badly for him, but he plays it well."

Two months later Robert was summoned by Peter of Amiens to join the parliament once again assembled at Soissons. Boniface of Montferrat was on his way from Italy to take the cross and accept command of the army. It had all fallen out as Gilo had predicted.

Aelis was smiling as she held the stirrup cup of farewell for her husband. He might be gone for a month or more, and though Lady Agatha would press aphrodisiacal herbs on her in his absence, herbs that guaranteed fertility and strengthened the female body against miscarriage, Aelis knew they would have no effect. Empty she was now, and empty she would remain. She looked fair and innocent, standing there in the late summer sunshine, her pale blond hair curling under the coif that proclaimed her married state, but she knew that the joy in her heart was sinful. She was praying that duty would keep Robert away from Clari at least until October, that Peter would keep him in Amiens even after the parliament was over, perhaps through Christmas. Nothing of this showed on her face as she raised herself on tiptoe to receive his formal kiss, then stood meekly beside Lady Agatha watching him ride off down the dusty road.

As they went back into the Hall, Aelis stumbled and clutched at her mother-in-law's arm to keep from falling. Lady Agatha steadied her, then stepped back a pace, holding her daughter-in-law at arm's length while her eyes ran speculatively over her body.

"Aelis, my child," she said, "I have sorely neglected you these past months. It is long past time that we two spoke together, not as mother and daughter-in-law, but as married women, one to the other, freely and openly. Gilo's health is much improved and he scarcely needs my special care now. While my son is away I shall devote my time to you alone, and willingly, for the sake of the future happiness I know you both desire."

Aelis kept her eyes fixed on the floor as she followed Lady Agatha toward the private corner of the Hall where the great loom stood.

"Sometimes it is not enough to do one's duty in a merely obedient fashion," Lady Agatha was saying. "Though I am sure you are as obedient a wife as any husband could ask for. Nature occasionally requires assistance from artifice. There are certain herbs and practices which many a wife has had recourse to. Do you understand what I am saying?"

Aelis nodded, miserable and humiliated, not daring to protest or speak the truth to this woman who believed her to be like every other female.

"I shall instruct you myself," Lady Agatha said, "while we work together." She picked up her spindle and began turning it deftly between her fingers. "It will make the time pass more quickly while your lord is gone, and who knows, perhaps by Christmas we shall have double cause to celebrate the feast." She smiled archly at her daughter-in-law.

Aelis smiled back, picked up her spindle and was soon lost in her own thoughts. She did not hear a word of Lady Agatha's very informative lecture.

IV

The noise of hammering drifted faintly into the Abbey of Our Lady of Soissons, mingling in the sultry August air with the curses of the men who toiled in the heat and the shouts of those who directed the building. Slowly a high platform was taking shape under the heavily laden fruit trees in the orchard, a flat stage crowned in the very center by the skeleton of an altar. The bare new wood gave off a sharp resinous smell softened by the sweet scent of ripening fruit. In a few days both odors would be lost in musky clouds of incense.

Mary of Flanders was comfortably lodged in the largest chamber of the abbey's guesthouse, a doubly honored visitor. As wife to Count Baldwin of Flanders and Hainault and sister to the late Count Thibaut of Champagne she was one of the most noble ladies in the land. But to the nuns of the abbey, bound forever to this house by their Benedictine vow of stability, she possessed an added attraction that was almost their sole topic of conversation during the short hours of community recreation. Sewn to the shoulders of the rather plain, dark-colored gowns she affected was the crusader's cross, for she had determined to accompany her husband to the Holy Land as once her grandmother, Eleanor of Aquitaine, had ridden with her first husband, Louis VII of France. The nuns who had assisted in the unpacking of her cases had burst into excited chatter as gown after gown had been shaken out, each bearing a marvelously embroidered cross of gold thread as its only adornment. Mary had smiled indulgently at their childlike enthusiasm, pleased that they compared the shining crosses to the finest cloths of their own altar.

"It is fitting that those who go about the Lord's business be

dressed soberly," she had told them, "putting away the orna-
ments of the flesh. But also fitting that His Cross blaze out in
such splendor that the infidel is blinded by its beauty and its
power."

Fitting indeed, the nuns agreed, almost smothered in the thick
woolen habits they wore year round. Having themselves chosen
the black and white suitable to Brides of Christ, their eyes
feasted all the more hungrily on the only magnificence left to
them, the greens and golds and scarlets of the liturgy and the
jewels that burned in altar vessels. The crosses on Mary of
Flanders' gowns were only miniatures of the great cross she had
worked for her husband, a thing of such surpassing beauty that
it was said to have lit up the whole cathedral of Bruges on the
dark, dank Ash Wednesday when both had pledged themselves
to the Holy Land. The nuns yearned for a sight of it, but Count
Baldwin had had little time to visit his lady. The great lords who
had assembled at Soissons to await the coming of Boniface of
Montferrat met daily and nightly, though for the most part the
subjects of their discussions were secret.

"Military strategy," explained Mary to the mystified nuns, as
courteous but uncommunicative messengers daily brought gifts
and inquiries about her health and well-being to the abbey.
"Men are curiously reluctant to discuss such matters with
women. We are not credited with much intelligence, good
dames, and our tongues are said to wag overmuch. But I shall
not remain long in ignorance, for there are no secrets in the bedchamber." She laughed as she spoke, for the nuns were supposed
to be unversed in the ways of men and the pleasures of the flesh.
A dark flush betrayed the avid curiosity and embarrassment of
the younger ones among them, those poor souls who, she imagined, had still to struggle with the forever unappeased longings
demanded by their vow of chastity.

Mary had not brought many of her women with her to Soissons. Indeed, she herself had had to argue mightily with the
Count over her own attendance at the parliament. Not for anything would she miss the sight of the Giant, as Montferrat was
nicknamed, receiving the cross from the hands of Fulk of
Neuilly, the famous preacher who had begun it all. And in addition, many of the lords who attended were her kinsmen and she

yearned for the sight of them and for news of their families. Who knew if she would ever see them again? Men were not the only casualties of the Holy Land.

Baldwin had given in to her pleadings, uncomfortably aware that the last of her arguments was undoubtedly true. He wished with all his heart that she had not taken the cross, for he feared that her fragile beauty was unequal to the rigors of the long sea voyage and the hot sun of the Holy Land. He had known from the beginning that it was useless to argue with a granddaughter of the most self-willed, stubborn woman in Christendom, for no man could long hold out against such single-mindedness. Reluctantly he had assented, saving face and asserting his authority by insisting that she confine herself to the abbey, well out of sight of the army's representatives—except, of course, for the occasions of ceremony, which she would be permitted to attend.

Mary had at first been satisfied with the Count's conditions, but as her stay at the abbey lengthened and each day was exactly like the one that had preceded it, a monotonous round of prayer and boring conversation over endless needlework, she grew restless.

She had begun by joining the nuns in the chanting of the Holy Office, even rising in the middle of the night, as they did, to sing Matins in the predawn chill of the chapel, keeping their same hours of silence, and gliding about the abbey and its garden with eyes ostentatiously fixed on the ground. But she was no nun, for Eleanor's blood ran too thickly in her veins, and gradually she abandoned the game. The nuns thought none the worse of her for having failed to live by the strict Rule they themselves struggled daily to maintain. Indeed they honored her for having tried, even for so brief a time, to enter fully into the life of the monastery.

"Few great ladies possess the piety of the Countess," the Mistress of Novices told her charges. "But our ways are not hers. God has placed her in the world and willed that she be given the privilege of seeing Jerusalem, a privilege He has denied us, my daughters. But to us He has given even greater gifts, if we will be worthy of them. We have been given the miracle of Himself and the honor of the total dedication of our lives in His service. Our prayers will strengthen and support the lady Mary, and in spirit we will accompany her on her quest. Do not be envious or restless in God's House, for there is no castle in Christendom that possesses a greater treasure than the one we bear in our hearts."

The novices discussed the Mistress's conference as they paced the cloister garden during the afternoon's hour of permitted conversation. There were three of them, and they walked abreast, ever conscious of the Rule's injunction that there was safety from particular friendships and charity in word and action when no two sought each other's exclusive company.

The senior among them, Agnes of Vailly, was to take her vows in three months' time, and was already fitted comfortably into the Benedictine mold. Since infancy she had been destined for this abbey, and she was fortunate that she possessed the gift of a true vocation. Claude of Chauny, her junior in the religious life by scarcely six weeks, found little joy in the calling her parents had chosen for her, but she had expected none. At times only the pride of her house upheld her, but with the passing of the years would come the peace of resignation and acceptance. She was strong-willed and clear-sighted, confident that someday she would wear the ring and cross of abbess, for she had a natural gift for organization and an air of authority strange in one so young. She was of high birth and her future was assured. She had only to wait.

They made a pretty picture as they walked to and fro on the green, close-clipped paths between well-tended squares in which grew the herbs used both for cooking and the making of medicines. The veils that framed their faces and billowed out behind them like the sails of small ships were of purest white, the color of innocence and virginity. The whiteness of the coifs and veils purified the fresh, unlined faces, endowing them for the moment with the slightly ethereal look often seen on the carved images of the saints, so that even Claude of Chauny, whose plainness verged on ugliness, seemed touched by beauty. It was purely a trick of the eyes in her case, as she herself had readily admitted the day she caught sight of her image reflected in the dark water of the washing pool. But on Anne of Nanteuil, the tallest and most slender of the three, the effect was startling.

Many of the nuns in the Benedictine monastery of Soissons

were comely, even handsome women. It was a prosperous house whose Abbess could usually afford to be selective in admitting candidates to the life. From time to time, in charity, she had accepted a girl who limped, who was hunchbacked, harelipped or so timid that she stuttered uncontrollably, but the feebleminded or the slow-witted she rejected. There were other, poorer religious houses to take them in, but not hers. Very beautiful young women were rarely made nuns, though some of the children who entered at ten or twelve years of age grew into a surprising and unexpected loveliness that faded as quickly as it had blossomed.

The weary priest who had brought Anne of Nanteuil to her had been almost unbelievably transparent. The Abbess had not believed for a moment that the girl who sat quietly beside him, never speaking unless questioned directly, was as eager to give herself to God as he claimed. But she did remember the sister who had begged to be left in her care so many years ago, and how gentle the lord of Nanteuil had been with his daughter.

"You'll come back," he had told the weeping nine-year-old. "I've given Lady Abbess the half of your dowry and she's promised to receive you when you've passed your twelfth birthday. I cannot bring myself to part with her before that," he had added, and the Abbess, a stern woman who seldom allowed herself the luxury of emotion, had been greatly touched.

Now the little black-haired, blue-eyed girl was dead, and a sister who might have been her twin had been ordered to take her place. The priest did not attempt to deny it, and the Abbess, who had received many other girls under exactly the same circumstances, asked only one final question.

"Do you come here of your own free will, and are you prepared to persevere in the life?" Few girls had, but the pretense was maintained.

Anne had not answered immediately. She had seemed to very carefully weigh both the question and the response she would give. The priest fidgeted nervously while they waited for her to speak, and the Abbess, far more worldly than he in spite of the walls behind which she lived, wondered what dreadful alternative she had been threatened with. Compassionate, guilt-ridden Father Antoine had treated her lips and fingers with a healing salve and dawdled so long on the road that her mouth appeared

head ache and run her fingers through her sweat-drenched hair, hair that she could tell by the feel of it now resembled the square, boxy cut of a young page.

She had begun to let it grow the day the leaders of the new crusade chose Soissons to be the site of their frequent parliaments. She had watched them assemble, had laughed with delight at the confusion of men and horses, tents and baggage carts that marked each arrival and departure, had known that one day Mary of Flanders would accompany her husband, and that with her would ride a bevy of brightly clad female attendants, ladies of noble birth, serving women, washerwomen, women to fetch and carry and amuse, a score of women in all manner of secular dress and headgear, so many, she hoped, that one extra could slip into their ranks unnoticed.

The other novices did not like Anne of Nanteuil. She revealed too little of herself, did not condescend to chat and gossip and exchange confidences, did not, in fact, act like a normal nun or woman at all. She was not afraid of mice or spiders, did not cross herself on entering a dark corridor, sought solitude rather than the comfort of companionship, and assessed her fellow religious, the old and fat and careless, the lean and harshly self-disciplined, the young and shy and nervous, with all the cool detachment and remembering eye of a paid informer. Her presence made all the nuns ill at ease, though it was only after she had been given the habit that the Mistress of Novices realized it. Until then the girl had moved through her assigned hours of study and religious duties in a state of dazed obedience, as if not quite certain where she was. But with the clothing had come this new personality, not the putting on of Christ, but the creeping out of slyness and a smile that mocked the injunction to be childlike in the Lord. The Mistress's initial dislike of Anne of Nanteuil had never changed, but until today the girl had done nothing, said nothing, to justify dismissal, and her dowry, while not enormous, had been fully paid.

Dame Joanna paused for a moment under the vaulted arches of the cloister. She was intensely angry, her face still red with the shame of having to meekly accept Lady Abbess's stern rebuke. It had been years since she had been spoken to so impolitely, as if she were a mere novice herself and not a senior nun with a truly exceptional gift for forming young souls. Pride was the subject she most frequently lectured her charges on, for she was proud herself, and not always certain that it was all that sinful.

The novices moved toward her, swaying from side to side with the religious dignity she had drilled into them, unhurried, serene, smiling expectantly at their Mistress.

"One of you has deliberately singularized herself," Dame Joanna said crisply. Two faces paled with fright and instant, guilty soul-searching. One was masklike in its stillness, and this one was Anne's. "The Countess of Flanders has asked that one of you play to her this afternoon. The heat has given her a headache. She asked for the novice who played so sweetly on the lute in the visitors' garden this morning after Mass. She asked for this novice by name, Sister Anne."

The girl's behavior was really intolerable. She had not even the grace to cast down her eyes in shame at having so boldly set herself apart. Singularization was one of the worst things a nun could do, one of the few infractions of the Rule that roused the bishop's anger and ensured his unwanted interference in the abbey's internal affairs.

"Since she has asked for you, you will have to go. Lady Abbess is displeased, I am displeased, and all the holy virgin saints upon whose lives we model ours must be hiding their eyes against the sight of one who professes to live a hidden life yet acts so brazenly. Go to her you must, but leave her chamber at the first stroke of None. You'll wear out your knees for this, Sister."

Anne stood outside the Countess's door, her hand upraised to knock. From what she had observed of the lady's conduct she judged Mary of Flanders to be fairly typical of her kind, easily aroused to enthusiastic espousal of anything that promised diversion, resentful of the passive role to which her husband had relegated her, soft-hearted and generous because it cost her so little to be bountiful, condescending to the nuns, whom she thought had little experience of the world. Not a plotter or a planner, not desperately determined to change the life fate destined her to live, above all, not the type to weigh an action overlong before committing herself to it. Mary was a careless young lady, a woman whose high position begged to be used.

"You play beautifully, Sister," the Countess said, "though I fear it has put my women to sleep."

Two ladies snored noisily in their chairs, veils askew, heads lolling forward as though their necks were boneless. A third, more forthrightly sweating in the heat, had hoisted her skirts above her knees and fallen asleep across the open window frame, her head pillowed on her arms.

"If they could only see how graceless they look at this moment." The Countess took the moist, mint-scented cloth from her forehead and delicately wiped her hands. "I wonder that any men can covet a lady who snores."

Anne waited patiently, her fingers plucking the strings of the lute. Chord after chord lingered in the air, but it was too near None to risk beginning another long ballad.

"I hope you are permitted to accept a small personal gift," Mary of Flanders said. "Hardly more than a token gesture of gratitude for the pleasure you've given me this afternoon, but I know that Holy Poverty forbids anything more costly." She held a delicately worked ivory statuette of the Virgin in her hand, a miniature of herself actually, for the artist had made it on commission and given his patroness's face to the Mother of God. "He flattered me, don't you think?" she asked, expecting the customary swift denial, but Anne of Nanteuil neither spoke nor reached out to accept the gift. She laid the lute aside as though never intending to pick it up again and fixed her steady, almond-shaped blue eyes on a point somewhere just over the Countess's head.

"An ivory statue is of no use to me at all, my lady," she said, "nor any of the other trinkets in this room."

Mary of Flanders was slightly shocked to hear her quite valuable possessions dismissed as trinkets. Shocked, but too bemused to be insulted. No one had ever refused a single one of the many gifts she had bestowed, nor had any creature so far beneath her in station dared to hint that she would prefer a reward of her own choosing.

"What would please you then, Sister? A new cloth for your altar? Some delicacy the community could share at recreation or in the refectory? Perhaps a gift of wine to ease the pains of those who lie in the infirmary? I had already planned to give something of the sort to repay Lady Abbess's hospitality, but I could make the donation a doubly generous one and tell your superior that I was moved to such largess by the amiability of one of her novices. And that would be quite true, you know."

"No, my lady, that's not what I want at all."

"Has no one ever told you, Sister, that those who refuse to accept what is offered them often end with nothing?"

"I have been told that, my lady. Many times. But I have also learned to reach out for what I want, to pass by the withered fruit at the bottom of a tree and reach for the tender, nearly unattainable fruit at the top."

"And what fruit are you reaching for today, little sister?"

"I want you to take me with you to the Holy Land."

Anne's penances were as severe as she had expected them to be. She knelt in the refectory that evening making her *amende* in full view of the entire community. With arms outstretched as if on a cross she confessed to the sin of pride and the fault of singularization. She recited the psalm of atonement, kissed Lady Abbess's feet, kissed Dame Joanna's feet, kissed the hard stone floor, ate her ration of stale bread while still kneeling, and heard herself ordered to repeat the performance at every community meal for a full two weeks.

For charity's sake and because the Rule ordained that it be so, her sisters would walk and talk and work with her as though she were as blamelessly obedient and humbly tamed as they. Only in the refectory, four times a day, would they sit listening to her catalog of offenses and wonder just exactly what she had done to singularize herself so magnificently.

"She's not humbled yet," Dame Joanna told the Abbess. "But she's tasting the bitterness of pride. I'll watch her more closely from now on, and set her additional penances to perform as soon as I judge her strong enough to accept them in faith. She has a rebellious soul, but it will be tempered and subdued in time."

"How much time?" Lady Abbess asked.

"As long as it takes," the Mistress of Novices replied firmly. "As long as it takes."

Three more days, Anne told herself again and again. Twelve more meals. Kiss the floor, choke down the crumbly dry bread, let no hint of anger show on your face. In three days the parliament would be over and she would be on her way to Bruges.

What did it matter that she had lied to the Countess of Flanders, had invented such a piteous story of persecution by Dame Joanna that Mary was moved to tears at hearing it? Or that she had played the lady's character as skillfully as she played the strings of her lute? Mary had passed from incredulous confidante to outraged champion to girlish intriguer with an ease and rapidity that had amazed even Anne herself. She had not known that she possessed so great an ability to charm. The Countess would regret the whole affair in the morning, of course, but Anne would not let her go, and she would be too embarrassed, too deeply ashamed of herself to reveal the novice's plan to Lady Abbess. To do so would be to inculpate herself as accessory. I made her bed for her, Anne thought complacently, but she climbed in all by herself and now she'll have to lie in it. Three more days!

V

Boniface of Montferrat arrived at the end of August, escorted by a large train of knights and servingmen. He had traveled from northern Italy with all the pomp of a monarch on a progress, and, like the king he felt he ought to be, he was lavishly welcomed. The lords who had so impatiently awaited him at Soissons rode out from the camp to greet him, their set speeches all the more flowery and praisesome for the crowds of lesser knights streaming in their wake. Many of these, battered, impoverished veterans of earlier expeditions to the Holy Land, listened with jaundiced ears, frankly and openly assessing the man they would be asked to follow.

It seemed to those who saw him from afar that for once a popular hero was proving to be larger than his legend. Montferrat towered a full head or more over the men among whom he rode and the watchful crowd sighed with satisfaction when he dismounted. The impressive height which had caused men to nickname him The Giant was no mere illusion gained on horseback, his air of authority no fleeting wish of the moment. Immensely tall, heavily muscled, a dark-complected, burly man with command and confidence engraved in every line of his weatherbeaten face, he strode briskly into Count Baldwin's tent where a welcoming feast had been prepared in his honor.

Rumor flew about the camp, and as men gathered around the cooking fires that were lit at twilight the talk was all of him. Most of them were familiar with the exploits of his house and the careers of his father, William the Old, and his eldest brother, William Long-Sword, who had been briefly married to the sister of Baldwin IV, the leper king of Jerusalem. They remembered a

second brother, Conrad, the defender of Tyre, whose obstinate
courage had won him first the hand of a sister of the Emperor of
Constantinople, then that of Queen Isabella of Jerusalem. With
that queen had come a crown, a kingdom and an Assassin's
dagger a few days after his election. And some even recalled the
tale of Renier, another brother, who had also married a princess
of the royal house of Constantinople and for a short time
reigned over the Greek kingdom of Salonika. The scions of the
House of Montferrat had long looked to the East to satisfy their
ambitions. And the East had always meant beleaguered Jerusalem. A very few men wondered that no marquis of Montferrat
had yet attempted to regain the kingdom lost by the inept
Renier. Salonika had been a prize almost beyond imagining.
Salonika, Constantinople. Every man who had ever listened
spellbound to travelers' tales felt the lure of Constantinople, the
city that was popularly called the Rome of the East. But even
these, with almost blind single-mindedness, eventually directed
their thoughts solely toward the Holy Land. This was an army
about to embark on a mission of righteous conquest. Every man
in it was guessing, speculating, planning. Constantinople, for all
its fabled glory, was a distraction quickly shrugged off and forgotten.

The broad outlines of the proposed campaign were common
knowledge; transportation overseas in Venetian ships, an overland march to Jerusalem, unavoidable pitched battles every step
of the way, an assault on the city, perhaps a long siege to be endured, then victory. Much would never be told them in advance,
for surprise was an important element in any war, and even the
most careless squire knew that the Sultan's spies were everywhere, trying desperately to learn the exact location of their
landing place. That must be the best-kept secret of all, for they
would be most vulnerable at the moment of debarkation from
their ships. Those who suspected that the target was Egypt were
careful to share their speculations with only the closest of
friends, for the logic of a sudden attack on the heart of the
infidel kingdom was so beautifully simple that they were convinced their assumptions were correct. Let the infidels call in
troops from far away to mass in a protective arc around
Jerusalem. A wise and crafty general would strike where least

expected so as to weaken the body in its most vulnerable part. Once the heart was dead the limbs could be chopped off almost at leisure.

Throughout the camp minstrels sang the songs composed by the troubadour Raimbaut of Vaqueiras, who had been Montferrat's constant companion for twenty-five years. The songs, dozens of them, celebrated the Marquis's bravery, his invincibility in battle, his prowess with women, his wide learning and his perfect courtesy. If only half the incidents they recounted were true the infidel would be confounded at every turn.

In the morning the Montferrat of legend, the real Montferrat, would be formally presented to those gathered at Soissons, and in the name of the entire army accepted by them and invested with its leadership. There was so great an air of excitement and anticipation in the camp that few bothered to make the pretense of sleep. The fires continued to burn long into the night.

Like many others, Peter of Amiens had found some excuse to stroll by the tent in which Boniface of Montferrat was being entertained by others of his rank. The personal guards of the Counts of Flanders, Blois and St. Pol lounged at its entrance in quiet conversation, ostensibly taking their ease. But the sharpness with which they scrutinized each passing man gave the lie to their apparent unconcern. Even here, almost in the heart of France, they were as alert as though in enemy territory. The drug-crazed Assassins of the Old Man of the Mountains could penetrate anywhere, and most felt that the leaders of the crusade were marked men.

One of St. Pol's men detached himself briefly from his fellows to greet Peter of Amiens. The count's kinsman was a favorite of his and well known to all Hugh's retainers.

"My lord," said the man, gravely saluting him.

"How goes it then, Eustache?" asked Peter of Amiens, returning the salute with a measure of the same gravity.

"Well enough, God be praised," came the answer. "And with yourself?"

"It's not a night for sleeping."

"Time enough for that when all is settled," agreed Eustache.

Peter of Amiens gestured questioningly toward the magnificent tent, from which came the faintest murmur of a man's voice, the words indecipherable even at this short distance.

"The Marshal of Champagne has joined them," said Eustache cautiously.

"No doubt the talk has turned serious then," commented Peter, half in jest. "Geoffrey of Villehardouin is a man upon whom the affairs of this world weigh heavily."

"The Marshal is sober-minded and serious," said Eustache approvingly. The finality in his voice indicated he would give them no further information.

Peter of Amiens smiled in the darkness. He approved the man's close-mouthedness. Whatever he had managed to overhear this night would never be passed on to any other, not even to a privileged kinsman of his liege lord.

"This is Robert of Clari, who will serve under my command," he said, introducing the companions who had been standing quietly in his shadow during the brief conversation with Eustache. "And his brother Aleaumes, clerk of the cathedral at Amiens. My brother Thomas I believe you know already."

Though he had feigned polite unawareness of their presence, Eustache had immediately assessed the three men accompanying Peter of Amiens, and as he approved of what he saw, he now greeted them warmly. They exchanged pleasantries for a few moments, then Eustache excused himself to return to his position near the tent's entrance.

"He's a good man," remarked Peter as they continued their stroll in the direction of the orchard. All was in readiness for the morrow and tonight the place drew men like a magnet. It was quiet under the trees, where the dark bulk of the abbey loomed over them like some huge bird with outstretched, protecting wings. They scarcely glanced at it as they passed beneath its walls; a house of holy women was of no interest to any of them.

"Fulk of Neuilly is here," commented Aleaumes. "I saw him arrive a short while ago."

"Will he preach tomorrow?" asked Robert.

"I doubt it," answered Aleaumes. "He looks exhausted, and I've heard that he's frequently ill nowadays. It's said that he's been on the point of dying more than once in the past six months. I don't know how much truth there is to the stories, but

I did see that he almost fell from his horse and had to be helped into his tent."

"No one here really needs his exhortations," said Thomas. "He would do well to save his strength and use it on those who must be persuaded to join us this coming year."

"Montferrat brought two white monks with him," continued Aleaumes, "and I've been told that the Bishop of Soissons himself will give him the cross tomorrow. Fulk will be on the altar with them, of course, but his presence here is more a matter of form than anything else. The news will be all over France that he approved Geoffrey of Villehardouin's choice and that will add strength and legitimacy to the Marquis's position."

"I wonder if it is wise that a preacher possess so much influence," said Peter of Amiens. "From now on there must be more emphasis placed on the military nature of the expedition. Prayer and mortification are all very well, and necessary too in their place, but men can't fight on empty bellies and visions."

"Have you heard him preach, my lord?" asked Robert of Clari.

"Only once. I was returning to Vignacourt and passed through a small town where a large crowd from the surrounding countryside had gathered in the marketplace to hear him. His manner of speaking put me off at first; he uses plain words and little of the imagery common to most preachers. On that particular day at least, he was vulgar and profane. But I could see that those who listened to him hung on his every word, and when he railed against the abuses of the moneylenders and the corruption of the clergy they cheered him. I think that, like a good minstrel, he suits himself to his audience, and as these men were poor farmers and craftsmen he spoke in a vernacular they could understand."

"He has never been universally popular," said Thomas. "The clergy of Lisieux had him thrown into jail when he dared to challenge their prerogatives."

"No man who speaks the truth as he sees it will be liked by everyone," said Aleaumes, "and God knows there is far too much corruption among clerics today. I'm sure that many a greasy monk and married priest prays daily for his swift departure from France."

"What place will he have with the army?" asked Robert.

"One of honor, I'm certain," said Peter of Amiens, "but of scant influence. The Giant will keep him so busy ministering to the spiritual needs of the foot soldiers that he will have no time to poke his nose into matters of strategy. His primary task, after all, is largely done. He preached the cross honestly and to good effect, but his hour of glory is almost over. It is we knights who will make his dream reality."

"We knights?" chided Thomas. The chanoine was far more content with the lot of a cleric than he knew his friend to be, but tonight, in this camp of men poised for war, his blood had begun to flow as hotly as it had on the evening when both he and Aleaumes had taken the cross, then slipped out of the cathedral precincts to mingle with the knights and common soldiers whose avowed intention had been to drink Amiens dry in the name of the glorious quest to which all of them were committed.

Peter laughed. "You are oversensitive, Thomas," he said, "you and Aleaumes both. Knights you may not be, but I've seen you fight and I know your worth. I would feel as vulnerable as a virgin without both your swords at my side. Just take care your bishop does not catch you practicing at swordplay in the sanctuary of his cathedral or it will be a dark cell and bread and water for the two of you!"

"Never fear, my lord," said Aleaumes confidently. "Our venerable bishop is half blind and so heavy with fat that one can hear him coming from half a league." He stuck out his belly and folded his hands piously over it, rolling from side to side in imitation of the bishop's waddling gait. "Which one are you, lad?" he intoned mournfully through his nose. "Ah, yes, the little farm boy from Clari. Stay pure, my son, stay pure."

"Your brother should have been a jester, Robert," said Peter of Amiens, wiping tears of laughter from his eyes. "Take care to warn him against turning his skill to imitating me. It would demoralize the troops."

"He is devoted to comedy, my lord," said Robert, "so you are safe from him."

"But there is comedy in every man, my lords," said Aleaumes. "And the more seriously a man takes himself, the funnier he becomes to those who have eyes to see and a brain to judge."

"Enough, enough," said Peter of Amiens. "Save your speeches,

Aleaumes, for the day when we shall welcome any new topic of conversation, even the learned commentaries of a clerk."

As they turned to retrace their steps back to camp, Peter of Amiens remarked casually to Robert, "It was most generous of your lady to spare me her bridegroom for this parliament." Probing delicately, he continued, "I trust she is in good health?"

"Excellent, my lord," answered Robert. "But after almost a year of marriage I can hardly be called a bridegroom." He paused a fraction of a second before adding, "Nor yet a father."

"That will come, in God's good time," said Peter reassuringly, having elicited the information he was seeking. "Your lady is still very young, is she not?"

"Not yet seventeen," answered Robert. The two clerks had dropped back and now followed behind, just out of earshot. "There is still time to beget an heir before I leave."

Peter of Amiens nodded soberly in agreement. No knight concerned himself overmuch with women's matters, but the birth of an heir was an intensely interesting subject to any man who owned land. A barren woman could and should be put away, though sometimes many years would pass before a husband's patience turned to bitterness.

"Present my compliments to your lady when you return to Clari," he said. "I should be pleased to meet her some day."

"She would be greatly honored, my lord," said Robert, wondering if Peter was about to invite them to his fief of Vignacourt for the Christmas festivities.

"You will have much to do at Clari before Pentecost," said Peter thoughtfully. "I shall probably be spending a great deal of time with my cousin of St. Pol, so I doubt that I'll need your service. You may remain at Clari until we set out for Venice. I've no doubt that will greatly please your lady."

"Yes, my lord," said Robert quietly. "I thank you."

"We should all spend time with our families in the coming months," continued Peter, thinking of his own wife and small sons. "It will certainly be years before we see them again. Our sons must not forget us."

"No, my lord." Those of us who are fortunate enough to have sons, Robert thought silently. He had been glad enough to es-

cape from Aelis's company for a few weeks, and did not doubt
that she had been equally delighted to see him go.

Everyone who saw her called her beautiful, but her complete
lack of passion made a mockery of her fairness. She was quiet,
docile and obedient before others, painfully silent and unreacha-
ble in private. Her body had scarcely changed since their marriage, but the sight of white, unresponsive flesh no longer
aroused him. To do his duty by her and his house, Robert now
had to take her in total darkness, imagining that his fingers
caressed one of the lusty, practiced wenches he had often tumbled in the past. Even that did not always work, particularly
when his lips met hers and found them dry with silent prayer.
Then he turned from her in disgust, his manhood defeated.

There was usually nothing more than polite disinterest between them, except in the rare moments when Robert's frustration and the fear of leaving no son behind him goaded him to a
cold anger akin to that he felt in battle. Several times in the past
few months he had beaten her, methodically and without
thought for the bruises she would have to conceal from others
by pretending illness and keeping to their chamber until the
blueness faded. But not even under a hail of blows did she display rage or passion. The body submitted, the lips moved, the
endless prayers continued. He was thoroughly sick of her, but
still determined to get her with child. Her mother had been fertile. She had borne nine children, though only Aelis had survived childhood. There was no reason to assume that the girl
was incapable of conceiving. He would continue to do his duty
by her, distasteful though it was. This winter would see his seed
take root. Only an heir could ensure that her lands would
remain his. Let her enjoy this temporary respite. Her body
would be rested and probably the more fertile because of it. It
had often proved so with the animals bred at Clari. And breeding was breeding, whether it be sow or woman.

The orchard was so thronged with men that the Abbess,
watching with all her nuns from the highest windows of the
monastery, feared for the safety of her precious harvest. "We
shall be lucky if half the fruit remains to us," she fretted, pointing out the bare lower limbs which had already been stripped of

their burden by the knights who had grown hungry and impatient while waiting for the Marquis to make his appearance.

Anne of Nanteuil, sandwiched in between the two other novices, scarcely heard the Abbess's remarks. Her eyes anxiously searched for Mary of Flanders, and her ears strained to catch the sound of the lady's distinctive, tinkling laugh. Surely the Countess would be among those closest to the altar. She sighed with relief when at last she made out the slender, delicate figure standing motionless and proud beside the Count, her husband. "There she is," she whispered.

"There who is?" questioned Claude of Chauny. Following Anne's intent gaze, she commented without great interest, "Oh, the Countess. Where else would she be?" She had had no personal contact with Mary of Flanders and was in fact hardly aware that the abbey's guest had removed herself, her ladies and all their baggage that very morning. "There they come!" she said, turning her attention to the procession that had begun to make its way through the crowd. "There's the bishop, and look, the tall man just behind the two white monks, that must be the Marquis."

At the end of the procession marched a rather slight man, the plainness of his dark robes startling amid the glittering throng, which murmured respectfully as he passed. "That is Fulk of Neuilly," she continued approvingly. "A holy man and one not puffed up with the pride of this world."

Anne heard nothing of the ceremony that followed; it passed like a silent dream before her eyes. Men knelt and crossed themselves and she saw their mouths move in acclaiming, soundless shouts. The Bishop of Soissons, gorgeously arrayed in vestments of cloth of gold, glittered like a sun spot as his arm rose and fell in the tracery of the cross. Geoffrey of Villehardouin spoke, and the Marquis delivered a speech that stirred the hearts and minds of the men now under his command so that they stamped their feet in a noise like thunder and shook the walls of the abbey with the roar, "Jerusalem, Jerusalem!"

The faces of the watching nuns shone with the excitement of the moment and their rapt, staring eyes mirrored the fanatic devotion being whipped anew into the men below. "Jerusalem, Jerusalem," they cried, the treble of their voices utterly lost in the bass rumble that engulfed them. "Jerusalem, Jerusalem," cried Anne with the rest, but her eyes never for an instant left the Countess.

At last it was over and the crowd fell silent. The Bishop of Soissons descended from the altar and began to make his way toward the Church of Notre Dame, where, in another ceremony, assisted by the two white monks and Fulk of Neuilly, he would fix the crusader's cross to the Marquis's shoulder. The space nearest the altar emptied as men fell in behind the priests in the order of their rank. A voice in the crowd began to sing the *Veni Creator,* and the hymn was immediately taken up by all, so that the procession moved in stately step past the abbey walls.

As the Countess approached beneath her Anne could see that she, too, was singing and that a look of purest joy was on her face. She has forgotten, Anne thought in sudden despair, willing with all her strength that it should not be so. But as the Countess passed her step faltered for an instant and as though she could not help herself, she looked upward to where the nuns stood. Her eyes found the three white veils almost immediately and she smiled up at them. The smile was for me, Anne thought, and she began to tremble all over like a dry leaf caught in the autumn wind.

Clouds drifted over the moon that night and it was very black when Anne slipped noiselessly from her cell an hour after Matins had been sung. She stood poised for a moment under the cloister arches like a wary animal who must hunt by dark and be safely hid in its burrow before light.

The night breeze ruffled her short hair and she welcomed its coolness. She wore only the black robe of her habit ripped off at the knees, lest she stumble on its hem picking her way over the rough ground of the orchard. She had left the white veil and coif folded in her chest, for in the blackness through which she must move they would surely betray her. Her long wooden rosary lay with them. Its beads clacked at the slightest movement with a sound so distinctive that any nun would recognize it. She carried her leather sandals in her hand and could feel the coldness of the stone floor beneath her feet. It was numbing and she knew that she must move quickly.

The silence in the monastery was complete and all-enveloping. Here and there a vigil light burned before a statue, and like a moth moving from flame to flame she darted quickly from one to the other, pausing for a few seconds by each, just long enough to peer through the darkness to reassure herself that she alone moved in the sleeping house.

In the kitchen she stopped for a few moments at the banked fire, rubbing her feet on the warm tiles until she felt the numbness go. She slipped her sandals on and fastened the straps tightly. Then she very carefully lifted the heavy wooden bar from the door and leaned it against the wall. In the morning they would find it there and chatter excitedly about the danger they had all been in during the night, sleeping the sleep of the innocent in an unlocked house where any evil might have crept in. Someone would be punished, even beaten, for having neglected her duty, and for hours the kitchen would be alive with suspicions and loud complaints. When finally it was discovered that she was missing, the Abbess would be informed that it must have been through the kitchen that she had left. She would come with her council to stand and stare at the open door and the bar beside it, and all would shake their heads and clack their tongues over her wickedness. Her flight and the manner of her going would be added to the store of Abbey tales that the nuns whispered to one another as they endlessly paced the stone corridors, and in all likelihood she would be accorded a line or two in the records book kept by the Abbess. It would all be very exciting for a day or two. Then she would be forgotten.

She dared not open the great door in the stone wall that encircled the monastery, for the hinges creaked badly and the nun who slept in the gatehouse was old and easily awakened. Nimbly as a cat she climbed into the branches of an apple tree that had been allowed to grow beside the wall, a tree the Abbess had been threatening to have cut down for years because ever-hungry novices filled their pockets with its forbidden fruit. From the top of the tree she could see campfires flickering in the field beyond the orchard and the dark shadows of sentries standing at their posts. She strained to see the Count's banner, but could not find it in the darkness. She would have to ask directions from a soldier, and that would be the most dangerous moment of the night. Somehow she would have to convince him that she had legitimate business with the Countess. She had no notion of what she would say, but neither had she any doubt that somehow she would succeed. She was utterly calm as she crouched for a moment on the top of the wall, then jumped to the ground below.

Robert of Clari could not sleep. Nor could Aleaumes. For a while they played at dice and drank wine with a few companions. As the hour grew late the heavy losers dropped out of the game and, grumbling over their misfortunes, went to bed. The winners remained for a time beside the fire, content to finger their new-won coins and discuss the great events of the day. They were unanimous in their praise of the Marquis of Montferrat, and unanimous too in their impatience with the year's wait that lay before them. The talk lagged, for there was no subject in dispute, and one by one they too retired to sleep briefly before breaking camp.

Finally only Robert and Aleaumes remained. In a few hours it would be dawn.

"I am uneasy, Robert," said Aleaumes, "though I don't think I could tell you why."

"Everything has gone very smoothly so far," mused Robert, though he too was conscious of an odd sense of restlessness which he could not explain.

"Perhaps too smoothly," continued Aleaumes thoughtfully. "I have been wondering all day long why the Marquis of Montferrat accepted leadership of the army after the others so openly scorned it. He is, after all, an Italian and a subject of the Empire while the army is almost entirely French."

"Piety perhaps. The Pope has said that the cause of Christ knows no boundaries of nationhood."

"Perhaps," Aleaumes agreed reluctantly. "But I think it is more than that. God knows he must have sins to expiate, but the look in his eyes tells me that he bothers little with the state of his soul."

"Ambition then," suggested Robert. "He has risen as high as he can within the Empire. There are no lands left in Europe to which he can aspire. Perhaps he intends to be King of Jerusalem as his brother was."

"There is no unwed Queen for him to marry. The man certainly has the air of one who dreams of being a king, but of what country? He has always had ambition and well-kept secret schemes. He's known for those two qualities. And now he has the tool to fulfill both."

"The army?"

"Exactly. We are his tools."

"But we are vowed for the Holy Land, all of us. I don't think that any of the barons could be persuaded to turn aside for any reason. Nor would Fulk of Neuilly allow it. And he is the real persuasive force behind our soldiers. One sermon from him and Montferrat, Flanders, Blois and St. Pol would find themselves without an army."

Aleaumes sighed tiredly. "There is something, Robert. I doubt that I will feel fully reassured until we stand in the Via Dolorosa, and then I shall not mind a bit if you accuse me of having been a worry-ridden old woman."

"Put it out of your mind, Aleaumes," said Robert, rising to his feet with arms stretched high above his head. "I'm stiff from the damp and the sitting. Let's walk out to the sentry lines and back. There's hardly any point in trying to sleep now."

"I've heard that Villehardouin visited the Marquis on his way back from Venice," said Aleaumes as they walked into the darkness away from the fires of the camp. "It's said that Montferrat expressed little interest in the expedition until he learned that Thibaut was dead and no one could be found to replace him. Have you ever wondered whose idea it really was that his name be proposed?"

Robert's answer was choked off by an oath and he bounded forward into the night, drawing his sword as he went. The alerted sentry whirled to face him and the thin black-clad figure which had just slipped past him was trapped between the two armed men.

Anne threw herself to the ground to escape the weapons which flashed above her, crying out, "Friend, friend, I am a friend," in a desperate, frightened voice that brought them up short.

The sentry reached down and dragged her to her feet. She ceased struggling and stood quiet, empty hands outthrust to show she carried no weapon.

"It's only a boy," said the sentry, relief mingling with the shame of having been caught so careless at his post. "What are you doing here, fellow? Speak up quick or you're dead."

"Please, my lord," she said to Robert, "I have business with the Countess of Flanders. She is expecting me."

"The Countess has no truck with boys who creep through the night," said the sentry angrily. "You'll have to think of a better story than that one, my lad. It's off to the watch sergeant with you."

"Just a moment," said Robert, peering at the white face and the pleading blue eyes that gazed at him with urgent intensity. "It's a girl you've collared there, not a boy."

The moon slid from behind the clouds and bathed them all in a clear white light. An unearthly glow lit up Anne's face. Her eyes were deep, still pools of the bluest water, and as Robert looked at her he felt himself drawn into their depths as though something waited there for him, something glimpsed only in dreams but familiar and promising. He felt himself caught in a spell, unable to move or speak or think, and the strength began to drain from his body so that his sword became a great weight he could not lift.

"God's Blood!" exclaimed Aleaumes. And as if it had never been, the spell was broken.

"Your name, girl," snapped out Robert.

"Anne of Nanteuil," she said, so quietly that the sentry could not make out her words. "Please, my lord, take me to the Countess's tent. She will explain everything to your satisfaction. I swear to you by Christ and His Holy Mother that I am no spy."

"No spy indeed," said Aleaumes, adding under his breath so that only Robert and Anne heard him, "she's a runaway nun. She's cut off her habit, but there's no mistaking the hang of it. And probably from the abbey over there. She'll have to be sent back to face her abbess."

Robert came quickly to a decision. "We'll take charge of her, sentry," he said. "You may return to your post. And see that in future you are more alert."

"I shall have to make a report," said the sentry stubbornly, realizing that he had been surprised by an unknown, somewhat shabby knight and a mere clerk.

"We'll do that for you," said Robert, "and see that you speak of this to no one but your sergeant. It's possible that the Countess will have reason to praise your discretion."

The mention of the Countess's name decided the matter. Great ladies often had secrets they paid well to keep. The sentry saluted them, muttered to himself for form's sake, then walked back to his post.

As the man moved out of earshot, Robert resheathed his sword. "I am Robert, knight of Clari," he said, "and this is my brother Aleaumes, clerk of the cathedral of Amiens."

"Clerk," repeated Anne, a disdainful challenge in her voice. She spoke directly to Robert, ignoring the black-robed man who had been so quick to see through her inadequate disguise. "Please, my lord, do not send me back there. I shall die if you do."

"You've broken your vows, girl," said Aleaumes sternly. "That's death to the soul and a far more serious matter than you seem to realize."

"Not so, Master Clerk," she said, turning on him in quick, cold fury. "I have taken no vows. I was only a novice and sent to that house against my will. The Church teaches that a vow imposed by force is empty and not binding. No one can force me to be a nun against my will. And I do not will it."

"Leave off, Aleaumes," said Robert. "I believe her."

"Why, so do I, brother," said Aleaumes easily, his unaccustomed pomposity falling from him like a poorly fitting garment. He smiled at Anne, who stood glaring at him, hands clenched at her sides. "She has too much spirit to be a nun."

"Why do you wish to see the Countess?" asked Robert.

"That is a matter I will not discuss with you," answered Anne with great dignity. "The lady herself may choose to enlighten you, but it is not my place to do so."

"You said she expects you?" asked Aleaumes, hardly able to keep from laughing at the sight of this undeniably beautiful but bedraggled creature facing them down.

"She expects me," said Anne, "and she will not thank you for keeping me from her."

With head held high she began to walk purposefully toward the camp. After a moment's hesitation the two men fell in beside her.

"Allow us to escort you safely to the Countess's tent," said Robert. There was a note of sincere homage in his voice which Aleaumes had never before heard him use in speaking with a woman.

Their interview with Mary of Flanders was brief but to the point. On no account were they to mention Anne's arrival in the camp, and the sentry must be bribed to silence. She counted on their loyal support as fellow soldiers of Christ. She herself would inform the Count, she told them, glancing back over her shoulder to where her husband snored peacefully in an inner room of the tent they shared, undisturbed and blissfully unaware of the conspiracy his wife had hatched.

As they bowed themselves from the tent they had one last glimpse of Anne, on her knees before the Countess. She was attempting to kiss the lady's hands in gratitude while Mary of Flanders whispered furiously at her.

"It's true she was expecting her," said Aleaumes as they began the walk out to the sentry with the purse of small coins the Countess had insisted on giving them. "She must have been waiting just inside the entrance to the tent ever since the Count fell asleep. Did you mark how she darted out as we approached and practically dragged us inside with her?"

"I wonder what she'll do with her?" mused Robert.

"Probably slip her in amongst her ladies and wait for the right moment to approach the Count on her behalf. He'll be furious, but I've no doubt she'll win him over in time."

"Who is she, and where did she come from?" continued Robert as if he had not heard Aleaumes' reply.

"Anne of Nanteuil, she said, but the name is unfamiliar to me." Aleaumes glanced at his brother as a new and amusing suspicion suddenly took root in his mind. "You could find out, if you wish. Discreetly, that is."

"She will ride with the Countess to the Holy Land," said Robert. Without knowing why, he was certain that that was the reason she had left her convent. "I shall see her again."

"No doubt, brother," said Aleaumes, "we shall both meet her again." With a touch of envy in his voice he added, "But I daresay you will see much more of her than I."

VI

Boniface did not return to Montferrat after the parliament at Soissons ended. He went instead to spend Christmas at the court of his suzerain, Philip of Swabia, now Holy Roman Emperor.

Philip's messenger had arrived at Montferrat hard on the heels of the French delegation sent by Geoffrey of Villehardouin. Leaving a score of foundered horses all along the road from Germany, he had ridden furiously to get there before the Marquis could frame a definite response to the offer being made him by the desperate envoys. The parchment he carried invited the lord of Montferrat to pass the festive Christmas season with his Emperor, but the urgency of the man's behavior suggested that there was more to the invitation than appeared on the surface.

The Emperor's man presented his master's compliments before the assembled court, the parchment was duly opened and read aloud for all to hear. Then Boniface summoned the messenger to his private apartments.

"Have you other letters for me?" he asked, dismissing his attendants.

"No, my lord. But the Emperor has entrusted me with an oral message which he instructed me to repeat to you in strictest privacy."

Boniface glanced at the one clerk who remained in the room. It was his function to take notes for the Marquis during private meetings and council deliberations, so that a man's words were not lost on the wind. Boniface had found that the sound of the clerk's scribblings had a salutary effect on even the most longwinded of his advisers. They chose their words more carefully and with greater deliberation, knowing that a day would come when the Marquis would quote them verbatim should their advice be proven ill-formulated or hasty. The clerk was a mute, but his ears had grown superhumanly sharp to compensate for his inability to ever repeat what he had heard.

"In strictest privacy," insisted the messenger.

"You may go, Alfredo," said Boniface. The clerk rose, bowed and left the room. Only the sound of the heavy wooden door closing behind him broke the silence in which Boniface and the man from Germany waited.

The messenger watched him go, then turned to face the Marquis. Montferrat had begun to drum his fingers impatiently on the arm of his chair.

"You may speak now. We are quite alone and your words cannot be heard outside this room."

The man cleared his throat nervously and began to recite the message he had learned by heart and repeated over and over during his journey.

"Greetings to Boniface, Marquis of Montferrat, from Philip of Swabia, Emperor. Remembering the joy of the Holy Family at Bethlehem, to which distant city wise men journeyed from afar to recognize their true King, we entreat you privily to attend our court, that together we may celebrate the anniversary of that Birth by which all good things were vouchsafed to mankind. To our own greetings we add those of the Empress Irene, our much loved spouse, for whose health and well-being we daily give thanks, that her house and ours may continue to find favor with the Father through the Son."

The Marquis's fingers no longer drummed. He sat very still for a long time after the messenger had finished speaking. There was virtually no expression on his face, but his eyes had a remote, farseeing, yet somehow inward look. His features remained blankly set and his voice betrayed none of the elation he was feeling when finally he gave his answer.

"Tell your master," he said, speaking slowly so that the messenger could commit his exact words to memory, "that I leave in a few days' time to attend the barons' parliament at Soissons. I shall next be at Cîteaux in September for the feast of the Holy Cross. It shall be my great pleasure to spend Christmas with him, during which season I pray that he will honor me with the wisdom of his conversation. His devotion to the Church and his special love for the Holy Family are well known by all and a source of great edification." Boniface paused, debating whether to say more. Philip's message had been extremely obscure, his own answer equally so. Enough had been said, he decided. The Emperor could not fail to catch his meaning.

"Can you repeat what I have said?" he asked the man who stood before him in respectful silence.

"Yes, my lord," he answered, and without hesitation he quoted the Marquis's words exactly, managing even to capture the lack of inflection with which Boniface had spoken.

"Good," said Boniface. "You will rest and refresh yourself this evening and tomorrow at dawn set out for Germany. Before you leave my clerk will provide you with money for the journey and a writ from me that will enable you to procure fast, sound horses all along your route."

He rang for Alfredo and instructed him to see to the messenger's comfort and to the necessities of his journey. "I am not to be disturbed," he added as he dismissed his clerk. "I shall ring for you when I want you. We must prepare an answer for the French envoys."

Until Philip's messenger had arrived the Marquis had not decided what reply he would send to the parliament at Soissons. True to the promise made in April, Villehardouin had sent messengers to Montferrat throughout the spring and summer months. The first to arrive had brought the startling news of Thibaut's death, and though Montferrat had expressed his sorrow at the loss of so exemplary a knight, he had held back from even hinting that he might be persuaded to take Champagne's place. Neutrality and patience were the cornerstones of his policy.

Between the lines of the letters which later arrived he read the Marshal's growing apprehension. Burgundy and Bar-le-Duc had spurned the crusade and Villehardouin was harsh in his condemnation of their self-serving. He remembered his last conversation with Boniface, how proudly the Marquis had spoken of his father and brothers. The name of Montferrat was respected, the Marquis himself the type of man born to lead. Finally had come the document he had been expecting, brought to him secretly by a gray-faced merchant who had paused only long enough to place it in the Marquis's hands, then had taken his leave hastily, fearing involvement in an intrigue at which he could not even begin to guess.

This time Villehardouin had dispensed with flattery. He had listed all the barons who had taken the cross, the numbers of men each had pledged to the army, given his best estimate of the expected total size of the force, revealed the existence of the treasury that Thibaut had bequeathed to his successor, and boldly asked Montferrat for permission to present his name to the upcoming parliament.

The Marshal had forced his hand. Reluctantly Boniface had agreed to allow his candidacy to become public, but only if two secret conditions could be met. If the barons sent for him, it must be by unanimous vote, and further, they must do so with the full intention of proclaiming him commander-in-chief of the army. He would be satisfied with nothing less. Let Villehardouin arrange it however he chose, the Marquis did not wish to know the details of the operation. He was interested only in results.

The weeks of waiting had ended with the appearance of this formal delegation from the parliament still sitting at Soissons. Somehow Villehardouin had contrived to meet the Marquis's conditions.

But even that was not enough. Although the world did not suspect it, and Villehardouin would have vigorously denied it, the Doge of Venice, not the French barons, controlled this army's destiny, and Montferrat had no intention of serving as Dandolo's stooge. The prize was not to be Jerusalem.

Though he was too cautious a man to voice what would be a universally unpopular opinion, Boniface was personally convinced that the cause of the Holy Sepulcher was forever lost. It was a conclusion he had come to hold gradually over the years, based on careful assessment of the information reported to him by knights returning from the Holy Land, a conclusion that grew logically and irrevocably from a consideration of the logistics involved in any large-scale plan of invasion and conquest. Piety and emotional attachment to Jerusalem did not in any way influence his judgment, for he was in every fiber of his body a military man, the veteran of many campaigns in Italy, the Empire and the Holy Land itself, and any invasion, whatever the motive behind it, was first and foremost a military matter. Purely from the military point of view, therefore, the crusade now being mounted was doomed to failure, though the French were too obstinate, too swayed by the rantings of Pope and itinerant preacher alike to see it.

He had been puzzled at first by the Venetian commitment to the affair. It was obvious that they would profit handsomely through the troopships they had agreed to supply, but the addition of fifty of their own war galleys to the fleet was surprising. Until he learned the price they had demanded. Then he was compelled to admire the shrewdness of the octogenarian Doge of Venice, a man whose mind worked along pathways as tortuous and well concealed as Boniface's own. Dandolo must have been certain when he signed the Treaty of Nolis that the French could never meet their financial commitment. And being the total merchant that he was, he would never lower his price or release them from the agreement. He had it in mind to use them for his own purposes, and the root and flower of his fame was his obsessive desire to increase the power and wealth of the republic he governed. The French would find themselves propositioned and the purity of their crusade compromised before they ever left Venice's harbor.

There were cities and trading centers all along the Mediterranean that had slipped from Venice's grasp during the past twenty years or so, places where the Doge's word had once been law but was no more. One in particular, he now remembered, was the important city of Zara, which had gone over to the King of Hungary in 1183. Venice had writhed in frustrated rage at that blow to its pride, but had been unable to mount an army large enough to recapture and subdue its errant vassal. Now the Doge had an army, and if Villehardouin's figures could be believed, one of the largest ever to be assembled in one place. The French would be so inflamed to reach Jerusalem that they would gladly accede to a slight delay to satisfy their ally and pay off their debt, and Zara, after all, did not lie far off their course.

Boniface chuckled to himself, hugely enjoying the deception which he felt sure Dandolo had envisioned from the very first moment the six earnest French envoys had appeared before his council. And now this extraordinary message from Philip of Swabia. Though he had instantly grasped its meaning, he focused his thoughts carefully on each separate sentence the messenger had spoken, reassessing the information therein contained, reevaluating the plan the Emperor was suggesting. It was plain that he too had correctly interpreted the Venetian involvement in the crusade and decided that they should not be the only ones to profit from it. A Hohenstaufen could teach even the magnificent Dandolo a lesson in statecraft.

The Holy Family to which he had referred could only mean that of Irene Angela, Philip's empress, daughter of the deposed and blinded Isaac Angelus, who had until six years ago been Emperor of Constantinople. Irene's brother, Prince Alexius, had during the summer escaped from the Greek Empire and made his way first to Italy, then to his brother-in-law's court. He had pleaded with the Pope to avenge the crime done to his family by the usurper, his father's own brother, who now called himself Alexius III, but Innocent had turned a deaf ear to his entreaties. Accompanied by a few companions as young and bitter as himself, the Greek prince had finally taken up what seemed to be permanent residence at Philip's court, for the Emperor, while sympathetic to his cause, had also declared himself unable to help.

Now the situation had changed. Philip's spies had undoubtedly informed him that his loyal vassal, the Marquis of Montferrat, was about to be offered command of an army which by its sheer size alone the ill-defended city of Constantinople would be unable to resist. And wasting no time, Philip had sent word to the Marquis that a kingdom was his for the taking. Alexius would have to be proclaimed emperor, but judging by the performances of his father and his uncle, he was no more inclined to bear the onerous work demanded of a king than any of the

House of Angelus. Boniface could expect to be the power behind the throne, allowing his protégé to disport himself in the baths and whorehouses for which Constantinople was famous.

The plan might be carried one step further, though that would depend on Philip's personal attachment to his wife's brother. Alexius would have to expose himself beneath the walls of Constantinople to rally his supporters inside the city to his cause. Who knew but that a stray crossbow quarrel might not tragically strike him down just as he was on the point of entering into his rightful glory? Once the army had been committed to the capture of Constantinople there could be no turning back. A Latin dynasty would replace the native Greek one, and the most likely, indeed the inevitable candidate would be the man who had led them to the East, Boniface himself. After a suitable interval those who wished to could continue on to the Holy Land, resupplied with food and weapons, tested and proved in battle, a more formidable force than when they had set out.

Philip had been very insistent that Boniface attend his Christmas court. It was imperative that the Marquis gain the prince's confidence, for the tool must trust its master. It was to be hoped that Alexius was the type of young man who could inspire others to risk their lives in his cause, for its legitimacy was vested solely in his person. The French had become almost fanatic in their defense of the right of legitimate inheritance by the eldest son and could be expected to assume that the Greeks likewise shared their peculiar conviction. That this was simply not so could easily be kept from them. And if Alexius could be persuaded to bring the Greek Church back under the authority of Rome, even Innocent III could not long withhold his support, though it would be far safer to present him with a fait accompli and risk excommunication in the meanwhile. No one could predict with any certainty what stand the new pope would take on any given issue.

As he rang for his clerk Boniface was already composing in his mind the letter the French delegation would carry back to Soissons, a letter in which he would appear both humbly grateful for the honor done him and fiercely determined to let no obstacle stand in the way of avenging the shame of Christ. The holy name of Jerusalem would henceforth be always in his heart and on his lips. He was almost convinced himself that this was so.

Boniface enjoyed the quiet anticipatory joy of the season of Advent as it was kept by the monkish Philip and his court. He found particular pleasure in long conversations with the Empress Irene, a young and very beautiful woman deeply in love with her husband. Montferrat had known of very few real love matches between members of ruling houses, and that an Emperor and his consort could actually have found true happiness with each other was a source of constant amazement, an accident that happened once perhaps in several hundred years, and for which, in this case, he was profoundly grateful.

The Empress had a great deal of influence with her husband and deep affection for her brother, the refugee Alexius. Soon after his arrival at Philip's court Alexius had poured out the story of their uncle's perfidy, recounting every detail of the coup which had dethroned their father. Irene had come to idolize Isaac over the years, for she had been sent from Constantinople at a very early age to marry the heir to the Sicilian throne and had known few happy moments since leaving her father's kingdom. Roger of Apulia had died within a year of their marriage and she had had no child by him. From future Queen of Sicily she had been reduced to useless appendage of the Norman House of Hauteville, and she had then suffered the horror of living through Henry of Hohenstaufen's conquest of her adopted country. She had been packed off to a convent in Germany with the emotionally destroyed Queen Sibylla and her daughters, and had heard that mother's lamentations even in her dreams. Henry VI had personally given the orders for the castration of Sibylla's only remaining son. What might he not do to an ex-Queen, that child's mother, and four unwanted princesses seemingly forgotten by the whole world?

Although she was too distraught to realize it, Irene herself was never in danger. She was of the blood of Isaac Angelus, Emperor of Constantinople, and Henry was ambitious. He had plucked her from the cold obscurity of her convent prison and married her to his brother, and though she had hated and feared the unnatural emperor she had fallen almost immediately in love with the gentle Philip.

One never knew where the Hand of God would fall, for now she, once the most miserable of women, was Empress of the Holy Roman Empire while her father, a great emperor, lay blinded and ill in a foul prison cell in Constantinople. She had been spared no detail of her father's blinding, for the shrewd Alexius had unmercifully taken full advantage of her love for her father, knowing that from his daughter's agony would grow the determination to force her husband into the role of Isaac's avenger. She had wept bitter tears, cried out in shared pain, and finally swooned when Alexius had spoken of the blood that streamed from their father's empty eye sockets and the stench of burned flesh under the cauterizing iron. But as he had correctly surmised, she had recovered herself, and although she still wept at the mention of her father's name, she had begun a campaign designed to erode her husband's determination not to risk his shaky throne and the welfare of the Empire in the pursuit of what he judged to be a hopeless cause.

Alexius no longer burst into the Emperor's council chamber, embarrassing Philip's staid advisers with his rantings and demands for vengeance. He had a formidable ally who would do his work for him and the result must be the same. He had only to wait, for Philip's resistance to his wife's pleadings was already wearing thin.

And now the Prince knew that his hopes were about to be realized. Boniface of Montferrat, supreme commander of an army vowed to Christian service, grew more friendly, more sympathetic, more respectful every day, and Alexius's spies, those eager Greek followers who shared his exile, reported that the Marquis and the Emperor were often closeted together for hours on end, with no witnesses to their conversations.

Alexius daily, hourly expected to be invited to join their private talks, but Advent and then Christmas came and went and no summons arrived. He grew impatient, fretful, angry, and finally careless. What right had they to put him off like this, deferring to him in public but no doubt sneering at his misfortune behind his back? He was heir to the throne of Constantinople, the greatest city and the greatest kingdom the world had ever known, the glory of the East. Nay, if Isaac had by now succumbed to the rigors of his prison, or more likely been quietly poisoned by one of his brother's minions, he might at this very moment be Emperor.

It would have been a sobering, dignifying thought to most young princes, but as Philip had already remarked to the Marquis of Montferrat, Alexius, alas, embodied all the worst and most degenerate characteristics of the House of Angelus. He was vain, proud, pleasure-loving, completely adverse to hard work, undisciplined, easily led, and stupid into the bargain. Philip had been amazed that for some two months now Alexius had managed to seem the model of princely deportment, but the strain was telling. At any moment he could be expected to crack.

The moment Philip had predicted did come, a few weeks after Christmas. Late one night Alexius and three companions, all heavily disguised, slipped from the palace and were soon made welcome in the taverns and whorehouses which had suffered a sharp decline in revenue during Alexius's self-imposed period of restraint. They had strange and perverse tastes, these Greeks, but the whores they frequented had learned to accommodate them with professional ease. Alexius was bitterly pleased that so many of the gold coins the pious Philip provided him with should end up in the greasy palms of tavern keepers and women who were bought and sold as casually as sheep.

The guard they had bribed let them through the palace gate with no show of the respect they were accustomed to receiving and so they believed that he was ignorant of their true identity. Hardly had they passed from sight when two other men also slipped by him, but these paused for a moment before disappearing into the darkness, and one of them nodded in the direction of the sleeping palace.

The guard made fast the gate, summoned another of his fellows to take his place, and went directly to the Emperor's private apartment to make his report.

"It will be tonight then, my friend," said Philip when the guard had returned to his post. "Alexius has been on his good behavior since your arrival. It is important that you also see him at his worst."

Boniface nodded in agreement. It would be hours before the Greeks stumbled back to the palace, but he was a man accustomed to waiting and there was still much he needed to discuss with the Emperor. The time would pass quickly.

The plan they had sketched out was a marvel of incontrovertible logic, but it all hinged on one very important contingency, and this was that the army's various leaders would be unable to pay the full sum of eighty-five thousand silver marks. The Venetians would refuse to release the fleet and the ensuing stalemate would drive the crusaders to the edge of despair and desperation. Philip and Boniface were sure that the Doge would propose a solution to the dilemma. Let the crusaders pay their debt in service rather than coin—and what better service than the reconquest of Venice's rebellious vassal city? Once the first diversion had become fact, the second could be easily arranged. The holy fervor would have worn thin, replaced by the lust for further conquest that always overcame a victorious army. Then Alexius would appear, and by bribery and piteous appeal for Christian knights to throw down a foul usurper, convince them that the road to Jerusalem lay through Constantinople. Once that was done Montferrat would see to it that no second thoughts disturbed the army's conscience. Henry VI had been the first Hohenstaufen to dream of conquering Constantinople. His brother would know the secret joy of fulfilling that dream. As long as the eighty-five thousand marks could not be paid. Might it be possible to influence the monks at Cîteaux to spend Fulk's treasury on other worthy beneficiaries already in the Holy Land? The hours passed, the tentacles reached out; the victim played on, unaware of his doom.

It was almost dawn before they were informed that Alexius and his friends were back in their own apartments. Only the thought of having to appear at morning Mass in some condition reasonably resembling that of sobriety had brought an end to their roistering. They had spent most of the night at the house of a Frenchwoman who boasted of being able to satisfy any whim, any desire a man could have. The spy casually reported the exact number of coins which had changed hands and Philip winced inwardly at the amount. The Frenchwoman would find herself out of business once Alexius had departed. One such place was an encouragement to others, and Philip had only ignored it this long because, if nothing else, it served the purpose of keeping the unpredictable Greek prince satiated and at times almost somnolent. The satisfaction of such lusts greatly drained a man, and although Alexius was only twenty, he was already addicted to them—another cord that bound him hand and foot to the men who had decided to control and manipulate the remainder of his life. Deny him his pleasures and he would promise anything, sign any document put before him, give away half his empire without a second thought.

Alexius had already fallen into a drunken sleep by the time Philip's most trusted servant presented himself at his door, but the man noted that when his message had finally been understood the prince snapped immediately awake. He seemed galvanized into sudden action and sprang from the bed to ring for an attendant, his face transformed with a semblance of royal pride and dignity.

"The Emperor has instructed that I alone am to assist Your Highness in dressing," the man said, "due to the lateness of the hour and the urgency with which he desires Your Highness's presence."

And Alexius knew that his time had come. Philip might insist on secrecy for the moment, but soon the news would be all over Europe, and in Constantinople his uncle would do well to tremble, for he must realize that a triumphant Alexius would not stop at blinding and imprisonment. Not even the gruesome death meted out to another usurper, the Emperor Andronicus, would be painful enough for the man who had driven him from his own country and made him the laughingstock of the Christian world. As he followed Philip's messenger along the silent corridors of the palace he grimly and with great relish envisioned the tortures he would inflict on his uncle. The crowds would be allowed, encouraged even, to mock and spit upon him, cover his naked body with dung and the refuse of their kitchens, then would come castration, disembowelment, dismemberment, hanging. No matter how careful the executioners were it could not last longer than a few hours, but Alexius promised himself that he would miss no moment of the spectacle.

His revengeful imaginings had so engrossed him that he ar-

rived at the door to the Emperor's cabinet without having
formulated a single thought of what he would say to his brother-
in-law and that other man who awaited him, the Marquis of
Montferrat. As the servant announced him, he was suddenly
overwhelmed by a rising panic which he could hardly control.
So much depended on this meeting. It did not help that wine
fumes were again clouding his mind so that he found it agoniz-
ingly difficult to focus his thoughts. The swift walk through the
palace had at first awakened all his senses to the small noises of
the night, but now the opposite reaction had set in. His body
was growing numb with the need to sleep off the evening's dis-
sipation and the palms of his hands were clammy with a cold
sweat. His stomach turned and heaved with nausea and an evil-
tasting liquid filled his mouth and coated his teeth. When he
opened his mouth to greet his brother-in-law he could feel the
grit of it against his tongue.

Philip had commanded a third chair to be placed by the fire
before which he and the Marquis sat; Alexius dropped into it
with a relief that he hoped was not too obvious. Over his head
the Emperor and the Marquis exchanged glances. So this was
how the pretender to the mighty throne of Constantinople
looked after a night of careless debauchery—so sickly pale and
miserably weak that they half expected he would at any moment
cry out for a basin in which to vomit up his filth. He was a pitiful sight, grimly amusing to the two men who had so correctly
judged the shallowness of his character.

"My dear Alexius," began Philip of Swabia sententiously, "all
Europe knows of the cruel injustices which your house has
suffered at the hands of the usurper who now presumes to occupy the throne of Constantinople, and everywhere men of
honor yearn to see you resume your rightful place. I myself, as
you well know, share the special grief of Isaac's children, because of the love which I bear for your sister, my Empress. God
has seen fit to link the House of Angelus to the House of Hohenstaufen by the holy bonds of matrimony, and as the head of that
house I do not take my obligations lightly. It has grieved me
greatly that I have so far been unable to avenge the great
wrongs done to my dear wife's family. My oath as Emperor
demands that my first duty be to defend and preserve this realm

He has placed in my care, and this has not always been an easy or a simple task."

"The Holy Roman Empire also has its would-be usurper." Boniface kept his voice low and mournful, as though this discussion of unlawful pretenders was almost too painful for a righteous man to bear.

"Otto of Brunswick must at all costs be defeated," agreed Alexius, hoping that for once he had said precisely what was expected of him.

"You have grasped the situation exactly," said Philip, smiling conspiratorially at his brother-in-law. "I hope that you will not be offended if I say that your comment shows an understanding of the difficult intricacies of statecraft unusual in one so young."

Glancing at the Marquis of Montferrat, Alexius saw that he too was smiling, and he began to relax. Apparently he had said something so profound that even these two greatly experienced men of the world were impressed by his wisdom. It was not going to be as difficult to persuade them to his will as he had thought. He was, after all, a Greek, and far superior in intellect to any Latin. Suddenly he remembered something.

"The House of Montferrat is also linked to the royal House of Angelus, is that not so, my lord?"

Boniface seemed not to have heard him, for he merely replied that His Highness might care for some refreshment and busied himself pouring wine into three crystal goblets, first proffering one to the Emperor, then to Alexius, who had been yearning for a drink from the first moment he had sat down and seen the decanter.

He sipped his wine slowly to cover his confusion. Surely anyone would be proud to acknowledge kinship with the Emperor of Constantinople. Could the Marquis really not have heard him? He knew he was not mistaken in believing that his aunt Theodora had married Conrad of Montferrat. There had been a double wedding which he recalled well, for Isaac had taken a second wife at the same time, Margaret-Maria, the daughter of the King of Hungary, who became the mother of Alexius's half brother, Manuel. He flushed then as he remembered that Conrad had abruptly abandoned the Emperor's sister to sail away to the Holy Land, where he eventually married the Queen of Jerusalem just as though he did not already have a legal wife in Constantinople. Aunt Theodora had entered a convent and his father had had one of his famous rages at the insult done him by an upstart Italian adventurer.

"As I was saying, this business of Otto of Brunswick has prevented me from giving you the assistance my heart and your honor demand." Philip's smooth voice ignored his brother-in-law's unfortunate comment. Alexius was sure that it would never be referred to again. "And it would seem that even the Pope chooses to ignore his duty to you."

"He hardly listened to me," Alexius whined. He had not forgotten a single moment of his humiliating interview with Innocent III.

"What can one expect of a lawyer?" Boniface's question was rhetorical yet comforting, for he managed to imply that he too had scant respect for the Vicar of Christ.

Philip spoke again. "Indeed, Alexius, it is my belief that you must expect no help at all from Rome unless it could be promised that through you the Eastern Church would once more be subject to the Throne of Peter."

"I told the Pope that I would be happy to be Rome's obedient son," said Alexius, reaching for more wine. "But he did not choose to believe me."

"He is negotiating even now with your uncle on that very matter," said Philip, "so we must assume that he had already decided that your cause was a hopeless one."

"But it is not, Philip," Alexius said, his voice rising and breaking with his anger. He had forgotten all the respect due his sister's husband. "I have told you over and over again that the people will rise in my name and throw out the usurper if only they have some hope that their revolt will succeed. Just a few well-manned ships is all I need. My uncle is so hated that he scarcely dares leave his palace."

"How is it then that his campaign against Manuel Camytzes was so successful?" Boniface was goading the irate prince, testing the limits of his self-control.

"He had to take me with him to deceive the people into believing that I supported him." Alexius was almost incoherent with rage. Why did no one seem to understand? "Don't you see, that's where he made his mistake. I only pretended to support him so that I could make my escape."

"Why was escape necessary if, as you claim, the people supported your cause?"

"In secret, my lord, in secret. They did not dare oppose him openly." Alexius paused to collect himself. He must make these Latins understand how revolutions were conducted in the Greek Empire. "My uncle has cruelly oppressed my people. His soldiers are everywhere. At the slightest rumor of discontent they pounce on a man and he disappears forever. That is why my father sent me to find help in the West. Merely a token force before the walls of Constantinople would so hearten its citizens that they would rise as one man. But they must have some sign of encouragement, some reassurance that they will not be alone in their fight."

Neither Boniface nor Philip believed that Isaac and his son had inspired such great love in their people that they were willing to risk their lives for them, but there were other potential allies in Constantinople and it was important to know how these would react.

"What of the Latin traders who live and work in Constantinople?" asked Boniface. "Could we count on their support?"

Alexius cursed himself for not having thought of them without the Marquis's prodding. The wine must have gone to his head more than he realized, for of course it was essential that the rich and powerful Latin traders, mostly from Italy, be on his side.

"My lord, it was two gentlemen of Pisa who made possible my escape, Count Rainerio of Segalari and Ildebrando Famagliati. It was they who arranged for the Pisan ship that picked me up at Athyra. And it was their idea, too, that I be disguised as a Pisan sailor so that even though my uncle's men searched the ship they did not recognize me. That is the kind of support I have among the Latin community."

Certain that his point had been well made, he poured himself more wine and did not see the look that hung in the air between the Emperor and the Marquis. Look how easily he betrays the names of those who conspired with him, it seemed to say. He is unworthy of their service and yet he was able to inspire them, two cautious, serious men, to risk all on his behalf. What effect might he not have, sober and dressed as befits a king, on an army of tautly drawn men who were feeling their hope of liberating Jerusalem slip through their fingers for want of a little gold?

"It may be, Alexius, that you shall have your army," said Philip of Swabia slowly, as though still struggling with a decision he was loath to make. "And no token force either."

Alexius sat very still.

"Your Highness has undoubtedly heard of the great force placed under my command a few months ago," continued Boniface of Montferrat. Alexius nodded, scarcely daring to breathe for fear his fragile dream would evaporate with the Marquis's next words. "It may be that these lords can be inspired to assist you. But they must be assured of some reward for their services, some tangible help from the Emperor of Constantinople that will guarantee their final victory in the Holy Land." He paused.

"Gold, my lord," stammered Alexius, spilling his wine in his excitement, not even feeling the heated liquid that stained his robe and dripped to the floor. "There is more gold in Constantinople than in all the rest of the world. And I will give it freely, a king's ransom. And supplies and weapons, horses, ships, whatever is necessary." Boniface sat silent, seemingly unmoved by the torrent of words that echoed through the small room. "And men also. Good fighting men supplied at my own expense. As many as you want. I shall not need them, for my people will welcome me with open arms and glad hearts." What more could he promise? "The treasury is full and overflowing; my uncle taxes the people hard. You shall have it all, all."

Alexius stared at the Marquis, his red-rimmed eyes glittering as he waited for a response from that unreadable face that seemed to hang disembodied in the firelight, filling his vision so that he saw nothing else. He could hear the sound of his breathing coming in painful gasps, and the beating of his heart. Vile-tasting liquid again filled his mouth and rushed, burning, into his nostrils. His knuckles were white; his hands gripped the arms of his chair so tightly that they were almost bloodless. Why didn't Montferrat speak?

"It has been a long night," said Philip of Swabia, "and the prince is understandably tired and grieved by all this talk of his sufferings. We must not presume further on him, Boniface." He thought the boy would puke right there, he looked so strange. "My man will escort you back to your apartments, Alexius. We will speak further about this at another time."

Am I not to have an answer, then, thought Alexius, unable to speak for fear he would lose all control over himself. Do they play cat and rat with me?

Philip's man had appeared and stood waiting patiently. Alexius had been dismissed. He stumbled to the door and turned with a last entreating look at the Marquis.

"Discuss this with no one," said the Emperor. Alexius, suddenly overcome with a trembling weakness, allowed himself to be led from the room.

They heard the sound of his footsteps diminishing in the distance, then the sound of his sickness.

Philip snorted in disgust. "His father and his uncle all over again," he said. "Only weaker and infinitely more stupid. I had not thought it possible."

"He is very anxious to give away the wealth of his kingdom even before he has regained it." Boniface was thoughtful. "He will look well in full armor, mounted on a horse. That red hair of his will flame in the sun and men will remember Coeur-de-Lion."

"Not too well, I hope," said Philip.

"Only what they want to remember. A young king setting out to regain his lawful inheritance and do a great service to the Church of Rome. And paying them well to share in his glory. I shall send for Alexius at the right moment. Meanwhile, you must do what you can to make a king of him."

"Or a reasonable facsimile thereof," laughed the Emperor. "Boniface," he continued seriously, "the Eastern Church must be reconciled to Rome. As things now stand they are heretics, and heresy is an abomination to me, as it must be to every good Christian."

"My lord, you know that I shall do everything in my power to bring that about." For the sake of Philip's peculiarly tender conscience Boniface was ready to swear to anything.

"I know that when the Patriarch makes his submission to Rome Innocent cannot but approve of all we will have done for him and for the Church."

"There is only one churchman whose opinion I fear now," said Boniface. "If a single word of what we propose should reach his ears he will instantly oppose us. And I cannot predict what effect his opposition will have on the army. Fulk of Neuilly is a man to be reckoned with."

"Could he not be persuaded?" asked Philip of Swabia doubtfully.

Boniface shook his head. "The man is a fanatic and immune to persuasion. Even bribery would not touch him." He stared at the dying fire as if in the depths of the coals lay the solution to his problem. "At Soissons he appeared to be very ill and later, at Cîteaux, even worse. He preached a sermon there that moved many Germans to take the cross, but afterward he was extremely weak and drained. It may be that he has overtaxed himself in God's service and that he shall enter into the bliss of heaven sooner than anyone expects."

Philip stared at the Marquis in horror. "I forbid it," he said, crossing himself on the forehead, the lips and the heart.

"Forbid what, my lord?"

"What you are thinking." Philip could not bring himself to utter the word poison, for a priest's life was doubly sacred and he was honestly appalled at the thought of murdering one of God's anointed.

"My lord, dismiss suspicion from your mind. Between us there are no secrets, nor will there ever be. I leave the priest to God, Who alone has the power over human life. Not even if Fulk proves troublesome would I do otherwise."

"Forgive me," said the Emperor, deeply ashamed at having momentarily doubted the honor of a friend and guest. "I spoke without thinking. It must be the lateness of the hour and the strain of my brother-in-law's presence."

"A presence you will not have to endure much longer," said the Marquis amiably. "I shall be taking that burden at least from your shoulders."

"Would that I could rid myself of the others," said Philip, rising and bidding the Marquis good night. "Or good morning, rather," he said, for the room was beginning to fill with the early light of dawn. "A good night's work, Boniface, and I wish you success of it."

I almost blundered, thought Boniface in the privacy of his own chambers. Fulk's decline will have to be a very slow one. Not as easy to manage now without suspicion, but not impossible. And certainly worth the risk.

VII

Peter of Amiens's summons came a few weeks before Pentecost, not a moment too soon for the restlessly waiting Robert of Clari. Since Easter the household had lived in such a state of anticipation that the sight of any stranger approaching the manor had been enough to distract the maids from their household duties and send Aelis scurrying up the tower steps to stand and peer down the winding road along the river. There were many men riding the roads that spring carrying messages from one crusading lord to another, and at last one of them, wearing Peter of Amiens's badge, turned aside to invite the heir of Clari to join his master's troops assembling in Amiens.

Now that he was really on the point of departure Robert was strangely reluctant to leave Clari. Several years would pass before he returned, if at all, and at least one familiar face would no longer be there to greet him in his hour of triumph. Gilo had been very ill all winter with pains in his chest and a racking cough that left him trembling and weak. No blood though, Lady Agatha reported, and took that for a hopeful sign. But with the coming of spring his old malady had returned to plague him, the gripes and purges worse than ever, much to his embarrassment and disgust. Too many of his days were now spent lying on a pallet in the sunshine under a heap of rugs, for he was always cold.

Lady Agatha had taken over most of the supervision of the manor's affairs, assisted by the unrepudiated Aelis, who had finally given up hope of ever reaching her quiet cloister, so that Robert was left free to spend several hours each day by his father's side. Both knew they were saying a final farewell.

In spite of his infirmities Gilo continued to consume prodigious quantities of the raw local wine, which he preferred above all others. He often said that it was the only pleasure left to him, and it did ease his pains as nothing else could. By midmorning his tongue was loosened and his mind, freed from the necessity of coping with pain, sharp and clear. Now that he felt his death creeping upon him he was almost pathetically anxious to bequeath to his son something more precious than Clari. And what more precious than the gift of life itself?

Gilo would never demean his own blood by suggesting that it was possible for a knight to avoid the most dangerous press of battle, but there were sensible precautions which could and should be taken to ensure that a fighting man's chances of survival were at least equal. A man's mount was his best friend and his first defense, for if the horse shied at the smell of danger and threw his rider, all hope was gone. Foot soldiers kept sharp eyes out for the floundering figures pinned to the ground by heavy armor, and their knives were quick and inescapable. Gilo had seen to it that Robert's charger was one any man would be proud to ride. Throughout the winter the great black beast had been fed the best grain available and daily put through its paces. Now, no less so than Robert himself, it was a formidable fighting machine. On that score all that was possible had been done, and the moneylenders the richer for it.

Try though he might, Gilo had not been able to furnish his son with the new, lighter-weight armor most suitable to the climate of the Holy Land. So he had contented himself with giving Robert the pieces he himself had worn in the time of Coeur-de-Lion. They had served him well and now, refurbished, rust-free and polished to a high gleam, each overlapping ring well oiled, he did not doubt they would be ample protection against the curved swords and arrows of the infidel. Robert's sword was his own, a gift at his knighting, carefully balanced and of a weight suitable to his rather slender frame.

Reviewing the arrangements he had made for his son's safety, Gilo was somewhat reassured. He hoped the army would be tested in those lightning skirmishes for which the Saracens were famous, for although such encounters were often more dangerous than pitched battle, they were the only means by which a man could gain the tactical experience which was the real difference between life and death. Over and over he described to Robert the infidel's manner of fighting, raising his voice in weak imitation of the bloodcurdling yells with which they terrified their opponents. "They scream like devils out of hell," he told Robert, "and you must throw the challenge back at them. 'Jerusalem, Jerusalem,' as loudly as you can. Once the fight has been joined you will hear them no longer. There will be so much noise all around you that you will seem to be above it, almost in a dream of which you will remember very little when it is over."

Now, on this last morning, knowing it would be this final sight of his son that he would carry to his grave, Gilo cast frantically about for one last piece of advice. "Salt," he stammered, horrified that he had almost forgotten this most important warning. "Eat it by the handful whenever you can get it. Buy sacks of it in Venice, no matter what the cost, and keep it closely guarded. In the Holy Land it is a treasure worth more than gold. At Acre our skins were crusted with the salt of our own sweat and for lack of it many who bore no wounds upon their bodies weakened and perished."

"I will, Father," answered Robert, "for you have given me more than enough silver for all my needs."

If only there were an heir, thought Gilo. I would not be so troubled. I could with greater resignation let my son go, knowing that the name and the flesh would continue. Why had he made Aleaumes a clerk? But then he had not known, when the promise to the Church was given, that only two sons would grow to manhood.

Aware that the two men who were to accompany Robert were standing impatiently at the far end of the courtyard, Gilo raised his hand to bless his son for the last time. Robert fell to his knees and a stifled moan rose from the group of women huddled together in the doorway. Gilo glanced at them reprovingly, noting that Lady Agatha and Aelis stood straight and tall, hands at their sides, their faces proud and tearless as befitted the mother and the wife of a knight who wore the cross. What was Robert saying? Something about a gift?

"The only one worthy of you, Father, and one I hope will be

to your great comfort while I am gone. Aelis told me two days ago. Her moon month is three weeks past due. If God wills, a grandson will be born before Lent."

Gilo let out his breath in a great sigh of satisfaction. "I will send you word somehow, for I cannot die until I hold your child in my arms."

I am glad I did not tell him earlier, thought Robert as he mounted his horse. Gilo's eyes were fastened hungrily on his daughter-in-law's slight frame. It makes the parting easier.

As he reached the bend in the river, Robert reined in his horse and turned for a last glimpse of Clari. Two figures were outlined at the top of the tower, standing motionless as statues. Seeing him halt, they raised bright-colored scarves which waved like pennants in the sunshine. He raised a gauntleted hand to return their salute, then urged his horse at a gallop toward Amiens.

Amiens was already crowded with assembling troops when he arrived, but Aleaumes had managed to save him sleeping space among the scores of knights who bedded down each night in Peter's Hall.

"And it was not easy to do either, brother," he said when arrangements had been made for Robert's two men and the all-important horses. "There are few billets left. Every merchant has been made to take his share and even the monks routed from their cells. There's not a tavern room to be had in the city." With a significant wink he added, "They were the first to go, as you may well imagine."

"I'd just as soon not carry the pox with me on this journey," said Robert. They were standing in Peter of Amiens's Hall, awaiting their lord's appearance and the serving of dinner. He pitched his voice lower so as not to be overheard by the groups of men that eddied and swirled around them. "Father is weakening. Our lady mother says it will be a miracle if he lasts the winter."

"I've known since Easter that he had not much time left to him," answered Aleaumes. "He's lived so close to death for so long that he's grown resigned to it, and I do not think he will be reluctant to be released from the pain he suffers. I've already paid for Masses to be said for him at the cathedral when the time comes."

Both the brothers knew that the relationship they shared with their father was an unusually close one, though they seldom spoke of it. Now that Gilo was in his final illness they were prepared to let him go without sadness. His sufferings were becoming well-nigh unbearable. Many clerks were bitter toward the fathers who had forced them into a life of celibacy and poverty, just as there were heirs who did all they could to hasten the day of their inheritance. But despite all his faults and the pleasures of the flesh he had indulged in, Gilo of Clari had always treated his sons with a gentleness surprising in a man whose first love was war. He had been firm with them and beaten them when they most needed it, but by his own example he tolerated no cruelty in his house, and rarest of all, from the time they were able to raise their baby faces to him in comprehension of what he said, he had spoken to them with the courtesy and frankness with which he addressed others of his own rank. If Aleaumes and Robert were a shade more thoughtful, a bit kinder and more considerate in their actions than the majority of their peers, it was because of this man's influence.

"There is another matter which demands our attention," began Aleaumes, but he was interrupted by the flurry of activity that greeted Peter of Amiens's arrival. "Make some excuse to leave as soon as the meal is over, then meet me at the west door of the cathedral. And come alone."

With no further explanation Aleaumes abruptly left his brother's side and made his way quickly from the crowded Hall. Mystified, Robert watched him go, then slipped into a vacant place at the long trestle table behind him. He knew slightly the two knights on either side of him, and greeted them with absentminded politeness. It was not like Aleaumes to have secrets. In fact, it was so foreign to his nature that Robert could not imagine what he might be concealing. Surely he could not have gotten himself involved with some woman at this late date.

"Just arrived?" asked the knight to his left, Anseau of Cayeaux. "I've never seen Amiens so crowded before."

"Nor I," put in Peter of Nêle, pushing a platter heaped with bits of roasted meat toward Robert. "A few more days, though, and we'll be out of it."

"This is nothing compared to what it'll be like in Venice," continued Anseau. "Have you ever been there?"

"No, I haven't," said Robert, unsure which question to answer first. "My men and I arrived a few hours ago."

"Then you haven't talked with Lord Peter yet." Anseau's mouth was full and it was hard to understand him. "No matter. He'll see you and anyone else who came in today as soon as we've finished here. Just a word of greeting and your assigned place in the train. He's no time for individual conversations."

Robert could see that even while eating, Peter of Amiens continued to direct the last-minute details of their departure. Messengers came and went from the high table, constantly interrupting the important men who were gathered around Peter in earnest conversation.

"We'll join up somewhere along the road with the Count of St. Pol," said Peter of Nêle. "That's about all I know at the moment."

Robert nodded. Although he would take his orders directly from Peter of Amiens, whose sworn man he was, they would all be serving under the command of Peter's kinsman, Hugh of St. Pol, who, along with Baldwin of Flanders and Louis of Blois, made up the triumvirate of great lords whose authority was only slightly less than that of Boniface of Montferrat himself. Within the army was a tight structure of command based entirely on the loyalties of overlord and vassal, a system so familiar that each man unquestioningly accepted his place within it.

This was no pleasant, leisurely paced feast at which they were assembled, Robert realized, for no minstrels attempted to make themselves heard above the din and each man ate and drank as quickly as he could.

Peter of Amiens rose from his chair and with a few loud raps of his dagger on the wooden table caught the attention of the diners. They turned on their benches to face him, and as the last voice died away he began to speak.

"I give you greetings in Christ's name," he said, "especially to those among you who have recently joined us. I will see the new arrivals in a few moments and my brother Thomas, who writes a rare clerkly hand, will give each of you the place he is to occupy during the march." A burst of laughter greeted the mention of

Thomas of Amiens's name, for Peter's brother was almost completely hidden behind the rolls of parchment heaped on the table before him, rolls on which were carefully inscribed the names of all those under Peter's command and the contents of the provision and arms wagons that were so important a part of this journey. "The day of our departure has been decided on. The Count of St. Pol sends word that we are to meet him at Bapaume, and to reach the rendezvous in time we must set out at first light the day after tomorrow."

The Hall once more resounded with noise as men jumped cheering to their feet and turned excitedly to clap their neighbors on the back. "Make whatever final preparations are necessary," continued Peter, raising his voice to a shout, "and say those last fond farewells." He grinned, knowing the whores would have no rest this night, then added, "Those I have not seen yet may come forward and present themselves."

The meal was over, but no one left the Hall, for there was still wine to be drunk and toasts to be exchanged with old friends. Robert drank a cup with Anseau of Cayeaux and Peter of Nêle, then pushed his way to the dais where he knelt and placed his hands between those of Peter of Amiens, renewing the promises he had made at his knighting. There was no time for private words as a line of other knights had formed behind him. He moved along the table and received his assignment from a harried-looking Thomas. "Aleaumes was looking for you," the clerk said.

"He found me," answered Robert, wondering if Thomas was privy to whatever it was his brother had done. But Peter's brother merely grunted and turned back to the rolls as another knight approached.

It was easy to slip unobserved from the Hall, and Robert resolutely pushed his way through the crowded streets to the cathedral. He hoped Aleaumes' business wouldn't take too long, for in a few hours it would be dark and he had not yet visited the stables to check on his horses and the two men he hoped were even now rubbing them down and seeing that there was plenty of water and good fodder available.

A cloaked and hooded figure detached itself from the shadow of the cathedral's most secluded entrance. Automatically Robert reached for his sword before recognizing the face that peered out from the depths of the black hood.

"I brought one for you, too," said Aleaumes urgently. "Duck in here and put it on. It's just as well we're not recognized."

Robert was too startled to reply, and after the first moment's shock, too convulsed with laughter at his brother's mysterious appearance to manage a word. Aleaumes, he could tell, was not laughing. He wrapped himself in the cloak and managed to choke down his amusement.

"Where are we going?" he asked as they emerged from the shadow of the cathedral and made their way down back streets that wound in and out so confusedly that no one could have followed them.

Aleaumes glanced back over his shoulder before replying, "To the Convent of the Holy Cross."

"The Convent of the Holy Cross? Aleaumes, you haven't got a nun pregnant, have you?" Robert could not imagine what other catastrophe could demand such precautions. "Because if you have . . ."

"Shut up, brother, and listen," Aleaumes interrupted. "There's not much time. We're almost there."

Robert shrugged his shoulders as if to say, "I'm all ears," and quickened his pace to match that of the long-legged Aleaumes.

"Do you remember that girl at Soissons, the one we took to the Countess of Flanders's tent?"

"Yes, I remember her." And the shock I felt at seeing such unearthly beauty in the moonlight, added Robert to himself. How could any man forget such a one?

"She's here now, waiting for us at the convent. Mary of Flanders is with child and Count Baldwin has forbidden her to make the journey to the Holy Land until after the babe is born. So she sent Anne to us."

"To us?" Robert seemed to be having difficulty breathing.

"She pleaded with the Countess to allow her to join the expedition by herself. Mary didn't know what to do with her, and I guess that's when the girl remembered our names."

"Our names?"

"There's no need to repeat everything I say," snapped Aleaumes. "The Countess dressed her up as a widow, gave her some money and sent her along to Amiens with a party of merchants. And probably only too glad to get her off her hands."

"What does my lady expect us to do with her?" asked Robert. He could not bring himself to say the name aloud, but the sweet sound of it filled him with pleasure. Anne, Anne. A scented whisper heard late at night through murmuring willow branches.

"We have a plan," said Aleaumes, "but the lady herself will have to tell it to you. We're here."

The bell was answered by a wrinkle-faced old nun who seemed to be expecting them.

"Two kinsmen of the widow of Guy of Bouchet," murmured Aleaumes in a voice so well disguised that Robert recognized nothing familiar about it.

They followed the portress to the visitors' parlor used by the pious laywomen who often spent periods of retreat in the convent.

"The lady is at her devotions, but will be with you presently," the nun said before leaving them alone in the tiny, whitewashed room whose sole furniture was three hard chairs and an enormous crucifix.

Robert would have liked to ask Aleaumes to tell him all he knew about Anne of Nanteuil's year in Flanders, but his brother was pacing restlessly about the parlor, obviously in no mood to answer questions. So instead he let his mind wander back to that night in Soissons. He made a great effort to analyze his thoughts and failed utterly. He could concentrate on nothing and his senses seemed in a state of confused revolt so that he was unaware of the passing of time.

Aleaumes abruptly stopped his pacing and stood looking up at the crucifix, from which hung a larger-than-life-size Christ. He seemed to be struggling with himself.

"How is Aelis?" he blurted out hoarsely.

Startled out of his reverie, Robert stared at his brother's stiff back. Aleaumes was no longer the careless young man with whom he had once shared the whores of Amiens. Nothing would ever quell his rebellious, adventurous temperament, but underneath it all lay the strict conscience of a man who was accustomed to facing his sins head on in long hours of prayer and meditation. Whatever else she might be, Anne of Nanteuil was a lady born, one who had sought the help and protection of gentlemen, and most certainly a virgin. There would be whores aplenty traveling with the army and catering to men's needs for a coin or two or a pitcher of wine. There was no sin, or very little at least, in such commerce, but a virgin of good family was another matter altogether. Robert felt a furious rage mount to his throat at the implied insult to his knightly honor, a rage which disappeared as quickly as it had come. Aleaumes is right to warn me, he thought. I should have warned myself.

"Aelis is pregnant. I told father just before I left. He seemed greatly strengthened by the news."

"God be thanked. I congratulate you, Robert."

Aleaumes turned, smiling, from his contemplation of the crucifix. There was no need to say any more. As always, they understood each other perfectly.

The inner door of the parlor opened and Anne of Nanteuil stood there, her hand on the latch, saying over her shoulder to some unseen nun, "Thank you, Dame. I shall not be long with my kinsmen."

Carefully she closed the door, listening to the sound of sandaled feet moving away toward the cloister.

"Nuns have an uncannily developed sense of hearing," she said. "It's all those long hours spent in silence." She nodded to Robert. "Have you told him, Aleaumes?"

"Only the barest outline of your predicament, my lady. There was no time to acquaint him with the details of our plan."

"Shall I do it then?" she asked, and without waiting for an answer seated herself and motioned them to bring their chairs closer to hers. "It is very simple, my lord." She spoke directly to Robert, her eyes fixed on his face as if demanding that he make no protest. "As you see, I am dressed as a widow, and the Countess has given me gold enough to reach the Holy Land and more besides. There are many pilgrims traveling with the army and I propose to join their ranks as a lady recently bereft of her husband who travels to join her closest living relative in the Holy Land. That much is true, for I have an uncle who serves at the court of King Almaric, and for my dead mother's sake he will make me welcome there. The difficulty is that no lady may travel with the army unless she be vouched for, and it is even better if she is sponsored by a knight. I do not think I need to explain why this is so."

"A sensible precaution," put in Aleaumes, "now that the Countess and her ladies will not be making the journey."

"Quite so," agreed Anne. "I will be safe among the pilgrims, particularly if it is known that I travel under your protection, Robert of Clari."

"But what excuse . . . ?" he began.

Anne interrupted him with an impatient wave of her hands. "You shall say that I am a distant kinswoman, a very distant kinswoman of some relative of yours, and you must appear very put out by the inconvenience demanded of you."

"That part is easy enough," said Aleaumes, knowing that Robert would be extremely embarrassed to make such a request of Peter of Amiens.

"I cannot lie to my lord," said Robert definitely.

"But it's probably not a lie at all," argued Anne. "Most of us are related to some degree anyway. Just because it was so long ago that no one remembers it doesn't mean that our families too might not once have been linked by marriage."

"I don't like it," said Robert stubbornly.

Anne stared at him in disbelief, her great blue eyes wide with anger and disappointment. "You can't deny me now," she said, while tears gathered and spilled down her cheeks. "Not after all I have been through, all I have risked."

"Lady, please." Robert reached for her hand. Anything to stop those tears.

She snatched her hand away from him and stood up. "If you will not help me I shall be forced to seek another protector. And if my soul be damned by despair or by blackest sin, the blame of it shall be yours."

"Nay, lady, there is no need for that," Robert said resignedly. "From this moment forward you are kinswoman to my second cousin and as such I take you under my protection. What was his name, Aleaumes?"

"Guy of Bouchet."

The tears instantly disappeared and Anne plunged immediately into a discussion of the things they must buy for her in the market, absolute essentials to her health and comfort on the long journey. Listening to her thrilled voice Aleaumes reflected that it was perhaps not so bad after all that he was denied intimate acquaintanceship with ladies, particularly as they seemed so easily able to twist a man to their desires in spite of himself.

Some women were more skilled at it than others, he thought. This one, so slender and beautiful that she seemed made of finely spun glass, had revealed an inner core of determination that was every bit as strong as tempered metal. She should have passed her days in the quiet routine of the cloister, meekly accepting the future ordained for her by the brother to whom she owed obedience. Thousands of other women, older, wiser, perhaps even more beautiful than she, had done so. But this one had without a second thought snapped her fingers in the face of duty, unashamedly taken advantage of a lady whose high birth she ought to have held in respectful awe, then abruptly quit that lady when she could be of no further use to her. And now she proposed to place herself under the protection of a man she hardly knew to undertake a journey most women would never dream of making.

A quick and easy friendship had sprung up between Anne and Aleaumes. She used no feminine wiles on him and spoke to him with the absentminded affection and utter frankness she might have employed had he been a favored older brother. He remembered her first words to him in this very parlor not three days ago. "I will not go back, Aleaumes. No matter what." Useless to argue with her and so he had not tried. "Some people accept what fate is sent them," she had continued. "I once did, but no longer. I know that my fate is what I choose to make it. And where once I thought it a weakness to be born a woman, I now know that it makes no difference. Male or female, I acknowledge no master and am well content to have it so."

"What of God, Who is Master to us all?" he had asked her.

But in reply she had merely shrugged her shoulders and fixed on him a long, knowing look that had penetrated to the inmost depths of his soul. The clerk in him struggled to form the conventional theological phrases, but lost the contest to the frustrated man. Once, years ago, he too could have said no, but now it was too late. His feet were firmly fixed on the path Gilo had chosen for him and there was no turning back. Bishop he might someday be; husband, lover, father, prince, never. But for her there were no limits, and in the arid wastes of the Holy Land her beauty and spirit might be enough to overcome the lack of dowry and the clouded past that she would always carry with her. In that instant he had promised to help her, forgetting that everything really depended on Robert. It was she who had serenely reminded him of that, she who had thought of the pilgrims, she who had insisted on haste and secrecy. The story of the runaway novice who had disappeared without a trace in the dead of night from a respected, scandal-free house was surely known to the nuns of Amiens, and the risk of discovery grew with each day she remained among them.

It wasn't until he and Robert had been left alone to wait for her that he had known the first misgivings. And then only because Robert's own voice had betrayed him, that and something he had once let slip some months ago. "Aelis is beautiful and obedient," Robert had confided late one night after the wine had loosened his tongue. "But there is neither excitement nor passion in her. She is like a body without a soul. When she has a child she will cease to hate me, but she will no longer need me, nor I her. We will grow old together, but like two strangers who travel the same road for convenience' sake, with never a word of understanding between them."

"That is what marriage is, Robert," Aleaumes had answered. "It is like a dance in which the figures touch briefly, then move apart. But if the forms of decency and politeness are observed it can be borne, for the sake of the children and the good of the soul."

"And do you think a man should be content with only that?" Robert had been very serious, as if certain that an answer to his question could be found, but Aleaumes knew there were no answers, only questions.

The anguished eyes of the Christ hanging on the parlor wall had reminded Aleaumes of that never-quite-forgotten conversation. In an intuitive flash of precognition he had known that Robert would soon come to believe that he had found the woman who should have existed only in his dreams. Unless he himself erected a guard and a barrier against her he would come to love her with an all-consuming passion, and if she returned his love, no power on earth could separate them. Many men in the East married a second time who still had living wives and children in countries to which they were determined never to return, and though this was grave sin, the Church could do little about it. Their own father had foreseen such a possibility. What then would become of Gilo's dream of the continuance of his line on the land for which so many sacrifices had been made? A child in Aelis's belly might make all the difference, particularly if it was a healthy boy. Aleaumes had sensed the almost imperceptible strengthening of Robert's will when he had spoken of the child to come and the effect the anticipation of the birth had had upon Gilo. That then would be the tie that would bind him to Clari, and Aleaumes prayed that it would not be too fragile to withstand the years of separation ahead of them.

Speculatively he looked at Anne of Nanteuil, who had at last fallen silent, her urgent instructions to Robert completed. She did not have the look about her of a woman who sensed anything out of the ordinary in the man seated beside her. She seemed almost oblivious of his presence as a man. Silently Aleaumes blessed the single-mindedness of her determination to join the pilgrims. She would be blind to all else but the necessity of playing her role well and convincingly. There was a compelling force in her that he devoutly hoped was worldly ambition, for if it was, she would disdain any liaison with a knight as poor and obscure as Robert. Such women used men to attain their own ends; they did not allow their hearts to soften and deceive them. For the moment she needed him, but once on board ship and certainly as soon as they reached the Holy Land his usefulness would be at an end. Off she would go to the king's court, where he did not doubt that her uncle would be easily persuaded to further her interests, while he and Robert and the rest of the army set about the difficult and dangerous business of recapturing Jerusalem. She would be forgotten in the urgency of survival. Robert's trained mind was that of a soldier and it would brook no soft, distracting thoughts while on campaign.

Someday, when they were both old and Robert's grandchildren played at their knees, it would be safe to mention her again, to wonder what had become of the fiery girl they had once befriended. Doubtless, like most other women, she would broaden with each child she bore, her breasts would sag and her belly grow slack, the black hair would turn gray and sparse and the vibrant blue of her eyes wash out into a runny paleness. Looking at her now he could not envision it, but, knowing that in the East the years took a terrible toll on women, he almost felt sorry for her.

Robert had stood up to take his leave. "When I speak to Peter of Amiens," he said, almost as an afterthought, "by what name shall I call you?"

"I shall continue to call myself simply the widow of Bouchet," she answered. She rang for the nun who would escort them from the parlor, then smiled devastatingly at Robert. In a low voice that throbbed with gratitude or some other, deeper emotion, she added, "But when we are alone, my lord, you may call me Anne."

Aleaumes' carefully reasoned hopes came crashing down around his ears. The silence was deafening.

PART
II

June, 1202-May, 1203

The barons and most noble lords of the army agreed
to what the Doge proposed, but all the rest of the
crusaders knew nothing about it. . . . The Marquis
of Montferrat was more determined than any other
that the army would go to Constantinople.

—La Conquête de Constantinople
Robert of Clari

I

Venice had decided to quarter the crusading army on the harbor island of St. Nicholas, a site well within view of the mainland but accessible only by boat. The city itself could not possibly absorb the thousands of men who began to arrive shortly before Pentecost, and while its citizens were used to the sight of foreigners on their canals and in their streets, they were uneasy at the thought of large bands of restless, bored, fully armed soldiers taking their pleasure where they could most easily find it. The crusaders would not have much money to spend in the wine shops and brothels anyway, they acknowledged realistically. Far better to isolate them in an area where no real harm could be done and where they could take out the frustrations of their wait by quarreling among themselves.

Tents mushroomed overnight until it seemed that the island must sink into the sea under the weight of the men crowded onto it. The choice locations where the breezes from the open sea brought some relief from the summer's heat and the stench of human waste were quickly gone, and as the months wore on late arrivals were squeezed in helter-skelter, wherever there was room to pitch a tent and tether a horse.

In spite of the overcrowding and the primitive conditions of camp life, spirits were high at first and there were remarkably few fights, for everyone wore the cross and a curious sense of exaltation pervaded the atmosphere. A few more weeks, they told each other, and we will be truly on our way. On to Jerusalem.

Count Baldwin of Flanders had been one of the first to arrive. The Countess Mary had had to be left behind, though once safely delivered she too would join the army. By that time, most agreed, the Holy City would be theirs, and the lovely young woman who had caught the imaginations of so many by her desire to share her husband's pilgrimage would be spared the rigors of the campaign. They chuckled over that, knowing her high spirits and her disappointment, but duty must come before inclination, and her duty was clearly to produce a healthy son for Flanders and Hainault.

Close by Baldwin's tent were those of Count Hugh of St. Pol and Geoffrey of Villehardouin. Hardly a day passed that these three did not spend many hours poring over maps and long lists of men and supplies, for there were fresh calculations and decisions to be made with each new group of arrivals. Often in the evening they would stroll together through the camp, a reassuring and heartening sight to those few who had begun to doubt the chances of success of this new effort to recapture the lost land of Christ. With leaders such as these, men of strong purpose and undeniable ability, argued the confident, it was foolish, almost treasonous to doubt. There is no rivalry among them such as destroyed the armies of Coeur-de-Lion and King Philip of France, was a frequently heard remark, and if an older knight commented on the youth of the Count of Flanders he was quickly reminded that Geoffrey of Villehardouin possessed wisdom and experience enough for two.

By July other questions were being asked, questions to which no one had an answer. Where were Boniface of Montferrat and Count Louis of Blois and Chartres? The original sailing date had come and gone, but the army's leader had not yet even left his court at Montferrat. Louis had been in Chartres as late as May, but surely he had left long since. No one knew for sure where he was.

Small groups were still arriving daily, and with them came rumors that many who had been expected in Venice, men whose passage had been contracted for over a year ago, had decided to sail from other ports. Still others, it was said, planned to join the Count of Brienne in Apulia, where the pay was good and the hazards fewer. Over thirty thousand men had been expected in Venice; less than ten thousand had arrived.

As the rumors spread, fed and embellished by speculation and lack of any real knowledge of what was going on in the country they had left behind them, it became apparent that there were two conflicting factions within the army. There were as yet no direct clashes, no outright challenges to the authority of the barons who led the host, but a gradual erosion of confidence began to make itself felt in the quarrels and discussions that soon occupied the time of each man and his neighbor. They had little to do but pass the long hours of each day in talk, for the Venetians had made sure that there were few boats available to ferry idle sightseers back and forth to the mainland. Boats came and went, but they were laden with supplies and newly arrived reinforcements, and though they returned empty to the port it was with good reason. A man might manage to get passage to the city, but how would he get back? The knights and pilgrims were so effectively isolated that the greatest trading city in the world, which they could clearly see from the island, might never have been there at all.

We sit here in idleness, virtual prisoners of the greedy Venetians, while others, wiser and less gullible than we, are already on their way to the Holy Land, went the argument. Even the Count of Flanders, who sits here with us, has authorized a fleet of his own, commanded by his most trusted companions and heavily laden with arms and supplies. Why, unless he also has doubts, does he risk gold and men on such an enterprise?

Villehardouin had exploded with anger when Baldwin first told him of this fleet. The argument had been fierce and entirely private, for when they had emerged at last from Baldwin's tent, they presented a united, smiling front to the army. But there were no secrets in such a crowded camp and inevitably the story leaked out. Baldwin had allowed himself to be persuaded by John of Nesle, Nicholas of Mailly and his nephew Thierri that the Flanders fleet would in no way detract from that provided by the Venetians. In fact, they had convinced him that more pilgrims would assemble at Venice than could be accommodated anyway. They swore on holy relics that they would join the fleet at whatever rendezvous Baldwin chose, that this was no private enterprise at all, and reluctantly the Count had given in. Privately Villehardouin damned the weakness of Baldwin's character, for to his strategist's clear mind it was obvious that the army was greatly weakened, its pool of common resources depleted.

He rejoiced that he had had the foresight to push the candidacy
of the Marquis of Montferrat, for Boniface was clear-sighted and
inflexible in the pursuit of his goals. Once he arrived, things
would go rapidly forward, and such was the force of his will
that no one would dare question his decisions.

He had sent word that he would arrive in mid-August, for
surely by that time all the stragglers would have drifted in.
Boniface did not want to be in the weak position of a leader
who is forced to wait helplessly for the assemblage of his troops.
When all was in readiness he would join them, and his authority
would be even greater for the impression that the pomp and ceremony of his arrival would undoubtedly make on the men whose
lives he would command for the next few years. Villehardouin
readily admitted the correctness of Montferrat's calculation, just
as he also admitted a growing concern about the weather the
fleet must encounter if sailing were to be postponed until nearly
autumn. He was not a sailor, but like everyone else he knew that
the passage was tricky enough during the calm of the summer
months. What would it be like in September?

There was nothing he could do about that, he knew, except to
trust to God, but there was another matter on which his
influence could be brought to bear. It was somewhat delicate
and would demand all his skill as a diplomat, but anything was
better than sitting frustrated in his tent day after day.

He laid his proposal before Count Hugh of St. Pol and Baldwin one hot summer evening. Count Louis of Blois and
Chartres, with a great company of men, was reported idling
somewhere in Lombardy. He was long overdue and it was common gossip in the camp that he was contemplating debarking
from another port, or worse yet, abandoning the enterprise entirely and returning to his own country. The rumors must be
scotched and Louis persuaded to make good speed to Venice.
Careful to allow no hint of doubt or criticism of the Count to
creep into the conversation, Villehardouin proposed that an embassy be sent to meet Louis and encourage him to delay no
longer. Hugh of St. Pol agreed, and himself chafing under the
strain of inaction and the oppressive heat and humidity of the island, proposed that he and Villehardouin, with a suitable company of knights, make the journey into Lombardy. Baldwin, by

virtue of his rank and the sincere respect he inspired among the
men, must remain behind to keep the host together. The project
was quickly agreed upon. They all knew that if the Count of
Blois and Chartres withdrew from the crusade the ships would
never sail.

Anne of Nanteuil, somber and pale in her widow's garb, was
in a fever of impatience. The rumors among the pilgrims were
far more exaggerated than those which disturbed the fighting
men of the army, for the former had little if any knowledge of
war or the lengthy preparations without which a campaign
would fail utterly. The knights and men-at-arms were accustomed to long periods of inactivity in camp, and busied themselves in the care of horses and the constant polishing and repair
of their gear, exchanging reminiscences of past campaigns over
the dice with which they whiled away the long, hot evenings.
They were contemptuous of the pilgrims who had attached
themselves to the army, for in battle they would be dangerous
encumbrances who would nevertheless be entitled to some sort
of protection. In fact, they delighted in concocting stories of the
dangers they would have to face on the long march to Jerusalem, gleefully watching the pilgrims' eyes widen with fear at the
descriptions of the endless marches through heat-shimmering
deserts and the dysentery and fevers that would decimate their
numbers. Anyone who drops out will be left to the buzzards,
they told them, to the buzzards and the infidels, and the pilgrims
crossed themselves in terror, for it was a well-known fact that no
one had ever surpassed the Saracens in the invention of tortur-
ous ways to end a man's life. What they did to women was simply unmentionable, but the few women among the pilgrims constantly discussed it in low-voiced horror.

Anne had struck up a friendship with two sisters from Rheims
whose tent and meals she now shared. Childless widows both,
they had somehow convinced themselves that their barrenness
was God's judgment on them for some unexpiated family sin
long since forgotten everywhere but in the Court of Heaven. For
years they had deviled their priest with it until in desperation he
had intimated that only a pilgrimage to Jerusalem would satisfy
God's justice. Soon after his suggestion Fulk of Neuilly had

begun to preach the new crusade. It was clearly a sign from heaven, one that could not be ignored. They were garrulous women in their fifties, lean, angular and singularly ugly, and Anne was very soon acquainted with every detail of their lives. She judged them to be a bit crazed, for after much discussion they had finally identified the sin for which they must atone, and had clasped it to their scrawny bosoms with all the passion so long dammed up within them.

Their father's first wife had died suddenly and mysteriously soon after giving birth to her fifth stillborn child. There was talk of poison at the time, but he had quickly remarried and fathered three healthy children and the old tale had been long forgotten. Only when their own barrenness could no longer be denied did they remember it. Now they were convinced that murder had indeed been done and that they had been chosen to suffer the wrath of a just God. True, their brother had fathered six children before he died, but that they took to be a sign of God's unfathomable mercy. The sin must be expiated by their generation, they whispered, else the curse of barrenness would be visited on their nephews and nieces. They viewed themselves as martyrs to their father's wickedness and walked proudly in acknowledgment of their holy burden.

Daily they urged Anne to confide in them, but she clung obstinately to her protecting mantle of widow's grief. Her dear husband was dead, and she too would resign herself to death after completing her vow to pray at the Holy Sepulcher, she told them, for although her closest living relative was at the Court of the King of Jerusalem, and would welcome her there, she had no desire to remarry. If God spared her life she would retire from the world into some convent in the Holy Land. Always at this point she was able to force tears to gather in her eyes, and the susceptible sisters found themselves busily comforting her while they too cried. It was immensely satisfying until they remembered that she had really told them nothing about herself at all.

"How much longer must we remain here?" Anne raged to Robert as they paced the shoreline in the gathering dusk of a late July evening. "I must be constantly on my guard with these women. One slip and it will be all over camp. And I don't doubt that one of these fanatic priests would think it his duty to shut me up in some convent here until I could be sent back to Soissons."

"Aleaumes says you worry unnecessarily," soothed Robert. "You took no vow, you were not bound there by any will but your own."

"Aleaumes does not know my sister-in-law," said Anne bitterly. "I begin to think that all men are weak fools who would rather give in to a woman at any price than be denied her bed."

"That is unjust, Anne."

"Oh, I did not mean you, Robert, nor Aleaumes either. I am grateful to you for all that you have done for me. I can never repay the debt, for I know that it was done through gallantry alone." She cast a sidelong glance at Robert, who stood gazing at the church spires across the port, black in the shallow light of evening. A muscle twitched along the line of his jaw. She knew that in the past few weeks he had fallen deeply in love with her. How much longer before he would declare himself? Were it not for Aleaumes' constant presence she was sure they would have long since been lovers. It would happen, she knew, for she would not dare deny him when the moment came.

Yet she would not be taken unawares, nor would she jeopardize her future. Husbands set a ridiculously high value on virginity and she intended to marry well. Her uncle would see to that. But if he suspected she were tarnished goods he would clap her in a convent as quickly as even her sister-in-law could wish, and all in the name of family pride. She would just have to be careful and above all discreet. Virginity could be faked; a tiny vial of blood concealed in the palm of one's hand, maidenly confusion and tears, a sudden cry of pain. And there were ways to terminate pregnancy; any girl who had listened to the whisperings of maidservants knew that. She sighed, for she was attracted to Robert and very conscious of his virility. If only he possessed more than the fifteen miserable acres of land he had told her about. If only his ambition matched her own.

Robert heard her sigh and felt his heart leap with hope. Could it be that she sighed for the barrier of knightly honor that by right protected her from his love? But in a moment his hope died as she turned from the shore to make her way back to the two old women who always looked at him so strangely. Whatever private conversation they had was in snatched moments like this, when under the pretext of inquiring for her well-being he visited the pilgrims' camp and casually suggested a walk for the sake of her health. She was chatting to him now in the same friendly, casual tone with which she always spoke. She might have been conversing with the celibate Aleaumes for all the hint there was in her voice of the difference between man and woman.

"I do not mean to burden you with my complaints, Robert," she was saying lightly. "I always resolve not to speak of them, but as you can see, the resolve is broken the moment we are alone. You and Aleaumes are the only friends I have, the only ones in whom I can confide without the fear of being betrayed, and when Aleaumes is not with us the whole burden falls on you."

"I count it no burden, Anne. The duty of a knight is to serve his lady."

"Robert, you have been listening to romances," she laughed, "and besides, I am not your lady. No one gives me a second glance in these horrible robes I wear."

"They are a good disguise, and more protection than I can give you." It had been on the tip of his tongue to tell her that he found her beautiful and desirable no matter what she wore, but they had reached the camp and he was aware of idle, listening ears and speculative eyes. The moment was not right. Would it ever be?

"What news can you give us, sir knight?" she said formally as they stood at the entrance to her tent. "We are all anxious to know when we shall sail."

"Yes, indeed," chimed in the two sisters, who had seen them coming and quickly ducked into the tent, where they had stood as close to the entrance as they dared in hopes of overhearing something more interesting than the news Anne was asking for. Now they popped out, unabashed by the obviousness of their sudden disappearance and quick reemergence. Standing one on either side of their tentmate, they urgently begged Robert to acquaint them with the latest rumor.

Robert greeted the widows with his usual courtesy, catching

the warning look in Anne's eyes, determined for her sake to appear nothing but what he pretended to be.

"Count Louis of Blois is only a few days' march from here," he said, "and will soon join his army to ours."

"How can you be certain of this?" snapped Sarah, the elder and leaner of the sisters. "We had it on good authority that he had already sailed from some place in Sicily."

"Peter of Amiens, whom I serve, returned this morning with the news." Robert's patience was being strained by these flapping crows who eagerly believed every piece of gossip that came their way and treated Anne with such proprietary airs. "He rode with his cousin of St. Pol and Geoffrey the Marshal to Pavia, where they met with the Count. The delay was caused by some illness of his, but he is now fully recovered and you will soon see him with your own eyes."

"God be praised," said Loma, the other sister. "We must offer a prayer of thanks that the Count has seen fit to do his duty." Grabbing Anne by the arm, she disappeared into the tent, followed by Sarah, who paused only long enough to give Robert a knowing, triumphant look. In a moment he heard the three women reciting the Ave, Anne's clear, low-pitched voice melodiously softening the cackle of her companions.

He had not dared reveal to them the whole of Peter of Amiens's report, for among those who were determined that the crusade succeed there was a tacit conspiracy to keep knowledge of new defections from spreading through the ranks. There were already enough opportunistic men who for reasons of their own were attempting to persuade friends and companions to desert the army.

Robert had not himself been approached by any of these, for his loyalty to Peter of Amiens was as well known as Peter's kinship to the Count of St. Pol. But others had come to him seeking reassurance and the grain of truth at the heart of each new rumor. Sometimes he had to laugh at the ridiculousness of the story told him, and the laugh itself was enough to hearten a confused and then thoroughly embarrassed soldier. At other times he freely confessed that he had no comforting information to give, but always the steadiness of his character and the calm assurance with which he trusted men such as Villehardouin and the Counts of Flanders and St. Pol made its impression.

Some important defections had indeed weakened the army, notably that of the Count of Brienne and the Champenois who had followed him to Apulia, but Robert was always quick to point out that it was far better for such men to pursue their own interests here in Europe than to suddenly disappear in Palestine. Every man who sailed must be a committed man; the passage was too expensive to tolerate weak or vacillating loyalties. The new Flanders fleet was disturbing, but not as serious as outright defection, for he did not really believe that Baldwin would have permitted its formation unless he were certain of his captains' allegiance.

Count Louis of Blois and Chartres was finally on his way, but there were others, men of lower rank but great popular renown because of their proven ability in the field, who would be sorely missed. One such was Villain of Neuilly, reputed to be one of the finest knights in the world. According to Peter of Amiens he was bound for Apulia and no argument or threat had succeeded in changing his mind. Because of his reputation many knights and sergeants had chosen to follow him, and Robert was certain that once the news was out there would be others slipping from the Isle of St. Nicholas by night. There were fortunes to be made in Sicily, while in the Holy Land a man could only be certain of hardship, privation and hordes of blood-crazed infidels. Glory and land there might be, and the soul's salvation was assured, it was true, but not all were anxious to realize salvation if the price were death. When it came right down to it, most men did not yearn for the bliss of heaven with quite the fervor advocated by the Church.

Robert hoped that the disgraceful conduct of Giles of Trasegnies would never be known, for it was a blow to the very heart of the most basic element of society, the sacred relationship of mutual service between vassal and suzerain. Peter of Amiens had choked out the story within hours of his return, so disgusted by it that he had seemed to spit the words out against his will. Giles of Trasegnies was Count Baldwin's liege man, and the Count had so valued him that he had given him five hundred livres out of his own purse to defray the expenses of the journey.

collected. "My lords, the Venetians will never accept less than the amount specified in the treaty."

"We could not expect them to," said Boniface smoothly. "They have fulfilled their part of the agreement and it is only right and honorable that we do the same."

"Perhaps if the situation were fully explained to the Doge," suggested Baldwin uncertainly. "Conon of Béthune has a silver tongue in his head and few can resist him when he chooses to exert himself."

"The Doge is immune to persuasion," Villehardouin told him bluntly. He was bitter and did not take the trouble to hide it. "He claims that for over a year his people have devoted themselves to nothing but this fleet, that they have suffered heavy losses in trade because of it, and that they must be paid all that is due them."

"We shall be forever dishonored if we do not keep our sworn oath," said Boniface. "Perhaps," he continued, "there are other terms the Venetians would consider."

Hugh of St. Pol looked at him speculatively. He had heard rumors that a dispossessed and impecunious Greek prince who called himself the rightful Emperor of Constantinople had found refuge at the court of Philip of Swabia. And Boniface had spent Christmas at this same court. It was an interesting thought.

Villehardouin was also unable to keep his eyes from Boniface's face, for the Marquis's suggestion was somehow too pat, too casually given. What other terms could he possibly mean?

Only Baldwin seemed oblivious of the situation. "Cousin," he said, turning to Louis of Blois, "I am willing to give all that I can spare and all that I can borrow to make up this debt. It will not be an insubstantial sum, but I fear it will not be enough."

Louis of Blois did not hesitate. "I too will gladly give more than my share, for I must point out, my lords, that we are virtual prisoners here on this island. We are already hard pressed to keep our people fed and our horses supplied with fodder. It would be an easy matter for the Venetians to refuse to supply us. We could die like flies here and no one would raise a hand to help us."

"You propose a second levy, then?" asked Boniface. "And that we and others who are able should attempt to make up the difference?"

"I see no other way," said Louis, wondering why the Marquis should even question the plan. "We are all wealthy men and can afford to be generous in the name of Christ." St. Pol had the air of a man who had just stumbled onto a great secret, and though his face was a mask of mournful propriety, his eyes gleamed as though they had suddenly lighted on a beautiful woman or a jewel of exceptional value. I must talk to him, decided Louis, privately and in strictest confidence. Something is hanging in the air between him and Boniface, and from the looks of him it has nothing to do with Jerusalem. Louis had his spies also, but as he had for a time toyed with the idea of joining the Count of Brienne he had not paid much attention to the vague reports they brought him from Germany. Now he was determined to interrogate them carefully and at length.

"If we are all in agreement then, my lords, I will give the clerks their instructions." Villehardouin was anxious to conclude this meeting.

"Do so, my lord Marshal," said Boniface. But as Villehardouin and Baldwin left the tent he echoed the Count's earlier comment, "But I fear it will not be enough."

The second levy was openly resented in the army. Many flatly refused to contribute, declaring that they had fulfilled their part of the bargain and that if the Venetians were not satisfied they would seek passage elsewhere.

Anne was one who claimed that she had no more to give, and as she was so obviously a widow and a pilgrim, she was believed. Not even Robert doubted her, for she had not revealed to him the true extent of Mary of Flanders's generosity. She ceased to complain about the hot, figure-concealing robes she was obliged to wear, for under them the bulkiness of the pouch in which lay hidden the gold and silver coins with which she must buy her freedom was easily hidden. When she was sure the two sisters were asleep, she wrapped each coin in scraps of cloth lest a quick movement cause them to clink against each other. Feelings ran high against those who held back and she feared that if the money were discovered it would be taken from her by force.

As the days passed the army was treated to a sight which secretly amused many. Gold and silver table services, jewel-encrusted crosses and altar vessals were hastily unpacked from the baggage trains of the great barons and under heavy guard ferried across to Venice where the populace gathered to see them ceremoniously borne to the Doge's palace. We were right to insist on full payment, the Venetians told one another. For here is proof that great wealth was concealed from us on the island of St. Nicholas.

The Venetians gladly provided boats to carry the wealthy barons of the army back and forth from the island, and guides to direct them to the quarter of the moneylenders. For a time business was brisk.

The Marquis of Montferrat, at the conclusion of one such visit, paid a personal call on the Doge, and it was remarked that he emerged from that private meeting with an air of confidence and satisfaction. The army breathed easier and praised the bountiful generosity of its leaders. There were still rumors, of course, that the full amount could not be raised, but these came chiefly from those who had held back from contributing to the second levy and who now sought to justify the care with which they had guarded their possessions. It was hopeless from the beginning, they maintained stubbornly, but now they mostly murmured among themselves, for no one knew for certain whether the commitment had been met.

"Thirty-four thousand silver marks remain to be paid," reported Villehardouin. "We have been defeated, nay, betrayed, and by our own countrymen." He was as close to despair as a man could be. For years he had worked tirelessly in this one cause, first in the difficult negotiations with the Venetians, then, after the death of Thibaut, in the long search for a leader to take his place. He had strained his own resources to the limit, as had the others who now sat in Boniface's tent, and he knew that not another coin was to be had anywhere. There was no help for it. The army must disband.

"A great sum," mused Boniface.

"Too great, my lord. We have no hope of raising it."

Boniface helped himself to some wine, carefully assessing the atmosphere of gloom which held them all in its grip.

Baldwin was thinking of his wife, and realizing that he might indeed manage to be in Flanders in time to greet the son he hoped she carried. She was a tempestuous woman, his Mary, but even she would be unable to find cause to reproach him.

Count Louis of Blois and Count Hugh of St. Pol waited patiently as the silence stretched on.

At last Boniface judged the moment to be right. He saw that Villehardouin had drained his cup and concluded from the expression on his face that the Marshal was already rehearsing the speech in which he would have to explain to the lesser barons of the army just why the force would not sail.

"The Doge has asked for an audience tomorrow and I have granted his request. I should like all of you to be present during our meeting."

Hugh of St. Pol and Louis of Blois exchanged quick, half-hidden glances. Baldwin of Flanders merely looked puzzled, but Villehardouin had risen angrily to his feet.

"What more have we to do with Venice?" he demanded. "They have flatly refused to allow the fleet to sail until we have paid the sum agreed on in the treaty. And they know that we cannot pay. Does Dandolo come to gloat at our misfortune?"

"Hardly, my lord Marshal. The Doge is a man greatly advanced in years and I doubt that he would stir from his palace merely to enjoy the spectacle of our embarrassment. I am not privy to the secrets of his council, but be assured that he comes to us on their behalf and that he will propose a solution to our dilemma."

The tone of Boniface's voice and the authority with which he had spoken could not be ignored. He had made it clear that he and only he wielded supreme command over the men camped on the Isle of St. Nicholas. Villehardouin sank back into his seat, reminded that it had been chiefly by his efforts that Boniface had attained this power. Do I really know this man, he wondered for the first time since the parliament at Soissons. Where is he leading us?

"My lord, I beg leave to interrupt you." A guard stood just inside the entrance to the tent, one hand still on the half-opened flap. "A messenger has arrived from France claiming he brings news of great urgency which he can reveal only to you personally. He wears your badge, my lord, and is most insistent. My men are hard put to restrain him."

"Let him enter," said Boniface quietly, motioning the others to remain. "We have no secrets from one another, my lords."

The man who stumbled into the tent and fell to his knees before the Marquis was travel-stained and clearly on the brink of exhaustion. Yet his voice did not tremble when, at a sign from Boniface, he began to speak.

"Fulk of Neuilly is dead, my lord, after a long illness. He has been buried in his own parish churchyard at Neuilly."

Boniface crossed himself reverently. "Jerusalem has lost a mighty champion," he said. "We will have Masses said for his soul without delay."

"Do you think it wise?" began Villehardouin. He was going to add that for the sake of morale this new blow to their hopes ought to be kept secret, at least until after the Doge's visit. But Boniface cut him off in mid-sentence, smiling mournfully.

"I do, my lord Marshal. Our people must be aware that only the Doge can help us now."

And God, added Villehardouin silently. He too crossed himself, but whether for the soul of Fulk of Neuilly or to ward off some new disaster from the already threatened crusade he did not know.

II

Early the next morning every priest traveling with the army said his Mass for the repose of the soul of Fulk of Neuilly. In the Church of St. Nicholas, which had given the island its name, the relics of the saint were exposed for the veneration of the people, and the sermon preached there was one of hope and comfort. Fulk had not abandoned them, the crusaders were told, for in death was everlasting life. Even now one could believe that he stood close to the throne of the Father, where his intercession on their behalf would certainly lead them to victory. And the knights and pilgrims allowed themselves to be comforted and their hopes renewed, for death was the lot of every man who lived, and surely the life of Fulk of Neuilly had been such that his salvation was not in doubt. Some declared him already a saint in all but name, and wondered how long it would be before the rite of canonization installed him for all eternity on the long roster of the Church's officially proclaimed champions. One ought not to weep when a holy man was gathered to the bosom of the Lord, the priests said, for such a one could find no true delight in the exile of life. After the initial tears and lamentations had spent themselves, the army went about its daily work with somber vigor, lest Fulk, looking down from Heaven, be displeased by his children.

Robert and Aleaumes were standing in quiet conversation on the shore of the island when the great gilded barge of the Doge first came into view. All around it were clustered other richly ornamented craft, a whole fleet of them bobbing attendance on the most venerated man in Venice. Even the tiny working boats that daily dotted the water's surface turned from their tasks and paid homage to the old man whose life seemed more legend than reality.

"What does it mean, his coming here?" Robert asked. Neither he nor Aleaumes had heard even the slightest rumor of a ducal visit.

"I don't know," he answered. "But, look, the Marquis stands waiting for him at the pier. He does not come unexpectedly."

They watched as the Doge's barge glided effortlessly to the dock and sailors in gold-embroidered livery leaped out to make it secure. The figure that embraced Boniface on both cheeks and bowed slightly to the other French lords who had gathered to greet him seemed hardly that of a living man, so stiffly embroidered with gleaming gold thread and sun-sparkling jewels were the robes that completely covered him and trailed behind in the dust as he walked the short distance to the Marquis's tent. At this distance they could make out little of his face, except for the high-bridged nose that jutted out sharply like the dark, pointed beak of a bird of prey.

"I must go," said Aleaumes. "Jean of La Force is ill with a fever and it may be that my lord of Montferrat will require the services of an extra scribe or two."

"And for once, brother, you look the part," said Robert. He watched Aleaumes dart off through the crowd that had gathered to watch the Doge's arrival. To pay full honor to the memory of Fulk of Neuilly Aleaumes had that morning freshly shaved his tonsure and donned the long black robe suitable to his station. He held its skirt bunched up in one hand as he hurried toward Boniface's tent; his brown, muscular legs betrayed the soldier in him. But as he neared the tent he let fall the robe and tucked his hands humbly into its wide sleeves. With lowered head he approached one of the guards, and in a few moments he and two other clerks had disappeared from view. Robert smiled. He and Aleaumes had no secrets from one another, and in a few hours neither would the Marquis of Montferrat.

Aleaumes blinked his eyes rapidly, adjusting his sight from the glare of the afternoon sun to the darkness of the tent's interior. It was a small and very select group that had gathered here. The

Doge occupied the seat of honor, a brilliant figure like some bizarre bird of exquisite plumage, and on either side of him sat the Marquis of Montferrat, the Counts of Blois, Flanders and St. Pol and the Marshal of Champagne.

"I sent for no clerks," said Boniface sharply to the three black-robed figures who stood uncertainly before him. They bowed deeply and backed respectfully from the tent. The Marquis watched them go, and with a thoughtful air rose from his place and spoke briefly to the guards outside. The men withdrew to a still-safe distance just out of earshot, and then with his own hands Boniface secured the flap that was the tent's only source of air and light.

We are in the belly of the whale, thought Villehardouin. Every face, though recognizable, was shadowed, and he could not trust his eyes to read the expression each wore.

"May we dispense with the formalities customary on such occasions, my lords?" The Doge's voice was in marked contrast to his appearance, for it was that of a far younger man, one who might still be expected to raise it on the field of battle. His hands did not tremble as did those of so many old men; only the deep lines that surrounded his dark eyes spoke of great age. Yet Villehardouin knew him to be eighty at least, and some incredulous souls claimed he could not be a day under ninety.

Villehardouin had heard many strange stories about the Doge, not the least of which was that he had lost his sight many years ago during a mission to the court of Constantinople, and that he had vowed to some day avenge himself on the Greeks who were responsible for the darkness in which he had lived since then. This story, Villehardouin had long since concluded, was yet one more exaggeration, for the Doge neither moved nor spoke like a blind man. Dandolo's eyesight might well be severely clouded, but one's awe of the man was not so great if one could believe that he was subject to the ordinary ravages of old age like any other mortal.

Dandolo was aware of Villehardouin's close scrutiny, of the difference between this man and the others among whom he sat. Boniface was greedy and ambitious, naturally secretive and hostile to the decadent Greek Empire that begged to be conquered and ruled by a strong hand. Louis of Blois was close enough to the French throne to yearn for it, but realistic enough to know without a doubt that too many other lives stood between him and kingship. He judged that St. Pol, too, had few moral scruples, and that once the obvious road to power and greater wealth was pointed out to him, he could be counted on to commit himself to follow it. Baldwin of Flanders would allow himself to be persuaded by the others, his kinsmen and fellow adventurers, for he knew that nothing could stop the ascendancy of Philip Augustus. That was, after all, why he had joined this expedition in the first place, to avoid having to make a clear choice between the kings of France and England and perhaps be crushed in the inevitable struggle that must soon break out.

Baldwin was not without ambition, but it did not consume him with an almost visible flame as it did Montferrat, St. Pol and Blois. That was why he commanded such universal respect and allegiance from the common mass of the soldiery, and why his participation in the scheme Dandolo had come to propose was so vital. Men would follow Baldwin of Flanders to hell and back with scarce a murmur of dissent, as they would have followed Thibaut of Champagne. It was a quality he had, the same the dead count had possessed, for his knights believed he truly cared for their welfare, and he in turn believed that the service they swore to render him was sacred and not to be betrayed.

Geoffrey of Villehardouin was really the only unknown quantity in the equation, yet Dandolo was sure that, properly handled, he, too, could serve the interests of Venice. The difference was that the Marshal of Champagne was a man of formidable intelligence, one whose education far surpassed that of most great lords. Yet in that very strength could also be found his weakness. For though he prided himself on being guided by sweet reason and delighted in the tortuous arguments of the diplomat's profession, he was no match for the intricate maneuverings of the wily Italian mind. The greatness of Venice lay in the men she bred, men who negotiated with infidel and pope alike, men whose bones were alive to the shifts of fortune and the wind of change, who did not scruple to change their allegiances as naturally as others changed their winter garments for those of summer. Convince Villehardouin intellectually that

Constantinople must fall in order to ensure the recapture of Jerusalem and he would devote all his energies to that task. Later he might demur, but privately, for he could be trusted never to take any action that might weaken the class to which he belonged, that small group of men whom God had placed at the apex of feudal society that they might rule it justly, yet beneficently, in His Name. Villehardouin had a passion for order, and nothing was more orderly than a world in which the place and function of lord, knight, monk and peasant was defined and accepted with the same fatality as life and death themselves. That the world might someday change, was perhaps even now stirring and rumbling in discontent, Dandolo accepted. But he would not be alive to see those changes, and a wise man left the future to take care of itself.

It is too soon to mention Constantinople, he reflected, for he, too, had his spies. Let them first accept Zara and the rest will follow.

The gloom of the tent had a hypnotic effect on the barons. From polite attentiveness they had each drifted into personal mental ramblings as the silence dragged on unbroken by either the Doge or the Marquis. For any of them to have spoken first would have been a grave breach of etiquette, and although the Doge had spoken of dispensing with formality, that itself was part of the circuitous and time-consuming formula to which they paid lip service. Among themselves, Louis of Blois, Hugh of St. Pol, Baldwin of Flanders, even the Marquis and the Marshal would exchange blunt soldier's remarks, but in the presence of the might of Venice they wore an unbroken, proud, yet respectful front.

When finally he did speak, the Doge's voice seemed to come from some faraway place.

"I deeply regret, my lords, the situation in which we now find ourselves. The Tomb of Christ calls out to us for vengeance, yet we are helpless to answer that cry."

The Doge looked around him at the men who nodded in pained agreement. Money would have to be mentioned, but he knew that none of these proud knights would broach the subject. It smelled of commerce, and already they had been humiliated and shamed by its touch. He stood above them in rank, for he was the lawful ruler of one of the greatest cities in the world, but he knew that although they feared him, they also despised him. How foolish the French are, he thought, for their ridiculous code of chivalry rests on the possession of the very thing they feign to ignore. Their king knew the real value of gold, and Dandolo respected the merchant in him, but he would never voice his approval of this side of the great Philip Augustus. It would shock and infuriate his nobles beyond bearing.

"Men of future generations will call us Christians unworthy of the name. Our shame will accompany us to our graves."

"Our shame is in your hands, my lord. You and you alone have it in your power to lift the burden from us."

It was Villehardouin who had spoken, and the Doge turned to answer him. He would address himself principally to this man, now that Fulk of Neuilly was so opportunely dead. The backbone of resistance must be made to bend, Boniface had told him, and the rest of the army would fall into line.

"My lord Marshal, perhaps you do not fully understand the system of government we of Venice have developed over the centuries and of which we are justifiably proud. We are a republic whose citizens look to God and lawfully elected representatives for guidance. I am head of this republic, it is true, but my powers are neither those of an elected pope nor those of a king. I must answer not to one council but to many, and on the matter which has brought us together my councillors speak with a single voice."

He paused, sensing the disdain with which these French lords had listened to his speech. To them a republic was a weak thing; it suited his purpose to allow them their illusion.

"My councillors have devised a way to end the predicament which we, as well as you, deplore with all our hearts." Dandolo had, in fact, exerted considerable pressure on various members of his council before they had seen the wisdom of his proposal. And in the end it had only been the memory of the losses suffered in trade and prestige after Zara's sudden shift to the King of Hungary that had won the day. The Mediterranean must once more be a Venetian sea, he had told them, and not one of them had been able to withstand this logic.

"My lords," continued the Doge, shifting his attention from

the suspicious Marshal, "we of Venice have for over a year devoted ourselves to one task and one only. And you have seen with your own eyes the results of our efforts, the largest and the finest fleet ever built by the Christian world. My people now face dishonor and poverty as a reward for this devotion, for if we refuse you possession of these ships all Christendom will condemn us. And yet, my lords, you cannot pay for these ships. This is not our fault, yet even now the citizens of Venice cry out that their children will starve this winter and go barefoot in the cold. My lords, I cannot allow this to happen. The oath I swore as Doge will not permit me to subject my people to such misery. It seems that we can neither abandon you nor let you go."

My God, thought Villehardouin, the man can force tears to his eyes as easily as a woman. And with as much effect, for Baldwin was growing obviously ill at ease.

"God, in His Wisdom, has caused you to remain here many months past the date on which you were to sail. It is now too late in the season to attempt a crossing to the Holy Land. But there is a place to which you could sail in safety, a rich city where ample supplies for both men and horses are yours for the taking. In this city you could pass the winter and strengthen yourselves for a spring offensive against the infidel."

There was expectancy on every man's face and tension in the bodies that leaned forward in the gloom, bodies pulled by invisible strings that found their knotted center in the heavily bejeweled fingers of the Doge.

"The name of this city is Zara. It lies on the coast of Dalmatia. Some years ago its citizens betrayed the oath they had sworn to Venice and sought the protection of the King of Hungary. I will not detail the atrocities these evil men perpetrated on the Venetians who could not escape the city in time, for in war one comes to expect these things. The point, my lords, is that if one vassal state is allowed to defy its sovereign ruler, others will be encouraged to do the same, and none among us can afford to let that happen."

He had struck just the right note, for the eyes of St. Pol, Blois and Flanders were already alight with the gleam of battle.

"These people are Christians, are they not, my lord?" Trust

Villehardouin to be troubled about the prohibitions of the Pope's mandate to the army.

"Obedience to one's temporal lord is an article of faith, my lord Marshal," said Boniface of Montferrat.

"This pope does not always seem to think so, as we in France have found to our sorrow." Villehardouin's pointed reference to the continuing quarrel between Philip Augustus and Innocent on the subject of the king's divorce from his long-repudiated Danish bride was lost on no one.

"My lords, I will not hide from you the fact that Innocent may initially condemn our actions. But in the end he will forgive, for the sake of Jerusalem. He is a lawyer; he understands compromise." The Doge was being unusually frank. He was a man who employed many tactics to achieve his end.

"We speak of conquest, then, my lord," said Villehardouin.

"We do. For I do not expect Zara to capitulate without resistance, though the sight of a mighty army encamped below its walls may well make the resistance merely a token one. Zara belongs to Venice, my lords, and if you will assist us to recapture what is rightfully ours, it will go far toward the payment of the debt I am, alas, obliged to remind you of."

"Eighty-five thousand silver marks," murmured Boniface, knowing that the mention of that enormous sum would be the last argument needed to swing the barons to his side. "Of which, I believe, we are short by some thirty-four thousand marks."

"Naturally," continued the Doge, "it is not to be expected that so much silver could be found even in the wealthy city of Zara. Much that is of value will be lost or destroyed if Zara unwisely decides to fight. My council has a further proposal, and it is this." He paused so that his words would have greater effect. "I am an old man, my lords, and not much time remains to me. I would feast my eyes on the Holy Land before I die."

"You yourself would take the cross?" The respect in Baldwin's voice spoke volumes; the Doge smiled paternally at him.

"I have determined to do so. And I have persuaded my council to accept my decision. My son will rule Venice in my stead. Not only I, but many other Venetians will join your holy cause. You have only to agree that the debt of thirty-four thousand silver marks will be paid to us out of the first conquests, jointly made, that shall fall to us."

Boniface looked around him, reading the answer on each man's face. Could he chance an immediate voice vote? Only Villehardouin looked uncertain. He would leave him to last.

"My lord of Flanders?"

"It is a noble offer and right gladly would I accept it."

"My lord of Blois?"

"I agree with my cousin of Flanders. For the sake of Jerusalem we must go to Zara."

"My lord of St. Pol?"

"I, too, accept."

"My lord Marshal?"

"It is a difficult decision, my lord, but I, too, see the wisdom of the Doge's proposal. And I accept the compromise, on one condition."

Beneath the masks of earnest perplexity both wore, Boniface and the Doge were instantly alert. There had been no mention of conditions.

"I do not think it wise, my lords, that the army know of the course of action we are considering. There is already much dissension in the ranks because of what some are calling our imprisonment on this island. If it became generally known that we propose to sail anywhere but directly to the Holy Land I believe that fully half the army would immediately desert. They are the sheep and we the shepherds. We will in truth lead them to Jerusalem, but by paths they might be reluctant to tread. We cannot expect the common soldier to understand the exigencies of command, and compromise only confuses him. If my lords will agree to keep the matter secret, then I will give my heartfelt approval to the Doge's proposal. Once Zara is before them, the men will fight, but I tremble to think what will happen if news leaks out that Christians will feel our swords before infidels."

Boniface felt the tension drain from his body, replaced by the sweet satisfaction of knowing that the first step in the plan he had discussed so many months ago with Philip of Swabia had become reality. The army was committed to the first diversion. He would send word to Philip to ready Alexius for the second. He looked admiringly at Villehardouin, who must bear the responsibility for suggesting the secrecy which Boniface had been on the point of proposing. The Marshal was now totally committed. Other compromises would follow each other with such sweet logic that Villehardouin would not doubt their necessity. He was reasoning and farsighted, and where Baldwin would require constant persuasion and frequent reassurances on the road to Constantinople, Villehardouin's own mind would do Boniface's work for him.

"My lords, it is time we showed ourselves to our people, lest they imagine that the worst has befallen us."

Smiling broadly, as two friends who share complete understanding of one another, Boniface and Dandolo, arm in arm, led the others out into the afternoon sunlight, and the camp soon began to prepare for a night of wild rejoicing.

By nightfall it seemed as if the whole camp were aflame. Torches burned before every tent and long lines of laughing, singing, dancing men snaked along the island's shores. They were as drunk on the good news that the debt had been settled as on the wine the Venetians had obligingly supplied them with. Whole casks had been brought by barge to the island, then rolled along the well-worn paths between the tents to central locations where they had been tapped so that every man could drink his fill. No one paused to prepare supper that night. Rations had been short of late anyway, and the smell and taste of good strong wine was greatly preferred to the anonymous messes most had resorted to eating in the last few weeks. Tomorrow, food in abundance would be brought to St. Nicholas, for the sad, undeclared state of semi-siege was ended. The Venetians were allies, friends, brothers in the Cross, and if their friendship had had to be bought, why that could no longer be held against them. There would be booty enough for all in the Holy Land. Everyone knew that the infidels had grown sinfully rich preying on innocent pilgrims and the brave Christian knights who had established the Kingdom after Godfrey of Bouillon's time. Soon the devil's spawn would be parted from their gold and their lives, too. We are invincible, went the cry. God with us! Jerusalem!

Aleaumes had been chagrined at his failure to become a wit-

ness to what had taken place in the tent of the Marquis of Montferrat, and uneasy at the extreme secrecy of the meeting.

"Boniface always has a clerk in attendance," he told Robert.
"It's a well-known fact, and one of the chief reasons for the success with which he rules Montferrat. You know when you enter
his presence that every word you say is being recorded and that
you will never be able to deny it."

"Perhaps the Doge does not care to have his words inscribed
for posterity," suggested Robert, not really paying much attention to what Aleaumes was saying.

"But it is so unlike him. A man does not suddenly change the
habit of years unless he has a good reason for doing so. Something is being deliberately concealed from us, and all this wine
and good fellowship is a blind." He waited, but Robert said
nothing, obviously trying to avoid becoming embroiled in a long
conversation with his brother.

He was waiting for Anne, his whole being focused on her.
Earlier in the evening he had gone to her tent, but found only
the two obnoxious sisters there, sitting spraddle-legged on the
damp ground with an empty wine pitcher between them. They
were arguing loudly about which of them should refill the jug
and had paid little attention to his inquiries. They hadn't seen
the young widow in hours, they told him, and would he please
render them the service of a noble knight and fetch them more
wine?

He had left them, still quarreling, and gone to the spot along
the shore where he and Anne had so often stood together, a
place he thought of as peculiarly theirs. Aleaumes had been
waiting for him there, certain that Robert would eventually turn
up. No, he hadn't seen Anne, he said. He had more important
things on his mind than a woman and had immediately begun
the conversation that Robert scarcely troubled himself to follow.

"Peter of Amiens was not in the tent, but St. Pol was,"
Aleaumes was saying. "Perhaps Thomas has heard something of
what was said."

"By all means, seek him out and ask him," said Robert. He
had seen a dark figure slowly, almost hesitantly approaching
them. Only Anne, of all the revelers, would come in secrecy
without a torch to light the dangerous beauty that no man could

resist. "Leave me your wineskin, Aleaumes. Mine is in my tent and Gaspard will gladly fill it for you."

Aleaumes saw a movement in the shadows and guessed that it was Anne. He hesitated, smelling the lust that hung heavy in the warm night air, knowing that if he did not remain, the fragile curtain of propriety that had so far protected his brother from this woman might all too easily be swept aside. But Aleaumes was on the scent of a puzzling riddle and he had drunk just enough wine to dull his perceptions. Robert was old enough to take care of himself, he decided, and what if he does tumble her? It might be the only way to get her out of his system for good.

He handed Robert the full wineskin, grinning so that his white teeth gleamed in the darkness, then strode off toward the camp, wetting the skirts of his robe in the incoming tide.

I haven't seen him that drunk since we prowled Amiens together, thought Robert, laying the dripping wineskin down on the soft sand. From behind the high rocks that made this small stretch of beach a perfect trysting place for lovers, the black-clad pilgrim widow moved toward him, glancing around as if to assure herself that no spying eyes observed them.

She stood for a moment as if deep in thought, then moved to within arm's reach. The moon was barely a crescent in the sky, but its pale light gleamed on the narrow white hands that slowly pushed back the widow's veil until it slid unprotestingly to the sand. Her hair was blacker than the night and shone with the reddish reflected light of the torches that played fitfully over the island. It smelt of the sea, for it was freshly washed, and released from its net it cascaded down her back and over her shoulders, hiding the ugly, coarse robe under its shimmering veil. The torchlight played on her face and settled in her eyes, defeated and absorbed in their blueness.

"My lord?" she breathed, question and answer becoming one.

"My lady."

Gently he cupped her serious face in his hands. Her lips moved as if to speak, but were silenced under his kiss, a kiss so gentle and so tender that it might have been a child who stood in his embrace. He felt her tremble at his touch and an answering thrill heightened the passion he had kept so long in check.

Not another word was spoken. They moved as one to the shelter of the rocks, nesting into the cool sand, touching one another hesitantly, as though this were a dream from which they might at any moment be brusquely awakened.

The noise of the camp revels reached them faintly, sounds of loud male laughter and singing, voices raised in hot argument quickly broken off lest bones be broken and blood be shed on this night of all nights. A woman's shrill laugh pealed out, and they knew that not all would sleep alone in their tents tonight. Wherever an obliging woman could be found men were bargaining for her favors. The thought was stimulating to them both, Anne's inexperience forgotten in the hot waves of desire that brought tears of longing to her eyes.

"Take me, Robert," she whispered, "take me quickly."

He stripped off his hose and surcoat, standing before her naked and proud like some pagan god newly risen from the sea. Snatches of dreary sermons flashed through her head as she looked at him. No wonder the Church declares hell to be the reward of the fornicator, she thought confusedly. Were it not for fear of the fiery pit not even a saint could restrain himself. His beauty and his maleness were overwhelming, and the scent that came from him was sharp and pungent like musk.

She raised her robe to her hips and, lying back, stretched out her arms to him.

"No," he said, "I would see all of you."

He knelt beside her and she felt his sure, strong fingers fumble briefly at her throat. The widow's dress lay in a heap beside her and droplets of sea spray mixed with the cool night breeze fell on her body. Almost reverently Robert caressed the sweet mounds of her breasts, bending over her until his mouth found the taut nipples. He sighed deeply, shuddering like a man who has despaired of finding surcease from his pain, his hand pressing the flesh of her belly, then moving more urgently to part her thighs.

Her body pressed itself into the sand beneath his weight and first she spread her legs, then clasped them tight around his waist as the pounding began. There was pain in her loins and an aching emptiness that teased and tormented her. He cried out hoarsely and she felt him start to go limp, but she would not let him go. She forced him deeper into her and writhed beneath him in anger that this should be all. She arched her back under the excruciating unknown delight and his hand stifled her cry.

He dressed quickly and, wetting her underskirt in the sea, tenderly wiped away the drops of blood and sticky moisture from her thighs.

"Now I shall call you my lady in all truth," he said, smiling as she drank thirstily from Aleaumes' wineskin. There was no shyness between them. It was as though they were lovers of many years' standing. She laughed, shaking out her tumbled hair, and frowned in annoyance as she slipped the black gown over her head. Not only was it ugly, but the coarseness of the weave scratched her skin, raising tiny red weals on her breasts and buttocks.

"Robert, when may I stop wearing this horrible disguise?"

"A few more weeks, beloved. Be patient for my sake."

"For your sake?"

"I have only one sword arm, you know, and it's not enough to stand off an entire army."

"I do not displease you then, my lord?" Deliberately she teased and flirted with him, swaying seductively just beyond his grasp.

"Shall I answer you with words? Or would that be too dull?" He made a sudden lunge, catching her about the knees. She fell across him, laughing, pushing at his chest with her hands.

"No, Robert, no. Not so soon. I fear I shan't be able to walk as it is."

He stopped his play and cradled her tenderly. "I did not mean to hurt you, my sweet. Lie back and rest."

She did as she was told, content for the moment to obey his commands. Later she would overcome the lassitude that now weakened her. Later she would make demands of him and he would do her bidding lest she deny him her body. He is mine now, she thought, and a slave to his passion. In his bondage I will find my freedom. How strange that it should be so.

"What are you thinking, my love?" asked Robert softly, stroking the silken hair that curled in tendrils around his fingers.

"I am thinking, my dear lord, that you have made me your

captive. I am yours through love and you have only to command me."

"Anne," said Robert seriously, "I would not have it so." He sat up, freeing his fingers from the clinging hair. "We are not figures in a romance who speak in courtly phrases the better to hide from one another. We are man and woman, and our love is as real as our flesh. I would have us be equals in love, Anne, free of the pretense that makes a woman treat a man as though he were an enemy she must conquer. I would have us be lovers of the spirit and the mind as well as of the body. I dreamed of such a love when I was young, but years ago I gave up hoping I would ever find it."

He would have gone on trying to explain, but she gently laid a hand on his lips.

"Robert, we are of one mind and one spirit," she said, "for I, too, have known this dream. And I, too, despaired because of it. We need not speak of it again, for we are one, and our love will only be confused by words."

Silently they shared the wine Aleaumes had provided, passing the heavy wineskin to one another as though it were a sacramental cup. Robert found he could not think. His half-formed thoughts bubbled to the surface of his mind and broke there like foam atop the waves. He was conscious only of an overwhelming joy that defied description, a sense of fulfillment that was soul-deep and strong. It would not fade with the morning light as other, more fragile joys had done in the past. This was forever.

The Doge took the cross on the Feast of the Nativity of the Virgin. On that Sunday all the most worthy citizens of Venice crowded into the Church of St. Mark to gape at the pilgrims and crusaders who had come to hear High Mass and witness Dandolo's extraordinary action. Few Venetians had at that time taken the cross, for most looked to the Doge to see which way the wind was blowing. For weeks it had been rumored that Dandolo would join the crusaders, and although no one knew why he had decided to leave the comforts of his palace for the hardships of army life, such was his influence that many had come to St. Mark's prepared to follow his example.

The decision to lead the army to Zara had remained a closely guarded secret from both the crusading army and the mass of the Venetian citizenry. A few of the Doge's councillors had confided Dandolo's plan to their eldest sons, but without exception this had been done in carefully lowered voices while their households slumbered on in ignorance, so that only the most ambitious of Venice's great families had had time to lay their plans. A new and entirely trustworthy governor would have to be appointed to administer the recaptured Zara, they reasoned, and why should not so great an honor fall to our family rather than to another?

When the church was full and the restless congregation had fallen silent, the Doge rose from his place and without assistance mounted the lectern. He gazed out over his people, tears gathering in his famous blind eyes, and quietly, like a father to his beloved children, he began to speak.

"I am an old man," he told them, "feeble and sick, one whose body cries out for rest and the comforts with which dutiful children yearn to lighten his declining years. But you have chosen me your lord and set me in this high place that I might command you. I have borne this honorable burden for many years, and it would be shame to lay it aside now. These men who have come amongst us, who wear the cross of Our Savior, are the most worthy in the world, and the undertaking to which they have committed themselves the most glorious. It is a great privilege to be joined to them in so holy a cause." He paused as murmurs of agreement rose and fell, a sound like rustling leaves. "Many of you will go to the Holy Land, but who shall command you?" The question hung in the air and all eyes were riveted on the Doge. Slowly he stretched out his arms as if asking their advice, an old, richly bejeweled Christ ascending his cross. "If you will consent, I myself will take the cross, for I am your lord and who else could lead you? If you will consent, I shall go to live or die with you as God wills, leaving my beloved son Renier to be your shield in this land."

For a few brief moments there was utter silence in the church, then a voice shouted out, "We pray you, consent. Come with us." And as if a spell had been broken the same cry came from hundreds of throats.

The Doge bowed his head, accepting the will of his people. Two priests led him to the foot of the altar, where he knelt and made his vow. Then one of them fixed the cross to the wide-brimmed hat that was the badge of his office and, turning, he humbly accepted the cheers of his people. From all over the church men pushed their way past their neighbors to kneel before the altar and make their promises, and as each man rose from his knees, the Doge greeted him with the kiss of peace.

When finally all who wished to do so had taken the cross, the High Mass was sung, and as the sweet soprano voices of the choirboys chanted the responses, men and women alike found release from their emotion in tears which they did not trouble to wipe from their cheeks.

Later that day there was a hastily called meeting of the Doge's private council. There were more than enough officers to command the Venetian contingent, and slaves aplenty to man the oars, but ordinary sailors and fighting men had not come forward in sufficient numbers to fill the fifty galleys. The Doge was angry and spoke with unaccustomed sharpness. It was the council's duty to recruit the necessary men. Did they want Venice to stand shamed before the world?

They moved quickly, afraid that their embarrassment would become public. A drawing of lots was arranged and Venetian men of military age were ordered to present themselves before the priest. Each man was made to choose between two balls of wax, inside one of which was concealed a tiny fragment of parchment. The priest made the sign of the cross over the two balls of wax, sanctifying with his gesture the whim of chance. The men who chose the ball containing the parchment were given the cross on the spot while their luckier companions looked on. By nightfall the drawing was completed, and the council reported to the Doge that the honor of Venice was safe.

Only a few crusaders witnessed the strange scene and brought the tale back to the island of St. Nicholas. But if they were disturbed by it, it was soon forgotten in the bustle of departure preparations. What matter if some Venetians had had to be persuaded to do God's work? They were, after all, a nation of merchants. What could one expect of such a people?

I I I

All Venice turned out to bid Godspeed to the departing fleet, pleased and excited that the ships would be under the Doge's command for at least the first leg of the voyage. Montferrat's departure had been unexpectedly delayed.

The crusaders and pilgrims crowded onto the narrow decks of the troopships had been disturbed by the news that the official leader of the crusade would not be sailing with his army, and for a few days there had been more rumors of defection in high places. But when it was announced that Stephen of Perche and Matthew of Montmorency would also remain in Venice because of sickness, the speculation died away. As soon as these two great lords were again able to travel they would rejoin the fleet, and for safety's sake other ships must also be left behind to escort them.

It was also rumored that Boniface planned to journey to Rome to personally inform the Pope of their still-secret destination. By the time he returned to Venice Perche and Montmorency would either be dead or cured of the fevers they had contracted. Within a few weeks, therefore, the fleet would be whole again. Meanwhile, the ships would linger along the coast of Dalmatia, putting in at hospitable ports to take on fresh water and additional supplies for the long voyage to the Holy Land.

Though all were anxious to reach Palestine, it was comforting to know that for a few weeks they would cruise the Adriatic within sight of a friendly coastline before striking out across the Mediterranean. The crusaders had picked up some of the sailors' jargon and spoke knowingly of the necessity for a shakedown cruise. Not that anyone doubted the seaworthiness of the Venetian ships, but it was certainly a good idea to make a test run in waters free of Saracen galleys.

Robert and Aleaumes accompanied Peter of Amiens on board the Count of St. Pol's vessel, a great honor in itself, for they had expected to sail with other knights of their own station on one of the smaller, less comfortable troopships. But Hugh had casually remarked to his cousin that he might choose several of his own knights to attend him during the voyage, and Peter's first thought was of the two brothers from Clari.

St. Pol had looked long and hard at Aleaumes in the first few minutes after boarding, as though trying to dredge up from his memory some recollection of where he had seen him before. But Aleaumes was once more indistinguishable from the crowd of knights who were lashing their blazoned shields along the sides of the ship and the Count had dismissed him with a puzzled shrug.

"The tonsure and the robes are a better disguise than I had thought," Aleaumes remarked under his breath to Robert. "I don't think he recognizes the humble clerk who invaded Montferrat's tent the day of the Doge's visit."

"What difference would it make if he did?" asked Robert.

"I'm not sure. Probably none. But I get a strange prickling at the back of my neck whenever I think of those men sitting silent and unobserved in the gloom that afternoon. I can't shake the feeling that something was decided that day that they are at great pains to conceal from us."

"You should have been a spy, Aleaumes, not a clerk."

"Perhaps I shall be some day. I don't like being manipulated without knowing why."

"You're too suspicious, Aleaumes. It will lead to trouble."

Aleaumes grunted in disgust. If anyone was destined for trouble it was Robert, not himself. His brother seldom spoke Anne's name now, and that alone was convincing proof that they were lovers. Aleaumes doubted that anyone else suspected it, except perhaps the nasty old crones with whom Anne traveled, and even if Peter of Amiens did learn the truth of the relationship he would hardly interfere in his vassal's private life. The trouble would start when they reached the Holy Land, for there the pilgrims would suffer far more than the mounted knights, and if

Robert's passion had not cooled by then, he would be frantic for his mistress's comfort and safety.

On a long march the pilgrims usually clustered around the slow-moving supply wagons, a prime target for ambitious bands of infidels, who found them easy pickings. Robert would want to be as close to those wagons as possible, yet his duty obliged him to ride at the side of Peter of Amiens, and that knight had never in his life ridden anywhere but in the vanguard of an army. Eventually Peter would be forced to confront his friend and vassal. Aleaumes could almost hear his stern voice saying, "Get rid of her, Robert. She will be your death and perhaps mine also. In battle and before it a man cannot afford to have a divided mind. And I want no knight beside me who prefers a woman's caress to the clash of swords." It would come to that, unless Anne was an early victim of the fevers which tormented every European who set foot in the Holy Land. He almost wished he could pray for her death, but such a prayer would be monstrous. Instead he prayed that her beauty would wither under the hot desert sun. Deprived of that, she might turn her heart to God instead of men, and to be an ugly nun was a far better fate than the one she now seemed determined to pursue.

"I don't even know which ship she's on," said Robert quietly, and guiltily Aleaumes wished he could cross himself. Sometimes the brothers' minds were uncannily focused on the same subject.

"She's safe enough wherever she is, Robert. The two old widows treat her like a daughter. Listen!"

Sounds of chanting drifted over the waters as each ship's passengers, led by a priest, begged God's protection on the journey. There was a moment's hush while all stood with bowed heads. Then the priests, standing on the highest point of each ship, began in unison to chant the *Veni Creator Spiritus*. When the hymn was ended cries of joy and lamentation were heard on every side as the ships moved in stately grace out of the harbor. Hundreds of brass and silver trumpets blew, and underlying their shrill blasts could be heard the muffled threats of drums and the light tattoo of tabors. The sun sparkled on the blue water and turned the vermilion galley of the Doge to blood red. Standing erect beneath his canopy, the Doge lifted his arm in a farewell salute to the only thing in life that mattered to him. And

Venice, understanding his gesture, returned the salute and cheered him on, certain that he would bring still greater glory to its name. He was old and none among them expected him to return, but he was glorious and very like a warrior chief of the legendary Norse countries. They were proud to let him go to a death that generations yet to come would sing about in awe.

It was indeed an army and a fleet to make the infidel tremble.

Not until after the fleet had landed at the rich city of Pola to resupply and allow the men and horses to exercise on dry land again did Aleaumes' discreet inquiries begin to bear fruit. He spent every spare moment in the company of the various clerks and scribes who attended the Marshal of Champagne and the Counts of Flanders, Blois and St. Pol, and at last he won the confidence of a timid little man who could not hold his wine.

Just before he passed out this clerk babbled incoherently of a plot that would bring excommunication on them all, and of the mysterious death of the man who had first discovered it. Unwilling to leave him at the mercy of the harbor scum who slit a man's throat before reaching for his purse, Aleaumes carried the fellow aboard his ship and left him lying on deck in the open air to sleep off the effects of the drink which had loosened his tongue. Early the next morning he went in search of him, but the deck on which he had lain was bare and newly scrubbed. He asked the ship's sailors what had become of the drunken clerk. No one knew. And no one, answering his questions, would meet his eyes. When he turned to leave the ship he found his way blocked by a knight he did not know, a man with an ugly, vicious face whose hand was laid lightly on the heavy sword at his side.

"You will come with me," the knight said, and the tone of his voice and the threatening stance of his legs allowed no argument.

Aleaumes waited just outside the richly furnished cabin of Louis of Blois while the knight who had conducted him there made his report. He stood quietly, feigning an interest in the activities of the sailors on deck who watched him covertly while they stowed away the provisions being brought on board. Aleaumes rehearsed his story quickly two or three times until he had it letter-perfect. No matter what questions the Count put to him he would have a ready answer. The important thing was not to be caught unawares.

"Your name, fellow." Louis of Blois was seated at a small table, the remains of his breakfast still before him.

"Aleaumes of Clari, my lord. I ride with Peter of Amiens." The strange-looking knight behind him blocked the door, and although he dared not look at him, Aleaumes knew the man's sword was at the ready.

"I am told you were asking for Peter of Landes."

"If that be the drunken clerk I carried on board last night, my lord. He was too far gone for speech, so I did not know his name."

"How did you come to be in his company?"

"I wasn't, my lord. He was sprawled on the ground just by the gangplank, and in the darkness I stumbled over him and nearly fell myself. I was of a mind to leave him there and almost did, for I supposed him dead. But then I thought it would not please my lord that one of his clerks should be gnawed on in the night by the rats, so I picked him up and carried him on board. That's when I discovered he was alive. He was still breathing and stank of wine. I rolled him into a corner of the deck and left him there."

"Did no one challenge you?"

"Oh, yes, my lord. The watch stopped me, but let me pass when I explained what had happened."

"What was the name of the officer who stopped you?"

"I do not know, my lord. I did not linger to talk with him because of the lateness of the hour."

"Had you ever seen this clerk before?"

"No, my lord."

"You are certain that you did not pass the night drinking with him?"

"Certain, my lord."

"And he said nothing to you?"

"Nothing, my lord. I did not even know his name until you spoke it."

Louis of Blois leaned back in his chair, unable to decide if Aleaumes spoke the truth. The man's eyes did not waver from his for an instant, he noted. He seemed a stolid enough fellow, not even curious as to why the Count himself had seen fit to interrogate him.

"It is a serious matter that one not assigned to this ship should have been allowed to come aboard in the middle of the night. We must be ever vigilant against the spies in our midst. You may think it a small thing of no account, and so it has proved to be. But the circumstances could easily have been otherwise." Louis of Blois hesitated, uncertain whether to say more. "You serve Peter of Amiens?"

"Yes, my lord."

"I will make inquiries. You may be quite sure of that. If you are not what you seem to be, you are a dead man. Do you understand me?"

"My lord, I am no spy. I swear it to you. My lord of Amiens will vouch for me. If my lord wishes, I will stay right here until my identity is proven."

"That will not be necessary. My men will always be able to find you. Always." The Count stood up and leaned across the table. Aleaumes could smell the wine on his breath. "You will speak of this to no one," he said. "The safety of our cause is involved. The man was a spy and has been dealt with. More than that you have no need to know."

"I have already forgotten it, my lord," said Aleaumes, keeping his face stupid and uncomprehending.

"You may go."

Aleaumes bowed and backed from the cabin. As he left the ship he could feel the strange knight's eyes boring into his back, and he quickly lost himself in the crowd on the dock.

He stayed lost for the remainder of their short stay in Pola, not even daring to return to St. Pol's ship at night. He sent word to Robert that he was fulfilling a secret penance, and as he had no assigned duties to perform no one inquired about his absence.

During the day he hid himself in a brothel where the woman in charge was not adverse to taking his coins even though he did not demand the customary services. At night, when the business was brisk and every room in use by a constant stream of sailors and soldiers, he found refuge in a nearby church, sleeping fitfully in a narrow space between one of the side altars and the exterior stone wall. If men came searching for him there he would be caught like a rat in a trap, but not even to the brothel keeper had he divulged the secret of where he spent his nights.

He slipped aboard St. Pol's ship a few hours before sailing, dirty and tired, smelling of incense, sweat and the strong perfume of the whores, but thankful to be alive.

Peter of Amiens greeted him jovially, wrinkling up his nose at the smell of him. "Penance indeed," he scoffed. "You'll have penance of a different sort to do if the Bishop hears of this." Aleaumes looked so alarmed that he hastened to reassure him. "No one missed you or even asked where you were, so there's no need to worry. I daresay Robert and I would have been glad to join you if my lord cousin had not kept us too busy for such sport. Your secret's safe with us, though if you don't wash the smell off, the whole fleet will soon know where you've been."

So the Count of Blois had not checked up on him after all. With what he now knew, Aleaumes was not at all surprised. He was no longer in danger, if he ever had been, for the whole secret would be out in the open at their next landfall.

"The name of the place is Zara." Robert had to strain his ears to hear Aleaumes' voice, for his brother was speaking in a whisper, his lips hardly moving.

They stood in an isolated place along the rail, a spot avoided by most of the ship's passengers, for the spray from the waves was thicker and colder here than anywhere else. They were leaning casually against the rail as if engaged in a few last moments of conversation before lying down on deck for the night. The sails of their sister ships in the fleet were ghostly in the moonlight and there were a few other knights along the rails enjoying the peaceful sight. In no way were they conspicuous. Aleaumes had assured himself of that while planning how to get his brother alone long enough to tell him his story.

"One of the sailors told me that just before dawn Peter of Landes woke from his stupor, stumbled to the rail on the starboard side and heaved himself over. No one saw it happen or heard the splash, but this was the story given out next morning."

"But why?"

"They were told that he was a spy and had been one from the beginning. That the Count's agents were watching him closely and had determined to place him under arrest before he could get away. The story is that he knew he was about to be discovered and that he had decided to feign drunkenness to put them off their guard. But he had not counted on the strength of the native wine, and having been careless enough to be discovered, was careless about that also. He's dead, I'm sure of that."

"But not by his own hand?"

Aleaumes shook his head. "He was in a deep sleep when I left him. Someone picked him up and slipped him into the sea before he ever woke up. He probably never even knew he was dead until he found himself in the company of the angels. He was a very frightened man and he's better off now than before, wherever he is."

"You came close to being among the angels yourself, brother."

"It was the mention of Peter of Amiens's name that saved me. The Count knew that if he had me killed, even if it was made to look like an accident, Peter would demand a full inquiry. And I don't think he wanted to chance that. Had I admitted to being a clerk though, he might have taken the risk."

"He didn't ask you?"

"I don't believe it even occurred to him. With no tonsure and no robes, he took me for what I pretended to be, just another stupid sergeant who had blundered onto a drunk while making his way back to his own ship. There's a weakness I've observed amongst most of the nobility. They assume that those who serve them cannot think for themselves. Or dare not. Whichever it is, it's a dangerous assumption, but one I owe my life to."

"That's not the way of my lord of Amiens."

"There are exceptions to every rule."

"Will you tell him what you have told me?"

"There's no point to it. The plan is a success already, and no one can stop it. The only other two outsiders who knew of it are already dead, and I see no point in adding to their number."

"Two are dead?"

"Jean of La Force also. He died of his fever, helped along by poison, I'm sure, before we left Venice. You remember I told you he was sick the day the Doge came to St. Nicholas."

"That was the clerk whose place you tried to take?"

Aleaumes nodded. "I almost wish now I'd never thought of it. He was feverish, but the kind of man who seeks to do his duty with his dying breath. Apparently he made his way to Montferrat's tent, but collapsed amongst the horses tethered just behind it. He laid there awhile, then started crawling along the ground, hoping someone would see him and come to his aid. He was too weak to cry out, and the guards were looking out for anyone trying to approach the tent from the front. He lay in the grass right up next to the back of the tent for a long time and he heard everything that was said inside. Peter of Landes found him there after the Doge and the others had left. By that time he was already delirious and babbling of what he had heard. Peter tended him himself for as long as he could, but Montferrat's leech came one day with medicines for Jean while Peter was out fetching water with which to cool his fever. He was bending over Jean when Peter came back. A few days later Jean died and Peter was given a place in Blois's entourage. Until the night I left him on the deck of Blois's ship Peter took care never to be alone. He said eyes watched him constantly, even in the night, though no one questioned him concerning what his friend had raved about during his illness."

"Are you sure he didn't make it all up just to keep you amused while you bought his wine?"

"He's dead now, and no one bothers to kill a man just because he makes up stories. No, I'm sure he was telling the truth."

"Where is this Zara?"

"Somewhere along the Dalmatian coast. It used to belong to Venice, but it's under the protection of the King of Hungary now. And that sticks in the Doge's craw. It's a Christian city, Robert."

"But we are forbidden to wage war against Christians. It would mean excommunication if we attacked them."

"Apparently that carries little weight with the Doge when money is concerned. We couldn't pay the debt, you know. Something like thirty-four thousand marks remained after the second levy."

"So the Doge bought himself an army for thirty-four thousand marks."

"And congratulated himself on the deal, I'm sure. We came cheap."

"Who else knows of this?"

"No one except the barons who agreed to it. Flanders, Blois, St. Pol, Montferrat and Villehardouin. Probably a few others who can be trusted to keep their mouths shut."

"Simon of Montfort?"

"Montfort wouldn't stand for it. He's vowed never to lift his sword against any but infidels and heretics. He's almost as much of a fanatic as Fulk of Neuilly was. No, I'm sure he's as much in the dark as the rest of the army."

"Aleaumes, you don't think that Fulk was . . . ?"

"Poisoned, too? No, he died long before anyone knew we'd be short of funds. But I'd wager a handsome sum that our leaders were not unduly saddened by the news. They'd never be able to get away with attacking Zara if he were here."

"What will happen when we reach Zara?"

"I don't know, Robert. I wish I did. The best thing would be for the city to switch allegiances again without a fight. And it very well may do so when its citizens see the size of our fleet."

"But if they don't?"

"Somehow the Doge will get his way. He and the others will convince everyone that the success of our cause depends on reducing Zara to rubble. And we'll all go along with it because we have no other choice."

"I think there will be opposition."

"You may be right. But Zara will be captured one way or another. Montfort and a few others will either stand aside and let it happen or leave the fleet entirely. It will make little difference in the end. Zara is a doomed city."

Robert thought of that unknown town whose citizens slept peacefully in their beds, unaware that an army of fellow Christians was rapidly approaching their shores, sailing through the night to bring them death and destruction. He no longer doubted the truth of what Aleaumes had told him. He thought of Anne and what might happen to her if he were to die in the attack on the city. He prayed that the people of Zara would have the good sense to surrender as soon as the fleet was sighted. If fight they did, he would be in the thick of it, for Peter of Amiens was St. Pol's cousin and vassal, and the double bond that tied him to the Count was unbreakable. St. Pol, Peter, Robert. Each linked to the other by sworn oath, and the vassal the victim.

Zara had no intention of surrendering.

As the fleet sailed into the harbor, sailors, crusaders and pilgrims alike murmured at the strange welcome with which they were being greeted. The gates of the city were tightly shut and armed men bristled on its walls. No one shouted or waved a welcome and no ship put out to invite them to land and refresh themselves as had happened at every other city along their route. At regular intervals along the walls huge white crosses had been painted and banners bearing the cross as their only device fluttered from every tower. It was as though the city was in mortal dread of the fleet and was desperately reminding those who sailed in it that they were as good Christians as could be found anywhere.

All that night the people of Zara remained on their protecting walls while the pilgrims watched in amazement. Surely they must know we mean them no harm, each man said to his fellow when at last they laid down to sleep. But all the same everyone was very uneasy, and by dawn the rails of every ship were crowded. Men could be heard shouting reassurances to the soldiers on the wall, but the wind blew their words back into their throats. No one could be heard. The distance between the ships and the wall was too great.

By midmorning the wind had shifted and the Venetian galleys, followed by a few warships, sailed through the harbor to the mouth of the port. A heavy chain was stretched across the entrance, and the pilgrims waited expectantly. Surely a ship would now put out to unloose the chain and allow them to enter.

What followed was never quite clear to anyone who observed it, and later a hundred different versions were circulated. Some said the Zareens attacked first, others the Venetians, but it hardly mattered which in the end. The chain was swiftly broken and slid beneath the waves without a sound. The Venetian galleys, followed by the rest of the fleet, sailed into the port, and once in shallow water men and horses swarmed onto the shore, meeting little resistance as they went. Those few soldiers whose duty it was to guard the port had hastily retreated into the city as soon as the chain had proved useless.

The Venetians quickly pitched a camp of sorts in the port area of the city, but most of the French crusaders and pilgrims remained on board their ships riding at anchor in the calm coastal waters. It was all very puzzling, especially as the priests could not tell them what sort of Christians these people claimed to be. If they were indeed heretics who sought to hide themselves behind the cross, then they were guilty of a double blasphemy which no true Christian could tolerate. If not, the army itself was in danger of committing mortal sin and could expect to feel the full wrath of Innocent III. It was another almost sleepless night for both sides, and the Feast of St. Martin passed uncelebrated.

Early the next morning a delegation from Zara slipped through the city's main gate and under a flag of truce made its way to the Doge's pavilion. He received them coldly, and to their offer to surrender the city on condition that their lives and goods be spared replied that he could do nothing without consulting the counts and barons of the army.

He left them standing outside his tent, a forlorn, frightened group of men huddled together under the dubious protection of their white flag while he had himself rowed out to Baldwin of Flanders's ship. He had no doubt that he could persuade the army's leaders to accept the city's surrender, for they had already committed themselves to its destruction if that should prove necessary. But how much more profitable to Venice if the city returned to the fold unpillaged and with its walls intact.

As soon as the Doge had disappeared inside Baldwin's cabin a small boat put out for shore from the vessel carrying the famous Simon of Montfort. As it touched land several men leaped out and hurried through the Venetian guards to where the envoys stood.

Aleaumes and Robert, still on board St. Pol's ship, recognized one of them. It was Enguerrand of Boves, who had been guest of honor at Robert's wedding. From the quickness of his step and the way he gestured repeatedly toward the fleet, they could tell that he was very angry. The Zareen envoys listened to him and watched as his brother, Robert of Boves, went to within shouting distance of the city's walls and stood there, arms upraised in a gesture of conciliation. They could not hear what he said, but a flutter of relief seemed to ripple through the tired soldiers who had watched through two nights now, and they were seen to raise their weapons aloft as if they were cheering good news. The envoys hesitated for a few minutes, consulting among themselves, then they clasped Enguerrand of Boves's out-stretched hands as though a compact had been sealed. Still under the flag of truce, but moving quickly now, they returned to the city and the gates clanged shut behind them.

Enguerrand of Boves, his brother Robert and the others of their party returned to their boat. For an endless moment they stood silhouetted like statues on the shore, and Robert and Aleaumes, turning to follow their gaze, saw that the Doge had emerged from Baldwin's cabin and was standing in the prow of the ship, staring at the men who had dared interfere with his grand design. Even at this distance they could feel Dandolo's malice reach out to envelop Gilo's friend and those who stood with him, and they trembled for the consequences.

"The opposition you spoke of, Robert," said Aleaumes under his breath.

Within the hour a parliament had been called to which all the lords and barons of the army were summoned. St. Pol allowed Peter of Amiens to accompany him, and Robert followed close on his suzerain's heels, almost unnoticed in the press of men who crowded even the Doge's huge pavilion. Aleaumes had chosen to remain behind, prudence for once overcoming his curiosity.

"My safety lies in obscurity," he had told Robert. "I would not care to have Louis of Blois's glance rest on me at this meeting. It might set him to thinking."

The Doge spoke first and at length, outlining the manifold wrongs the city of Zara had committed against Venice. He would have immediately accepted the city's offer of surrender, he told them, had he not been bound by courtesy to consult the other leaders of the army. And then, during the few moments of his absence, indeed, as soon as his back was turned, certain perfidious knights unworthy of the name had taken it upon themselves to promise that no attack would be made upon the city. Whereupon the negotiations had been broken off and a terrible insult dealt to all of them. If the crusaders were not prepared to honor the agreement made in Venice, the Doge had no choice but to demand forthwith the payment of the thirty-four thousand silver marks still owed him. With interest.

He sat back in his great armchair, his arms folded sternly across his chest while a chorus of bewildered protests and questions broke out among the men whom he had summoned to his tent. For most of them this was the first inkling they had that the debt had not been paid, and they were angry to the point of drawing weapons at the treachery that had been done to them.

It was Villehardouin who at last managed to restore a semblance of calm among the barons and knights, explaining in his reasonable way that there had been no other alternative. Over and over he praised the Doge for allowing the army to work off its monstrously huge deficit by an action that was impeccably correct. Zara was a vassal state of Venice which had broken its sacred oath to its sovereign lord, he reminded them. If a similar situation arose in France they would not hesitate. This might be Dalmatia, but even here the oath between vassal and lord was unbreakable.

As he had foreseen, this argument was unanswerable, and though he had been careful to steer clear of any mention of the plunder that might be gained by the subjection of the city, a few greedy tongues flickered over dry lips and many more were already engrossed in calculating the wealth they expected to find within Zara's walls.

Robert listened closely, fascinated at the ease with which both the Doge and Villehardouin were manipulating the angry men. St. Pol, Blois and Flanders had remained silent throughout the wrangling, but only Baldwin had the grace to look embarrassed.

From the rear of the tent where he had been standing unnoticed, a Cistercian priest worked his way through the throng until he stood directly before the Doge. His name was Guy, Abbot of Vaux and Cerny, and in his hands he carried a roll of heavy parchment from which dangled the papal seals of Rome. He looked with open disgust at the old Italian who had thought to profit handsomely from the shame of Christ, his eyes sliding over Dandolo's rich robes and the sparkling jewels that weighed on his long, thin fingers. Grasping hands, he mused, but this time they would come up empty.

Then he turned his back to Dandolo, unrolled the parchment and began to read. His sonorous voice carried to the farthest corners of the tent, so that no man there could in future claim he had been ignorant of the Pope's command. Each count, baron, knight, sergeant and man-at-arms, each sailor and each pilgrim was individually and collectively forbidden to do harm to Christians who might be encountered on the journey to the Holy Land. On pain of excommunication. On pain of eternal damnation. By the authority of Pope Innocent III, Bishop of Rome, God's lawful representative on earth.

In the stillness that followed the reading of the Pope's decree, Guy of Vaux added that the citizens of Zara so feared the hatred of Venice that they had had the foresight to demand and obtain a document from Rome similar in every respect to the one he had just read. Now he added his own not inconsiderable authority to that of the Pope, urging them to leave the port of Zara immediately, threatening that if they did not, he and the other Cistercian priests of the army would read the Pope's command aboard every ship of the fleet, so that no one, not even the most illiterate sailor, would be in any doubt of the danger in which his soul stood.

Two or three of the men closest to the abbot suddenly reached out and seized him, knocking the papal parchment to the ground. Angry shouts filled the tent and there was a surge toward where the Cistercian's white robe could be glimpsed through a hail of upraised fists.

The Doge sat immobile while the long ribbons of the papal seals fluttered at his feet. There was a way to mollify Innocent, he knew, but in the meantime he would gladly run the risk of excommunication. Another and unexpected obstacle to his grand design was being removed before his eyes, and being a fastidious man, he moved his feet slightly lest the priest's blood stain his robe.

Baldwin of Flanders had half risen, uncertain whether to go to the abbot's assistance, but before he could reach any decision, Simon of Montfort and the brothers Enguerrand and Robert of Boves had drawn their swords and formed a tight circle of glittering steel around the Cistercian. Guy of Vaux got painfully to his feet and retrieved the trampled document which he ostentatiously smoothed out, rerolled and placed in one of his voluminous sleeves.

"I and my men, and any of like mind who wish to join us, will have no part in the sacrilege you propose. We are good Christians, sworn to the Cross, and obedient to our Holy Father in Rome. We shall withdraw from this camp and this fleet, but you shall feel our presence. I have sworn never to let my sword taste Christian blood, and so you need not fear that I and my men will attack you from the rear. But while you assault the walls of this Christian city, pause to glance over your shoulders, for we shall bear witness of your shame and your sin to the Holy Father himself and to the rest of Christendom." Simon of Montfort raked his eyes over the faces of those who stood in awe of his upraised sword. No one would challenge him, for his vow did not prevent him from running through an attacker with all the ease and precision of a practiced cook spitting a chicken. "The Abbot of Vaux is under my protection and all other priests who seek to do their duty. Anyone who lays a hand on a man of God will answer to God. In person."

Simon and his followers left the tent, the abbot in their midst. As they passed, Enguerrand of Boves paused for a moment to speak to Robert. "You are welcome to join us," he said.

"I am bound to follow my lord of Amiens," Robert replied, hoping that no one was observing their conversation.

"Peter, too, is welcome," Enguerrand said.

"My lord, we have been friends in the past, and I trust our friendship will continue," said Peter of Amiens formally. "But I am Count Hugh of St. Pol's man, and his cousin, too, as you well know."

"Then I wish you ease of your conscience," remarked the lord of Boves ambiguously. "I will remember you in my prayers when I kneel before the Holy Sepulcher."

"What was that supposed to mean?" Robert asked after Enguerrand had moved on. "Surely we will reach Jerusalem long before he does. They'll have to resupply elsewhere and that will delay them even more."

"Hold your tongue," snapped Peter of Amiens. "You forget your place, Robert."

Long afterward Robert would remember the brusqueness with which Peter of Amiens had cut him off in mid-speculation, but only then would he attach any significance to it. For the moment he put his commander's flash of temper down to his desire to hear the plan of battle that had begun to be discussed as soon as the tent flap had come down behind the departing knights.

True to his word, Simon of Montfort drew off from the main body of the fleet and maintained a careful watch on the army during the five days of siege that followed. Somehow word of the Pope's prohibition was spread throughout the camp and the text of his letter read to groups of dismayed soldiers and pilgrims.

But not all the Cistercians and priests of the other orders in whose care the spiritual well-being of the army had been placed shared the opinion of the brave Abbot of Vaux. These were quick to point out that the actual wording of the Pope's decree was imprecise enough to need interpretation. They were forbidden to attack Christian cities *unless* their inhabitants should wickedly oppose them or some just or necessary cause should arise. The letter with which the Zareens had fortified themselves specified that the Venetians and only the Venetians were forbidden to attack Zara, and thus only they ran the risk of excommunication. The French were excluded from the ban, a fortuitous oversight in the opinion of the barons, and were therefore free to do as they saw fit.

Zara fell on the twenty-fourth of November, the Feast of St. John Chrysogonus. Its inhabitants had held out bravely against the barrage of stones hurled by the catapults and mangonels, huge deadly missiles that smashed into the walls and collapsed the roofs of houses, burying their inhabitants in the rubble. When they saw the sappers move in to tunnel under the towers and the walls, they made one last appeal for help to Simon of

Montfort, smuggling a messenger out to his ship in the dead of night.

Twenty-four hours later he returned to the city with the news that the great Montfort could or would do nothing. "I have not come here to do harm to fellow Christians," he was reported to have said. "Whatever the others do, you need fear nothing from me or mine." It was merely a repetition of assurances he had earlier given them and it was greeted with bitter, derisive hoots. He did not participate in the attack, nor did he do much of anything to stop it. They had had enough of his self-righteousness and immediately sued for peace.

The Doge accepted their surrender, but agreed to only one of their conditions. Their lives would be spared, and that was all. The envoys pleaded with him and assured him of their deep loyalty to Venice, offered tribute and hostages, but his will was unbendable. Their lives only. For the rest they must take their chances. Hopefully, they counted on the well-known avarice of Venice as protection against wholesale pillaging and destruction of the city. When the Doge sailed away he would doubtless wish to leave behind him an humbled colony that could only add to Venice's wealth and power. They did not realize that they had tried to deal him a mortal blow by their defection to the King of Hungary, nor that he never forgot a slight. His pride could not be bought, but this he hid from them by hints of reconciliation and honeyed words.

The city was divided and fully occupied, the Venetians taking the half of Zara that bordered the port area, while the crusaders and pilgrims contented themselves with the rest. The weather had already turned cold, and the news that the army would winter in Zara was welcomed by all. By Easter the seas would again be calm enough to cross in safety to the Holy Land. After the casualties suffered during the siege, most thought it wise to allow the wounded to recuperate fully on land. The Zareens offered their homes; they were pitifully eager to serve the army's best interests.

On the third night of the occupation fighting broke out between a group of Venetians and some of the common soldiers of the army. The battle lasted most of the night as first one, then another rushed to the help of his countrymen until most of the

city streets were filled with shouting, angry men. The people of
Zara huddled inside their houses in terror of the bloodshed
going on around them. If this was the way allies treated each
other, how might they act toward those whom they had conquered?

Knights on horseback were finally summoned to ride the
streets, slashing out indiscriminately at any who defied their orders to disperse. By midmorning over a hundred corpses lay in
the gutters and at least one high-born lord, Giles of Landas, a
liege man of Flanders, was dead. But peace had been restored,
though no one ever knew what had caused the disturbance. Idleness, too much wine and national jealousy, concluded the
barons. From now on Venetians and Franks would be kept
strictly apart.

Robert had spent the night of the battle worrying about
Anne. Most of the pilgrims, the last to disembark, were lodged
near one another in the section of the city assigned to the
crusaders, but the shelters they had found were the hovels of the
poor and the stables of the rich. Already many of them were
suffering from the cold and the scarcity of provisions, but they
dared not protest, for they were barely tolerated by the knights
and soldiers who, they were told scathingly, at least earned their
keep.

Once the city was again secure and the dead had been buried,
Robert set about finding a place of safety and comfort for the
woman he had seldom seen since the departure from Venice.
When he stumbled on a small stone house tucked behind one of
the several large cathedrals of the city, he breathed a sigh of relief. Though the place was not large, it was easily defendable,
being entirely enclosed by a high wall pierced only by a heavy
wooden door.

The old couple who opened the gate to him agreed without
argument to house him and his lady, relieved that their unwelcome guests would at least be people of quality. They were
Greeks, they told him, originally from Constantinople, who had
come to Zara barely a year before the city's change of loyalty.
Nicholas Tripsychos was a scholar and former teacher, his wife
Theodora adept at the brewing of medicinal herbs.

Robert offered to pay for his keep and that of the lady also, and with surprising graciousness they showed him about the house and garden. He and Anne would have the entire house to themselves, while its rightful owners made do on pallets in the kitchen. If Robert wished, they would engage a reliable cook and a maid or two to do the heavy work and see to his lady's personal needs. He did wish, but sternly warned that these Zareen servants must not remain in the house after sunset. One could not be too careful.

When all had been arranged to everyone's satisfaction Robert had his coat of arms painted on the wooden gate to seal his claim to this house and announce his protection of those who dwelt within. Then he hurried off to Anne to bring her the good news.

IV

Food and fuel had already become scarce in Zara when Boniface of Montferrat, Matthew of Montmorency, Pierre of Bracieux and those others who had remained in Venice arrived in the newly conquered city in mid-December. They were warmly welcomed for the badly needed supplies they brought, but it was noted with alarm that many familiar faces were missing from their party.

Stephen of Perche had recovered from his illness almost as soon as the fleet was out of sight, reported Matthew of Montmorency bitterly. He himself had come close to death, had even received the last sacraments, but his life had been spared that he might make up for the perfidy of others. With no forewarning Stephen had disappeared from his lodgings one night, accompanied by Rotrou of Montfort, Ives of La Jaille and many other knights who had taken the cross with Stephen's brother. By now they were in Apulia, from where they intended to sail to Syria in the spring, according to a frightened servant who had been left behind. If only Geoffrey, Count of Perche, had not died, lamented Villehardouin. He might have controlled his wild younger brother. Now the name and honor of yet another noble family was besmirched beyond redemption.

The Marquis of Montferrat wasted little time on recriminations. The army was still badly divided over the issues which had been raised prior to the conquest of Zara. Simon of Montfort and the Abbot of Vaux continually reminded the crusaders that they were in fact excommunicants, that every breath they drew was nothing more than a temporary reprieve from the fiery pits of hell. The frightened men turned to other priests who calmed them with reassuring words, but the situation was a potentially explosive one and could not long be tolerated.

It was decided that an embassy should be sent to the Pope, to explain to him why it had been necessary to besiege Zara and to receive his absolution for the crusaders who had taken part in the battle. The Bishop of Halberstadt, a German who had joined the army late the previous summer, and Nevelon, Bishop of Soissons, were of the opinion that this was not strictly necessary. Under the conditions of war, they argued, they themselves could absolve in the Pope's name, and this they proposed to do. The Abbot of Loos, a Cistercian, agreed with them, but pointed out cautiously that no harm could come from informing Rome, after the fact, that the army was once more in a state of grace.

Surprisingly, the Doge would have no part in the affair, nor would he agree to allow any of his Venetians to join the group chosen to make the long journey back to Rome. "We in Italy know the Pope too well to bow the knee to him when we are in the right," he told the amazed barons. "Vicar of Christ he may be, but his robes cover the body of a man, and no man can presume to dictate to Venice." They stared at him in disbelief, while the Marquis of Montferrat, who privately shared his opinion, chuckled in amusement. "My Venetians are not divided in their loyalties," Dandolo continued pridefully. "They need no pats on the back from the Bishop of Rome to comfort them. Only one voice is law to them, and that voice is mine." With that he marched triumphantly out of the meeting, disdaining to notice the envious looks that followed him.

So the embassy departed without Venetian representation, and the army settled back to await the Pope's pleasure, confident that the Bishop of Soissons, who headed the delegation, would prove Innocent's equal in face-to-face debate.

To assist the Bishop in his delicate task, Baldwin had sent his learned chancellor, Master John of Noyon, and lest it seem that army and Church were not united in the action which had been taken against Zara, two knights also made the trip to Rome. One of them, John of Friaise, was among Count Louis's most trusted advisers, a man whose loyalty was beyond question and whose worth had been proved during the original negotiations with

Venice that had resulted in the Treaty of Nolis. In diplomacy he was second only to Villehardouin, who, it was agreed by all, could not be spared for even a mission as important as this one. The men of Champagne now looked to the Marshal as their natural leader, having transferred their loyalty easily and completely from the dead Thibaut to his most able vassal. There was a new Count of Champagne, but the child was barely walking and had moreover been placed by his anxious mother under the protection of the French king. The Champenois felt themselves adrift; it would be many years before Champagne's lord could take his natural place as the head of his people.

The fourth envoy was Robert of Boves, who had almost single-handedly destroyed the army's hopes of capturing Zara without a fight. His choice had been hotly debated, for he represented the party of Simon of Montfort and those who had sided with him against the Doge and the principal barons. But Robert seemed to have undergone a change of heart, claiming that his opposition had been based solely on religious grounds. He was quite prepared to bow to Innocent's judgment, he asserted and, with the others, swore on holy relics to perform his mission faithfully and return as soon as possible to Zara.

The night before the envoys left he paid a long visit to Simon of Montfort. This was duly reported to the barons, but it was too late to send another in his place. Suspicious and uneasy, they watched the ships sail from Zara's harbor, wondering if yet another defector had sailed away never to return.

Robert and Anne were indifferent to the crosscurrents of intrigue that made the first few weeks of Zara's occupation so interesting to Aleaumes. Peter of Amiens, at last aware of Robert's interest in the lady who was so patently not the kinswoman she claimed to be, had reacted with his habitual easygoing generosity. As was his duty, he had chided Robert severely for the deception practiced on his lord, but his anger did not ring true.

"I don't want to see you in my presence for at least the next ten days," Peter said severely. "I suggest you spend that time in serious activity of a sort that will return you to your previous high level of service."

Get her out of your system was what he meant, Robert knew. He tried to keep his voice suitably dismayed and repentant. "Yes, my lord. I shall devote myself to it night and day."

As he bent the knee before the lord of Amiens he heard Peter whisper, "Enjoy yourself, Robert. Duty will soon take you from her."

"Peter has given us ten days, my love," he told Anne that night, "surely the best Christmas gift I have ever received."

"Then in his honor we shall make this a Christmas that neither of us will ever forget," she replied sweetly, twining her arms around his neck and raising her lips for his kiss.

Her beauty was greater than ever, for she had replaced her widow's garb with a soft woolen robe whose blue matched her eyes. At Robert's urging she no longer bound her hair, but let it flow loose over her shoulders, and on her feet she wore shoes of soft blue leather, the finest she had ever owned. She had had to part with one of her precious silver coins to purchase this finery, but so tightly had she clenched it in her fist before surrendering it to the seamstress who had made her gown that no one in the house suspected the size of the hoard she had hidden away in the bedroom which had in better days been occupied by their hosts.

Early on the morning of the second day of January, Aleaumes paid a visit to his brother's new house. He banged on the door of the room shared by Anne and Robert, shouting in a voice that echoed all through the small dwelling that it was past time for Robert to return to his duties. Peter of Amiens had inquired after him yesterday and a parliament had been called for this morning which all barons and knights of the army were commanded to attend. He would wait for Robert, but not for long. Haste was imperative, for already the streets were thronged with men answering the summons to assemble, and Aleaumes for one did not wish to arrive late.

Grumbling to himself, Aleaumes descended the staircase and shouted for wine. Theodora brought it to him, explaining courteously that the servants were worthless creatures who disappeared as soon as one needed them. Aleaumes glanced sharply at her, admiring the clearness of the black eyes that stared unblinkingly back at him. For an old woman she held herself remarkably straight and her skin was amazingly smooth and unwrinkled. What had Robert said? Oh, yes, she dealt in herbs. No doubt she concocted secret potions in the dead of night and whispered to her gullible clients of remedies that promised eternal beauty—nasty, greasy creams, foul-tasting drinks and poultices that burned off the top layer of skin. He had to admit, though, that she was a good advertisement for her wares.

"No, sir clerk," she said, interrupting his train of thought, "I offer no miracles, only simple healthful brews that any housewife can easily learn to prepare if she but have the patience."

"But, alas, patience and common sense are the rarest of human qualities." An old man stood in the doorway regally inclining his head as if welcoming this stranger to a palace. "I am Nicholas Tripsychos," he said, coming forward, "and this is my wife, Theodora. We have the honor of providing your lord brother and his lady with this humble refuge from the distractions of the world. Perhaps you will permit me to join you in a cup of wine while you are waiting."

Aleaumes was too surprised to do more than nod politely and allow himself to be ensconced in a comfortable chair by the fire. His host sat opposite, stretching his legs toward the warmth.

"One grows steadily colder with age," he remarked, as though the idea amused him, "a natural preparation for the coldness of the grave, I presume. The body, even in death, does not care for sudden shocks."

"How is it that you speak French, sir?" Aleaumes asked, uncertain how he should address this interesting apparition whose thin white hair stood out all over his head like wisps of soft fleece.

"Actually I speak some thirteen languages, but not all of them well. I have no more students on whom to practice the more exotic tongues, and so I bedevil my dear companion by following her about the house jabbering away in the three or four she understands."

He raised his cup to Theodora, who was disappearing toward the back of the house through a tiny door that Aleaumes guessed led to the kitchens. The woman turned and smiled affectionately at her husband. "They come in handy sometimes, my dear, though it is a bit distracting to switch about in midsentence as you will persist in doing."

"Her French is very good, is it not? Actually I think her accent is better than mine."

"Very good. She might easily be taken for a native." With a start Aleaumes realized that Nicholas had abruptly switched to Latin and that he had answered him in that same language. He shook his head ruefully. "I see what she meant."

"A little test, sir clerk, a harmless amusement for my old age. My wife is almost never wrong, but I cannot resist the temptation to verify her conclusions. Though to my eyes you are a knight indistinguishable in dress or bearing from all the others, she knew you for a clerk. I really don't know how she does it."

"But a knight could not be expected to understand Latin."

"Precisely. I hope you will forgive me."

"On the contrary, I congratulate you. It was very skillfully done. I, too, enjoy the study of my fellow human beings."

"Do you? When I was young I preferred parchments to people. They were so much more predictable and far easier to understand, no matter what language they were written in. But as I grew older I found that the only study worthy of the true scholar is the continuing discovery of man. And so I became a teacher, and found that often my students revealed more to me than I did to them."

"I think I should very much have liked being your pupil." Aleaumes was enjoying the conversation and had almost forgotten the original purpose of his coming.

"I doubt that you would have stayed with me long. You are a man torn between two worlds, a natural lover of freedom, too restless for the quiet contemplation so dear to a true scholar. The vows sit heavy on your spirit."

Aleaumes did not answer and Nicholas sighed in disappointment.

"As one grows older and becomes acutely aware of the swift passage of time, one tends to dispense with the niceties of polite conversation," he said. "Idle commentary on the vagaries of the weather and the exchange of mutually meaningless compliments become insufferably boring. One bears right in to the heart of the matter." He smiled apologetically. "Alexius Angelus is a depraved young idiot, like all the rest of his family. You will find him treacherous and ungrateful."

Aleaumes stared. How did this old man know that envoys had arrived yesterday bearing credentials from both the German Emperor and a Greek prince who claimed to be the son of Isaac Angelus? And that this prince's name was Alexius?

"I think you will enjoy Constantinople if you don't destroy too much of it during the siege," continued Nicholas. "It is one of the most marvelous cities in the world. I was born there, you know. Perhaps it's time for me to return. There's no longer much security in Zara."

"Aleaumes, what's this all about?" Robert stood buckling on his sword, still tousled from sleep and obviously annoyed at having been so unceremoniously awakened.

"You might as well ask him," said Aleaumes, gesturing toward Nicholas, who had risen from his chair as his guest entered the room. "He seems to know more about it than I do."

"Mere speculation, sir clerk," Nicholas said smoothly. "There is nothing like a mystery to keep the wits sharp and the spirit active. Perhaps you will be kind enough to return after the parliament is ended and take another cup of wine with me. I have enjoyed our conversation immensely, and I am certain that we shall soon have many more topics of mutual interest to discuss."

Robert shrugged his shoulders impatiently. "Let's go, Aleaumes. You can tell me about it as we walk."

"Your host is a very unusual man," Aleaumes said as he and Robert hurried toward the square where the parliament was to take place.

"Is he? I don't think I've exchanged more than a dozen words with him in the last ten days."

"I think I will accept his invitation," said Aleaumes, a glint in his eye. "Unless you object to my presence there, Robert."

"You are welcome anytime, Aleaumes. Just don't expect me to be on hand to entertain you every time you have an idle hour to kill. I've better things to do."

"I've no doubt you do," said Aleaumes. "How is the lady Anne, by the way?"

As speech succeeded speech Aleaumes marveled at the worldly sagacity of Nicholas Tripsychos. What was being proposed was outrageous, but so logical that all around him in the crowd of listening men heads nodded in agreement. Sheep, he thought disgustedly, men of no brains who all their lives have quickly bent the knee to authority or even the semblance of authority, willing themselves blind, deaf and dumb to all but a king's flattery and honeyed words. There were some angry faces in the crowd, and there would be more when the full realization of what the Emperor was proposing had sunk in. That thought at least was comforting. There had been trouble over Zara in the beginning, but many had choked back their rebellion, though secretly they yearned to speak out with the frankness of Simon of Montfort. Could anyone expect these same men to meekly submit to a second diversion? There was utter silence as Philip's letter was read aloud.

"Lords," wrote the Emperor, "I will send to you my wife's brother, thus placing him in God's Hand and in yours. Because you journey for God, the right and justice, you owe to those who have been wrongfully disinherited the return, if it lies within your power, of what is theirs. Alexius will deal with you in a manner more generous than has ever before been known, and will aid you in all ways to conquer the Holy Land.

"Firstly, if God grants that you restore him to his rightful eminence, he will place the entire kingdom under obedience to Rome, from which it has long been separated. He knows that you have beggared yourselves in your cause and that you are poor, so he will give you two hundred thousand silver marks and meat enough to feed every man in the army, noble or common. He personally will go with you to Babylon, or send in his place, if you think it wiser, ten thousand men maintained at his own expense. And these he will maintain for a full year; and for all the days of his life he will maintain a force of five hundred knights in the Holy Land, to guard and preserve what you have won."

When the envoy ceased reading an angry growl arose from the crowd, like the protest of some somnolent wild beast pricked and poked in its lair by a persistent hunter. As the tumult grew a few loud voices rose over the hubbub, and men shifted their positions to draw closer to those whose opinions they shared. At last they were openly divided, for an empty space some ten paces wide stretched the length of the square, and men shouted and raised their fists at one another across the neutral ground.

The German and Greek envoys were quickly spirited back to the palace occupied by the Doge. There they waited, in uncertainty and real fear for their lives, for the dispute could be heard even at that distance.

The Marquis of Montferrat stood alone on the platform the envoys had so hastily and gratefully left. Had any of the inflamed quarrelers below him glanced up they would have been silenced by the calm arrogance with which he surveyed the scene. His eyes followed the figures of Villehardouin and Baldwin of Flanders as they moved from group to group, soothing, reasoning, pleading for unity. As was to be expected, their personal prestige and the universal respect accorded them were having their effect. Many drifted from the fringes of the crowd back toward their lodgings, where no doubt the discussion would continue, even though they must now know that the final outcome was inevitable.

Louis of Blois and Hugh of St. Pol stood chatting quietly with Matthew of Montmorency, Pierre of Bracieux, Miles the Brabant and the poet, Conon of Béthune. These were men who could be depended upon to do their duty without question. At a sign from Montferrat they began making their way unobtrusively toward the palace, joined by the Bishops of Halberstadt and Troyes, who shook their heads despairingly at the commotion behind them.

The Abbots of Vaux and Loos, Cistercians both, stood sandal to sandal fiercely arguing, their flushed faces all the redder for the white of their habits. As each man made a telling point it was taken up by his listeners and passed from one to another until, inevitably, a challenger dared to question it. Eventually, when tempers cooled, a more formal debate would emerge from the confusion as preachers contested one another for the edification of all who cared to listen. The talk would go on for days, weeks perhaps, for there were monks and clerks aplenty in each party and Simon of Montfort seemed determined to split the army in two.

Boniface knew that many would defect in the coming months, and he would willingly let others go, some to Syria or Hungary, others back to Apulia and the Count of Brienne. The remainder would be enough to conquer decadent Constantinople, and as he had known all along, Jerusalem was a lost cause not worth shedding one's blood over.

Twelve men signed a solemn covenant that afternoon agreeing to reinstate the heir of Constantinople on his throne, though two of them, Count Baldwin of Flanders and Geoffrey of Villehardouin, arrived late to the ceremony. As they affixed their signatures to the document they reported that sizable groups of knights and priests still lingered in the square, though by now their debate was strictly academic.

The covenant to which their seals were then attached fixed the date of Alexius's arrival in Zara for two weeks after Easter.

Since the day of the parliament Robert had had little free time to spend with his beloved Anne, and she grew increasingly restless and impatient with her too-often-absent lover. Gradually she fell into the habit of spending many hours each day in the company of Theodora, who instructed her in the art of herb brewing. At Anne's request the old woman spoke to her almost entirely in Greek, and in a few months' time she was able to make herself understood in that language.

"She has a remarkably good ear for it," Theodora told her husband, "and a single-minded determination to master the fine points of the language that I do not quite understand. After all, once she leaves this house she will probably never hear Greek again."

"As usual, my dear, you are too kind," replied Nicholas. "That is a very ambitious young woman, who has an eye to her future. When she sits with Aleaumes and me listening to my old man's stories of life in Constantinople her eyes betray her thoughts. By our standards the life Robert and Aleaumes were accustomed to on those pitifully few acres of theirs in Picardy is shockingly primitive, their ideas of comfort far below anything we would tolerate. Robert will eventually return to his home if he lives through this ridiculous adventure, but there is no place there for her. Even if there were no long-suffering wife I doubt that she would go with him. She needs Robert for a while longer, but once Constantinople is taken, she will set her sights on higher game. Greek, Frank, German or Venetian, it will make little difference to her if the man be wealthy and powerful. I think, however, that she rather prefers to dream of herself as a Greek princess. Obviously she has no idea what our nobles are like. But believe me, she will kick her faithful knight aside without a backward glance the moment her prospects improve."

Theodora considered her husband's words for a moment. "I believe he is already puzzled, though probably grateful, at her failure to conceive. Begetting children seems to be a proof of manhood to these Franks."

"She has taken precautions?"

"Almost from the first. She was lucky, it seems, in Venice, but came to me in secret as soon as she learned about my medicines. Every morning I prepare a drink for her, but he knows nothing of it."

"Nor will he, unless she grows careless."

"I have taught her how to make the brew and promised to give her a supply of dried herbs to take with her when she leaves."

"I like Robert. There is something very honest about him, though he has not the depth of his brother. But I suppose that comes of being a soldier. They are not trained to think when they are young, and when the void makes itself felt in manhood, they do not recognize it for what it is. Give her the herbs she desires, for if she is not caught in the bonds of parenthood Robert's freedom will come all the sooner. I shudder to think what she might demand of him if she became ambitious for a child as well as herself."

They sat in companionable silence for a while, their minds so attuned that there was no further need to speak. There was no malice in the assessment they had made of Anne's character. Indeed, they felt rather sad that so beautiful a young woman should have proved to be so shallow. But they were resigned to it. She was not unlike so many others they had known. Robert would be grievously hurt by her, but he would recover. No matter how great the unrequited love, it was only in romances that it brought the lover to his grave.

"Aleaumes will return to his cathedral in Amiens," said Nicholas musingly, "unless by some miracle the army does finally reach the Holy Land, which I very much doubt. If it weren't for the narrowness of his faith, he could be a very fine scholar. But the time of the warrior-bishop is past, and he will have to abandon that illusion along with many others. It will be a dreadful waste, but he will no doubt end up a monk in some dank monastery chanting away his life."

"Surely he would be miserable in such a place."

"Miserable, my dear, but saved. He will subdue his mind and his body for the sake of his soul."

"Which he has never seen." Theodora's remark was as gently spoken as all of her utterances.

"My dear, I hope that my skepticism has not robbed you of a belief which might bring you comfort," said Nicholas sadly.

"My doubts began with the first poor woman who bled to death while I stood by helpless to prevent it. And when I prepared her cold, empty body for the grave and thought of the twelve pregnancies she had endured without complaint and of the husband who was already planning to replace her so that he could beget still more children, an anger began in me that has never diminished in all the years since."

"You should have been a man, Theodora. You would have made a truly great doctor."

"But I would not have been able to do the little I have for other women, for doctors all believe that childbirth and female ailments are beneath them. And I would not have had these years with you."

Anne was amused at the sight of the two old people who sat before the fire holding hands and gazing into one another's eyes like a pair of starstruck young lovers. For some minutes there had been a knocking at the gate that she had heard even in the tiny room off the kitchen where Theodora's herbs were dried and stored. But these two had heard nothing. As she bustled into the room she wondered for a brief moment how it felt to be in love like that. But she quickly dismissed the thought, for it did not really interest her. Love was an emotion that weakened the will, and she rejoiced in the strength of her own immunity. She had known a few hours of that weakness in Venice after she and Robert had first become lovers, but the long separation of the sea voyage to Zara had cooled her ardor and given her time to think. Her healthy young female body had almost betrayed her by the unexpected force of its response to Robert's passion, but she had learned that passion could be easily and pleasurably sated without damaging the private core of self that had become her strength.

"I think that is Aleaumes at the gate," she said as she walked quickly by Theodora and Nicholas. "Were you expecting him today?"

"I expect him every day that there is news to tell," said Nicholas as Theodora rose unbidden to fetch a certain wine that Aleaumes preferred to all others. "Lately there has been much to tell of the army and its doings."

Aleaumes' face as he greeted Nicholas was tightly drawn by the continuous effort he had been making all day to restrain his anger. He seldom bothered anymore to attempt to conceal his feelings from Nicholas and Theodora, for it was a useless game. They often knew of the latest defection before he did, even to the names, ranks and destinations of the knights and men-at-arms who had been slipping away from Zara throughout the winter.

"I don't approve of this plan to capture Constantinople," he said angrily, accepting the cup Theodora handed him. "I never did. But unless the army stays together we never shall reach the Holy Land. If enough of us who oppose it were to band together and present Montferrat with an ultimatum there might be a chance that he would give it up. But every time someone slips away on his own the rest of us are weakened."

"Who now, Aleaumes?" asked Anne.

"Renaud of Montmirail. He was one of the first to take the cross, you know, at Ecri with Count Thibaut and Count Louis. And he left with Count Louis's approval, on an embassy to Syria. They made him swear on the Host to return within fifteen days after reaching Syria, but he won't. And Easter is only a week away."

"Who else went with him?"

"His nephew, Hervée of Châtel, William of Ferrières, the Vidame of Chartres, John of Frouville and his brother Peter, and quite a few others I don't know."

"When men of reputation begin to desert a cause, it's usually for a good reason," said Nicholas. "They can't walk away unnoticed like common soldiers."

"Simon of Montfort is behind it all," said Aleaumes. "But no one can figure out what motivates him. After Constantinople he'll have plenty of infidels to raise his sword against if only he would stay with the army. But he won't listen to reason."

"Perhaps he knows that after Constantinople there will be nothing," said Nicholas. "Personally I don't like Montfort. He is narrow-minded and a fanatic who sees heresy in the most innocent of philosophic theses, but in spite of that he's the most honest man in your whole army. He has vowed to kill unbelievers and that's what he intends to do. He sees Constantinople for what it really is, a tempting, easy alternative to Jerusalem, a place where a good fighting man in these times can become rich and powerful. And in his stubborn honesty he rejects it utterly. It wouldn't surprise me a bit to hear him call it the Devil's own temptation. For him it's Jerusalem or nothing."

"But Nicholas," said Aleaumes, "we've been over this so many times. We need the men and money Alexius has promised us. We've lost over two thousand this winter alone through desertion, not to mention those who have died from their wounds and other causes. And the army needs experience. Except for the siege of Zara, which was no true test, these men have never fought together. They come from all over France and many from Germany. A lot of them can't even understand each other's speech. The way things are now, we'd never succeed in the Holy Land. It takes a good battle to make men forget the differences of the past and come to trust one another again."

"You've spent a lot of time listening to the Abbot of Loos, my friend."

"What he says makes more sense than what the Abbot of Vaux and Montfort are preaching. And Alexius's cause is a just one, after all. It might even be considered sinful were we to refuse to help a legitimate ruler regain the throne God has willed him to occupy."

"Aleaumes, sometimes you Franks are so childlike that I wonder how you manage to live in this world," said Nicholas. "Everything is so simple to you. Something is either right or wrong, true or false, with no gradations of compromise between. Alexius has no more right to the throne of Constantinople than I have. We Greeks have only one guiding principle to the succession; whoever is strong enough and vicious enough to pull down his predecessor rules. And only until another ambitious man rises up to do the same to him. Our revolts are all palace revolts; the people care nothing for who wears the crown. And I promise you that when Alexius is shown to the people of Constantinople they won't even recognize his name. They'll shrug their shoulders and turn their backs on him, and then where will your righteous cause be?"

"What does Robert think, Aleaumes?" asked Anne. "When we are together he never speaks of it."

"He feels much the way I do," answered Aleaumes. "But he is very certain of one thing. He will follow Peter of Amiens because that is where his duty lies. And I think that Peter is reserving final judgment until he sees Alexius for himself. If the prince is noble and worthy he will fight for him. If not, I don't know what he will do."

"Montferrat would never commit us to a man who was too weak or unstable to fulfill his promises," said Anne. "Nor would the others in authority. I have no doubt that the prince is all he is reputed to be and that under his rule the Church in Constantinople will return to Rome and the people of the Empire prosper in Christian harmony with their European brethren."

Well done, thought Nicholas, glancing at Theodora, whose eyes twinkled in amused understanding. The minx means to get to Constantinople at all costs, and she will swear to the truth of any outrageous story to make sure that Robert gets there too.

Aleaumes was looking speculatively at Anne, who sat demurely beside him, her hands folded gracefully in her lap. Her face and eyes shone with the same light that had transfigured the faces of the men who had listened to Fulk of Neuilly so long ago. It was as if she saw a holy vision and was illuminated by it. How could a woman who wallowed so willfully in adultery remain so pure and innocent looking? The ravages of her sin ought by all that was holy to be taking their toll on that slim body and clear, unlined face. If anything, Aleaumes decided, she seemed more beautiful every time he saw her. He understood some of the fascination she held for Robert, for he was not wholly immune to it himself. One wanted to believe what she said. She had an air about her that demanded trust and devotion as though she were entitled to it.

"I must go," he said, shaking himself from his reverie. "I had only a few hours free and could think of no better place to spend them than here."

Nicholas bowed in acknowledgment of the compliment. "You are always welcome, Aleaumes," he said. "Your presence brings a light into this house."

"Did you bring me no message from Robert?" asked Anne as she walked with Aleaumes through the small courtyard toward the door that opened onto the street.

"Anne, forgive me," said Aleaumes, "I was so caught up with Renaud of Montmirail's defection that I forgot. He asked me to tell you that he completes his week's duty at sunset tonight and will be here as soon as possible." The rest of Robert's message was too tender and intimate for Aleaumes to repeat, for his brother had told him to assure his lady of his love and devotion and tell her how much he longed for the sight of her. The words stuck in Aleaumes' throat and he could not get them out.

"Anne," he said, pausing with his hand on the latch of the half-opened gate, "have you given thought to the performance of your Easter duty? Lent is almost over, yet you have neither confessed nor told me whether you will receive the sacrament next week."

"You are not my confessor, Aleaumes," she said firmly, "nor Robert's either. Have a care for your own soul, but do not presume to interfere in a matter you cannot understand."

He flushed at her pointed reference to his celibacy. It was on the point of his tongue to tell her that she was living in sin and dragging his brother along with her, but her face was already closed to him and he knew she would pay no attention to what he said. If he spoke now, if he antagonized her, she would build a wall between the brothers that he would be powerless to scale.

"Good-bye, Aleaumes," she said, and he found himself out on the street, the wooden door bearing Robert's arms latched shut behind him.

V

The Venetians destroyed Zara the day after Easter while the crusaders and pilgrims watched the grim business from the neutrality of their ships. It was methodically done, so that when the Doge at last declared himself satisfied not a house, not a tower, not even the city wall itself remained standing above the rubble.

There were many among the crusaders who would have gladly joined in the sack of the city for the sake of the valuables any man could easily pick up in the course of the operation, but Montferrat had strictly forbidden any Frank or German to take part. The Bishop of Soissons and Master John of Noyon had earlier returned from Rome with the welcome news that the Pope had forgiven them for their role in the capture of Zara. He absolved them from their sin and sent them his special blessing, along with an urgent appeal to work for unity within the army, so that God's holy work might be accomplished. Robert of Boves, to no one's surprise, had forsworn his oath and gone to Syria.

When the destruction of Zara had been completed there was one last confrontation between Simon of Montfort and the leaders of the army. At Simon's specific request the Doge was not present at the meeting. He and all his Venetians were still excommunicant and as far as Montfort was concerned they were as good as damned.

The parley was brief and to the point; there was no time left for argument and persuasion. The city was in ruins and could no longer supply the needs of the army. The winds and weather were perfect for the long sail to Constantinople.

"This is the devil's work you propose to do," Simon told them. "Will you not turn aside and join those of us who wish only to serve God and the cause of Christ with no thought for worldly advantage? It is not too late."

"It is we who have the Pope's blessing," the Bishop of Soissons replied. "I would remind you that he particularly desires that the army remain whole and united in spirit as well as fact."

"He cannot know that you mean to attack Constantinople," said Simon, guessing that pains had been taken to make sure Innocent suspected nothing of the scheme until it was too late to stop it. When his accusation was not immediately denied he felt sure that he was right. Innocent would be enraged when he learned of the deception and Montfort wanted no part of the consequences of the Pope's wrath.

"We shall leave then, my lords. The King of Hungary will welcome those of us who from the beginning opposed the unprovoked attack upon his city. Do you deny us our right to go?"

"We will not stop you, Montfort, if that is what you mean," said Boniface of Montferrat. "We want no traitors in our ranks."

Simon of Montfort's face turned scarlet at the insult and he would have struck Montferrat had not the Abbot of Vaux laid a cautionary hand on his arm. They were outnumbered at this meeting and must swallow the slur as best they could. The important thing was to get away safely with as many men and ships as possible.

As Montfort strode toward the quay where his ship lay waiting he paused frequently to announce in a loud voice that anyone who wished to join him would be made welcome. Few who were not already committed did, for the bulk of the army assumed that the Pope's blessing included tacit permission to reach the Holy Land by way of Constantinople. And many had come to the same conclusion as Peter of Amiens. They would suspend judgment until they had seen Alexius for themselves. There was some question as to whether the new promises made on their behalf by Montferrat and the others really bound them. There would still be time to go their own ways after the arrival of the Greek prince.

A few days after Simon of Montfort's departure Enguerrand of Boves came looking for Robert and Aleaumes. Robert had been exercising his destrier for the last time before it must again be confined aboard ship. The horse was restless and full of stored-up energy, as were most of the men, who had had little to do since Zara's destruction. The rubble of the city was an eerie landscape behind them and they seldom left the security of the port area. At least in the bustle of activity that was a part of each sailing one was unlikely to meet any of the wraithlike creatures who haunted the ruins of their once-great city, piteously searching for missing friends and family or for a few valuable or long-cherished objects to take with them into exile.

"I have decided to go to Hungary," said Enguerrand of Boves, laying a quieting hand on the horse's mane.

"Why didn't you sail with Montfort, then?" asked Robert.

"I almost did," replied Enguerrand, "but I don't like the idea of being beholden to any man, and Montfort has a way about him that sets my teeth on edge."

"I don't understand," said Aleaumes.

"It's a hard thing to speak of," said Enguerrand slowly. "When your father and I served in the Holy Land together there were many things we saw there that sat ill on our consciences. I am not one to shirk my duty nor does it trouble me to kill an enemy in battle. I have dispatched many a poor wretch, Christian and infidel alike, who cried out for my sword to end the agony of a wound from which there was no hope of recovery. I would expect a friend to do the same for me."

Robert and Aleaumes nodded gravely in agreement. No knight wanted to prolong his life if it meant a lingering death from putrefaction or a maiming that would turn him into one of the indescribably miserable beggars one saw crawling the roads and huddling on cathedral steps after every war.

"But there is a bloodlust that comes over some men that has nothing to do with honest fighting. It turns a knight into a soulless devil who would spit a child or a woman on the end of his sword and laugh to see their entrails spill into the dust. Coeur-de-Lion became one such at Acre, when he ordered five thousand infidel hostages butchered."

"Infidels are not men such as we know them," said Aleaumes. "Their souls already belong to the devil."

"They think differently," said Enguerrand. "Have you ever talked to a Saracen or even seen one?"

Aleaumes shook his head. "No," he admitted, "but that doesn't matter. Have you spoken like this to others besides us?"

"Only to my brother and your father. That was many years ago and he has probably forgotten. The bloodlust I spoke of—Simon of Montfort has it, though he doesn't know it yet. Someday, if he is given the opportunity, he will engineer massacres that will make Coeur-de-Lion's pale by comparison. If my duty calls me to fight at his side, then I will do it, but for now we are all free to choose our own paths."

Enguerrand waited expectantly for some response from the sons of his old friend, but Robert and Aleaumes could not meet his eyes. They knew he was inviting them to sail with him to Hungary and that were Gilo there he might counsel them to go. Finally, after a nod from Aleaumes, Robert spoke.

"There is a party, my lord," he began hesitantly.

"I know," interrupted Enguerrand, "though some will label it a conspiracy. I, too, was approached to join it, and I almost did. But when I learned that the army would await Alexius at Corfu, I changed my mind. I don't much like the idea of being trapped on an island as we were on St. Nicholas for so long. Once Alexius joins the army Montferrat and the others will be so committed that they will no longer permit anyone to leave peaceably. You will have to fight your way out. The time to choose is now."

"We have already chosen, my lord," said Robert respectfully, "as have you."

"Then let us hope each of us has made the right decision." Enguerrand clasped their hands in farewell. "God go with you and the saints protect you. I pray that I am wrong and that you don't find the Greek princeling and those who support him as treacherous and ungrateful as I fear they will prove to be."

Aleaumes stared after the retreating figure he had known from childhood. "Robert," he said in a hushed voice, "those are the very words Nicholas used the first time he spoke to me of Alexius. Treacherous and ungrateful." He crossed himself against the coincidence.

After the hardships and privations of the winter spent in Zara and the tensions caused by the rift in the army, Corfu was a delight. The island was rich and for once there were no short-ages of either food or drink. The people, too, were friendly and the camp very quickly took on a holiday air. Almost everyone was eager to forget, for a few weeks at least, that Alexius would soon be among them.

The tents and pavilions were spread out all around the city and the horses taken from the transports to graze in the rich pas-tures that the people of Corfu obligingly offered their guests. The Doge and the Marquis of Montferrat had stayed behind at anchor in the port of Zara to await Prince Alexius and provide him with a suitable escort to Corfu. Baldwin of Flanders was in command on the island and the strict discipline that Montferrat imposed was temporarily dispensed with. Watches were posted around the camp and the ships, but they were frequently relieved so that even the most humble soldier had time to wan-der the island and enjoy its wine and its women.

Robert and Anne contrived to be together as much as possi-ble, knowing that another long shipboard separation lay before them. On one lovely May afternoon not quite a week after their arrival they rode up into the hills, carrying with them a lovers' feast of wine, cheese and fresh fruit. It was Anne who had suggested the ride, anxious to get away for a whole afternoon from the two old sisters who had once more closed in around her, like two raucous black crows, she told Robert.

"They bedevil me night and day with questions about Zara. Where exactly was the house in which I stayed? What sort of Christians are Nicholas and Theodora? Why did I choose to leave the pilgrims in the first place? Have I already forgotten my dear husband and the sacred vows I took after his death? They give me no peace at all, Robert. And they are becoming vindic-tive because I will not satisfy their curiosity."

"Bear with them for my sake, my love. For at least a few more weeks. After that you may no longer need their protection."

"What do you mean, Robert?"

"Only that there are plans being discussed which it were bet-ter you remained ignorant of, for your own safety." Not even to Anne was Robert willing to confide how determined and how well organized the opposition to Alexius was becoming. There were frequent secret meetings held at odd moments in out-of-the-way places all over the island, meetings attended by five or six men at most, the better to conceal the conspiracy from Baldwin of Flanders and Geoffrey of Villehardouin. No action would be taken until after the arrival of Alexius, for it was just possible that the young man would turn out to be as worthy and noble a prince as had been promised them, just possible that a union of Greek and French forces would guarantee victory over the infidel. The army had so dwindled in size since Zara that many experienced soldiers believed that without reinforcements they would stand no chance whatsoever against the massed armies of the infidel.

This morning, when Robert had told Peter of Amiens that unless his lord had need of him he would spend the day riding with Anne in the hills, Peter had entrusted him with an urgent task.

"Find a secluded valley far from camp or any human habitation," he had told Robert, "where we may all meet in parliament if it becomes necessary to do so. We are of so many minds that we are weak and fragmented. If we leave this army we must do so in unity, with a clear and agreed-upon course of action before us. Else we are but a rabble and unworthy of the cross we wear."

And Robert had promised that he would find such a place if one existed on the island. He had become used to the fact that Peter of Amiens was one of the most important leaders of the conspiracy, even as he had grown accustomed to the sight of his lord's haggard face and the dullness of his eyes. Peter of Amiens had not come lightly to the opposition party and indeed if ever a man's struggle with his conscience showed on his face, it showed on Peter's. He was unhappy with the choice he had made, but caught between betrayal of his vow to Christ and his vow of obedience to Hugh of St. Pol, he had had no alternative but to plot behind the back of his cousin and liege lord.

On Aleaumes' advice Peter kept close to his tent these days, pleading a fever he was unable to completely shake off. Aleaumes had a healthy respect for the sharp eyes of Louis of Blois and feared that Peter's honest nature would not survive the strain of a confrontation with that lord.

"Secrecy is our best hope of success," he had told the restless

Peter. "It is to you that many of us look for leadership if what
we fear comes to pass. When and if we meet in parliament those
who are with us in this must be given a definite alternative.
Here in the quiet and privacy of your tent you can weigh the
options which are open to us. You can decide which of them will
bring us most swiftly to Jerusalem."

"I have thought of little else these past weeks," Peter had admitted. "Our choice is a limited one, for we are trapped on this
island just as your friend the lord of Boves predicted we would
be. We will need ships and there are only two men to whom we
can petition for them, the King of Hungary and the Count of
Brienne. It would be far better to be under obligation to a
fellow countryman than to a foreign king. I do not know what
conditions Hungary would impose in return for its support. I
have no wish to turn mercenary. But the Count of Brienne rules
Brindisi and enjoys the support of the Pope. He is, moreover,
still vowed to the Holy Land and obliged to assist us in the
fulfillment of our mutual promises. Many of those who went
with him to Apulia may now be ready to continue their interrupted journey to Jerusalem. There are many considerations to
be weighed, Aleaumes, but I am certain that we must somehow
return to Sicily or the Pope's domains to regroup and seek reinforcements. We are hardly an army any longer."

Anne did not dare ply Robert with questions when he was lost
in the moody silences that often fell on him nowadays. He had
little patience with anyone at such times and even she had felt
the lash of his tongue. He was changing somehow, growing
away from her in some subtle way she could not understand,
and even when he made love to her there was a distance between them. He was still an ardent and considerate lover, and to
the unobservant eye a paragon of respectful attentiveness, but
there was a detached air to all he said and did, as though part of
him moved and spoke while another part, the inner, invisible
self that was the man, stood aside as though listening for a call
that might never come.

She knew more about the conspiracy than Robert suspected,
for Sarah and Loma were incurable gossips and heard every
rumor that circulated in the camp. Few people paid any attention to the two old women. They were too skinny and withered

to arouse any feelings of lust even among soldiers notorious for their ability to enjoy females of any age and condition of disease, so they moved freely wherever their curiosity took them. They overheard snatches of conversation around the campfires and at the wells, and often, in return for doing his washing, a soldier would recount in great detail what he had overheard standing guard outside some baron's tent. They could not believe that Robert told her nothing of what was going on and so repeated every tidbit of information that came their way in the hope that she would confirm their suspicions and be led to gossip herself. But Anne had nothing to tell. She was forced to use her wits and her own judgment, picking her way through the maze of conflicting stories they recounted at the end of each long day.

She was certain that Nicholas Tripsychos was responsible for Robert's silence, and she could not forgive him for that. He was an interfering old man, no longer the harmless scholar whose company she had enjoyed in Zara. He had briefly been of some use to her, when with Theodora he had taught her Greek, but now he was a threat and she avoided him whenever possible. He was polite and courteous, almost fatherly in the way he spoke to her, but his old eyes bored into her and she knew that her character had been weighed and found wanting.

She was angry with herself for ever having suggested that his talents could be of use to the army. She had made a grave error there. It was really Theodora's company she had wanted—the herbs that kept her from conceiving and the assurance that if she did conceive, Theodora would find some safe means of aborting her. She had allowed herself to believe that the elderly Greek woman would drift into the habit of serving her, would in fact become her personal maid, thus freeing her from the necessary companionship of the widows. She had seen herself and Robert in the role of benefactors, but it had not worked out like that at all.

Nicholas had gained an audience with Geoffrey of Villehardouin and had had little difficulty in persuading the Marshal that his services as interpreter would be invaluable when the army reached Constantinople. Villehardouin, a man of learning himself, respected and enjoyed Nicholas's scholarship. Among

other things, they shared a sense of history. Villehardouin, much
to his own surprise, found himself telling the Greek about his
plan to write a history of this crusade, so that all men might
know the true causes of the divisions and defections that had
plagued the army almost from the beginning. "I have no time
now to begin such a task," Villehardouin said, "but once Jerusalem is secure, I have promised myself a period of rest and retreat far away from military duties. The whole world must know
what we have done and why. The names of the faithful must
serve as examples to those who will follow us, and those who
deserted our cause will no longer be able to hide their shame."

"Your lordship might be wise to spend a few hours whenever
possible dictating notes to your clerk," Nicholas suggested. "The
mind has a way of forgetting the details of a difficult struggle
when victory has been attained."

"I have already begun to do this," said Villehardouin, "for if I
come to write this record it must be as truthful as is in my
power to make it."

"I hope someday I may have the honor and pleasure of reading it," said Nicholas. "I believe that this crusade will stand out
from all the others for reasons yet unknown to us."

"He looked at me most strangely," Nicholas had told Robert
and Aleaumes, "as though he would question me further. But he
thought better of it and made instead some passing remark
about old men who thought themselves prophets. He knows
there is much discontent in the ranks and even among the
barons, but for the moment at least he chooses to ignore it. If it
were not for him Montferrat might still be in Italy and Baldwin
the leader of this crusade. I think he is deliberately cultivating a
blind spot where the Marquis is concerned. He does not dare
admit that he might have misjudged the man, for in a strict
moral sense he shares responsibility for Montferrat's decisions.
Montferrat has sworn that Alexius is a noble prince and he is the
only one of the barons ever to have seen the young man, so
Villehardouin must perforce believe him. But he is uneasy in his
own mind. One can read it in his eyes."

"Did he question you about Alexius?" asked Robert.

"No, and that in itself is strange, for I did not hide from him
the fact that most of my life was lived in Constantinople amongst

people who frequented the court. I had already left, of course, by the time Isaac came to power, but there is much I could have told him about the Empire and the ways of its kings. It seems that he prefers to remain in ignorance for as long as possible, fearing perhaps that knowledge will shatter the spell which Montferrat has woven around all your leaders. But the effort goes against his character, and he begins to wear much the same look as your own liege lord, though for a different reason of course."

"I wonder if he knows about us," mused Robert.

"I am certain he does, but there also he will turn a blind eye and a deaf ear against the day of Alexius's arrival. But if you move from mere grumblings and formless discontent to open rebellion he will judge you harshly. You will find yourselves named as traitors and cowards in that chronicle he intends to compose. In fact, your actions will compel him to write it, and because of you it will be an apologia of this whole sorry expedition."

"You haven't much faith in anything, have you, Nicholas?"

"None at all where human beings are concerned. Faith and hope are misspent emotions. I prefer to deal in realities."

"And what are the realities, as you see them?" Robert's question was a mocking one in spite of his natural liking for Nicholas. It was hard to endure an old man who believed that he alone was capable of sound judgment, who viewed with amusement and skepticism the sincere aspirations of the Frankish knights to whom the crusade was no mere "expedition."

"There is no need to be angry with me, my young friend. You know my mind, for I have spoken freely to you and to Aleaumes on many occasions. But since you ask the question I will answer it yet one more time, and this will be the last you shall hear me say on the subject. Alexius will betray you. He will refuse to pay what has been promised and you will have to fight him to get it. If you capture Constantinople you will never see Jerusalem. The Greek Empire will leech your strength and determination from you so that you will forget you ever hoped to tread the ground of the Holy Land. Ambition and conquest will consume you utterly." Nicholas felt very old as he looked at the unbelieving faces turned to him. When he was as young as they, he, too, had believed that he controlled his own destiny. Now, of course, he accepted the fact that if you were neither prince nor patriarch destiny swept you along in the current of other men's decisions.

One more warning he must give them, certain that it would strain and perhaps destroy the fragile bond that existed between him and Robert. Aleaumes would understand and probably concur, and perhaps he would impress it more strongly on his brother than it was in Nicholas's power to do.

"Robert, divulge none of your plans to Anne, neither the place nor the time of any of your meetings, and especially not the names of those who conspire with you. I advise it as a friend who cares greatly that you be allowed at least one opportunity in your life to make a choice that is truly your own."

Robert had been too stunned to become angry, and by the time he had grasped Nicholas's meaning, the scholar had retired to his own tent where he was instructing the brighter clerks in the rudiments of spoken Greek.

Aleaumes, surprisingly, agreed with Nicholas, though he chose to spare his brother's feelings by emphasizing the constant strain Anne was under, a strain which might cause her quite inadvertently to blurt out something of what she knew to the two sisters. And that would be the same thing as hiring a crier to inform the whole camp.

So Robert adopted a policy of silence with Anne, and then because she did often try to extract information from him, he was frequently annoyed by her obvious maneuverings. He fought against his vague uneasiness and explained her curiosity as the natural interest and worry a devoted woman might be expected to display when the man she loved was in a situation as difficult as his. Sometimes he cursed Nicholas for having planted the seed of he knew not what doubt. At other times, such as this afternoon, he forgot it entirely in the pleasure of her company and the beauty of the day.

They had ridden for hours before finding the one perfect place both had been searching for. It was a grassy bank almost at the summit of a thickly wooded hill, a tiny hollow of soft green where the only sound was the whisper of swiftly flowing water that eddied around moss-covered stones.

With no prying eyes fastened disapprovingly on them, they

were freed from the constraints they had imposed upon themselves in the roles they were obliged to play out in the presence
of others. They waded in the stream and splashed one another
with the icy water and their unguarded laughter rang out
through the woods where there was no human ear to hear it.

They made love fiercely and exhaustingly, refreshed themselves with the wine and the food they had brought, dozed
naked in the dappled sunlight of their Eden, and woke to share
an even deeper passion. They spoke of the tiny house in Zara
and the long winter during which their love had grown and
flourished while the world about them lay chill and brown, and
first one, then the other asked, "Do you remember?"

It was Anne who spoke of the night they became lovers in the
sands of the island of St. Nicholas.

"Are you sorry?" asked Robert.

"No, my love. I rejoice that I came to you freely and of my
own will. In a strange way I am glad too that my brother's wife
insisted I be placed in the convent at Soissons. She could not
know that her selfishness would preserve me for you. If it had
not been for her I would have been married off to some boorish
widower who needed a servant more than a wife. We would
never have met, or if we had I would have been so work-worn
and bowed down with care that you would have looked on me
with pity and disgust. From the time she can walk, Robert, a girl
is taught to guard her virginity, not for a love gift, but as barter
for security and her family's profit. I daily thank the understanding saint who preserved me from such a fate."

She really was not sorry that she had become Robert's mistress. Without the fear of an unwanted pregnancy to inhibit her
she gave herself over completely to the enjoyment of lovemak-
ing, playing her own body like a finely tuned instrument and
deriving deep pleasure from the act. She could let herself sink
into the oblivion of the moment, knowing in the far recesses of
her mind that cool control of her feelings would return as soon
as her lover left her. And since their periods of separation were
frequent and as inevitable as the rising of each day's new sun,
she was in no danger of being overwhelmed like many a poor
woman who loved too well.

More than anything else she sought to reassure Robert of her

constancy, binding him to her with the thousand frail ties of
shared moments of intimacy and danger, ties she reinforced with
pleasant reminiscences until they had the strength of a tightly
woven cord which bound the heart and spirit yet did not chafe.

It was not without calculation that she had mentioned her virginity, for she well remembered Robert's sudden guilty tenderness when the blood proof of her innocence had flowed
warmly down her thighs. She had long ceased to think of it with
any hint of regret, but to him, as to most men, she knew it was
no light matter. Somehow it put him deeply in her debt, and obscure though the notion seemed, she did not dismiss it lightly.
Nor would she have him forget.

"Robert?"

"It's getting late, Anne. We must be on our way."

"Something is troubling you, Robert. Won't you tell me what
it is?"

He busied himself loosing the hobbles that bound their horses'
legs and did not answer her. He had let his mind wander back
in time and space to Picardy, to the only other virgin he had
possessed, the pale, unresponsive Aelis who, had she been allowed the choice, would have preferred a convent to the marriage bed. What a strange contrast these two women made, one
so dark and passionate, the other so fair and remote. Had their
births been reversed how uncomplicated his own life would now
be.

As he mounted his horse he counted swiftly on his fingers,
hiding them in the tangled reins. Eleven months since he had
ridden so lightheartedly from Clari. The child must be about
three months old, if it had lived. What must it be like to hold
one's firstborn son in one's arms? Had they named it for him?
Was there a small Robert in faraway France who would never
know his father's face?

He felt stifled, suffocated in the midst of these trees that rose
on all sides. He longed for clear, open air and the wind of a fast
ride to clear the miasma from his head.

"We'll ride to the top of the hill," he said urgently, "and see if
there are plains below. We'll get back to camp faster if we can
follow level ground."

She followed him up the slope, letting her horse pick its careful way over the rock-strewn ground while Robert swore under his breath at the slowness of their ascent. He had told Anne long ago that he was married and she had taken it as a matter of course that a man in his position would naturally have a wife. She had asked him softly if he had sons, and he had answered no, no children. He had never mentioned the new life in Aelis's womb. Now he wished only to forget, to live for the present and the future and let the past lie buried.

They reached the crest of the hill and paused to let the winded horses rest. Before them stretched a small green valley closed in on three sides by steep, rocky slopes. The stream in which they had frolicked meandered down the hillside and widened as it reached the valley floor, flowing through a wide cleft in the hills which Robert felt certain led back to their camp.

"This is it," he said, unaware that he spoke aloud. "It's perfect."

"Perfect for what?" Anne's leg pressed against his as though demanding that he share his far-off thoughts.

He almost said, "Perfect for the parliament that must come," but something of Nicholas's warning had stayed in his mind. This is not women's business, he thought. She will forgive me later when everything is out in the open.

"We can follow that river all the way from camp and have this whole valley to ourselves, my love. And a far more pleasant ride than scrambling up and down the hillsides. Faster too, I warrant. We could probably be here in an hour's time."

"I liked the spot by the stream, Robert. It was like a private little bower no one else could enter but us."

He seemed not to hear her, so intent was he on studying the size and shape of the hidden valley. It was just large enough to hold the men who would meet there. Peter of Amiens estimated that fully half the army was ready to abandon the Constantinople venture, but not all would declare themselves openly until an ultimatum had been formally presented to the barons. Perhaps a hundred or more would risk meeting here. There was natural security on all sides, for no one could descend the slopes without sending a cascade of rocks and boulders crashing down to the valley floor, and on the fourth side it would be necessary for an approaching band of men to splash noisily through the waters of the small river. No force could come upon them by stealth. Robert was well content with his find.

The ships bearing the Doge, the Marquis of Montferrat and Prince Alexius arrived the week before Pentecost. In their honor an elaborate procession was staged that wound its way through the camp and down to the port area. Baldwin of Flanders, Louis of Blois, Hugh of St. Pol, Geoffrey of Villehardouin and the noble bishops of the army marched at its head while the lesser barons and common soldiers fell in behind them as best they could. The priests waved incense-filled censers so that the air was fragrant with clouds of perfumed smoke, and hymns of thanksgiving drowned out the mutterings of those who were determined to judge for themselves the worth of this stranger who was being foisted upon them.

The scene had the air of a carefully stage-managed morality play as Alexius, gorgeously arrayed in jewel-encrusted dalmatic robes worthy of an emperor slowly descended the gangplank of Montferrat's ship, pausing every few steps to raise his arms in stately acknowledgment of the welcoming cheers of the crowd. Behind him walked the Marquis, coolly scanning the crowd as if to assess the depth of sincerity behind the shouting.

To the rear of the throng, somewhat apart, stood Peter of Amiens, Robert, Aleaumes and Peter's brother, Thomas. They watched in silence as Alexius mounted a white horse and began a progress through the camp to show himself to those who had not been able to crowd into the port area. Dandolo had joined the Marquis and the two stood looking after their protégé. They exchanged guarded looks and a few low words, then Dandolo disappeared in the midst of a crowd of his Venetians.

Montferrat's eyes raked the crowd in a final assessment of the situation, coming briefly to rest on the little group surrounding Peter of Amiens. He motioned to Baldwin of Flanders, who hurried quickly to his side. Flanders shrugged his shoulders and shook his head as if unable to answer the Marquis's questions. Villehardouin joined them and the conversation became more animated. Then he walked over to Louis of Blois. One by one the lords began to make their way unobtrusively toward Mont-ferrat's tent.

"It's beginning," said Peter of Amiens succinctly.

Alexius personally agreed to all the terms that had previously been proposed by Philip of Swabia's envoys speaking in his name. Furthermore, he assured the French barons, their stay in Constantinople would be a very short one, for his people were anxiously awaiting his return and would rise in revolt against the usurper as soon as he showed himself outside the walls of the city. He intimated that the sum of two hundred thousand marks was of scant concern to the wealthy Greek Empire and that his position would be so secure that he could easily spare them an army of ten thousand men. He spoke with respect of the Pope and told the amazed French lords that union with Rome was something the Eastern Church had long desired. There seemed no end to his generosity and good intentions.

"He speaks and moves like a puppet on a string," was Peter of Amiens's conclusion after having attended a meeting at which Alexius addressed the high lords and barons of the army. "And Montferrat pulls the strings. He has ordered Alexius's tent to be placed immediately beside his own and no one can approach the prince without his permission. The prince says nothing and goes nowhere without Montferrat at his side."

"Many were mightily impressed by the figure Alexius cut on horseback," said Robert. "With that red hair of his they compare him to Coeur-de-Lion in his prime."

Aleaumes snorted in disgust. "He's weak and easily led, some-thing Coeur-de-Lion never was, in spite of all his other queer predilections. I watched him closely when he rode through the camp. His eyes were glazed over and he moved without con-scious thought, like a body without a soul. His smile was a gri-mace, totally devoid of warmth, and he has no chin whatsoever. I begin to think Nicholas was right. If we help him to regain his throne we will also have to help him keep it, for he will never be able to do it alone. We'll end up spending years riding all over his Empire putting down insurrections. He's buying himself an army of mercenaries, just as surely as Dandolo did."

"But this time our price is higher." Peter of Amiens's voice was bitter. "I wonder what reward he promised Montferrat."

"King of someplace or other, you may be sure of that, brother," said Thomas. "It sickens me to think of it."

"At midnight in three days' time we meet in Robert's valley," said Peter of Amiens. "The time for talk is past."

Anne could not sleep. She had lain down at dark as usual in the tent she called her Purgatory, but the night was so still that not a breath of air stirred. The stench from the unwashed bodies of her two companions filled the small space, and her stomach heaved. She would never understand why the pious held cleanliness in such disdain, but they did. Many of the nuns at Soissons had smelled so of stale wine and old sweat that she could not bear to approach them. It was certainly no stimulus to charitable thoughts.

She stirred restlessly on her pallet, willing sleep to come and end yet another long, hot day of waiting. In a way this was worse than the Isle of St. Nicholas, for now she had a goal and a plan. They were so close and yet so far from Constantinople. She gritted her teeth in frustration, seeing with her mind's eye the gorgeous palaces and fine churches Nicholas had described to her. The richest and most beautiful city in the world, he had called it. The Rome of the East. She, too, was beautiful, she knew, but her beauty was wasted here in this miserable camp. She had come to hate the sound of the word Jerusalem and all it meant. Endless prayers, hardship, sacrifice, sour wine and maggoty food, humility and self-abnegation, and the supreme honor of dying in some barren desert in the name of Christ.

Lately she had grown more honest with herself, for she had little to do to occupy her time. Robert had not taken her to ride in their valley as he had promised. Indeed he had seemed anxious to avoid mention of the place. He had even seemed to want to avoid her. Ever since the arrival of the Greek prince he had been constantly at the side of Peter of Amiens and there was a shut look about his face that warned her not to ask any questions. Useless to try to wheedle anything out of Aleaumes or Nicholas. Both seemed immune to her charms and even at times openly hostile. They considered her a threat to their precious Robert, but soon enough they could have him all to themselves. She would no longer need any of them once they stood in the Hippodrome.

The thought pleased her and calmed her restlessness. She lay still, planning her future, seeing herself garbed in silken robes and hung with a king's ransom of jewels. Power would be hers and she would know how to use it.

Gradually she became aware that there was movement outside her tent, muffled footsteps and quickly stifled oaths. Some soldier had blundered into the pilgrims' section of the camp in search of his whore and lost his way in the rows of small tents that looked exactly alike in the darkness. She waited for the sound of drunken curses, then crept cautiously past the two snoring sisters and raised the flap which hung across the tent's entrance.

The moon was three-quarters full and cast a silvery glow over the sleeping camp. Not a soul stirred. She wondered what had become of the soldier, then stepped outside to cleanse her lungs in the fresh air.

It seemed quieter than usual, and she glanced toward the cluster of large tents nearer the sea, looking for the small campfires around which sleepless knights and soldiers usually gathered to toss dice and exchange stories of past campaigns. Slowly she realized that only the moonlight illuminated the camp and that no shadowy figures paced the alleyways between the tents. There were guards stationed outside the tents where Montferrat, Alexius and the other noble lords slept, but there were no guards at all along the far perimeter of the camp. There was no one to be seen in the direction she was looking, where the river stretched silver toward the interior of the island.

A wave of panic engulfed her. There had been an incident a few days ago; some of the people from the city had shouted insults and thrown stones at the ship in which Alexius had traveled to the island. They had been quickly dealt with and the shameful occurrence hushed up, but it was painfully obvious to everyone that here at least Alexius was not welcome. Had the guards been bribed or drugged? Was there even now a party of

Assassins creeping their silent way through the camp, bent on murdering the prince and his supporters?

She fought for control, dismissing the idea of danger from the people of Corfu. It was too preposterous. The army would wreak the same vengeance on them as it had on the unfortunate citizens of Zara. But what other explanation was there? And then she realized that only one answer was possible. Anger flared up in her and she spat out a mouthful of bile. Whatever it cost her she would not be dragged back to Italy or France. She had set her face to the East and to the East she would go.

In a few minutes she had made her way far from the center of the camp to where Peter of Amiens and Robert had pitched their tents on the pretext that Peter's illness would be more quickly cured away from the hubbub of activity in which the great lords moved.

The campfire outside Robert's tent was long dead and cold, and though she held her breath to listen, she could hear no snores from peacefully sleeping men. The tent was empty. So, too, was Peter of Amiens's. Men and weapons alike were missing, vanished into the night as though they had never existed at all.

The glint of moonlight on the river caught her eye as she emerged from the blackness of Peter's tent. She stood entranced, staring at the silvery ribbon in the distance, as all the pieces of the puzzle fell into place. Robert's strangeness, his silences, Peter's drawn, tense look, the whispered conferences hastily broken up at her approach, the discontent that had festered since Zara, Nicholas's gloomy prediction of failure, the smug sarcasm with which many spoke Alexius's name, and finally, Robert's pleasure at finding the small valley he had never again visited.

Would they listen to her, she wondered, if she went and pleaded with them? Would she even be allowed to speak? Of all the men there not one would pay her any heed, except perhaps Robert. If she could get to him. But too many others stood in her way, and if Aleaumes was there, as he surely must be, he would drag her roughly back to camp for her own protection. And Robert would agree. It was no place for a woman.

She began to run, her head a jumble of confused thoughts.

Not to Villehardouin, no, Nicholas and Theodora had pitched their tent close to their patron's and old men slept lightly if at all. Flanders might not believe her, would perhaps dismiss her as a hysterical woman with childish fancies. St. Pol or Blois? Would they act quickly enough? She could not take the chance. The stakes were too high. It must be Montferrat himself.

By the time Montferrat's bodyguard challenged her she had regained control of herself. She was breathing heavily from her headlong run, but her voice was steady as, imitating the cold tone of command she had often heard Mary of Flanders use, she demanded that she be shown into the Marquis's presence immediately.

"The hour is late and my lord is asleep," said the guard, not certain what to do with this woman who had appeared out of nowhere. He cleared his throat, then continued hesitantly, "If you were sent for earlier, it would seem that my lord has changed his mind."

"I am no whore," said Anne bluntly. "I come not for my own pleasure, nor for his, but in the name of Christ, to warn him of foul treason." She stood there obstinately and it was obvious that she had no intention of allowing herself to be frightened off. The effect of her words began to sink in.

"Treason," repeated the guard dully.

Anne raised her voice as loudly as she dared. "The crime of desertion is accounted treason, is it not?"

There was a flicker of light from within the tent as someone lit a candle. The tall shape of a man was outlined against the canvas, then filled the doorway of the tent with its dark bulk. As she looked up at the man they called the Giant, Anne had a moment of shivering doubt before he spoke, but it was too late to change her mind.

"Someone spoke of treason," he said, his voice low yet heavy like the sound of the death drum.

"I did, my lord," said Anne, quickly recovering herself before the guard could speak. "I have proof of treason, but it is for your ears only."

With a quick motion of his hand he cut off the guard's flustered attempt at explanation.

"It seems I will entertain a lady tonight after all," he said in the same low voice, and Anne realized that he spoke for the benefit of the guard, who had visibly relaxed at the comment. Standing aside, he gestured her into the tent, and as she stood uncertainly inside she heard him tell the guard to remain at his post unless called for.

"You said you had proof, madam. I hope for your sake that you speak the truth, for I have no interest in rumors." He did not ask her to be seated, and remained standing himself, towering over her in the sure knowledge that his height alone would intimidate.

"My lord, before I speak, I must have a promise from you."

"It is not my habit to promise informers anything."

"My lord, it is a simple thing." Frightened though she was, Anne knew she must match him in this and best him, otherwise some one of the men meeting in Robert's valley would see that she could never again betray anyone. "You do not know my name, my lord, nor can you ever. And my face you must forget the instant I leave this tent."

"Your face is hidden in your hood, madam."

"Nor," she continued inexorably, "must you reveal to anyone that a woman brought you this information. There are those who would know that only one woman in this camp could possibly have knowledge of their plans and the place of their meeting. Those are my terms, my lord."

"I am a reasonable and realistic man," said Montferrat finally. "Some who speak of me thus do so in criticism, but I take it as a compliment, as a realistic man might be expected to do. I grant you your terms."

"Thank you, my lord. You will not regret it."

"Don't waste my time now, madam. I am growing impatient."

"There is a parliament meeting in a valley one hour's ride from here. You have only to follow the river and you will come upon them before they can know of your approach. I know nothing of their plans except that they will not go to Constantinople, and that whether they remain behind on this island or demand that ships be supplied them from the fleet, they will take the half of your army with them, to Syria, Hungary or back to Italy."

"Names, madam."

"I can name no man."

"Names, madam. Or you do not leave this tent alive."

No one doubted the word of the Marquis of Montferrat. Slowly she began to name the men she had seen talking to Robert or Peter in the past few days, men who came from all the divisions of the army and all the regions of France. "Guy of Coucy, James of Avesnes, Odo of Champlitte, Richard of Dampierre and his brother Odo, William of Aunoi." The list went on until at last she could remember no others.

"There is one you have not mentioned, madam, one whom I suspect is at the very core of this conspiracy."

"My lord?"

"Search your memory, madam. I would have you forget nothing of importance to me in this matter."

The threat was plain. It was no use attempting to conceal anything from this man who knew everything.

"Peter of Amiens."

"I thought so. It is good that you did not forget to mention him after all. As far as I am concerned you have never existed. You may go."

"Please, my lord. What will you do?"

"That is no concern of yours. You have betrayed someone who trusted you, and while I shall profit from your betrayal, I am not obliged to tolerate your presence any longer. I do not like snakes and other low creatures."

It was unbearable that he should speak to her like that. Her taut nerves hummed with anger at the insult and she drew herself to her full height and stared pointedly at the cross stitched to his shirt, the cross that represented Jerusalem.

"Snakes are often found in one another's company, my lord, and in the darkness of the night one snake looks much like any other."

She slipped quickly past him and fled back toward her tent, half fearing she would be stopped. But he had made no move to block her exit from the tent, and the guard had studiously averted his eyes from the distraught woman who dashed past him. I am not even important enough to rouse his anger, she

thought furiously. But we shall meet again some day, my great
lord, in the daylight, and perhaps then you will wonder at the
scorn a noble lady shows you. I shall have my revenge on you,
and it will be sweet. But you will never know the cause of your
despair.

The secret parliament ended in confusion and a compromise,
for Montferrat, as Anne had hoped, moved swiftly and decisively, with the impressive threatricality that marked all his actions.

Before she had reached her own tent, the Counts of Flanders,
Blois and St. Pol had been awakened and summoned to Montferrat's presence. In a few words he told them of the conspiracy
and outlined the means they would use to combat it. There was
no argument, no discussion even, for they had to move speedily
and the Marquis's instinct was sure.

Within a half hour a long column of mounted men had set out
along the riverbank, their horses' hooves bound in cloth to
deaden the sound of their approach. Montferrat rode at the head
of the column, Alexius beside him, his ears straining to catch the
Marquis's instructions. He was not to speak, only to show himself, to sit his horse in majestic splendor, and to compose his face
in sorrowful yet noble lines. He could do it, he assured the
Marquis, but perhaps a stirring speech to the malcontents might
also be in order? Montferrat did not even bother to reply.

The Counts of Flanders, Blois and St. Pol had spaced themselves along the length of the column, for in it rode a near relative or friend of almost every man in the valley. They were
being urged to use all the persuasions of kinship and comrade-
ship to sway the decision that could spell the end of the crusade.
Villehardouin, too, rode up and down the line, for many of the
deserters were from Champagne, and again he had been shamed
by his countrymen. Even if they do repent their treachery, he
promised himself, their names and the action they attempted
shall not be forgotten. He would confound them utterly with the
power of the written word.

The Bishops of Halberstadt and Soissons rode in the midst of
a group of priests and monks, a silent force of group prayer.

Montferrat had left nothing to chance. If a man did not respond to a relative's entreaty, then Holy Mother Church would move in with prayer, exhortation and the threat of eternal damnation.

As they moved into the valley it became obvious that in spite of their precautions they had been heard. The sound of splashing water carried far in the night air, and there had been no way to avoid it. A solid phalanx of silent men stood waiting for them, while here and there a grim face glowed for a moment in the torchlight.

Obedient to the Marquis's instructions, Alexius sat his horse in silence, but he could not resist a gesture all his own. He moved the white horse forward until he was within a few yards of the men he sought to impress, allowing it to prance and caper as though it were being ridden on parade. And all the while he himself wore what he fondly assumed was the look of a great leader wounded to his heart's blood by the treachery of the men at whose head he would gladly lay down his life in battle. He was enjoying the scene and picturing how it would look reproduced in mosaic tile on the walls of the Blachernae Palace. Indeed, some emotion at last seemed to be stirring on the faces of the dissidents.

My God, thought the Marquis, as he watched Alexius pose and posture in the moonlight. After all I taught him he still can't carry it off. He looks like a grinning monkey on horseback. Damn the fool! A few faces in the crowd seemed to be smiling. If they began laughing out loud at him it was all over with.

Montferrat looked significantly at the barons and bishops who had drawn their horses around him in a semicircle. He saw dismay written on their faces, and heard St. Pol hiss in his ear, "Draw their attention away from him before it's too late."

"Follow me and do exactly as I do," he hissed back, then he leaped from his horse and ran to kneel before the astonished Peter of Amiens. Hugh of St. Pol knelt beside him, weeping as loudly as Montferrat, and in the confusion that followed, as all who had ridden so urgently through the night followed his example, Alexius on his white horse was pushed aside unnoticed until he found himself on the dark edge of the crowd in the midst of the now riderless horses.

One after another the barons spoke, pleading with the dissidents to remember their vows of knighthood and their more sacred promise to do all in their power to liberate the Holy Land. Men moved through the crowd seeking their relatives and friends, adding their entreaties to those of their leaders until the two parties were inextricably mixed and all pretense of order was gone.

Peter of Amiens tried to speak above the clamor, but his voice, even when raised to a shout, was drowned by other, more insistent voices, and no one heard what he said. At last, in desperation, he rudely shoved the Bishop of Halberstadt aside and, seizing a brightly flaring torch, began marching up one of the rocky slopes. Robert, Aleaumes and Thomas, also carrying torches, followed him, and as the moving lights attracted the attention of the crowd, a hush fell over it.

Peter's voice rang out in the darkness. "My lords, you have interrupted a parliament of free men whose only desire is to obey the voice of conscience. You seek to divide us with your accusations and your entreaties. Yet we will not be divided. Draw apart, men of honor, and join me here on this hillside. We will consult together and answer our accusers with one voice. Each man shall have his say and none shall be coerced. I pledge myself to abide by the decision reached in lawful parliament, whatever it may be, and I ask each of you to do likewise."

Montferrat watched the silent men troop toward the light under which Peter of Amiens stood like some prophet of old preaching to his people from a stony hillside in the Holy Land. He brushed the dirt from his knees and to Baldwin of Flanders's worried question answered only, "They are ours."

"Until Michaelmas, my lord," said Guy of Coucy, avoiding the eye of his uncle, Matthew of Montmorency, who had a short time before called him names it were better to forget. "We will loyally perform whatever duty you demand of us, but only until Michaelmas, and only on condition that after that date, you will furnish us ships, if we request them, within fifteen days of our demand."

Four months, thought Montferrat. That should be time enough and to spare.

"Gladly will I and all other men of good faith keep that covenant with you and yours, and we will swear to it on holy relics." Montferrat clasped Guy of Coucy's hand in a bone-crushing grip, and as the poet grimaced in pain, shouts of laughter broke out on all sides.

The revolt was over.

PART III

June, 1203-March, 1204

Alas! Why did my eyes gaze at her,
That sweet, False Friend?
She mocks me, and I have wept so over her.
No man has ever been so gently betrayed.
When I was master of myself, all was well.
But now I am hers, and she brings me death,
For no other reason but that I have loved her with
  all my heart.
    I can find no other cause.

—Chanson de croisade
Guy of Coucy

I

Behind them lay a long string of dubious conquests: the city of
Zara razed to the ground, Corfu punished for its insult to Prince
Alexius and its ineffectual, halfhearted attack on the fleet, islands such as Andros overrun, impoverished by their attempts to
buy off the crusaders, fields picked clean and storehouses emptied by the army's need for grain. The latest victim had been
the rich city of Abydos, where for eight days part of the fleet
had lain at anchor awaiting the slower transports and the foraging Venetian galleys. The corn had been standing tall and green-
gold in the fields around Abydos when the crusaders accepted
the city's hasty surrender; not an ear remained when they left,
and even the stripped stalks had been carried on board the ships
to feed the horses. The city would starve this winter, but no one
cared, for at last the ships had entered the Straits of St. George
and the towers of Constantinople shimmered in the distance.

Tomorrow was the Feast of St. John the Baptist, an important
day in the Church's calendar and one which would live in every
crusader's memory as the day on which the fleet sailed past the
sea walls of Mickle Garth, the almost legendary city whose
wealth and grandeur had long fascinated Western Christendom.

Knights and soldiers crowded to the ships' rails, gazing at the
walls of Constantinople, pointing out to one another the high
roofs of its many palaces and the domes of its churches, assessing the strength of the defensive towers which rose at regular intervals as far as the eye could see. They were still three leagues
away from the city, clustered in the small port area of the
fortified Abbey of St. George, and the bright rays of the summer's sun reflecting on the blue waters of the Straits dazzled and

blinded them. Men turned from the glare to hang their blazoned shields over the ships' sides, but found themselves irresistibly drawn back to the rails, straining their eyes to pierce through the tantalizing haze that veiled the city.

The counts and barons of the army had assembled in parliament with the Doge in the Church of St. Stephen to decide the course the vessels would take the following day. Many of the French wanted to disembark immediately; the cramped quarters on board ship had taken their toll on men and horses alike. Now the barons were anxious to re-form their companies, to exercise muscles slack and weakened from disuse, to recapture the discipline and the precise interaction between man and beast that would be all-important in the assault on the city whose land walls beckoned in the distance. The Doge shook his head despairingly at their naïveté. The land walls of Constantinople had stood impregnable for eight hundred years, a triple barricade running outward from the city, closely studded with easily defensible towers, further protected by a deep and enormously wide ditch which could be flooded at will. There was not the slightest hope of passing these defenses, and once the army had seen their might, despair would quickly erode morale. None of the barons could guarantee that their hungry men would not leave the main body to forage and loot on their own, and many would be killed or uselessly maimed by the soldiers and populace of the surrounding countryside.

Constantinople did have one fatal weakness, however. Its navy was practically nonexistent. No new ships had been constructed for years now because the Emperor would not permit the tall trees of his favorite hunting grounds to be cut down. The shipbuilders of the Arsenal had been grimly amused at such folly; it was further evidence of Greek decadence. Venice's spies had reported that there were perhaps twenty seaworthy ships of war that could be expected to sail against them, but their captains and crews were inferior sailors and it was highly unlikely that they would be capable of anything but the merest token show of force. Protected as they had been for so many generations by their land walls, the people of Constantinople had become complacent and overconfident. They lived in the past glories of their city and forgot that the sea was a broader highway than any the Romans had ever built. The men of the sea, the keen-eyed men who looked always to the future, would teach them a bitter lesson.

A subtle shift of leadership took place during that parliament in St. Stephen's, as Boniface of Montferrat deferred to the clearly reasoned logic of Venice's Doge. His presence with the army took on added value, for he alone among them possessed any personal knowledge of Constantinople and the waters that guarded it on two sides. Thirty years ago he had come here on a trading mission; some said that it was the Greeks of this very city who had by treachery deprived him of his sight. Sightless he might now be, but in his mind's eye he carried details of the city's harbors and of the swift-moving currents they must sail against. Even the opposite shore, where the pleasure palaces of the rich lay, was no secret to him.

It was to this shore that he now counseled them to sail, to the group of islands known as the Princes' Islands, where the fields awaited the harvest and the people were without defense. Supplies could be gathered at their leisure and the horses could be exercised while the people of Constantinople, watching on their walls, grew fainthearted and despairing at the sight of so much power amassed against them. When there was no hope of a surprise attack on an enemy, his will could be weakened by an overwhelming display of strength.

The barons brought news of the decision back to their ships and throughout the night preparations for a landing on the Princes' Islands continued. Not all were strictly warlike, however, for the barons were confident that little resistance would be met the next day. It was a strangely leisurely evening on board most of the ships as the night breezes revived spirits that had labored under the day's unaccustomed heat. Beards were trimmed and faces shaved that had not known a razor in weeks. The sailors hauled buckets of seawater onto the decks and the grime- and salt-encrusted knights for once enjoyed the chore of bathing. There would be wine and women aplenty on the islands; it was a last respite before the hot and dirty business of fighting began again.

As the moon rose and the stars twinkled above them, so close, it seemed, that you had only to reach out a hand to touch them, the men sprawled on the open decks, some to fall asleep with a smile on their lips for the pleasures the morrow would bring, others to talk quietly, reminiscently, of the events of the voyage now nearly ended.

Sir Guy of Coucy had died somewhere on the open sea between Andros and Abydos and his weighted body had been slipped overboard to disappear forever under the foam-topped waves. His fellow knights shook their heads over it. A man's body ought to lie in a grave of his own choosing, before the altar on which Masses for his soul would be sung, in a hallowed place where his widow and his descendants could come to pay him homage and remember the joy of his living. The sailors laughed. What difference if the flesh were consumed by the fishes of the ocean or the worms of the ground? The end was the same and all men were mortal. But something of the Castellan of Coucy lived on, for he had been a skilled poet, and the minstrels were singing his sweet laments into the night air. He had written of the pain of parting from one's beloved and of the mutual sufferings and unrequited longings during the years of separation, his words so simple and his emotions so nakedly exposed that each man felt the lord of Coucy had spoken for him alone. Years might pass before the lucky ones saw their wives and children again, yet even the joy of homecoming would not be without its sorrow, for there would be the widows and orphans of friends to console and there would always be the memory of broken bodies in hastily dug graves.

Lately some of the bitterness toward those who had deserted the army had softened because of an incident that had occurred near Maléa. The fleet had met two of the ships that had sailed on their own from Marseilles to Syria. The knights and pilgrims aboard had been defiant and a little fearful, knowing full well that their failure to join the army in Venice had been the cause of the strange alliance between the Doge and the crusaders. They had heard of the destruction of Zara, of the Pope's anger, and of the rumors that the entire army was excommunicant. Nevertheless, one of their number, a sergeant, had himself rowed to Count Baldwin's ship where he announced that he was quit of his former companions and was prepared to sail with the fleet to conquer new lands. If one such, and he not even a knight, could see the error of his ways and be brought by God to a change of heart, might not others also? True, they would be too late to help in the restoration of Alexius to his rightful place and could claim no part in the glorious work of reuniting the heretic Greeks to Rome, but they would still be made welcome in the Holy Land. There might be many empty places to fill in the ranks, and these new men, if they came, would fight the harder to wipe out the stain of their past shame.

Robert and Aleaumes, sitting in the prow of St. Pol's ship with Peter and Thomas of Amiens, wondered aloud if perhaps Enguerrand and Robert of Boves might not rejoin the army someday. The events on Corfu, and in particular the fulfillment of Enguerrand's gloomy prediction, had weighed on all their minds in the last weeks. Even now Peter brooded on the ease with which Montferrat had appeased them.

"Did we do right to give in so quickly?" he often asked. "Could we not have held out longer, driven a harder bargain?"

"We have Montferrat's sworn word that he will do our bidding after Michaelmas," Robert reassured him. "There are hundreds of witnesses to it. He will not dare break the agreement."

Peter was no longer a leader of the dissident faction in the army, simply because that faction had ceased to exist. A strange metamorphosis had taken place after Corfu. It was almost as though there had never been any opposition to the Marquis's plans, as though the challenge to his leadership had never taken place, and many men, when reminded of the active part they had played in the conspiracy, responded with blank stares. Conscience had been served and salved; now it was time to get on with the business of conquest.

Even Peter shared this mentality to some extent, as his deep-felt loyalty to Hugh of St. Pol reasserted itself and his soldier's impatience for battle increased. Only occasionally, as tonight, did he sink into preoccupied silence. Most of his days were spent at his cousin's side, and though St. Pol shared few confidences with him, being still unsure of his shaken loyalty, he managed to convey the impression that all was forgiven and forgotten and that he looked to Peter as to his strong right arm.

Robert had grown tired of the problem. It had never been

much of a moral dilemma to him anyway, more a question of clash of duty, with the fealty owed directly to Peter easily winning out over the more distant service due the Count. He yearned for Anne and his arms ached to hold her again. The lord of Coucy's songs were an agony to listen to, yet he frequently sought out one of the minstrels and slipped him a coin to play one of Guy's bittersweet *chansons*. Whatever else Constantinople held for him, the promise of reunion with his beloved was enough to inspire him to fight with all the pent-up fury of a legion of devils. Tomorrow the promise would be fulfilled and the future would begin to open up at last.

Early on the morning of the feast of the Baptist the fleet began to sail past the walls of Constantinople. The wind was carrying them, not to the Princes' Islands as planned, but toward Chalcedon on the Asiatic coast where one of the Emperor Alexius III's finest palaces stood. If the Doge was dismayed by this, he did not show it; all men of the sea know that the wind is a capricious mistress at best.

The sea walls of Constantinople were densely packed with people, some of whom had waited all night to catch a glimpse of the strangers who had appeared so suddenly, so menacingly, from the Western European countries they despised for their poverty and barbaric customs. The Emperor himself was surely among those crowds or perhaps watching from the rooftop of the Boucoleon Palace, and the Doge stood the taller in his gaily painted galley for knowing that his enemy's eyes were upon him.

Innocent had thought to warn the Emperor that there was a plan afoot to attack Constantinople, but had assured him that the plot would come to naught. He, the Pope, had discovered it in time and forbidden it on pain of excommunication. After Zara the Pope had written the leaders of the crusade, bluntly exposing their treacherous design and condemning it in strong words. But the letter had never reached them, and though the barons were certain that the Pope's messengers were vainly trying to catch up to them, the main body of fighting men thought that they had Innocent's blessing on the enterprise. It mattered little to the Doge, either the Pope's anger or the fact that the Emperor had probably been put on his guard. He ought to have

known that one day Venice would come to right the injustices
done to its majesty. Alexius III had sealed his city's doom on the
day he had flagrantly broken the long and preferential treaty the
Venetians had enjoyed with the Greek Empire. Genoese and
Pisan traders were the new favorites, but their hour was almost
done. This stripling nephew of the Greek Emperor who strutted
so arrogantly on the deck of Montferrat's ship, Montferrat himself, his barons and his army, with their hypocritical lip service
to Jerusalem, all were merely pawns in the Doge's grand scheme
—pawns to be deployed, then swept from the board when the
game was over.

The sun rose higher, its rays blinding the watchers on the
walls so that they shaded their eyes with their hands, unwilling
to believe that the more than two hundred ships passing before
them were anything but tricks played by sun and water, like the
mirages that sometimes appeared in the early morning mists,
ghostly reflections of ships that sailed other seas. But these vessels refused to disappear; they sailed closer and closer to the
wall and the people of Constantinople could make out the
figures of steel-clad men standing shoulder to shoulder on the
decks, so close-packed that they seemed to grow out of one another's sides like some monstrous beast of many members.

For hours they remained on their walls, yet still more ships
came sailing up the Straits. Those in the distance looked like
glittering jewels floating above the water, the chain-link armor
and highly polished shields of the knights casting the sun's glitter back into the increasingly more frightened faces of the
beholders. The far-off sails were like a never-ending, cloud-filled
sky, while the huge red crosses painted on them spoke of the
fiery vengeance of a bloodthirsty god. The vanguard of the fleet
was already anchored at Chalcedon, its ships disgorging horses
and men who swarmed like ants toward the Emperor's palace
when the slower vessels at last wallowed past the city. From the
decks of the laggards a rain of catapults was fired at the nearest
towers and at the Greek fishing vessels peacefully at anchor in
their small harbors. It was as though they defiantly assured the
city that though the ships on which they sailed might be slower

and more clumsy than the others, the men on board were not to
be despised.

All that day and throughout the one that followed, Constantinople waited, its Emperor hourly expecting an envoy to appear
at the city's gates. If it was war the foreigners wanted, there
would be a formal *défi* to be answered. Such was the custom
among Western knights. If, as Innocent had promised him, the
plans were not to conquer, then perhaps the ships were in need
of supplies. In that case the envoy would be properly humble
and Alexius III was prepared to meet his requests, no matter
how outrageous. Other greedy invaders had been bought off
many times in the past. That was the highly successful Greek
custom. But though the watch regularly reported to the Emperor, the story was always the same. No vessel of any size had
put out from the opposite shore, nor could even the keenest eye
discern any being readied to sail.

Spies sent to Chalcedon brought back even grimmer news. A
Frankish lord had slept the night in the Emperor's own bed, the
pleasure palaces that often housed the court swarmed with gog-
gle-eyed knights who were efficiently despoiling them of anything of value, even carrying off the sacred icons and gold altar
vessels of the private palace chapels, and all the houses of the
city had been taken over, their owners chased out with just the
clothes on their backs. Tents had been pitched everywhere and
the streets were clogged with the dung of thousands of horses.
Some of the people had hidden themselves in the fields, but even
that refuge was denied them, for the crops were being brought
in, not by the farmers who had planted them, but by the common soldiers of the Western army under the direction of their
leaders.

Still Alexius III waited, more ready to be influenced by those
of his councillors who reminded him of Constantinople's invul-
nerability than by the few who urged a massive attack before
the invaders had time to provision and strengthen themselves.
He had noted the presence of the distinctive Venetian war galleys among the large troop and supply vessels of the fleet, and
he had been informed by the Pope that the Doge himself had
taken the cross, but it seemed impossible that a man of over
eighty could have survived the long voyage. If Dandolo was in-

deed resting his aged bones in Chalcedon then war was probably inevitable, but, he reminded his two sons-in-law, Theodore
Lascaris and Alexius Dukas, no one had yet positively identified
Dandolo, though some claimed to have seen him yesterday
standing beneath the vermilion canopy of an elaborately painted
galley.

"He is there," Alexius Dukas declared positively. "And though
the others may secretly desire to be bought off with gold, that
man alone will never agree to it."

"We must attack now," urged Lascaris, "while they think us
unprepared and awed by their numbers."

"We are safe within the city," was the Emperor's decision.
"We will wait."

Late that night another spy was admitted to the Emperor's
presence and Lascaris and Dukas were hastily summoned from
their beds to hear his report. The man had been discovered and
had been wounded making his escape through the narrow
streets of Chalcedon, but the news he brought was so important
that he had refused to have his wound treated until after he had
seen the Emperor.

"Enrico Dandolo is there," he told them. "I saw him with my
own eyes, a man so old that age has no more meaning for him. I
heard other names also, the Counts of Flanders, St. Pol and
Blois, and the commander, a cousin of the King of France,
Boniface, Marquis of Montferrat. There will be no *défi*, though
an attack on the city is being planned even now. The Frankish
lords would have proclaimed their intent, but Dandolo stood
against them. He said that his presence was all the *défi* required
and they gave in to him. The ships will move again tomorrow
morning, but I could not learn where. Not even the captains
have been informed yet."

"Dandolo will lead them to Scutari. The harbor there provides
good anchorage and it is a short sail across it to the mouth of the
Horn. He knows our coastline well, too well." Alexius Dukas's
voice was bitter, and the thick black eyebrows meeting over his
hawk nose that had given him the nickname Murtzuphles made
him seem blacker and more warlike than usual.

"The Horn is protected by its chain and by the Galata tower.
The tower will never fall and the chain will remain in place. The

Doge's ships will dance on the waves in their frustration, but they will never sail up the Golden Horn. Nevertheless, the army will prepare tonight to march to the shore opposite Scutari in case your prediction should prove correct. If necessary, I myself will lead them." The Emperor's voice was calm. He had no doubt that the mere sight of his imperial presence would be enough to frighten the Frankish lords into a compromise, and somehow Dandolo could be dealt with also.

The messenger lay prostrate on the floor before his emperor, but now he raised his head slowly, forcing himself to divulge the last and most bitter of his intelligences. "Prince Alexius also lies in Chalcedon palace," he said, as every eye was fixed on him. "Among the soldiers it is said that he prays nightly for his father's deliverance, with much weeping and great lamentation. He claims the scarlet buskins in Isaac's name."

The Emperor grimaced, unsurprised. The Pope had been most explicit. "I should have had him blinded, too, and gelded for good measure. More likely he prays that my brother has long since died so that he can call himself emperor with an easy conscience. He was ever a treacherous, sniveling stripling, though once I found him useful to me. This time, however, I will see to him personally, and father and son will share the same executioner."

The messenger was dismissed with a purse of gold to reward his efforts, but Theodore Lascaris and Alexius Dukas lingered. There was strategy to be planned and the crusaders' tactics to be guessed at in the little time that they felt remained to them. But the Emperor soon sent them away, for dawn was only a few hours hence and he loved the soft pleasures of his bed. Even now, with the mightiest army of Western Christendom mustered against him, he would turn for distraction to the willing body of a woman and the cool taste of a fine wine.

From that day forward Alexius Dukas wore such a look that men seldom spoke his given name. Murtzuphles he became in truth, a name that had begun as a jest but now bespoke a force as dark and unyielding as the face of the man itself. That night, as he heard Alexius III, Emperor of the Byzantines, call for a eunuch to summon a certain Nubian slave from his well-filled harem, loathing for his father-in-law filled his heart, and he knew deep shame that such a one should call himself Emperor of Constantinople. If I were Emperor, he thought, these Franks and Venetians would be crushed beneath my foot like insects. If I were Emperor. The thought and the ambition it awoke lodged themselves permanently in his soul and would one day bear strange fruit.

The fleet sailed to Scutari the next day as Murtzuphles had said it would and another of the Emperor's summer palaces was defiled by the foreigners. As the knights and foot soldiers marched northward along the coast to where their ships already lay at anchor in Scutari harbor, they could see a vast army streaming out of Constantinople's mighty gates. The Greeks made their camp opposite the crusaders' own, and as the Franks continued to forage in the rich fields around the Emperor's palace, they often paused to gaze across the Straits to where Alexius's men had pitched their tents. The Greeks waited patiently, lined up in deep, stretched-out ranks before their city, ready to repel a landing from the high-sided transports. The moment of landing was the most vulnerable for a seaborne force; horses often grew excited at the cold shock of the sea and attempted to pitch off their heavily armored riders, while the less-well-protected sergeants and common soldiers plunged through the waves under a hail of arrows and deadly crossbolts. All dreaded that moment, knowing it must come, for the triangle that was Constantinople was protected on two sides by the waters of the Sea of Marmara and the Golden Horn, yet no other approach to the city was possible.

One of the foraging parties, composed of some eighty knights led by Count Girard of Lombardy, met and defeated a Greek contingent of over five hundred knights, and the heartening tale soon spread throughout the army. The Emperor had sent his own brother-in-law, the Grand Duke of Constantinople, with a band of handpicked Greek knights to spy on the Franks and pick off any who wandered too far from their fellows. The Grand Duke, Michael Stryphnos, made a splendid camp at the base of a mountain three leagues away from where the crusaders were assembled and it was the sight of all this luxury in the field that had whetted the appetites of the men who rode with Count Girard.

"I thought it a good time to test the Greek fighting mettle," the Count said afterward, "for with the mountain at their backs they would have to stand firm against us. We divided ourselves into four battalions and the Greeks likewise formed their ranks, but almost as soon as we fell upon them they threw down their weapons and scattered in all directions, running like frightened rats back to their city."

"Odds of more than six to one against us, and still they fled," said Odo of Champlitte in disgust. "We were so few in number we were hard pressed to bring back all the horses and mules they left behind them."

The camp cheered the return of Count Girard's party and from all over Scutari men gathered to gaze with envy on the rich booty they brought back. The fine war stallions and handsome palfreys were led away to be gentled and mingled with the herds of horses brought from Europe, while a hundred or more tents and gold-emblazoned pavilions were unloaded from the pack mules. Even in the field it seemed the Greeks dined off gold and silver plate and brought with them the exotic jewel-encrusted icons before which they bent themselves in prayer. If riches such as these could be won in a skirmish that had lasted but a few minutes, a fight in which not a single Frank had even been wounded, what glories awaited them inside the city itself? They raised their voices in derisive hoots, lifting their arms in obscene gestures at the weakling army across the Straits. It was going to be an easy campaign after all. The Greeks were no better fighters than women.

Villehardouin heard a report of the fight from Odo of Champlitte, immensely pleased that so many men of Champagne had been numbered in the party which had made the first contact with the Greeks. The names of his daring countrymen sang in his ears, Manasses of l'Isle and Oger of Saint-Chéron, who had taken the cross at Ecri and never faltered in their loyalty since that day, Odo himself and his brother William, who had pledged themselves later at Cîteaux. Fine men all, whose actions deserved recognition and whose names would burn brighter for the contrast with the many Champenois who had deserted. Villehardouin was not fooled by this first easy victory. He knew that it had been a chance encounter, a fluke that would not be repeated unless the Greeks were really more stupid than anyone imagined, but like the others his spirits rose at the thought of it and with good heart he entered into the general rejoicing.

The incident, and the sight of his Grand Duke cowering before him, frightened Alexius III more than he cared to admit even to himself. He flew into a violent rage, screamed cruelly descriptive epithets and obscenities at his brother-in-law, and descended from his throne to beat and kick the man who had covered the name of Angelus with shame. Even blind Isaac would not have run as swiftly from the field as their sister's weak-livered husband.

Theodore Lascaris and Murtzuphles watched their father-in-law's display, unmoved by pity for Michael Stryphnos. The man was unbelievably corrupt and had sought office only for the wealth he could acquire by bribery and fear. As Admiral of the Fleet he had even sold the sails and anchors from the few ships he commanded. If blame lay anywhere for Constantinople's weakness on the sea, it lay on the head of the Grand Duke. It might be too late to undo the damage he had done over the years, but it was grim satisfaction to know that he had at last fallen from his high eminence. Alexius III threatened him with blinding, castration and beheading, but as his rage spent itself and his speech became more intelligible, Stryphnos heard with relief the word imprisonment. Some of the watching courtiers realized that every man might soon be needed, even such a one as the now-disgraced Duke. Fortunes at the Greek court rose and fell with dizzying rapidity; even as Michael Stryphnos was being led away to the place of his confinement he saw smiles of sympathy on faces turned carefully away from the Emperor's view.

The army would stay where it was, just in case the Franks, emboldened by their easy victory, chanced a surprise attack on the region around the Galata tower. In the meantime an envoy would be sent to the crusaders' camp. He would bear letters of credit from the Emperor and would touch not at all on the sinister aspect of the Frankish army's actions. Flattery spoken in their own language would be the strategy employed against the barbarians, and just in case they were immune to subtleties, an outright bribe would be offered in the plainest possible words. Nicholas Roux, a Lombard who had lived long and prosperously in Constantinople, was the man chosen for the task.

The counts, barons and commanders of the army were gathered in council in the throne room of the Scutari Palace when word was brought them that the long-expected envoy of Alexius III had presented himself at the palace gates. A flurry of speculation broke out, abruptly cut short by Boniface of Montferrat, who reminded them all that no matter what terms the Emperor had chosen to offer, the restoration of Prince Alexius to his rightful place in the land must be the primary condition for peace.

The barons tended to forget the prince's presence among them, for he was usually excluded from the council meetings and had never, since the disastrous night on Corfu, been allowed to address them formally. Boniface saw to it that he was kept amused and out of the way, and the young man had seemingly accepted the obvious slur with no thought for his own pride of rank. Now he was quickly sent for, and as Boniface escorted him to his uncle's throne the knights and barons bowed respectfully at his passing.

He certainly looked the king, for he was garbed in Byzantine robes heavily encrusted with jewels and gold-embroidered devices of fantastic intricacy. He glittered as he walked, swaying slightly under the heaviness of his garments. Louis of Blois caught the distinctive scent of wine as the prince brushed against him to mount the steps to the throne. He repressed a snicker and met the eye of St. Pol, who stood just opposite. This peacock clad in the loot found in the Emperor's wardrobe was already unsteady on his feet and the sun not yet at its zenith.

Louis and St. Pol both inclined their heads a bit more than was necessary, the better to remind the others fanned out at the foot of the throne that there was a game to be played here. Let no one forget that the strongest argument for their presence in Constantinople was the person of the prince. When the Pope's wrath fell upon them, and none of the barons doubted that it would, Alexius alone could turn it to approval by restoring the Greek Church to Rome.

Nicholas Tripsychos slipped quietly through a small door behind the throne and came to stand slightly behind Villehardouin. The envoy, waiting now on the other side of the massive oak doors at the far end of the chamber, had identified himself as a Lombard, but if the Emperor's letters were written in Greek as they surely would be, a trustworthy interpreter committed to the Frankish cause would be needed to verify the accuracy of translation.

When all were in place the Marquis stationed Conon of Béthune at his side. He would speak in all of their names, for even Montferrat was impressed by the brilliance with which the poet could argue a point with only the sketchiest of preliminary briefings. A few whispered words in the ear of Prince Alexius, who sat up straighter on the hard throne and laid his hands majestically on the armrests, and all was ready.

The doors swung open silently and Nicholas Roux entered the room, all eyes fixed on him as he paced slowly toward the throne. He seemed not to see the glittering figure of the prince, or chose perhaps to pretend he was not there, too visible a slap in the face of his own emperor, for he came to a halt before Montferrat and presented his letters to the Marquis with a polite though undeferential bow.

Some were written in Greek, some in Latin, and Nicholas Tripsychos quickly scanned them in the total silence that lay heavily on the room. He verified that the Latin documents were true copies of the Greek, and they were read aloud to the barons by the mellifluous-voiced Conon of Béthune.

When all had agreed that the bearer, Nicholas Roux, was properly accredited to speak in the name of the Emperor, he was invited to present Alexius III's message to the assembly.

The Lombard's eyes had never strayed from the Marquis's face during the reading of his credentials. He was a fellow countryman, though his lot was cast with other interests, and he seemed to be trying to penetrate the inscrutable look with which Boniface regarded him. To those watching it seemed a duel of the eyes, with no advantage won by either side. Both men were cold and impassive. They looked at each other without real interest, for both knew that strength and avarice alone would decide the outcome of this confrontation. But Nicholas Roux had been so long in Constantinople that he had become slightly Byzantine, insular, a bit fatalistic. He was thus the weaker of the two, though he did not know it.

"Lords," he began, after clearing his throat loudly, "the Emperor Alexius acknowledges that you are, of those who wear no crowns, the finest people in the world, and from the best of countries. He marvels greatly at your coming, why and to what purpose you have entered his kingdom; you are Christians and he is Christian, and he knows that you are journeying to the Holy Land to the relief of the Holy Sepulcher. If you are poor and in need he will freely give you of his goods and his wealth so that you may leave his lands. He wishes that no evil be done you, yet he has the power to do so, for even if your numbers were twenty times as great as they are, he could, if he wished, prevent your leaving or destroy you utterly."

The bribe had been offered and the threat behind it unveiled. Though his person as envoy was sacred, Nicholas Roux knew a moment's fear as the men who had listened to his short speech began to mutter and growl low in their throats. Then Conon of Béthune descended to the bottom step of the dais and raised his hand for silence. When it came, he paused to bow low before the stiff figure of the prince and the man who towered beside him, then turned to speak directly to Nicholas Roux. His voice was so soft that men leaned forward to hear him, a calculated bit of showmanship that contrasted sharply with the loud, rasping tone the Lombard had employed.

"Fair sir," he said, smiling gravely as a teacher does when forced to explain a simple problem to a dull student, "you have told us that your lord is perplexed and wonders why our lords and barons have entered his lands and kingdom. But we have not entered his land, for he holds it wrongly and sinfully, against God and all reason. Behold his nephew who sits enthroned amongst us, he who is true son of your lord's brother, the Emperor Isaac. If your lord wishes to place himself at the mercy of his nephew, if he will return to him his crown and his kingdom, we will use all our power to persuade the prince to pardon his uncle, and to assure that he may live freely here and in great wealth." He paused long enough for everyone to realize that Nicholas Roux's glance had at last rested on the prince. "And if you do not come with words of surrender on your lips, then do not come to us again." He bowed gracefully to the ambassador, then turned to bend the knee to his prince, his gesture so smooth and so spontaneous that it had the ring of sincerity to it. No one else moved.

"I will take my leave then, my lords, for I am not authorized to say more." As he left the throne room, Nicholas Roux had the eerie feeling that not a man there noticed his leaving. It would seem that the Franks were not disposed to negotiate. The Emperor would be furious and disbelieving.

As he passed through the anteroom, he felt a hand clutch his sleeve and he was drawn into a small alcove. "I am Nicholas Tripsychos, formerly of this city," said the man who now waved back the ambassador's escort. "And I would have a few words with you."

"I have heard your name spoken often, sir, by former pupils who continue to hold you in great respect."

"I am gratified to know that I am not forgotten in my birthplace. Will you sit beside me on this bench for a moment? I am too old to be running through the back corridors of a palace." Nicholas smiled and the ambassador relaxed. Old scholars seldom carried knives hidden in their sleeves.

"The Emperor will not yield." It was more a statement than a question.

"Never," replied Nicholas Roux. "He came to the throne bloodily and only in blood will he be forced from it."

"The men I serve have been told that the people of the city will rise spontaneously against the Emperor, for the grievances they bear against him. And further, that they will acclaim this army as saviors who restore to them their rightful ruler."

Nicholas Roux stared at this Greek who should have known better than to believe such nonsense. "Your leaders have been lied to and grossly misled. The people care nothing for Isaac's son, nor for Isaac himself. No one has lifted a finger in their behalf, nor will anyone now take notice of their claim. You are a Greek, Nicholas. You know I speak the truth. Can you not persuade these Franks of their folly?"

Nicholas shrugged. "They are more your people than mine. You saw them, did you not?"

"I saw the Doge and Montferrat."

"Then you know that they are set on a course from which there will be no turning back. They are fierce fighters who give no quarter. The city will not be able to hold against them."

"Constantinople has withstood many hordes of barbarians battering against its gates. You will exhaust yourselves to no purpose and finally we shall in charity bury the dead you will leave behind." Nicholas Roux had become the ambassador again, and rose from the bench where Nicholas Tripsychos continued to sit in silence. "Do not attempt to probe the Emperor's defenses through me. It is not worthy of you to play the spy."

"I play at nothing, my lord. But I forgive you your suspicions, for you serve a suspicious man and it is true we shall not meet again in peace. The lines have been too clearly drawn today. There is still time for flight and I counsel you to it, as one old man to another, for you are not a soldier."

"Nor am I a coward."

The ambassador stalked off, his back rigid with anger. The escort closed in behind him and he disappeared from sight. Nicholas, sighing, rose from the bench to return by the hidden door to the throne room from where he could already hear loud, excited voices. In times like these no one listened to the voice of reason.

II

Nicholas Roux did not return to Scutari, nor was there any change in the disposition of the Greek army. It remained encamped in full view of the crusaders, amply supplied from the city, seemingly willing and able to hold its position indefinitely. Now was the moment, argued the barons, to light the tinder of rebellion inside the city. None better would present itself.

They met in council to debate the matter, for in this army every baron and every knight now felt strongly that leadership was a shared responsibility. Montferrat's control had been temporarily shaken by the compromise he had been forced to make on Corfu and his commanders were determined that no more secret agreements would be engineered such as the one that had taken them to Zara. They no longer bore him a grudge for his partnership with the Doge, for the fruits of that deception promised to be sweet. Constantinople would be theirs and, after all, the knights who still held portions of the Holy Land were accustomed to waiting. But once burned, twice really, if Prince Alexius's cause was considered a separate matter, they were far more wary than in the days when they had first gathered together in Venice.

Their reasoning was eminently logical, but they could not know that the facts upon which their argument was based were a mere will-o'-the-wisp, having no basis in truth. Over and over they had been told that Constantinople yearned for the return of its rightful prince, that Alexius had only to present himself and the city's gates would open to receive him. They were so steeped in their own concept of lawful inheritance by the eldest son that they readily believed the story, for none among them was familiar with the long history of bloody usurpations which were common practice in Byzantium. In their own way they were honest men, and bewildered now by the way Nicholas Roux had remained unaffected by the sight of his lawful prince. He ought to have paled and trembled, given some sign of guilty fear at the reappearance of God's anointed heir. Even John Lackland had not dared hold out against Coeur-de-Lion once that king had returned from captivity. His own barons would have torn him to shreds, for by turning felon he would have damned their souls and their honor as well as his own. He had been forced to acknowledge his brother and play the loyal servitor, as this false emperor would also have to do. Upon the crusaders' heads rested the responsibility for initiating the action which in the natural course of events the Byzantines themselves would carry to its conclusion. The barons had a plan which they believed could not possibly fail.

Let the Venetian galleys draw apart from the rest of the fleet, they proposed, and let each galley be manned by a skeleton crew. The knights and barons, resplendent and dignified in their finest garments and polished armor, would board the galleys to form an impressive escort to the prince, who would stand in the prow of the Doge's own vessel with the highest lords of the army beside him. To the sound of regal trumpeting the galleys would sail as close as possible to the walls of Constantinople, avoiding that plain at the far north end of the city where the Emperor's army lay. Alexius's name and rank would be proclaimed to the people, who would not fail to crowd the walls at such a sight, and the rightness of his cause would then be made known to them. The barons did not doubt that revolt would break out immediately in the city, and as the Emperor had committed the tactical error of amassing his forces outside the walls, the citizenry would quickly overcome the remaining guards, locking the gates against the troops on the plain. It would all be over almost before anyone knew what had happened. The Emperor's army, trapped between the crusaders and the newly aroused and determined populace, would be forced to surrender. Then negotiations could begin in earnest.

They were immensely pleased with their plan and urged its immediate adoption. Cries of "Aye, aye," rang out all over the hall, a wave of sound that pounded against the silent opposition of the Doge and the Marquis. There was an element of danger in what was being proposed which the two men weighed carefully against the advantages to be gained, and they conferred quickly in whispers while the eager barons continued to press them with loud voices.

Alexius would be rejected, that much was certain. If they were lucky, silence would be his only reception; if not, there was always the chance that some determined Greek soldier would wound or kill the prince as he passed too close to one of the wall's towers. His safety could only be guaranteed if the galleys sailed carefully just out of bowshot range. Dandolo assured Boniface that his sailors were fully capable of keeping to that distance. But what would be the barons' reaction when the prince was spurned? Were there still those among them who would, even at this late date and with untold plunder before them, hold back from an attack on the city? Would they abandon Alexius, even as his people had abandoned him, and demand ships to sail immediately to the Holy Land? If they did, the last hope of conquering the city would disappear. Dandolo was willing to take the chance, willing to gamble on the pride and cupidity of the Franks, on the tremendous anger and righteous wrath they would feel at the sinful people of Constantinople. As much as the thought of the Holy Sepulcher in pagan hands was the driving force behind the crusade, so was the concept of loyalty to one's prince the cement that bound them all to the code of chivalry. And Alexius had sworn to turn his people from heresy. The barons would destroy Constantinople for the good of the souls within; there were still preachers in the army who would interpret Constantinople's obstinacy as a sign from God that such blindness and stubbornness in the face of right could only be cured by the sword. Their colloquy had taken only a few minutes, agreement reached almost instantly. The chance must be taken.

Boniface rose from his seat, taller, more massive than any other man in the chamber. Proudly he stood before his soldiers, and proudly he inclined his head, signifying his willingness to do as they bid him. They loved him for that gesture. He was strong and wise, the finest soldier among them, a man among men, yet superior because his rank lay so lightly on his pride. The reins of real command were fully restored to his fingers; Zara and Corfu might never have been.

The galleys rowed up and down before the walls of Constantinople, close enough to the city so that the people could hear the proclamation being read aloud to them, but far enough away so that the few arrows directed at the ships fell harmlessly into the blue waters.

Over and over the heralds shouted their message: "Behold your rightful lord, son and heir to Isaac, foully blinded and cast into prison, his throne and kingdom torn from him by an unnatural brother, he whom you now obey as your lord. Return to righteousness, cast out the usurper and bend the knee in obedience to your true Prince. Fear naught from us if you return to your duty, but know that if you do not, we will come against you in great numbers and you will be destroyed."

At first, silence was the only answer to this puzzling demand. The people gazed uncomprehendingly at the red-haired youth who raised his arms to them. They were more interested in the legendary Doge of Venice, who stood beside this new Alexius, and in the huge man from Montferrat who dwarfed them both. Two of this giant's brothers were known in Constantinople. Both had achieved royal favor; both had resisted the smooth Byzantine way of life with its under-the-surface complexities, and both had finally fled to other lands. Now a third member of that house was come. These men seemed drawn to Constantinople as flies to honey. Doubtless this one too would sail away. They had only to wait, and centuries of practice in the art.

"They seem not to recognize him," said Robert of Clari. "Is that possible?"

"The Emperor may have more soldiers on those walls than we imagined," answered Peter of Amiens. "And we do not know if the people have arms enough to overcome them. It may be that they will wait for darkness, the better to conceal their movements."

"There will be no revolt," said Aleaumes. "Nicholas has been right from the first. These people care nothing for their rulers. Their lives have gone on for centuries unchanged by the men

who sit on the throne. And the emperors care nothing for them.
There are two separate worlds here, the world of the streets and
the world of the palaces. Only their Church unites the two, but
even that bond is not strong enough to make them one."

"We too have our kings."

"Yes, Robert, but the best of our kings have learned to be
responsive to the needs of the people, and the oaths of fealty we
swear bind us one to the other in a way that is foreign to these
people. We are a new nation, strong and ambitious. Though our
roots go back to Rome as do those of Constantinople, we have
carved out a new world for ourselves, while they have been content to sit in the decay of the old. Nicholas has much to say
about nationhood, and though at first I thought him over-skep-
tical and world-weary, I have come to believe that there is truth
in the opinions he holds."

The voice of the herald who stood near them drowned out
Peter of Amiens's reply. They listened once more to the words of
the proclamation, heads turned toward Constantinople to see
what effect, if any, it was having. A white-haired man, a noble
judging by the richness of his garments, stepped forward to the
very edge of the wall and stood with hands cupped to his mouth
as if he alone would answer the challenge flung at his city.

"We do not recognize this youth who stands in your midst."
The words came plainly to them across the intervening stretch
of water. "You say that he is the son of Isaac who once was emperor here, but we say that we do not know him. Alexius III
Angelus is our lord, and so he will remain until God wills that
another sit in his place."

"We do not know this youth. We will not have him." Other
voices took up the defiant shout, other men stepped forward to
raise their fists against the crusaders. "Go back where you came
from. We will have none of you." The heralds shouted back their
proclamation, but their voices were drowned out. In the lead
galley, Alexius seemed to be arguing with the Marquis of Montferrat, his gestures indicating that he wished to be rowed closer
to the walls. But the Marquis shook his head and Dandolo ordered his oarsmen to pull away. Slowly they made their way
back to the Scutari shore, mocked and derided by the defiant

Greeks, whose army now howled after them as loudly as the citizens who hooted from the safety of their walls.

The next morning, after Mass had been heard, another parliament was held. This time the crusaders assembled on horseback in the open, ruined fields near the palace, the better to display their strength before the city's defenders and the Emperor's army. Each knight, in full armor, sat his finest destrier, the ranks drawn close around the various commanders. As each battalion was decided upon and its battle assignment given and accepted, the men of that company drew a little apart from the others until there were seven separate divisions on the field. The actual sequence of the attack would be decided later; for the moment it was enough that each man should know his place within the army.

Count Baldwin of Flanders would command the advance guard, the first division, because his Flemish archers and crossbowmen were more highly skilled than any others. Under the deadly rain of arrows and iron crossbolts the enemy could be expected to recoil and fall back in confusion while the mounted divisions rushed forward to the attack.

Henry, Baldwin's brother, was given the second division, composed largely of the mounted knights of Flanders and Hainault, including the wealthy Matthew of Wallincourt and Baldwin of Beauvoir, both of whom had taken the cross with Baldwin in Bruges. They had brought a large number of retainers with them and would be jointly seconds-in-command after the Count's brother.

Count Hugh of St. Pol commanded the third division, in which Peter of Amiens and Robert would fight, and Count Louis of Blois and Chartres the fourth. The fifth division was composed of the men of Champagne, led by the experienced Matthew of Montmorency, to whom Geoffrey of Villehardouin had willingly ceded command. The sixth division was made up largely of Burgundians, while the seventh, which would act as a rearguard, included the Germans sent by Philip of Swabia and the Lombards and Tuscans, whose sympathies lay naturally with the Marquis of Montferrat. Boniface had assigned command of this division to himself, for it was the position most likely to provide an overview of the entire engagement. The Doge, who took no part in this parliament, remained in sole command of his galleys, a force too important and too independent to be assigned to any lesser figure. It was agreed that the attack would be launched on the morning of July 5.

During the few days preceding the planned attack, each man in the army made his confession and received the sacrament. Those who had not made their final testaments before leaving Venice were urged to do so now, for the Emperor's army remained drawn up against them and it was plain to all that a great battle with heavy losses on both sides would very soon take place.

Almost alone among the crusaders, Robert of Clari did not seek out the priests who were hearing confessions and giving rapid absolution in dozens of places all around the camp. He shunned the long lines stretching out from the dark-robed figures seated in the open air, lines of men who for once were silent in their waiting. To confess properly he would have to promise to amend his life should he be spared in battle, to give up the cause of his past sin, and obstinately he refused to humble himself and expose Anne and their love to the condemnation of some weakling celibate.

The pilgrims remained aboard their ships, the smallest and most overcrowded in the fleet, forbidden by the Marquis to land either at Chalcedon or Scutari. It was pointless for them to protest this harsh treatment, for they were useless appendages to the army who must nevertheless be provided with the minimum of food and drink by the soldiers detailed to protect them. It was duty greatly resented by those assigned to it, men who for reasons of ill health or infractions of discipline were temporarily separated from their fellows. The pilgrims were few in number now, for many had left the army at Zara and Corfu, but those who remained hung like dead weights around the neck of the Marquis. They were a quarrelsome, discontented group who intrigued among themselves for the smallest of privileges, so jealous of their positions that they remained leaderless. The strongest among them, the most sincere, had long since given up hope that this army would reach Jerusalem and had departed to make their own way through unknown dangers and uncharted lands, confident that somehow Christ and His Holy Mother would protect them on their journey. Only the very old, the feeble, the sick and the greedy were left, and these pestered the Marquis with querulous petitions for better food, medicines and more spacious living quarters. He was heartily sick of them and would gladly have turned them out to fend for themselves had not the Doge counseled otherwise and contributed to their support from his own purse.

"As long as these are with us," he reminded Boniface, "not even the Pope will dare to question our sincerity. For would an army whose sole purpose was conquest weigh itself down with this band of noncombatants? The answer is obvious. These people are our shield against the world's criticism, for their goal is Jerusalem and so, it must seem to our detractors, is ours. Send them away now, and it will be said of us that we never intended to reach the Holy City at all, that from the first our object was an unholy one. It must appear that each delay we have encountered has been thrust upon us by the force of circumstance, that even the conquest of Constantinople is but added assurance of our eventual success in the Holy Land. We need these pilgrims yet awhile. Michaelmas is but three months away. Suffer them with good grace until then."

"Not many will leave Constantinople in spite of the promises made on Corfu," said Boniface. "Else I am a poor judge of human nature."

"There will be a few," answered Dandolo, "and to these you must keep your word. The pilgrims will sail with them willingly, for it will seem that they only precede us. Once gone from these waters we and the world will never hear of them again. The infidels will cut them down without mercy and they will seem fools, while to us will go the praise for a truly Christian achievement. Rome and the entire Christian world will applaud the heretics' return to the True Faith and the men who made that return possible."

So the pilgrims were indulged and a priest assigned to act as their official representative to the Marquis, a man so soon loaded down with petitions, complaints and suggestions as to how Constantinople could be best overcome that he often spent his hours ashore trying to inveigle another to take his place, knowing that it was a waste of time to attempt to gain an audience with the army's commander.

At least one of Anne's dreams had been realized, for shortly after Nicholas Roux's visit to the Scutari Palace, Theodora had joined her on one of the pilgrim ships, and she had been able to shun the company of the two widows she had come close to openly despising. Theodora attended Anne assiduously, acting almost as maidservant instead of chaperone, and Anne found some of her earlier affection for the woman returning.

"Nicholas was unwell, you know," Theodora confided, "else I would never have left you to the company of these others. But the Marshal himself bade me see to my husband's health, even to sharing his quarters aboard Villehardouin's ship. Nicholas knows more about Constantinople and the workings of the court than anyone else, and even the Doge has seen fit to consult with him. But now, may the Virgin be praised, he is fully recovered, and his first thought was to send me to you."

"He is kind," Anne said. "I thought at one time that he was angry with me."

"We look upon you as the daughter we never had," said Theodora, enfolding Anne in a comforting embrace. "How could we be angry with you?"

"I thought that because of Robert . . ."

"Robert, also, we regard with great affection," interrupted Theodora. "Your love reminds us of our own young days. Aleaumes, too, loves you as a sister, but you must remember that his conscience is oversensitive, and he suffers greatly for it. He is bound by his vows to be suspicious of all earthly loves, but he is young and he will learn."

Nicholas had indeed sent Theodora to Anne, both for her own safety, as none could predict the course of the fighting, and because he knew that Anne was one of those who would survive and prosper anywhere. "Make yourself necessary to her, my dear," he had said, "and then no matter what happens to me I will know that your future is assured."

"It is preposterous, Nicholas, to think that this girl could protect me. She is one woman virtually alone in the midst of a conquering army that may or may not succeed in laying waste the greatest city the world has ever known. She, if anyone, is supremely vulnerable."

"She is the kind of woman who will always be protected by a man, my love. And when she chooses her next protector it will not be from among the humbler ranks of the army. Trust me." Nicholas seldom demanded that Theodora do anything she herself did not want to do, and she had finally given in to his persuasions, although secretly she could see nothing of the unusual in the girl he seemed so confident of.

"I know women, my dear," he said succinctly. "Did I not choose you out of all others to be my wife? You are worth a thousand Annes, but she too has a certain value, not to be scorned or underrated. She is a survivor, as we have been in the past and as we must continue to be in the uncertain future."

At the Marquis's command a continuous chain of prayer had been organized aboard the pilgrim ships. One group after another took its place in the vigil so that a never-ending stream of petitions arose in the clear air to assault the Throne of Heaven. They prayed for military victory and that God's Holy Will be made manifest among the heretics and saw no contradictions in the asking.

Anne stood at the ship's railing, gazing at the walls of Constantinople and the tiled roofs of its palaces. She scarcely saw the army encamped on the plain and, except for noting their richness, paid little heed to the gold-gilded church domes that blazed in the summer sun. Her knees ached from their recent contact with the hard plank deck and she knew that they were calloused from the long hours of prayer, red and sore like nun's knees. When next her turn came to keep the vigil she would plead faintness or some woman's weakness even if it meant being temporarily confined to the foul-smelling darkness below deck. She knew from past experience that long hours on one's knees disfigured shapely legs; Theodora would have to procure some healing, soothing cream to rub into the cracked flesh. It was a wonder that her teeth had not loosened in her head, as had happened to so many others on this journey. In stealth she had brewed the herbs Theodora had given her against shipboard disease; in secret she had drunk them, sharing with no one, not even those who had weakened and died for lack of a few dried leaves to restore their health. And though she pitied them their miserable deaths the emotion was so weak and fleeting that it disappeared with the bodies consigned to the waves.

"Theodora, tell me again about the emperor's palaces."

"They are so rich and so vast that even I cannot remember all their details. Everywhere you look you see gold and silver; even the doors of the rooms are encrusted with precious gems. The walls are covered with mosaics, brilliantly colored pictures made of tiny pieces of enamel and colored glass, some very ancient. The whole history of Constantinople is depicted in those mosaics, its glories and even its long-dead emperors. But the palaces are not the greatest achievements of this city, though you have never seen their like in the West. In our convents and monasteries lie manuscripts that preserve all the learning of long-dead generations of philosophers and scholars; we have libraries here that contain treasures undreamed of by your people. And holy relics. Constantinople is very much a city of God, for it is the storehouse of His saints and even of the Passion of Christ Himself. Pieces of the True Cross have been preserved in our churches, and the people revere the nails that pierced His Hands and Feet, the garment stripped from Him by the soldiers, even some of His Precious Blood."

"I am no more interested in relics than you are, Theodora, or Nicholas either for that matter. They are for the priests to exclaim over and for children to bow down before. Of what use to me is a withered finger from a dead man? In our convent we had many relics, but I never saw a miracle worked by any of them."

"Hush, little one. You must not say such things where others can overhear you. The prudent man or woman does not openly go against the spirit of the times."

"I have learned much in the two years since Soissons, Theodora. Do you deny that we three, you, Nicholas and I, are kindred spirits in this at least and perhaps in many other matters?"

"I deny nothing, nor do I admit to anything. In neutrality also lies safety." Theodora was surprised and worried by Anne's sudden frankness, so unlike the carefully calculated opinions she was used to hearing from her. The heat and the close confinement aboard ship had made her reckless in her speech and even in her actions, for she loosened the widow's hood she wore and pushed it back upon her shoulders, allowing the slight breeze from the sea to cool her brow and the bright sun to shine on her hair. She was openly flaunting her beauty, challenging any casual beholder to guess at the perfection of body hidden beneath the widow's robe, hinting that hair so fine and black would cascade smoothly against white flesh if once it were loosed from its coils.

"Your hood, Anne," Theodora hissed, as a flurry of excitement behind them reminded her that now was not the time to do away with caution.

Robert had come on board and was standing in the midst of a group of eagerly questioning pilgrims, calmly answering their queries while his eyes swept the deck in search of his beloved. The captain sent the pilgrims back to their devotions and the two men stood quietly talking, their heads turning toward the Venetian galleys, then back to the opposite shore as Robert told him all he knew about tomorrow's planned attack.

Bowing politely, the captain pointed toward the spot where Theodora and Anne stood waiting, then returned to his duties. Robert approached gravely, holding out to Theodora a small cylinder of parchment which she quickly unrolled.

"Robert, there is nothing written on it," she whispered.

"Nevertheless you must pretend to read it through," he answered. "It was the only way I could come on board. It is an important message for you on the state of health of our valued Greek interpreter."

"Who continues in good health, I presume?"

"In excellent health, Theodora. He sends you his best wishes and bids you remember him in your prayers."

"So shall we all," breathed Anne, inching forward to stand beside Theodora, whose head was bent low over the parchment. "I have longed for the sight of you, my lord."

"And I for you, lady." He did not dare draw her aside for private conversation; the pilgrims keeping vigil had become suddenly alert for hints of sinful dalliance among their company.

"It is a well-known medical fact that old women are as deaf as stones," Theodora said.

"Robert, will it be tomorrow as we have heard?"

"We move at dawn. St. Pol commands the third division."

"I shall watch for sight of you and pray without ceasing for your safety."

"At this distance you will be unable to tell one division from another, but I shall be in good company, with Peter of Amiens on one side and Aleaumes on the other."

"Aleaumes?"

"He has armor and a sword and by bribery or theft will have a horse too before the night is out. Don't turn your head, but listen. There is a tall tower on the far shore, Galata it is called. A chain stretches from this tower across the mouth of the harbor to the point opposite. Once the tower is taken and the chain lowered, the fleet will enter the Golden Horn. Keep your eyes fixed on the Galata tower tomorrow and I in turn will be gazing back at you."

"Robert, you should not be telling me this."

"I shall fight the harder for knowing your eyes are fixed on me."

"Will there be much danger at the tower?"

"There is always danger in any fight." He shrugged his shoulders impassively. "But I am a soldier, my love, and danger is an old companion. I fear it not."

"Have you confessed?"

"Why waste the priest's time, when there is no sin to be absolved?"

"Robert."

"I love you, Anne. Remember that. I have loved you from the first moment I saw you, and I shall love you at the hour of my death."

"Don't speak of death, not now."

"Anne, if something happens to me tomorrow, look to Aleaumes or to Nicholas for help. I have spoken also to Peter of Amiens, and he will befriend you for my sake." There was an urgency in his voice that dismayed her, as though he had some presentiment of disaster he would warn her of, but not fully share. "Anne, I would not leave you unprotected or unprepared. Peter has promised to see you safely to Almaric's court, and Aleaumes will remain at your side until you are in your uncle's care."

"Someone is coming," whispered Theodora. In a loud voice she thanked Robert for bringing her Nicholas's message and gave him back the parchment.

"Farewell, my lady," he answered her, his eyes linked to Anne's.

"Godspeed, my lord." Both women turned from him and as they walked away he heard Theodora's voice, resonant with religious fervor. "Come, Anne. It is our vigil hour. We must not keep our companions waiting."

It was an unsatisfactory parting at best, but at least he knew that she would be safe no matter what happened to him. He would carry the memory of her tear-misted blue eyes with him into battle, and the strength and surety of her love would be his shield.

By dawn the next day every man was in his place. The sun rose higher in the heavens; its gentle warmth burned away the early-morning mists, shining down with impartial benignity on Greek and Frank alike. Now it heartened them after the chill of the night; later in the day, sweating in their heavy armor, they would curse its sultry heat and the brightness glinting off thousands of helmets, a dazzling light that blinded red-rimmed eyes and caused a pounding like a thousand devils' hammers in the head.

The morning hymn to the Virgin burst from thousands of throats, a pulsing, throbbing sound that rose and fell on the still morning air, dying softly into silence. The Emperor Alexius had come from his palace to lead his troops, the golden icon of the Virgin held proudly aloft where every Greek eye could see it plainly. The stillness of the morning was stretched and taut as the two forces awaited the command of the one man who could set them in motion.

The Marquis of Montferrat, his eyes fixed on the beckoning icon, nodded his head and at once a deafening blast sounded from hundreds of silver and brass trumpets. The drums and tabors began a heavy beat, and as though impelled solely by the force of sound, the galleys began to move toward the waiting Greeks. Each galley towed a heavily laden transport behind it, and the other ships followed in their wake until the waters were

entirely covered with the crusaders' craft. The noise of the trumpets and the drums grew louder and louder, their rhythm punctuated by flights of arrows and crossbolts that flew dark against
the sun and landed closer and closer to the Greek army until
finally they found their range and cries of pain mingled with the
music. Greek soldiers in the front ranks were falling among their
fellows long before the first barges were beached, but though
the lines wavered and thrashed about like a living beast, they
were holding firm. The transports came close behind the barges
on which crouched the crossbowmen, and as each touched the
sloping shore, mounted knights crashed through the shallow
waters until it seemed to the astonished Greeks that the huge
ports in the ships' sides would never be emptied. The knights
came all at a rush, lances lowered; fierce war howls issued from
the iron helmets which protected and hid their faces, making
them all the more terrible to behold.

The second division followed close on the first, but as Henry
of Flanders's men touched shore bellows of rage and disappointment rose from their ranks and from the other ships jockey-
ing for position behind them. The Greek line had broken and
the entire army was fleeing back across the plain toward the city
gates now swinging ponderously open to receive them.

The pilgrims on board their tiny ships could see it all; the
Greek soldiers flung aside their heavy weapons the better to run
for safety, leaving tents and supply wagons scattered in their
wake while the first divison harried the laggards, slashing indiscriminately from side to side, their numbers not great enough to
pursue the main body of the Greek army. It was a total rout,
and the pilgrims slapped one another on the back joyfully,
laughing and shouting obscenities at the discomfited Greek civil-
ians who watched unbelieving from the walls. The soldiers left
behind to guard them snorted derisively; the Greek army had
yet to be destroyed and one day's retreat did not win a war. The
crusaders lacked the supplies necessary for a siege of the city;
there would have to be an assault on the famous walls of Constantinople and in that engagement the advantages would be all
on the other side.

A band of fifty or so knights was pounding furiously after a
detachment of Greek cavalry that alone among its fellows rode

without breaking its close-knit ranks. A shout went up, "The Emperor, the Emperor flees," and the pilgrims held their breath. But the Greek lead was too great and as the riders swirled into the mass of foot soldiers, the ranks opened for their passage, then closed behind them. Trumpets blew from the shore and the Frankish knights obediently turned back. Alexius III had made good his escape.

Within minutes not a single Greek remained on the plain. The gates of the city were shut fast; its walls presented a blank face to the invaders, while from its towers came the mocking cries of its defenders. They were well prepared to sit out a siege.

The crusaders made camp that afternoon all around the Galata tower, ringing it in securely yet keeping their distance, for the tower was still in Greek hands and could not be approached without calling forth a deadly fire from the garrison within. The Galata shore was actually a suburb of the city itself, for most of the foreign traders lived there and also the Jews, in a section of their own called Stenon.

Late in the afternoon the pilgrim ships and the supply ships which had remained at Scutari made the crossing and came to anchor in the Galata harbor. The pilgrims were ordered to debark and find shelter for themselves wherever they could, either in the homes of the foreign traders or in the Jewry. Every ship, even the most leaky, unseaworthy vessel of the fleet, would be needed in the assault on the walls, and late into the night there was a constant flow of soldiers and sailors in the harbor area as ship after ship was unloaded and stripped for action.

Anne was hurried off by Theodora to the home of a rich Venetian trader whose sons Nicholas had once tutored. The family welcomed them, plied them with questions and food and assured the two women that they could stay in that place of comfort and safety for as long as it pleased them.

The head of the household, Baldassare Pareto, a withered old man in his seventies, rubbed his hands in glee. "Now they will learn what it means to spurn the might of Venice," he said over and over to the tired women. "I have waited patiently through the years while the Pisans and Genoese prospered at my expense. They told me to go home, that Venice's day in Constantinople was past, but though I listened to their advice politely and with good grace, I knew that our decline was merely temporary. I never left and I never doubted. And now the Doge himself has come! It is almost more joy than an old man can bear."

His worried wife and sons at last persuaded him to seek his bed, fearful that so much excitement would bring about a sudden weakness of the heart.

"Do all foreigners living here feel that way?" Anne asked.

"All but the Pisans, the Genoese and the Jews," replied Baldassare's eldest son, Matteo, an old man himself. "Where Venice reigns supreme she suffers no competitors, so the Pisans and the Genoese will attempt to stiffen the Emperor's back while seeming to remain neutral. The Jews are too much tolerated by the Greeks, given many privileges in this city that are rightfully denied them elsewhere. There has been wailing in their synagogue since your fleet was first sighted. Many will leave when Alexius falls."

"And you are certain that he will?"

"Theodora is a Greek. She can tell you better than I."

"He will fall, and the city with him," Theodora said with mournful certainty. "I only hope his fall will be swift so the city is spared destruction."

Anne would have questioned Signor Matteo further, but Francesca Pareto returned from her husband's chamber and bustled them all off to bed, very much the busy matron proud of the fine guest chambers into which she ushered them. "Tomorrow," she said, "there will be ample time for talk and much else. Theodora, your gown is in a disgraceful condition, and my lady Anne's also if you will forgive my frankness. We have robes aplenty in this house and will have you decently clad before Tierce, else I shall stand forever disgraced in the eyes of every other woman in the community."

"I will leave off the widow's garb," said Anne quietly, expecting that Theodora would object. But she did not.

"And so you should, my dear. It is unbecoming a young woman to mourn an old husband too long, is it not, Francesca?"

"There is the future to think of, and it does no good to dwell too long in the past," answered their hostess, her shrewd eyes taking in every detail of Anne's body as she deftly helped her to disrobe. "My lady does not intend to take the veil then?"

"Such was my intention when I first set out on this journey," Anne lied, sensing that here was a powerful and willing ally, "but it came to me in a dream that God did not wish it of me."

"My lady has friends or family in the Holy Land perhaps?"

"My uncle serves at the court of the King of Jerusalem."

"A most worthy lord, I am certain, to be so near the king."

"Most worthy and most powerful."

Francesca digested this bit of information carefully, and after bidding her guests good night, hurried off to acquaint her son with it.

"She is a highborn lady of noble birth," she told him, "with family connections at the court of King Almaric."

"Our ships sailed often to that court in the past," he mused contentedly, "until others used their influence to supplant us. I shall express my gratitude to Nicholas for allowing us the opportunity to extend hospitality to the lady. No doubt her uncle will be anxious to reward us for our good care of his niece during the perilous times to come. See that she lacks for nothing, Mother, and if she offers payment for her keep, refuse it. A few gifts will cost us little but may bring great returns."

While Anne and Theodora slept peacefully in the unaccustomed comfort of soft feather beds, Robert and Aleaumes snatched what sleep they could on the hard ground near the Galata tower where a detachment of Baldwin's men were standing guard. One of them, James of Avesnes, had been an outspoken member of the Corfu conspiracy and a friendship had sprung up between them. They stood guard with him for a while, chatting quietly in the soft darkness, their eyes pulled back and forth from the silent, dark tower to the torches that flared on the city walls. The tower would have to be taken on the morrow, and if help were sent from the city it would be during the night. But all seemed unearthly peaceful, though enemy eyes undoubtedly watched their every movement. Gradually the guard relaxed its vigilance, only a skeleton force remaining awake while the rest dozed fitfully, heads pillowed on their helmets, hands resting on their sword hilts.

By dawn there was still no sign of reinforcements; neither was there any evidence of movement within the tower. Robert and the others drifted toward the campfires where a thin gruel was being prepared, an unappetizing but strengthening brew that made a man's nose wrinkle in disgust, but warmed and filled his belly. An attack on the tower was being planned in Montferrat's tent, but meanwhile the business of unloading the ships and setting up a permanent camp continued. The morning wore on and the tower became a familiar sight, too familiar to seem dangerous.

Suddenly, just before Tierce, the doors in the base of the tower opened and a horde of screaming Byzantine soldiers came pouring out in numbers so great that it was evident that they had somehow been reinforced during the night. Even as the first creak of the tower doors cracked through the fringes of the crusaders' camp, barges loaded with Greek fighting men began to set out from the opposite shore, and more barges came into view from the far side of the promontory on which the tower stood.

It was clearly a diversionary move, carefully planned and organized to permit more men, weapons and supplies to be lodged within the tower. Properly reinforced it could hold out indefinitely, and the chain that prevented the fleet from sailing up the Golden Horn would remain in place. The Byzantines fought like madmen, scattering the few crusaders who came against them while their heavily laden barges were run up on shore.

It was James of Avesnes who rallied the Franks, running on foot, helmetless, with his sword upraised and glittering in the sun, straight into the thickest knot of Greek soldiers. As he ran he shouted the rallying cry of his house, and those who owed him allegiance and every other man who saw the danger and sensed the opportunity threw down his gruel cup, picked up whatever weapon lay at hand and charged after him. Robert and Aleaumes were at his side in moments, forming a small triangle of flashing swords that moved forward slowly but steadily toward the still open tower door. If they could reach that door there was a chance that they could back through it and slam it shut in the very faces of its defenders. The Greek soldiers seemed to have forgotten the purpose of their sortie, seemed to have gone berserk, as if their new fury would wipe out the shame of their Emperor's ignominious retreat.

Robert's shoulders touched those of James and Aleaumes. He could feel the shocks of the blows they took and the tensing of their muscles as they struck. Aleaumes was grunting like a man or a beast at the moment of his body's greatest release, and when a short grim laugh punctuated the grunts Robert knew that another Greek soldier had fallen. He was facing backward, toward the camp now alive with men swarming to the fight. Most were coming on foot, but there were a few mounted knights among them and these and others who were running to horse would scatter the Greeks like chaff before the wind.

"James is down. Keep him between us." Robert stumbled as the heavy weight of the wounded knight fell against his legs. He dared not look, but braced himself against his companion's body, a heavy, inert mass from which no sound came.

"To us, to us," he called out, and the nearest mounted Frankish knight abruptly swerved his horse from the tower path and came thundering toward them. The Greeks fell back at his approach and seemed to realize for the first time that safety and the unguarded tower lay behind them. They broke off the fight and began to run, but it was already too late, for the crusaders were attacking them from all sides. The mass of men heaved backward and forward, Greeks and Franks inextricably mixed in dozens of individual hand-to-hand combats, the precious tower the goal of both sides.

Nicholas of Jenlain reined his horse in with a cruelly sharp jerk of the reins, his face breaking into lines of dismay at the sight of the bloody mess that was James of Avesnes.

"Put him up before me," he shouted fiercely. "I'll get him back to the leech while there's still time to save him. My God, his face is completely gone."

Robert's gorge rose in his throat as he and Aleaumes lifted the unconscious James. "He took a lance in the face," said Aleaumes briefly, "but he's still breathing." It hardly looked like the face of a man, a featureless red pulp out of which one eye stared glassily, its companion socket empty and spurting blood. The lips were moving soundlessly and suddenly James laughed and spat out a stream of vomit, blood and teeth. Nicholas of Jenlain cradled him before him as gently as he could, then turned his horse and spurred furiously back to camp.

Robert touched Aleaumes lightly on the arm. "For James," he whispered grimly. They fought their way to the tower over ground littered with fallen Greek soldiers. The heart seemed to have gone out of those who remained standing, for they fought in a desultory fashion, as men who know themselves beaten, and here and there, in twos and threes, they were throwing aside their arms and crying out for mercy.

The barges had disappeared, ordered back to Constantinople only partially unloaded by frightened captains who cursed the folly of a venture that had been hopeless from the start. It was no secret that Theodore Lascaris had urged it on the Emperor, and his name and the names of all the other commanders who had remained in the safety of the palaces were roundly cursed.

The tower fell quickly; the press of men at its base was so great that the Greeks who had managed to get back inside could not close the door for the bodies wedged tightly in the entrance. Those who were mortally wounded were dispatched with a swift sword thrust through the throat; the others were rounded up and marched back, prisoners, to the camp.

Robert and Aleaumes stared in awe at the gigantic windlass from which stretched the heavy iron links of the harbor's chain. The chain at Zara had been a child's plaything compared to this one, whose individual links looked to be too heavy for a single man to lift unaided. The chain was drawn up tight just below the surface of the water, and with their eyes they followed its path through the waves across the entrance to the Golden Horn. Through the narrow slits in the tower walls they could see the fleet still at anchor just beyond the forbidding chain that barred their passage. Already a few of the Venetian galleys were preparing to enter the Horn; the drumbeat that set the rowers' rhythm floated across the water.

A band of six Venetian sailors pushed their way through the crowd of knights, laughing and chattering to one another in their own tongue. With rapid gestures they made the knights understand that they must stand back from the mechanism, then swiftly they set to work on it, shaking their heads over the unfamiliar aspects of the machinery, giving loud triumphant shouts at winches known to all men of the sea. Within minutes they seemed to have the problem solved, for they ceased their busy working and stood quietly joking among themselves while one of their number went to a window slit and stood there as if awaiting a signal. After several minutes he nodded his head and waved an arm to someone below, then turned to his men and gave a quick order in which the Franks could make out only the name of the Doge, spoken with great respect.

The machinery creaked and groaned protestingly, the noise of its turning drowned out by the sound of the enormous links gathering together as the tension was released and the chain unwound. It was a never-ending sound that echoed through the tower and kept the knights rooted to the spot, unable even to raise hands to ears to keep out the deafening cacophony.

The spell was broken when the last enormous link rolled from the spindle. They rushed to the window slits to watch it disappear beneath the water; almost before it slipped from sight the fleet began to move past them, sails outspread to the wind. They could see the sweat on the backs of the slaves bent over their oars and the exultant, grimly triumphant expressions on the captains' faces as each man turned briefly to salute the tower's conquerors.

As the last ship passed and their view of Constantinople was once more unobstructed by tall wooden masts and billowing sails, they seemed to gaze at half the city's population, silent crowds of people atop the ramparts of the invincible walls. Victory was in the air at the Galata tower, but from across the Golden Horn the wind brought the sour smell of a great city's defeat. The people were utterly silent, for it was beyond their comprehension that an invading fleet had come to anchor in waters where for hundreds of years only Greek ships and friendly trading vessels had penetrated. Their first and most important defense had been overcome. Now they were cut off, locked in behind their walls, imprisoned by the ships which sailed arrogantly and unopposed on a sea that had once known only Byzantine masters. From this moment on the walls would be fully manned, day and night, for none knew when the Franks would attack—only that an attack would surely come.

III

Eleven days later they were ready.

A small garrison had been left at the Galata tower, but the rest of the army had marched more than a league eastward toward the most poorly defended portion of the walls that faced the Golden Horn. This was opposite the palace of Blachernae, the Emperor's favorite residence, where the Barbyssa River flowed into the Horn. The Greeks had destroyed the narrow stone bridge that spanned the river, thinking to force the crusaders into attempting a dangerous fording of the waters. But after a day and a night of steady labor a wider, more solid bridge stood in place of the old and the army crossed to make camp in and around a fortified abbey that stood outside the walls. The place was named after one of the most famous crusaders of all time, the great Boemund I of Antioch, who more than a hundred years ago had led the only truly successful army to fight in the Holy Land. To this new generation of cross-signed men, it was a favorable omen.

Catapults, mangonels and other siege engines lumbered across the stone bridge in heavily guarded wagons and were set up on the plain within easy range of the Emperor's palace. The sight of these formidable weapons, which would soon begin a continuous bombardment of their walls, stiffened the backs of the beleaguered Greeks within the city. Bands of knights and soldiers seemingly bent on suicide burst from the landward gates with maddening regularity, sweeping down on the engineers who were supervising the assembling of the war engines, inflicting many casualties and actually managing to destroy several of the machines with pitch-soaked fire arrows. Day and night these bands harassed the crusaders, while those within the city began a steady bombardment of their own that sent huge missiles whistling through the air to land well within the perimeter of the crusaders' camp.

The situation became so perilous that work on the siege engines ceased after a few days and the whole army was employed on the building of a high wooden palisade that completely encircled the camp. Added to that basic defense was a deep ditch on their most vulnerable side, the only possible way to impede a Greek cavalry charge.

The men worked all the harder for the knowledge that time was running out on them. Supplies had fallen alarmingly low; there was hardly anything fit to eat in the camp. Since leaving Galata they had subsisted largely on flour and salted meat, but now the barrels of flour were alive with weevils and other insects and the bacon was so covered with green slime that it was barely edible. Once in a while a sick or lamed horse was killed and the aroma of its roasting flesh tortured the half-starved soldiers, who knew that only their leaders and their wounded would partake of the delicacy. They starved and grew weak while within the city before whose gates they sat was food enough to satiate even the hungriest among them. The guards who patrolled the walls and towers were well aware of the camp's hunger and taunted them with half-chewed bones on which clung tempting morsels of meat. They tossed these from the walls well within their bowshot range, and the few soldiers who crawled out on their bellies to retrieve them were sometimes allowed one mouthful of tender roasted lamb or kid before their bodies were riddled with arrows. It was a grim sight, for it was impossible to bring back their corpses and the buzzards soon settled on human and animal flesh alike, picking and ripping indiscriminately.

The whole camp was waiting for the Doge to declare his ships ready for the assault, but though his men worked swiftly, he would not be hurried. Day after day he could be seen pacing the deck of his galley, receiving the reports of his captains and overseers, and as the days wore on the ships took on a new and fearsome aspect. The chief product of Dandolo's genius was a forest of hide-covered ramps that stretched higher than the masts to which they were secured. As soon as the ships were beached the ramps would crash down onto the walls beside the towers of the city. They were in reality long tunnels through which the Venetian soldiers could race two abreast, completely protected from crossbow quarrels and the terrifying fire arrows. Until these ramps were completed and water-soaked hides nailed securely to the sides of his ships and spread over every inch of the wooden decks, the Doge would not move.

"We must expect to be met with fire," he told his sailors, "and there must be no dry wood to feed their arrows, else we shall be aflame and at the bottom of the Horn within minutes." Knowing that he spoke the truth, they praised him for his farsightedness and continued their heavy work without complaint.

On the night of July 16, the Doge dined with the Frankish leaders, adding the last fine wine of his private store to the bacon and the flat, sour-tasting bread they offered him.

"We are ready," he told them. "All that could be done has been accomplished. The rest is in God's Hands."

"Tomorrow morning then?" queried the Marquis of Montferrat, and the others nodded their heads in agreement. "The attack will be two-pronged as previously agreed upon. The Venetians will attack from the sea, at a point where the walls lie close to the shore, while we attack the gate of Blachernae and the palace itself. Four divisions will form the body of the assault while three remain behind to guard the camp should the Emperor decide to counterattack from the rear. I very much doubt that he will leave the security of the city to meet us in open battle, but our preparedness must at least equal that of our illustrious ally."

"I crave the vanguard of the assault," said Baldwin. "My men are over-thirsty for this battle. They will not falter."

"The vanguard is yours, Baldwin," answered Montferrat, "and with you will ride the divisions of your brother Henry and the two led by Hugh of St. Pol and Louis of Blois. I and my men will content ourselves with the guarding of the camp and the siege engines, and the Champenois and Burgundians will also remain behind. Is there anyone who would question these arrangements?"

The query was a mere formality, for the battle assignments had been thoroughly discussed at many previous meetings, and though Villehardouin was disappointed that the Champenois would not lead the attack, he had accepted Matthew of Montmorency's decision not to quarrel with the Marquis's plan.

"If all are agreed, my lords, I suggest we see to our men and then try to get a few hours' sleep ourselves. The assault begins at first light."

They separated, each to his own tent for a last conference with their captains. For safety's sake two men in each division would have the power to order advances and retreats, the commander himself and one other, the steadiest, most battle-experienced knight under his command.

In St. Pol's tent Peter of Amiens was given the honor of being second-in-command, and Robert, who had accompanied him there, grimly promised himself that he would remain at Peter's side no matter where his lord led.

At dawn the next morning the anxious citizens of Constantinople, who had watched with great fear the transformation of the Venetian galleys and large transports, saw the anchors of these ships drawn up and heard the overseers shout the command to row. It was too beautiful a morning for any man to die, yet as the ships drew closer to the walls, the Byzantine soldiers made the sign of the cross three times, took careful aim, and filled the clear sky with arrows that flamed briefly on the hide-protected decks of the oncoming ships, then guttered and went out. The Venetians easily sidestepped these missiles, laughing and praising the Doge as they stamped them underfoot while from the decks of the large transports the mangonels hurled rocks at the walls, testing their range, finding it, and causing the defenders to scurry within their towers to avoid the crushing missiles. Their own mangonels fired haphazardly, for they were located behind the walls and their engineers depended on lookouts who were reluctant to raise their heads to ensure an accurate range.

As the long line of ships touched the shore, the ramps were lowered onto the walls, a whole series of thick, impossible-to-sever umbilical cords that joined invaders and defenders in a bloody struggle that would end only when the wall was in Venetian hands.

The land force was having less success. Only a few scaling

ladders had been thrown up against the walls and the few knights and sergeants who managed to reach the top of the wall alive were either thrown from its height or captured by the Emperor's men. The mangonels and catapults were doing their work, but slowly, and Baldwin ordered his force to draw back. The siege engines were concentrating now on a small section of the wall near the Blachernae gate, and bits of rubble began to fall onto the plain. As soon as an effective breach was made he would order a new advance, and this time the army would break through into the city itself. It was impossible to tell at this distance what advances the Doge's men were making. Their objective was to draw men from the region of the Blachernae gate, secure a portion of the wall and hold it until the Franks could enter the city and crush the Byzantines between them. The wounded who had managed a safe retreat from the first probing land attack reported that the strategy seemed to be working. They had expected to see the mass of the Greek army drawn up just inside the walls, but the quick glimpses they had had before being driven back had revealed strangely empty streets, and though the odd-looking soldiers they had encountered during the attack fought fiercely, they were few in number.

"They are not Greeks, but mercenaries of a type I've not met before," said one experienced sergeant. "Tall, blond, heavily bearded men who fight with axes rather than swords."

"But you saw nothing of the Emperor or the main body of his army?" Montferrat himself had come to question the wounded.

"Nothing, my lord. There were sounds of a great battle being fought to the east where the Doge's ships made their landing, but I could see nothing of the conflict itself."

"That's where the Emperor and his men are," said Villehardouin positively. "He does not dare allow Dandolo to penetrate the city. When he saw us pull back he drew his army off to repel the Venetians, leaving this section of the wall undermanned and ripe for a second assault. As you said he would, my lord. He has not sufficient forces to fight on two fronts at the same time."

"Rather he wishes to choose his battlefield. He will not have it forced upon him by his attackers. A very wise decision. Look yonder, my lord Marshal."

Villehardouin turned to follow the direction of Montferrat's upraised arm. A huge army was stretched across the plain, moving steadily toward them from the southwest. More men issued from the farthest land gates, joining the main body until it seemed there was no end to the marching ranks. They drew steadily closer until the crusaders' camp was entirely ringed in on the landward side. Behind them lay the narrow bridge which led to Galata and before them the plain beneath the city walls, a plain now black with Byzantine soldiers who had slipped out of the gates at first sight of the Emperor's force. The crusaders were caught in a vise not of their own making, and from the front rank of the Flanders division, drawn up with the three others in tight formation near the palisades, Baldwin's messenger sped across the plain to Montferrat.

"My lord of Flanders is to advance toward the main body of the Emperor's army," Montferrat instructed the sweating herald, "until he is just out of bowshot range. On no account is he to initiate the battle and neither is he to expect any assistance from the camp. He is to sit his horse in face of the Emperor and await his pleasure. Tell him further that I have sent word to the Doge that Alexius has come out of the city against us and threatens the camp. Once he has found his position he is to hold it at all costs."

The messenger spurred his horse back to where the four divisions awaited Montferrat's command, then slowly that portion of the army swung past the camp and advanced over the plain. Montferrat ordered the three remaining divisions to watch carefully for any sign of movement from the direction of the city, then mounted his horse and rode to the highest place of safety to watch the pageant unfolding before him.

The Count of Flanders rode at the head of his mounted knights, closely followed by several individual companies of foot soldiers and sergeants. On either side, but a little behind, rode the divisions commanded by Hugh of St. Pol and Henry of Hainault, while the men of the Count of Blois and Chartres formed the rearguard. They rode in silence, without the customary blaring of trumpets and beating of drums, and the only sound to be heard was the jingling of harness and the steady tramp of thousands of marching feet. They were outnumbered by at least ten to one, Montferrat judged, but true to his promise

Baldwin did not falter and in the clear morning sunshine the silk-covered horses and glittering lance tips made a brave sight.

They came to a halt two bowshots from the camp and then Montferrat saw a sight that made him clench his fists in anger and rise to his full height in the stirrups, not believing what was happening before him.

A cluster of barons had broken from the ranks and appeared to be arguing with the Count of Flanders, pointing back toward the palisades that lay behind them. Baldwin seemed uncertain; he rode his horse back and forth at a little space before his confused troops, followed by the small band of battalion commanders. Now Henry of Hainault rode across the plain to join them and the argument seemed to grow fiercer. Montferrat willed that the weak and vacillating Emperor would not choose this moment to attack the isolated four divisions and saw with alarm that Alexius's commanders too had left their ranks and were gathering beneath the golden icon where the Emperor and his bodyguard stood.

Peter of Amiens would never forget the shame of what happened next. Baldwin of Flanders raised his arm and signaled his division to move back, and his brother, Henry of Hainault, arm upraised in the same signal, was also leading his men in retreat. The two divisions were moving slowly, reluctantly, the mounted knights cursing and swearing as they followed the shameful order, but there was no longer any doubt about it. Baldwin and Henry had been advised to await the Emperor's attack from behind the already well-fortified and well-manned palisades, and they had given in to their weak-livered councillors. Louis of Blois, far to the rear, seemed not to know what was happening, but he and his men stood their ground as the Flemish troops moved slowly backward toward their position.

Within a few minutes St. Pol and his division stood in the advance position, a little to one side of the center of the field, but the only force remaining face to face with the Emperor.

"We will not turn back," he told his captains, and Peter of Amiens seconded the decision.

"The Count of Flanders has given us the van, and in God's Name we will take it!"

Slowly the division moved to the center of the field, eyes

never for a moment leaving the Emperor's golden icon, until at last they stood in close ranks before him, with vast empty stretches of plain on either side where the other crusading troops should have stood.

Baldwin's herald was sent out with a message ordering them to retreat while there was still time. The Count of St. Pol heard the man out in respect for the livery he wore, but his reply was barely civil. "The Count of Flanders shames us all by his retreat. Tell him that, in plain words. And tell him further that I and my men have taken the van and will not turn back. We value our honor more highly than our lives and have placed both in the hands of Jesus Christ, who will not confound us."

The herald, who himself was burning with shame at the role he was obliged to play in this business, rode angrily back to Baldwin where he delivered St. Pol's message word for word, exulting at the flush it brought to the Count's pale cheeks.

"My lords, we cannot leave the field." He argued with his advisers and with Henry, his brother, but they pointed out that St. Pol was begging for a massacre and talked of strategy until Baldwin's head rang with their confusing logic. Two more messengers were sent to St. Pol, but they returned with an even blunter refusal and stinging remarks on the bravery and honor of knights who left the field before the fight was even joined. Halfway between the camp and St. Pol's position, Baldwin called a halt to the retreat and ordered his men to stand fast. Unable to make an independent, final decision on his own, he hoped that St. Pol would make it for him.

He watched as Peter of Amiens and Eustace of Canteleux took up positions on the division's two flanks. St. Pol remained at the center, in the most dangerous position of all. Slowly the Count's standard dipped, then slowly rose to float in the morning breeze. The command to advance rang out and St. Pol, Peter of Amiens, Eustace of Canteleux and all the men who followed them began a steady march alone toward the entire Byzantine army drawn up against them.

They moved slowly, proudly forward, a miniature army from out of chivalry's finest legends. The sun blazed on their unsheathed weapons and picked out the gold thread of blazoned surcoats. Even the foot soldiers in their plain garb marched with an almost royal dignity, heads held high, backs stiffened by blind courage. This is what we voyaged half the world round to do, they seemed to say—watch and you will see how jauntily we go to meet death.

Conon of Béthune left his place in the ranks and, using the flat of his sword, pushed his way through the small crowd of highborn knights who tried to keep him from reaching Baldwin's side. With sword still unsheathed and now raised high in open defiance of his liege, he spoke in that quiet, far-carrying voice that had won him a reputation as the best singer of his own poetry.

"My lord, I served you well and honestly in Venice and in the Scutari Palace, defending our righteous cause against our enemies with the words God saw fit to place in my mouth. But in my hand He has also seen fit to place a sword and were I to sheathe it in the face of His enemies I would suffer shame and disgrace so great that never again could I return to my own country, for I would be accounted a base thing not fit to share the company of brother knight or fair lady. My lord, you cause me to break sacred vows not lightly taken, and if you will not advance then I will no longer hold myself bound to you in fealty."

"Conon . . ." began Baldwin helplessly.

"Look behind you, my lord, at the honest knights you shame."

Baldwin looked and saw row upon row of eyes that stared defiantly back at him; he heard the hiss of many swords being drawn from their scabbards. The sergeants and foot soldiers shuffled their feet and muttered among themselves, unwilling to meet his eyes, but it was plain that shame was not a knight's prerogative alone.

"My lord, it is not too late," urged Conon.

"Henry, what say you?"

"We are four divisions against ten times that number, and even though we be in dire peril, Montferrat will send no reinforcements. It is madness, brother, useless suicide. None of us will leave this field alive. Yet if we retreat now, we live to fight another day on ground of our own choosing."

"My lord Henry's words are wise, as the world judges wisdom." Conon's voice was mournful, yet there was scorn in every word. "But what has worldly wisdom to do with honor? Farewell, my lord."

"He is a fool," said Henry, watching the lone knight ride away from them. "A brave man, but a fool."

"There are those who would dispute your judgment, Henry," said Baldwin, as knights singly and then in twos and threes rode past them from the ranks, pausing to bow a grave and courteous farewell to their Count before spurring forward to follow the poet whose voice, raised in song, drifted back to mock the fainthearted. "My lady Mary will never forgive me if I leave this field alive." So saying he raised his voice in a great shout, "À Flanders," and spurred his horse to a gallop, leaving behind him his startled brother, who paused only long enough to mutter through his teeth, "I always thought he had more sense than that," before putting the spurs to his own horse. The companies streamed across the ground so lately given up, screaming their war cries at the top of their lungs, all mixed up together in their haste to be the first to reach St. Pol's division.

"My lord," said Robert, who had turned in his saddle, startled, at the sudden burst of noise behind them. "They are returning."

The news spread quickly along the line and St. Pol halted his troops just long enough to allow the Flemish divisions to regroup on either side. He gave no other sign of welcome, a gracious gesture that ignored the ignominious retreat, but sat his horse patiently until Baldwin's herald reached him.

"My lord awaits your pleasure, for the vanguard is yours and yours the command," said the herald, the same who had brought the first order to retreat. Now he held himself proudly and met the Count's appraising stare unashamed.

"Our scouts report that the main body of the Emperor's army lies just beyond that rise," said St. Pol slowly, deciding on his strategy even as he spoke. "What we see directly before us is merely his right flank. Another large body of men is to the north, sealing off the camp. But those divisions we will leave to Montferrat to entertain. Tell my lord of Flanders to string his division out as thinly as he dares, knights in the front rank, crossbowmen and foot soldiers behind. Our two divisions will mount the rise together, the others following, so that when we reach the top it will seem to the Emperor that all Christendom is poised against him. He moves slowly because of his great numbers, but the high place must be ours."

Baldwin disposed his troops as he was bid, and all together, to the sound of silver trumpets, the army advanced at a trot up the slight incline which momentarily hid the full Byzantine army from their sight. As they marched, the crossbowmen halted now and then to return the fire that had begun to inflict casualties among them, kneeling to let loose their quarrels blindly, then running quickly to keep up with the line of knights before them. The fire was coming from both sides, from the stationary flanks of the Emperor's army which were far in advance of the main force.

As they burst over the top of the rise the four divisions came to a sudden halt, though no command had been given. The knights sat their horses as if transfixed, staring at the valley floor below them, and the crossbowmen, struggling to rewind their heavy weapons, paused to cross themselves with trembling fingers. No one broke rank, but each man silently said his last prayer. Massed against them was an army greater than any dreamed could exist in one place.

They could see the figure of the Emperor sitting a white horse beneath his golden icon, a little apart from his troops, surrounded by a bodyguard of blond giants who hefted enormous billed axes as though they were children's playthings. Behind and on both sides of him stretched his army, each division a little separated from the next.

"How many?" asked Peter of Amiens. Robert shaded his eyes and began to count.

"Give it up, Robert," said Aleaumes. "They outnumber us, but I do not think I care to know by exactly how many."

"He has split the army and sent the half of it to attack Montferrat," reported Robert, twisting in his saddle to look at the palisaded camp behind them, so tiny and vulnerable at this distance. "But I judge there are at least fifty thousand horsemen on the plain."

"I make it forty divisions," said Peter, "not counting the foot soldiers."

"Since you insist on playing with numbers, my lords, it works out very simply," laughed Aleaumes. "Each of us has but ten mounted knights to kill and the day is ours. A good morning's work to whet the appetite."

The men nearest him burst out laughing at the remark and the tension eased. The crossbowmen held their weapons at the ready and each knight whispered last words of encouragement to the beast upon whom his life depended. At any moment St. Pol would give the word and they would charge. How they would cross the wide canal that lay at the base of the hill no one cared to consider. Their casualties would be heavy unless the Emperor could be enticed to make the crossing himself.

The minutes dragged on while the Byzantine army continued its slow advance and messengers galloped back and forth between St. Pol, Flanders, Henry of Hainault and Louis of Blois. There were still those who counseled caution, though the Emperor could not know it. From the valley floor he looked up to a long rise of ground on which a formidable army was stretched out, an army whose front exactly matched his own in length. Though Theodore Lascaris and Murtzuphles assured him that the crusaders' line had no depth to it and could be easily broken, he obstinately refused to believe them. He was mortally afraid of being wounded in the flesh, and though he could order the cruelest of executions and watch them with the greatest amusement, the thought of his own blood being spilled on that dusty ground made him yearn to flee back to the safety and voluptuous comfort of his palace. He was in no personal danger, Murtzuphles promised, for the Waring Guard would die to a man before allowing any harm to come to their emperor. Their loyalty was above question. Alexius knew that he spoke the truth and his flesh shrank under his son-in-law's scorn, but long before they reached the canal, he ordered his troops to halt. The divisions which had been sent to attack the Frankish camp, hastily recalled, came thundering into the valley expecting to find their emperor in pitched and heavy battle. Winded by their precipitous ride and thoroughly confused by the sight of the Emperor's unbloodied troops standing as peacefully as if they had halted momentarily while on parade, they took up positions at the rear of the army as ordered, wondering at the strangeness of it.

The sun rose higher until it stood directly overhead; the heavily mailed Franks sweated in the mid-July heat, staring thirstily at the water running cool and clear through the canal into the city. Montferrat's original order was being adhered to. The Emperor's army must strike the first blow, and to do so it must risk a fording of the canal or swing wide on the plain to march around it. The Byzantines, lightly armored, stood at their ease and awaited the Emperor's command.

The golden icon had become the focal point of each man's gaze, so that when it first began to move, all thought it a trick of the heat. But like a tiny second sun it moved steadily over the heads of the Byzantine soldiers, and not until the sound of loud weeping and wailing broke from the watchers on the wall did the Franks realize that the Emperor and all his forces were withdrawing.

"Why?" asked Robert, unable to believe that with certain victory within his grasp Alexius III had fled the field.

"Who knows?" answered Aleaumes. "Probably not even the Emperor himself. They are a people grown soft through years of safe living, decadent and weak as Nicholas said they were. At least that is true of their leaders. The soldiers seem willing enough to fight, but without strong commanders they are sheep without a shepherd and can do nothing. The will of a commander is everything to an army." He looked significantly at St. Pol, that strange, silent man with a will of iron who seemed driven and upheld by secret inner forces. Was it honor or ambition which rode his soul? Today it had not mattered which, but when the city fell, so perhaps would his guard and then, thought Aleaumes, then we shall know the true man.

They remained where they were until the plain beyond the canal was once more barren and deserted. In challenge and *défi* they turned then to face the city, inviting combat, but none came. Constantinople seemed dead and deserted, its walls patrolled by men who no longer had the heart to shout insults at their attackers or loose a defiant missile at them.

A heavy pall of black smoke hung over that portion of the wall where the Venetians had made their landing. The sight of the Emperor's enormous army had driven all thought of their allies from their minds, but now they were anxious to return to camp and learn the meaning of the fire that seemed to be burning within the city. In good order, like the conquerors they felt themselves to be, they put their horses to the trot and swept down the slope of the little rise which had served them so well. To their amazement they heard sounds of cheering and shouts of praise; the walls were suddenly alive with the scarves and veils of women, women who had watched and judged these men finer, braver, more splendid than their own. They laughed at the sight, making ribald jokes about Byzantine manhood, and each man thought hungrily of the welcome these women seemed to be promising.

Montferrat did not come out to meet them, for he was locked in an angry struggle with the Doge, but the rest of the camp overran the palisades and came whooping out to hear the story of the Emperor's defeat and to tell the tale of those who had remained behind. The cooks and horseboys capered all in a group, still clad in the ragged quilts and horse blankets with which they had been fitted out, copper cooking pots on their heads in grotesque parody of helmets, brandishing pestles and long-handled spoons. The sight of these dirty, goblinlike creatures had so unnerved the Emperor's foot soldiers ranged along the walls that not a single arrow had been fired at them. Like devils from hell they had hooted and danced for the Emperor's men until the superstitious Greeks could bear it no longer and fled away from them into the city. It was a fine tale, told and re-told with great relish and ever more detail until at last the knights tired of it and sent the horseboys back to their duties. The cooks took the copper pots from their heads and returned to their barrels of weeviled flour and rancid bacon, muttering among themselves that perhaps the pots as helmets would better serve the army than when they were filled with the stomach-turning messes that had lately shamed their well-polished sides.

But there was another tale to be heard, and as the knights disarmed and gathered here and there in small groups, the wonder of it spread and another legend was added to the store of marvels that had become the Doge.

In the crucial moments before the Venetian ramps crashed down on Constantinople's walls, when the repulse was fierce and it seemed the shore would be denied them, Dandolo had given a command that for once his men were loath to obey. Over eighty years old, more than half blind, unable to raise in self-defense the heavy sword he carried, he had ordered that he be put on shore where the arrows and quarrels fell the thickest. To their agonized pleadings he turned a deaf ear, threatening to snatch the standard of St. Mark from its bearer and plant it himself on Constantinople's highest tower. He had his way, of course. His galley was the first to touch land and he himself the first of his men to wade ashore. Somehow the standard was planted in the sandy soil, and somehow, miraculously, many believed, though all around him men were falling, the Doge remained untouched, as though he walked protected by an invisible cloak. The Hand of God. The assault began then in earnest and one by one the Venetian galleys and the transports reached the shore and let down their ramps, unstoppable then because a frail old man led them on.

Twenty-five towers fell within an hour's time, for there was no defense against the ramps and the men who poured from them. The Byzantines threw down their weapons and fled further into the city, spreading the story as they went. The Devil himself had left the fires of Hades and come to plant his cloven hooves outside God's city.

The Doge sent a triumphant message to Montferrat, urging him to hurry his divisions to that section of the wall that had fallen so easily. The breach could be held for perhaps an hour without reinforcements, but there were already signs that the Greeks were conquering their fear and massing for a counterattack. The Venetians were spread out too thinly in their twenty-five towers to withstand a concentrated assault, and much of their weaponry had been expended on the first attack. Above all, urged Dandolo, send bowmen to harass the Greeks. The knights could follow afterward. Abandon the two-pronged attack. What was needed now was a single crushing wave of men who would sweep through the city, driving its defenders before them.

Back the messengers went to Dandolo with Montferrat's reply. No reinforcements, no weapons. Alexius had made his move and they were outplayed. His entire army marched to destroy the Franks and their camp. They were surrounded and vastly outnumbered.

Dandolo never wasted time on regrets, but he allowed himself the luxury of cursing Alexius III and all his line to the last gen-

eration before giving the order to withdraw. To cover their retreat the Venetians set fire to the wooden hovels and the shops
that clustered near the wall, and the dry timbers flared and
burned gaily in the crackling flames. The wind was right and the
fire spread quickly inward, totally destroying everything in its
path. Black smoke obscured the wall and under its cover the Venetians took ship and sailed to aid the men they believed to be
desperately fighting for their lives.

The sight of the camp, safe, untouched, filled with riotously
rejoicing men was a bitter one. Was it for this that the Venetians
had fought, tasted victory, then been forced to abandon their
hard-won gains? Where was the great army whose size alone
had thrown Montferrat into despair? Once again Dandolo's foot
was the first to touch shore. He scorned a litter, refused a horse,
and marched angrily, his famous masklike face contorted in a
terrible rage, to Montferrat's tent. The argument was vicious but
brief, and for the sake of the alliance quickly patched up. They
would attack again tomorrow. The camp settled down to uneasy
slumber, and soon only the guards patrolling its perimeters continued to discuss the strange events of the day. Finally even
their hushed whispers ceased, and only the noise of the fire still
burning in the city broke the dark night's silence.

Early the next morning the Blachernae gate was opened and a
small party of highborn Byzantine nobles under a flag of truce
walked to within calling distance of the palisades. They came
seeking audience with the most noble Prince Alexius Angelus,
they told the astonished guards, but refused to answer any other
questions. The camp was fully awake and arming for the
planned attack, but as the Byzantine lords in their splendid
robes were led to Alexius's tent rumor spread that they were
come to discuss the terms of peace, perhaps even to surrender
the city. Some laid aside their weapons and rushed to interrogate the sentries, only to hear that none knew why the Byzantines had come. Most of the knights merely shrugged their
shoulders, reminding one another that no Greek could be
trusted, and returned to the burnishing of their swords and the
fitting on of their armor.

The Byzantines entered Alexius's tent and after a time that

seemed endless to the curious crowd gathered outside, the Prince appeared briefly, ordering a soldier to conduct the Marquis of Montferrat into his presence. The manner of his ordering, the tone of his voice, the slight disrespect of his words, all astonished the barons who had closely observed his conduct for the past two months. Montferrat had kept the Prince tightly under his thumb, giving him no duties to perform, no regiment to command and practically no contact with any but himself, the Doge and one or two others. The Prince had squirmed under this restraint at first, but had gradually drifted into the habit of easy, deferential obedience to the Marquis's wishes. Even his tone of voice had the whine in it of a dog who begs favors from a hard master. Now suddenly the dog was giving orders, and it seemed that the master would jump, for Montferrat appeared as ordered, with Flanders, Blois, St. Pol and Villehardouin to round out his personal escort.

They found Alexius sitting enthroned on a common wooden campstool, the Byzantine nobles ranged behind him, motionless and gorgeously appareled, like statues on an altar. He did not rise in courtesy to greet them, nor did he invite them to be seated. Indeed, to further increase the aura of a makeshift throne room, Alexius had had the tent emptied of its usual furnishings. The Franks and the Byzantines stood, regarding one another uneasily, while the Prince alone sat, smiling broadly at the discomfort he fervently hoped he was causing. He hated Montferrat and feared him above all men; now he would show him that his place was not at royalty's side but beneath its foot.

"My lords, the Emperor Alexius III, him you have called the usurper, has fled the city and abandoned his people." It was Nicholas Roux speaking, no longer the proud and defiant ambassador who had scorned this very prince scarcely two weeks before in the audience chamber of the Scutari Palace. He seemed in that short space of time to have aged and shriveled up like a grape left too long on the vine. Had it not been for his voice he would have been a stranger to them. Although it was personally painful and humiliating to him, he had determined to tell these men the true details of Alexius's flight, omitting nothing, for fantastic stories and rumors were already rife in the city. These foreign lords, as he thought of them, must know that there was strength and courage still in Constantinople's citizens and great opposition to their continued presence in Greek lands.

"During the night, the Emperor, accompanied only by a favorite daughter and a small number of supporters, slipped from the city and sailed away from us on a ship he had secretly made ready for his purpose. He took with him a large sum of gold and many jewels from the Royal Treasury. Where he goes we care not, for he had made an oath to attack this camp and he has betrayed his word. When his flight was discovered we counseled together, the high princes and noble lords of the Empire, whether to fight and destroy you utterly or to seek a peaceful solution to the quarrel that has arisen between us. We are Christians and loath to spill Christian blood. You would have forced us to it, to our shame and yours. You say you come against us to right a great wrong, to restore a lawful ruler to his throne, and that when this is done your quarrel with us is ended, that you are not conquerors and despoilers but instruments of God's Will. Behold then, lords, the deed has been accomplished and we ourselves have done it. Isaac sits his throne in the Blachernae Palace even as he did before his brother's ambition took it from him, and he awaits impatiently the coming of his son and heir whom you have restored to him. We do not surrender to you, for there is no war, but we invite you as guests into our city, to rest and refresh yourselves as long as needful to ensure a safe passage to the Holy Land."

"We rejoice with you and with this prince in the restoration of the true line of the House of Angelus." Villehardouin's smooth diplomat's voice rose and fell in even, calming cadences. He spoke at length, praising the decision of the Greek princes and nobles, reviewing for their edification the sorrowful tale of their prince's exile and the manner in which the Franks had come to espouse his cause, careful to give no hint of the differences that had almost split the army in two. It was a splendid performance, worthy of his talents, but most important, it bought them time, time for the angry sparks to fade from Montferrat's eyes, time to consider the terms they must demand, time enough for Prince Alexius to grow bored and begin to shift about on his ridiculous stool in a most unprincely fashion.

"My lords, the Prince Alexius, as you have heard, has suffered many wrongs at the hands of his countrymen." Montferrat had taken over, no hint of his anger in the voice pitched so solicitously low that it carried just to his listeners' ears and no further. "Amongst us he has occupied a place of honor and respect, and I, who am a man of some years, have been privileged to stand for a time in the place of the father who was taken from him." Alexius felt the net tighten around him again. He had almost forgotten that all these thousands of men stood between him and his city, and that they were not his to command. "We would be remiss in our duty were we to allow you to take this prince so abruptly from our midst. What if harm should come to him after he has passed from our hands? Can you guarantee his safety when, as you yourselves have admitted, there are many who oppose his coming? I think not. And there are other matters also. There exist certain covenants between this prince and us, covenants which the Emperor Isaac must swear to as his own, else we stand, duty done, naked and bereft, unable to fulfill our greater vow. This we will do. We will send envoys into the city to parley with the Emperor and to see with their own eyes the loyalty and goodwill of his people. If their report is a favorable one, then we ourselves will escort Prince Alexius to his noble father. But if we or they are scorned, the prince will not enter his father's city save in the wake of its destruction."

"Your envoys will be made welcome, my lord." If the Byzantines were angered by Montferrat's threat, if they were dismayed at having to return to Isaac without his son safely in their charge, they did not show it either by word or manner. They abased themselves before Alexius, bowed low before the Frankish commanders and, still under the protection of their white flag, returned to the city.

Matthew of Montmorency, Geoffrey of Villehardouin and two of the Doge's Venetians were the first crusaders to enter the city in peace, unarmed, with no military escort. The Blachernae gate was opened wide to receive them, and the Franks had a brief glimpse of a long double line of the strange blond, ax-wielding men who had thrown them back from this very wall before the four envoys disappeared from sight. For more than three hours the camp waited and fretted, trying to picture the scene that must be taking place in Isaac's throne room. It seemed a very long time for such a simple business. There was, after all, nothing to negotiate, no long speeches to be made. Either Isaac agreed to ratify his son's promises or he did not, and if the latter proved to be the case, why nothing much had changed except the name of the emperor who must be brought low.

Somehow a shift had taken place in all of their thinking. No longer was it enough that rightful rule had been restored, and by the Byzantines themselves. Rich Constantinople owed them something for the trouble they had taken on its behalf, for the expense of the journey, the hunger and privation they had suffered, the men who lay wounded and the men who had died. The crusaders intended to collect the debt in full, and if it meant that the Holy Sepulcher must bide a while longer in infidel hands, that no longer seemed too great a shame for them to bear. They had gotten used to saying "*when* we reach the Holy Land." Like those who dwelt in eternity, they no longer had a sharp sense of moments passing, of days, weeks, months that slipped away unsavored and unremarked. They had not even entered the most fabled city of Christendom, but already its allure, its promise of easily-come-by wealth and soft living, its Easternness, was sapping their will.

The envoys returned, moving slowly like men in a daze. The news was good, they told the men who crowded around their horses, unable to await official word from the criers. Isaac agreed to everything. A great victory has been vouchsafed us.

"My lords, I have seen nothing like it in all my travels, and I am not a man who is easily impressed by the riches and splendor of this world." The barons were meeting once again in private, serious men with serious matters to discuss, while outside the tent in which they had gathered the common soldiers had given themselves up entirely to rejoicing. The noise of their joy reached even into this separate place and their shouts and laughter made sharp discordant background music to Villehardouin's recital.

"We passed between a double row of the Emperor's private bodyguard, so many men that it stretched unbroken to the foot of the throne itself. These men are descendants of the old race of England, Danes and Saxons who would not bend the neck to

Norman masters. They call themselves the Waring Guard and never, my lords, not even among the Germans, have I seen such giants."

"I had heard of them before, of course," broke in Matthew of Montmorency, speaking with the sincere admiration of a soldier for one who promises to be a worthy opponent on the field. "But spoken of as figures in a tale, like the legends of bare-breasted women who fought more fiercely than men in the time before Christ walked the earth. But these men are real, as real as the hatred they nurture in their hearts against all who call themselves Frank. There was murder in their eyes as they looked at us; only the Emperor's command kept them from falling on us and tearing us to pieces. I shuddered as I passed between them. It was like an honor guard from hell, was it not, Geoffrey?"

"Worse," agreed Villehardouin, "because these devils were of flesh and blood."

The Venetians said nothing. The Franks often amused them, and never more than when they showed themselves children, easily awed by palaces and potentates for whom the Doge cared nothing. The real wealth and power of a nation lay not in its monuments and the finery of its citizens, but in the ships that plowed the sea and the trade that made all else possible.

"What said Isaac?" asked the Doge, weary of the tales, the sights, the impressions that did not cut to the heart of the matter.

"We had private speech with him in a small chamber, the Empress and his interpreter his sole attendants. We told him of the convenant, of the two hundred thousand marks promised us and of the men he must send to the Holy Land, and he groaned and wrung his hands at the great expense, cursing his brother for the gold he smuggled from the city at his flight. When we told him that the kingdom must return to Rome and that his Patriarch would henceforth be subject to the Pope, he would not at first believe that his son had made such a promise. But at last, and largely through the Empress's pleadings, he agreed to all and sat us down to a great banquet and feasted us well. Before we left he asked one favor of us, and this seemed to come, not from his own will, but from the lords who form his council. We agreed to his condition, for it seems reasonable and to our advantage."

"There is a military loss," admitted Montmorency, "but we gain good favor with the Emperor and the citizenry. We are to withdraw from this camp and quarter ourselves at Galata and in the Jewry, where supplies will be brought us and all else we may desire. The Emperor fears that if our troops enter the city in great numbers many quarrels will arise and armed clashes that will rouse the people against us. There is much anger already because of the fire. A large section of the city was completely destroyed, with much loss of life."

"What we crossed once, we can do again if need be," remarked the Doge. "We shall lie more easily amongst the Westerners in the Galata region than in the streets of the perfidious Greeks. I see no danger in agreeing to the Emperor's proposal."

"What of the other matter?" asked Montferrat.

"He agreed to that also, though with greater reluctance," answered Villehardouin, watching the lines of tension fade from Montferrat's tight-set face at his reply. "At first he said it was unnecessary and seemed angered, but again the Empress soothed him, and though I could not understand her speech, she seemed to be reminding him of his blindness and the sickness that weakened him in prison. Alexius will be crowned co-Emperor in two weeks' time, on the Feast of St. Peter."

"A fitting way to celebrate the saint's day," commented Montferrat, rubbing his hands together in satisfaction. "Meanwhile?"

"We are free to enter the city as often as we wish, provided we do so in small groups and carry no weapons on our persons other than those a man normally carries. None will molest or hinder us, neither in the streets nor in the churches. And at the coronation itself we are to be honored guests."

"Then nothing remains but to deliver Alexius to his father as we promised. My lords, we ourselves will form his honor guard, but some will need to remain behind to organize the move to Galata." Montferrat looked questioningly at Montmorency, the most skilled commander among them.

"My lord, I shall remain, if it please you," said Matthew. "I have been inside the city once already today. Let another take my place."

"The Waring Guard will miss you, my lord," said Montferrat

in rare good humor. "But I shall leave all in your hands, knowing that no other could perform the task so well."

He rose and stretched himself as if a great weight had suddenly fallen from shoulders stiff with the carrying. "My lords, Constantinople awaits."

"As does the Prince," said Louis of Blois.

"The Prince, yes. I had almost forgotten him." Montferrat laughed. "By all means, let us go inform His Royal Highness that we have won him his throne."

IV

Reluctantly, politely, firmly, Matteo Pareto refused to quarter Robert of Clari in his home. There were unmarried girls in the house, sick children, relatives who had crowded in after their own homes had been burned, Theodora and Nicholas, the latter still prey to some mysterious ailment that kept him from his duties with the army and, of course, the lady Anne, who by virtue of her rank occupied a chamber all to herself.

"Her rank!" Robert exploded to Aleaumes. "She is made so much of in that house that today, with all the airs of a queen, she 'received' me with an old dowager chaperone in attendance. And to make matters even worse she feigned shock and amazement when I suggested dismissing the woman. For almost a year, Aleaumes, we shared the same bed in Zara; we made love on the sands of beaches, in soldiers' tents and on the bare ground of Corfu's hills, yet now she is too virginal to be left alone in my presence."

"You quarreled?"

"Bitterly and to no purpose. Both of us said things that can never be forgotten, though even now I feel I could forgive her anything. Even now when she denies our love."

"To deny love is to prove that it never existed."

"She didn't mean what she said. Her temper has always matched mine and she was carried away by the heat of her anger. But Aleaumes, I must get her away from those people. They cling around her with cloying sweetness, plying her with gifts of jewelry and gowns, praising her beauty, her wit and her skill with languages. While I was there she spoke to them in their own tongue, knowing that I could not understand a word of what she said. They all laughed, and I knew the laughter was at my expense."

"Brother, it is hard for me to say this, but I must, in duty and in love." Was this the moment, wondered Aleaumes as he searched for words to soften what he knew Robert would take hard. "Though we have had no word from Clari, nor can we expect any, Aelis's time is long past. Your wife has borne you a child, and that child may be a son who lives and grows stronger each day. Your son, Robert, your son and heir."

"I have no son," answered Robert bitterly, "or I would know it in my bones. Aelis miscarried of the child. The women greatly feared it. I often heard them whispering in those last days before I left. No son, and no wife either. Aelis, if she lives, would do well to take the veil, as she wanted right from the first. She might as well be a nun, for she'll never again lie in my bed."

"Robert, think what you're saying, think of Father and your duty to our house."

"I have decided not to go back, Aleaumes. And you waste your words when you speak of duty and our house as though we were men of importance. We barely scraped out a living at Clari. No one knew our name or our blazon, and it will be the same if you are foolish enough to return there. Father is dead by now, and our mother is a lusty, practical woman. Lady Maud may have remained a widow, but be assured our mother won't. Aleaumes, you once said to me that you were a man who had learned that true wisdom lies in accepting one's fate, and I praised you for it. But there are fates to be accepted and fates to be created out of the sweat of one's brow and the widening of one's ambition. We thought to find ourselves in the Holy Land, but ambitious men brought us to Constantinople instead. We have been used and lied to over and over again, and I for one am ready to take the blinders from my eyes. Whether a man find his fortune here in this Empire or in the Holy Land it is all the same. It is the winning of it that matters."

"You mean that she will not have you in your poverty, and so to keep her love you will sell your soul."

"My soul is a burden I would willingly discard; it weighs too heavily on my manhood. Anne has suffered more on this journey than any woman should be asked to bear. She is weakened by it, embittered and afraid, an easy prey for these greedy Venetians who would use her for their own sake. She thinks she no longer loves, but the love is there, hidden, waiting to burst into flame again. I mean to have her, Aleaumes, and I will."

"You contradict yourself, brother."

"I only begin to awaken from an overlong sleep of innocence. Montferrat's ambition is nothing compared to what mine now is."

"You'll have to find a house willing to shelter both of you," said Aleaumes wearily, unable to abandon his brother even in this new madness that had come upon him. "I will help you."

But even with Aleaumes' indefatigable efforts the brothers found no house rich enough to tempt Anne from the Pareto dwelling. The palaces and summer houses of the Emperor's nobles had all been reserved for the highest barons of the army and there they installed themselves in splendid isolation from their troops. The poorer knights and the common soldiers were billeted in the Jewry, where the living conditions were overcrowded and far from luxurious. Many of them preferred to remain in their tents rather than be forced into daily intimate contact with Jews, and as the army expected to stay only long enough to collect the monies promised them, it hardly mattered anyway.

As a last resort Aleaumes finally spoke to Peter of Amiens, and Robert unexpectedly found himself called to daily personal attendance on his lord, no longer able to slip away to force himself into a house where he was obviously an unwelcome visitor. Anne sent him a sweet message of reconciliation when she learned of his new duties, begging him to think kindly of her and not to be aggrieved if she seemed to prefer her hosts' company to his. "I do it for both our sakes," she wrote, "for the future we will share and to serve your ambition as well as your love."

"She doesn't know yet which way the land lies," commented Aleaumes, who had brought the letter to Robert. "She protects her flanks like a seasoned veteran of many battles."

But to Robert it was a reassuring communication, and as he sought a deeper meaning to her words, he came to believe that she spoke the truth when she said her love served his ambition.

Great women stood behind great men in all the tales of history, making them greater though they themselves remained hidden. He relaxed and began to enjoy his attendance on Peter of Amiens and their frequent trips into Constantinople, for Aleaumes also reported that there were no suitors in Signor Matteo's house. Theodora kept close watch over her protégée and, though Anne's days were spent in luxury unlike any of them had ever known, her nights were unquestionably chaste.

The coronation of Alexius IV took place on August 1, the Feast of St. Peter. It was richly, royally done, so that even those who had become accustomed to the wealth of the Blachernae Palace during the intervening weeks were awestruck at the splendor of the ceremony.

Robert had been at Peter of Amiens's side night and day since Aleaumes' request had been made and granted, and both men had dropped into an easy camaraderie that in private at least ignored the gap of rank that separated them. Peter, too, had changed. He no longer spoke yearningly of the Holy Land, nor did he care for reminiscences of Corfu and the troubles they had shared there. At St. Pol's personal direction he was often at the palace, Robert accompanying him. Alexius IV seemed to have conceived an admiration for Peter that St. Pol considered valuable, for the newly crowned co-Emperor had allowed his dislike for Montferrat to become obvious, going to elaborate lengths to play the unapproachable monarch whenever the Marquis sought an audience.

In his own court Alexius was apparently sole master, and the barons hesitated to bring up the business of the payment still owed them. Isaac could be reasoned with and approached with dignity, but he was in rapidly failing health and a new party of discontents was forming around the prince, who as yet could not bring himself to apply his energies to the task of ruling.

Some monies had been paid, less than half the total agreed upon, and as the pressure grew from Murtzuphles' party to resist further payment, Alexius sought distraction wherever he could find it. Full payment was forthcoming, he assured the barons as he sat among their knights dicing and drinking heavily while his disapproving suite awaited his pleasure. Resist, drag your feet, delay, counseled his countrymen. Give up as little as possible. They will weaken with the waiting. The walls are being rebuilt and strengthened every night, though no Frank has spied it out yet. Delay long enough and they will sail away, never to return, for soon our strength will be greater than theirs.

He played both sides, one day the staunchest of the Greek patriots, vowing to drive the foreigners from their sacred soil, the next the compliant, beleaguered prince who must needs escape the protocol of his position lest it smother him. In reality his fear of what might happen to him at the hands of his own people was slowly overcoming his hatred of Montferrat. In his cups he recalled the fatherly way the Marquis had always directed him, for his own good, he readily admitted, for was not the Marquis in reality acting on behalf of Philip of Swabia, his own sister's loving husband? Each time he returned to his palace after an afternoon or evening spent at the crusaders' camp he was greeted first by a stony wall of disapproving silence from his senior councillors, then by urgent exhortations to mend his ways from his now partially bedridden father. Intrigues abounded on all sides and gradually he became convinced that if he did not feign to actively lead the party that wanted to oust the crusaders from their comfortable *séjour* in Galata he himself would be the victim of yet another palace revolt.

One truth was continually impressed on him: the Treasury was empty, or very nearly so. There was no possible way to raise the funds to pay the debt owed the Franks, especially as no revenue was coming in from the many cities of the Empire which still held to his uncle, Alexius III. He was ruler only of Constantinople itself and the immediate countryside, and that by virtue of the foreigners' army. Day after day he refused to come to grips with the problem, day after day his will weakened and his fears increased. He commanded that every new visitor to the city, every freak who could entertain or amuse, be brought to the palace to distract and amaze his visitors, for he had by now become distrustful of even the loyal Waring Guard and feared to leave the grounds of the Blachernae Palace.

"The Warings are sworn to protect the Emperor with their lives," he told Peter of Amiens one afternoon, "and they will always do their duty. They are the one constant in the life of this court. But they have no personal loyalties at all. If another should proclaim himself Emperor and seek to rule in my place, how could I be certain they would not choose him?"

"Little in life is certain, sire," replied Peter of Amiens. He was not overly fond of Alexius, but through much recent contact with him he had come to feel pity for this young Emperor who was so obviously a pawn in a game without rules. "The barons await your pleasure, my lord."

"I know why they've come," Alexius moaned, wringing his hands together in a familiar gesture of despair. "They come to remind me of my promises; they are growing impatient with the delay. Everyone at this court is impatient. But it will do no good. There is nothing I can do, nothing."

"They will be insulted if you do not receive them, sire."

"I know, Peter, I know. I tread warily these days, lest one side or another take offense. I will receive them, for friendship's sake, and also the Nubian king who begs audience. Together we will distract ourselves listening to this man's tale, and perhaps your barons will then leave me in peace for a while."

Peter doubted that any diversion, no matter how unusual or amusing, would cause the barons to forget even for the space of a single hour the unpaid debt that was the despair of Alexius's days and wakeful nights. The crusaders' mood was growing ugly; the first glow of easy success had faded, replaced by a restlessness and uneasiness which no amount of sightseeing in the city could satisfy. Some had begun to murmur that Michaelmas was barely six weeks away, Michaelmas when their covenant with Montferrat would end and they would be free to demand ships and provisions to continue the interrupted voyage to the Holy Land. It was amazing how that had been forgotten in the days when everyone had believed Constantinople would not willingly surrender. Now that there was no longer the probability of a war to occupy their minds, the crusaders had begun to split along the old lines established at Corfu. Alexius was not the only one to spend sleepless nights this hot month of August.

The Nubian king was a tall man, entirely black of skin, and as he approached the throne Alexius rose to greet him, such a signal honor that the French barons were amazed and bowed lower before this strange king than they had intended. An ugly scar disfigured the center of his forehead, and as they craned their necks for a better look at it, they whispered among themselves that it appeared to be a cross burned into the living flesh. What manner of strange vow had been fulfilled in such a painful way?

Alexius made much of him, calling him brother, inviting him to sit in the imperial presence, summoning an interpreter that all might hear his story from his own lips. His robes were of snowy white, simply cut and made of a coarse material resembling sacking, and above them his shaven head glowed smooth except where the horrible scar stood out in ridges of tortured flesh. He wore no crown, but no one there doubted that in his own country he was a very great king indeed. Majesty filled his being and flowed from him with every calm gesture. Even his guttural and utterly incomprehensible speech was kingly, for his voice was low, measured, the tones those of a man accustomed to instant, total obedience.

Through the interpreter he told them that his land lay one hundred days' march beyond Jerusalem and that his people were old Christians among whom the apostles had once walked. Every man and woman in his country wore the mark of the cross upon the forehead, for at baptism a hot iron burned it into the skin so that not only was the soul marked, but the body also.

To fulfill a vow he had given up his throne and gone on pilgrimage to Jerusalem, accompanied by sixty of his nobles. Fifty had died along the route, uncomplainingly surrendering their souls to a demanding God. Only he and two others survived to reach Constantinople, where they had been living the life of monks in one of the city's abbeys. God had restored their health and strength and tomorrow they would begin the long trek overland to Rome and thence to the shrine of Compostela to venerate the miraculously preserved body of St. James. It was their humble ambition to return to Jerusalem to die. As he rose to leave them the crusaders fell to their knees and begged his blessing, for he was the holiest man any had ever met. Reluctantly he sketched the cross over their heads and blessed even the Emperor who knelt briefly before him, then strode from the audience chamber with impassive, awesome dignity.

As Alexius had intended, the barons could think and talk of

nothing else for several days. It was a reprieve, but a short one; a week later came the command, phrased as an invitation, that he had been dreading. The lords and barons were meeting in parliament; would the Emperor honor them with his presence? A guard of honor would escort him to the quarters of the Count of Flanders and Hainault where the meeting was to take place.

There was no refusing the summons, but though he hated this Frankish custom of frequent parliaments at which every man of rank felt free to raise his voice in debate, he concealed his distaste with unusual skill. Politely, before any had the chance to harangue him about the debt, he asked permission to address the assembly, and the Doge and Montferrat, perhaps guessing what Alexius would propose, readily assented. Not all the barons were present, only the most noble and important commanders, and this made Alexius's task easier, for he was well aware of the ambitions that drove these men.

"My lords," he said, rising to his feet to do them honor, "by your help and God's Will I am Emperor and I have come into my lawful inheritance. Yet among the Greeks there are those who deny me my rights and there are enemies who seek my destruction. Michaelmas is almost upon us; the term of the covenant which binds you together is drawing to an end. Alas, I am unable in so short a time to fulfill the pledges I made to you in good faith. It is not my will that this should be so, but the will of my enemies, who are also yours. Because of my love for you the Greeks hate me, and if you depart from here at Michaelmas, they will kill me. I would make a new covenant with you, that you remain here until March, and during that time assist me in the reconquest and pacification of the lands that are mine by holy ordinance. By this means my Treasury, despoiled and emptied by the usurper, will be filled again, and I shall be able to pay you the monies agreed upon and more, for I shall bear all your expenses during the time of your stay. And the advantage will be yours, for if you remain until March you shall have the whole of the spring and summer in which to conduct your war against the infidels, whereas if you sail at Michaelmas winter will soon be upon you, and the seas and lands treacherous and unfriendly. What say you to my proposal?"

Silence was the only answer to his question, the same un-

fathomable silence into which he had spoken his carefully rehearsed speech.

"We will consult together and tomorrow we will meet in general parliament," said Montferrat, a trace of condescension in his
voice now that Alexius had finally admitted the vulnerability of
his new-won throne. "It is our custom to do nothing without
the full consent of the entire army, for we are all brother soldiers
in Christ. You shall have our answer in two days' time."

The general parliament lasted a whole day, from early morning until late into the night, and the wrangling was so fierce that
meals remained uncooked and even the precious horses were
neglected. It was Corfu all over again, only this time there were
no uninvolved parties standing calmly aside from the fray, content to see which side would carry the day before committing
themselves. Even the foot soldiers debated among themselves,
taking the part of whichever baron had won their allegiance.

There was one important defector from the ranks of the Corfu
conspiracy, and this was the leader himself, Peter of Amiens. His
support of their commanders' wishes weakened the opposition
and caused it finally to collapse. If a man like Peter of Amiens,
whose honor was above question, conceded the wisdom of
remaining where they were throughout the winter, then perhaps
there was no new betrayal being plotted by the army's leaders.
It was hard to face another long period of inactivity when the
very stones of the Holy Land cried out for the Holy Sepulcher's
tardy rescuers, but if a man could but cool his passions and
think clearly, it was obvious that a spring and summer campaign
stood a far greater chance of success than one begun in the chill
of autumn.

Messengers were sent to bring the good news to the Emperor.
The crusaders would remain until March at least, and half their
number would ride the countryside with Alexius. Montferrat,
who would lead them, counseled speed. Could the Emperor be
ready to leave within three days' time? He could indeed, came
the reply, and he rejoiced that once more the army had placed
duty and honor above all other considerations. Almost as an afterthought he hinted that those who followed Montferrat could
expect to profit personally during the expedition. The Emperor

was prepared to close his eyes to a little private looting, provided that it did not get out of control and did not impose undue hardship on the people whose loyalty he was bent on winning.

Inevitably the news leaked out and there were many who envied the men chosen to accompany the Greeks. There might be hard fighting and, of course, the discomforts of life in the field—but no one had so far profited from their stay in Constantinople, and the constant display of untouchable wealth just beyond their grasp had whetted many appetites. Three divisions would ride with the Emperor, those under the command of the Marquis of Montferrat, the Count of St. Pol and Henry of Flanders. Baldwin would remain as commander-in-chief of the other divisions, assisted by Villehardouin and Louis of Blois and Chartres. The Doge had the sole charge of the Venetians and no desire whatever to take his men far from the sea.

The day before they left Robert received permission to put his private affairs in order. Peter had looked pityingly at his most trusted vassal, the young man he had honored with his friendship, and had with great difficulty held his tongue. A fine man like Robert of Clari ought not to demean himself by thralldom to a woman. The whole situation was incomprehensible to Peter, who had never in his life given any thought to love. In his world one married and begat sons for duty's sake, slaked one's lust with easily available whores and conserved one's energies for the wars and intrigues that brought power, wealth and new lands to rule. Had Robert asked his advice he would have told him to avoid this strange ex-nun, for Aleaumes in his agitation had told him everything. What had she to offer but the dubious patronage of an uncle she had never met, an uncle who might have died years ago for all anyone knew, so undependable and infrequent were communications with the court of the Kingdom of Jerusalem. To Peter's mind his vassal's best hope of advancement lay in returning to his own lands with as much loot as he could carry back from the Holy Land and from this new campaign. He had already doubled his fief by marriage, and by his bravery in the field and his good service had won the respect of lords who would grant him many marks of preference when all were home again. The slow, sure, time-honored ways of advancement were the best and the most certain. To throw it all away by a stubborn alliance with a woman who, according to Aleaumes, was herself consumed with an ambition that made a mockery of love, was folly of the highest order. Stupidity, Peter would have called it had it been anyone but Robert who acted thus. As it was, he sent him off to bid farewell to his Anne, hoping that their projected three months' absence would cool his ardor.

"This is an opportunity I hardly dared hope for," he told her. "When I return I will bring with me the gold that will free both of us, but it will be only the beginning of what I shall one day lay at your feet." For once the duenna had been dismissed so that Robert and Anne could converse without restraint in the cool shade of Signor Matteo's garden. The high walls of this impressive house rose all around them, and as Robert gazed at the stone carvings of the gallery he promised himself a dwelling that would put this one to shame.

In spite of the distrust and dislike he instinctively felt for the Venetian merchant, he was grateful now for the care Anne had received from this family. She had bloomed under their ministrations like an exotic flower too long cut off from the life-giving sun. Her skin, reddened by sunburn and roughened by salt air, had become smooth again, pale and delicate, and the luxuriant masses of her hair, bound discreetly in a net of gold thread, gleamed with health and subtly perfumed oils. She wore a dress of gold-embroidered blue silk, for no other color suited her quite as well, and in her ears, around her throat and on her fingers sapphires winked and sparkled in the dappled sunlight. She was a vision to send any man's blood boiling through his veins, and Robert hungrily drank her in, consciously choosing to carry this new image of her to whichever Greek cities the army journeyed.

"Will Aleaumes be going with you?"

"Mounted, armored and sword in hand. He seems to have forgotten he was ever made a clerk."

"I shall miss you both dreadfully."

"Though differently, I hope."

"Robert, do not chide me. You know what I mean."

"Nay, Anne. I would not spoil this hour with a quarrel."

"We have quarreled a great deal lately, Robert, and most of

the time it has been my fault. Each time I have wished I could take back the words I spoke in anger, and each time I have sworn to hold my tongue in future. But the anger bubbles out against my will and I cannot hold it in check. I have been very unfair to you." Anne's head dropped forward on her breast in the attitude of a willful child who seeks to soften an angry parent.

"Anne, my love, look at me." Robert held both her hands in his and slowly she raised her head, though still she did not seem able to meet his eyes. "The poets and the Courts of Love hold that unless a love is hard won and oft tested it is false, shallow and of no value, that those whose love is easy are not true lovers. Whatever else men may say of the love that binds us together, they cannot claim that it has been lightly given."

"Or that I have not tested my knight almost beyond human endurance. But each test I have imposed upon him has been met and overcome with grace and generosity of spirit. And so he well deserves my love." Anne smiled. Here in this peaceful garden, dressed more richly than any Western princess, she could in truth imagine herself a great lady whose mind busied itself with nothing more dangerous or unpleasant than a casual toying with her lover's affections. The shameful flight from her convent cell into a camp of soldiers, the long months of servile attendance on Mary of Flanders, the widow's disguise and the months of hiding amid a crowd of smelly, half-deranged, fanatic pilgrims, even the moldy crusts of bread and slimy bacon that had added to the horror of her seasickness and the constant fear of shipwreck, all these she had begun mercifully to forget. In fact, though she dared not mention it to Robert, who would most surely forbid it, Signor Matteo had recently hinted that a change in her uncertain status might be simple to effect and far more to her liking than continued residence in his busy household, where the close quarters and many extra guests had already given birth to tensions among the many women gathered under that one roof.

As he said his last farewell Robert begged her not to accompany him to the massive wooden door that gave onto the street. He wanted to remember her just as she was, the fairest flower in a fair garden, and she kept her seat, amused at the many backward glances he cast at her as he disappeared into the house. For some reason he felt obliged to assure Signor Matteo that the monies lavished on Anne would be repaid with interest from the plunder he was certain would fall into his hands in the next few months. Anne had no wish to witness the anger with which the Venetian would receive this further proof of a knight's disdain, nor to see Robert make such a fool of himself.

When she heard the noise of the great door opening, then closing with a heavy, somehow final sound, she let out her breath in a long, relieved sigh. Three months or more, Robert had said, three months of blessed freedom from the difficult double game she had played so long. For a while at least she would not be forced to act the gentle, loving maiden whose heart and will were no longer her own, the lover to whose lips sweet words seemed spontaneously to spring at the mere sight of her knight's glowing, tender face. Though nothing had been said, she knew that Signor Matteo was not fooled by her masquerade. She had very prettily begged him to receive her lover courteously, hinting that it would pain her should the obvious dislike he had conceived for Robert during the first days of her stay continue. She herself might quarrel with her knight, greet him coldly and almost rudely, but this was the way she held him, at times yielding him everything, at other moments withholding even her hand from his kiss of greeting.

Now that he was safely gone from the house and by tomorrow would have ridden many leagues from the city, she put him as easily from her mind as though he had never begged her to think of him each time she sat in the garden. "You will find me here, on this bench, when you return," she had promised him, "and it will be as though you had only stepped from the garden for the space of a few brief moments." Men were such fools, she thought, beginning to pace up and down the close-cropped path, and though some women would have thought the thought with laughing tenderness, knowing it was only half true, it came to Anne's mind with cold calculation.

Now she turned Signor Matteo's recent proposal over in her mind, testing it for weaknesses, assessing the gains that could be expected to accrue from the service he had suggested, weighing the manner in which the merchant would use her against her own willingness to profit from such use. She wasn't proud, just careful, and she knew that the merchant, and even Theodora and Nicholas, valued her steeliness of purpose and willingness to abase herself if necessary to attain her ends far more than they respected the much-vaunted, useless qualities that the empty code of chivalry professed to serve.

In Constantinople lived a great lady, Matteo had told her, called by everyone the French Empress because she was sister to King Philip Augustus and had wed the Emperor Alexius II at the age of eight or nine. Her child husband had been overthrown and strangled by Andronicus Comnenus and, though he was over sixty years of age and she barely twelve when the revolt took place, he had forced her to marry him and share his bed. For two years this unnatural union had been the scandal of the entire world until Andronicus had been overthrown in his turn by Isaac. Agnes of France, or Anna as she had been rechristened when she had first come to Constantinople, was forced by her husband into ignominious flight and a mercifully brief exile, her only female companion Andronicus's favorite concubine. The former Emperor was quickly apprehended and brought back to Constantinople, where Isaac had him publicly tortured and then executed in a manner that was still talked of with ghoulish delight by all who had witnessed it. It had been whispered throughout the city that Agnes-Anna, still in her early teens, had avidly watched the mangling of her husband's body, urging the torturers on to greater refinements of their profession, chortling with an almost maniacal glee as Andronicus's eyes were put out, his bones cracked and the blood spilled upon the ground. That night, so the story went, she had held a great feast in the luxurious apartments Isaac had given her, and though she was always called the French Empress, everyone knew that her sufferings had caused her to become more Byzantine than the Byzantines themselves.

Isaac had married her off to a great noble, Theodore Branas, and when he himself took a second wife, the ten-year-old Margaret-Maria of Hungary, the French Empress, so young herself, had befriended Isaac's bride, even during the period of Isaac's own blinding and imprisonment. The two Empresses were closely linked by ties of suffering no mere man could even begin to fathom, and by the hatreds each nourished against the families that had sent them so young to such glory and such despair. Never, during all the years that Agnes-Anna had suffered outrages few women would have survived, had her brother, the King of France, so much as lifted a finger to help her, and Hungary likewise had ignored its daughter. Agnes-Anna hated her brother with every fiber of her body, and because of his indifference to her, she hated all the men of his nation. When Louis of Blois and Chartres had sought her out she had hissed and spat at him in angry Greek, having long ago decided never again to speak the language of her childhood. Louis's mother, Alix, was her half sister, and Agnes-Anna thus the Count's own aunt, but kinship was no longer a remedy for the venomous hatred she felt for all Franks.

It was an interesting situation, was it not, Matteo had commented, and then had begun to speak of other, more mundane things, topics which held no interest at all now for Anne, whose fertile mind was entirely concerned with the story of the French Empress. A few days later he had told her that another, even more interesting development was taking place. Louis of Blois had not, it seemed, accepted his aunt's rejection. He had made repeated visits to the palace where she lived in royal state and, always through an interpreter, had managed to express his profound sympathy for the sufferings of her early life and his admiration for the way she had risen above them. She had gradually softened toward this nephew, even to the point of exchanging family confidences, and when Louis had told her the whole story of her half sister Alice's misfortunes at the English court, she had been moved to tears, the only tears she had been known to shed since the murder of her first husband. Louis had very cautiously allowed a note of criticism to creep into his voice as he spoke of Alice's seduction by her intended father-in-law, Henry II, the years she had been his secret mistress, and the cold way in which Coeur-de-Lion, who ought to have married her, had spurned her as "spoiled goods."

"Was there ever such a brother?" Agnes-Anna had cried out. Even this heartfelt cry had to pass through the interpreter. Now she regretted that she no longer spoke French, for here was a kinsman to whom at last she could pour out her heart.

So Louis of Blois and Chartres was caught in a dilemma of his own making, for there were things he longed to discuss with his powerful kinswoman, practically a friend and ally now, that could not be allowed to be heard by any ears but their own.

The solution to the Count's problem came, of course, from Nicholas, who always and in every circumstance kept a sensitive finger on the pulse of events that might concern him. Let Louis suggest to Agnes-Anna that she include a Frenchwoman in her suite, a woman of noble birth who had also been a victim of life's misfortunes and for whom such an act would be a charity pleasing to God. Anne was skilled in languages; she spoke perfect Greek and near-perfect Italian, and she was familiar with Nicholas's time-proven methods of teaching foreign tongues. Within a few weeks' attendance on the Empress, during which time Anne would converse with her mistress only in French, Agnes-Anna's knowledge of her girlhood tongue would come flooding back. The knowledge was not lost, merely buried in the farthest recesses of the Empress's brain. Nicholas guaranteed that long before Michaelmas aunt and nephew would be conversing as easily as if Agnes-Anna had never left France.

Agnes-Anna, when the plan had been explained to her, was almost pathetically eager to welcome her new attendant, and Louis of Blois impatiently demanded that Anne be conducted to the Empress's palace immediately. He took it ill when told that for reasons that could not be revealed, the young noblewoman in question could not leave her present residence until the Emperor's army had left the city. He too was anxious for them to be gone, but for reasons of his own. He chafed and fumed at the delay while Anne restlessly paced her garden paths. Matteo and Nicholas, two patient men of the world, marveled at how easily fate could be bent to the service of the farseeing.

V

Agnes-Anna conceived an immediate liking for Anne, and in the weeks that followed, as the Empress's command of the French tongue did indeed return with truly amazing swiftness, she pressed many rich gifts on her tutor, rings she stripped from her own fingers, gowns that cost a king's ransom but which the Empress would wear only once, bolts of new, uncut cloth stiff with gold and silver thread. Always Anne received these presents with the dignity of one who bestows rather than receives, and long before Robert had deposited the first plundered cup in his saddlebags, Anne was possessed of a rich assortment of easily negotiable goods, all of which she sent to Signor Matteo's house for safekeeping. Although no one in the Empress's palace dared speak against her, she knew that because she was a Frank she was hated there and an easy prey to petty viciousness.

Toward the end of August a fire broke out in Constantinople that forced Agnes-Anna and her household to move for safety's sake into the Blachernae Palace, well away from the flames that raged through the heart of the city and threatened for a while to destroy Santa Sophia itself. For two days and two nights the city burned; churches, palaces and the wooden shacks of the poor all were destroyed with terrible equality. Hundreds of men, women and children were burned to death in the narrow, twisting streets, and in the Blachernae Palace the women covered their ears to deaden the sound of a screaming which not even the roar of the flames and the crash of falling buildings could drown out.

When at last the fire burned itself out, a strange exodus began. Every foreign trader in the city, no matter what his nationality, gathered whatever goods he could carry and fled with his family to Galata and the safety of the crusading army. Those who scorned such flight were hunted down and beaten to death with bare fists by enraged Greeks, men whose hair had been singed from their bodies by the fearsome heat, fathers and husbands whose families had perished in the flames, patriots who could no longer stomach the horrors that had come upon them with the return of Alexius Angelus to the land of his fathers.

Villehardouin sent messengers spurring after Alexius and the army, urging them to return to the capital where, he said, the situation was urgent and every Frank walked in danger of his life. While he waited for a reply and daily struggled with the problem of how to provide for the fifteen thousand refugees who had reached Galata safely, he cursed the Greek emperors whose softness and laxity in matters of religion had been the indirect cause of the fire.

There had been fights aplenty between Frank, Italian and Greek, street skirmishes that were quickly quelled with little damage other than a few broken bones and bruised heads, but it was the presence of a Saracen mosque in Christian Constantinople that had caused this last and greatest disaster. After having drunk themselves almost into insensibility, a band of Pisan residents, joined by Flemish and Venetian soldiers from the camp, had conceived the grandiose scheme of pillaging this rich temple, which was an abomination to every right-thinking Christian. Resentment of the mosque had smoldered for years. Pisans and Venetians, usually the most bitter of rivals, had at least one prejudice in common, and it made them bold to the point of rashness. But the Greeks were a tolerant people who had long ago made peace with Moslem beliefs, and many had come rushing through the streets to help in the defense of the mosque, obliging the Westerners to flee for their lives. The Venetians had once before successfully covered a retreat with fire; they quickly set their torches to the same work. This time they had succeeded beyond their wildest dreams.

From Villehardouin's vantage point in the tower of Galata, it seemed that fully a third of the city had been laid waste. The crusaders were safe as long as they did not try to enter the city, but what would happen when the Emperor's army returned to find its loved ones dead, maimed or homeless, he did not dare to dwell on. Yet still he had impressed on the messengers the necessity of urging the Marquis and the Emperor to return with all speed. If somehow they did so, and quickly, reparations could be made, assistance given in burying the dead, housing the homeless, caring for the bewildered survivors. Prayers and Masses could be offered, they could mourn together as Christians and perhaps repair the terrible damage and close the widening breach between them.

But the answer, when it came, was a curt refusal to interrupt a triumphant and important progress merely because a few old buildings had gone up in flames. Were Villehardouin and Flanders incapable of taking hold of the situation? If so, Louis of Blois could take command. The army and the Emperor would not return until the conquest of the Empire was complete.

Men later said that the Marshal of Champagne grew old and whiteheaded in a single night, and they were not far from the truth.

Alexius and the army did not return until the Feast of St. Martin in early November. The day on which they marched triumphantly toward the devastated city was bitterly cold, with low-hanging gray clouds that promised an early snow, yet almost the entire populace went out to escort the Emperor on the last league of his journey. Crowds of crusaders left their camp at Galata and streamed over the plain, eager to gaze at the booty their countrymen had won, eager too to tell the story of the great fire and the months of fear and near-starvation that had followed it. For the first time since the holocaust Greeks and Franks mingled and met without open hostility, for many ladies had been carried out on the plain in their litters, their bright-colored garments and richly decorated vehicles lending an air of festival to this long-awaited homecoming.

The Greeks appeared overjoyed to see Alexius, an attitude that astounded many of the Frankish barons, who remembered with what fear and loathing the young Emperor had spoken of his people. Were these cheering crowds composed of the same men and women whom Alexius had accused of plotting his death? Either the Emperor had deliberately misled the crusaders or the capital had undergone a sudden and complete change of heart. Any monarch greeted in such an enthusiastic, loving way would bask in their adulation, as Alexius was now doing, confident that his throne was both unshakable and unassailable.

Alexius was surprised and frightened at the first sight of the mob advancing to meet him, but as their cries of praise and welcome reached his ears and became distinct, he straightened in his saddle and handed his helmet to an aide. The red hair he had inherited from his father blazed out in the gloomy damp of that winter's day, making him easily identifiable both to the Greeks and to the Franks, who excitedly compared those fiery locks to the red-gold hair that had been Coeur-de-Lion's trademark.

It was a theatrical gesture, one that the English king himself had often employed, and the crowd roared its approval, closing in around their handsome young sovereign, cutting him off from the Marquis of Montferrat, who struggled to hide his rage at such interference. Alexius was borne off to the city, sparing not even a backward glance or word of farewell to the Franks who had so loyally served him and who now made their way back to Galata on the other side of the Horn.

There was great rejoicing in Constantinople that afternoon, celebrations that lasted far into the night in every palace and hovel. Much of the Empire had now acknowledged Alexius IV, only a very few of the far-outlying cities still holding obstinately to Alexius III. The former Emperor was still at large, still riding the fringes of the kingdom fomenting dissent and uttering terrible threats against his nephew and his Western supporters, but his cause was a hopeless one and, eventually, perhaps during the spring campaigns, he would be captured and dragged back to Constantinople to endure a terrifying, thoroughly entertaining public execution. Alexius IV had proved himself a man and a Greek, for had he not used the crusaders to his own advantage? And they all unknowing? To the Emperor had fallen whole cities and vast stretches of fertile land, a promise of wealth and a renewal of prosperity in the reunified Empire, while no Greek had failed to notice that the packhorses and saddlebags of the Franks were scarcely more full than when they had left.

There was rejoicing in the crusaders' camp also, but it was dampened by a bitter disappointment. The cities they had conquered had all chosen easy, swift surrender, abject pledges of obedience to the restored Isaac and his son, and though they had provided provisions and entertainment aplenty, there had been no plausible excuse for the wholesale looting that the common soldiers in particular had counted on. Knowing their disappointment, Montferrat had wrung a promise from Alexius that each man who had marched with him would be paid a certain sum, according to his rank, from the revenues that would shortly begin flowing into the Emperor's coffers. With this the crusaders had to be content, but knowing Alexius's past record in the discharge of his debts, they were uneasy and openly disbelieving.

Of all the crusaders, none was as bitterly disappointed as Robert of Clari. All during the long march back to Constantinople he had prepared himself for the moment when he must face Anne and confess to her that his great dream had been as insubstantial as the morning mist. All he had to show for his three months of campaigning was a single gold cup that a frightened abbot had thrust into his hands when he and a small party of advance scouts had suddenly appeared at the monastery gates to demand a night's shelter for the Emperor. Upon learning that his monastery was not to be razed to the ground by foreign invaders, the abbot had thought to ask for the return of his chalice, but changed his mind and called it a gift of hospitality after one look at the knight's angry scowl. That and a few silver coins won at dice were Robert's sole acquisitions for three months of hard service, and he had kept the cup at peril of his life, for once it became apparent that little if any fighting would take place, strict orders against looting or extortions from the populace had come from the Marquis and the other commanders.

During the short walk to the Pareto house from the lodgings that he and Aleaumes shared, he decided that he would present the cup to Anne as a love gift, the first he had been able to give her. She would be pleased, for it was a delicately worked object, admirably suited to an altar or a lady's table. In the joy of their reunion after so long a separation there would be much to talk about, and perhaps she would not ask him outright about the other riches he had promised to bring back. He had only an hour to spend with her; Peter of Amiens had informed him that he expected Robert to attend him as closely as he had done in

August. An hour was scarcely enough time for all he wished to tell her of his experiences, of the loneliness and longing for her that had made the hours and the days pass with agonizing slowness, but as he knocked on Signor Matteo's door he was humming to himself one of the happy little tunes heard often in the marketplaces of France, a song that recounted the story of a lovers' reunion in endless bawdy verses.

The servant who peered through the barred wicket at him was a new man, and very reluctant to admit this unknown knight to his master's house. Repeatedly Robert gave his name and the purpose of his visit, to pay his compliments to the lady Anne of Nanteuil, who was Signor Matteo's honored guest. The servant was obviously dim-witted, insisting that the knight had mistaken this house for another. No Frankish lady of that name dwelt within, though yes, to be sure, the dwelling did belong to the Pareto family.

Robert had just drawn his sword and was about to hammer with its heavy pommel on the door when Signor Matteo himself opened it, apologizing profusely for his servant's stupidity.

"The man is newly come to service in this house, and has never fully recovered from the shocks he suffered during the great fire," Signor Matteo explained as he led Robert into the small, richly appointed chamber where most of his business was conducted. "He was servant to a kinsman of mine who perished in the disaster. But for that I would not have taken him in." The Venetian continued talking as he poured wine for himself and his guest and saw Robert ensconced in a comfortable, thronelike chair close to the blazing fire, seemingly unaware of Robert's attempts to interrupt him. He whispered some instructions to the woman servant who had brought the wine, and Robert, certain that Anne was being sent for and would in a very few minutes join them, began to pay attention to what his host was saying.

"It was a terrible disaster, the worst I have ever known, and the suffering of the people was heartbreaking. The Greeks have sought to place the blame on us, of course, and have driven our people from the city, which is why this quarter is so crowded now. It's common knowledge that it was a gang of ruffians, Pisans and some of your people, who set the flames, but do the Greeks care for justice? Not at all. Every respectable trader in the city has been blamed, and I needn't tell you that the business losses have been tremendous. It will take years to recoup them. We live in a sad time, sir knight, a sad time, and the future is black indeed."

Signor Matteo shook his head mournfully, and in the few seconds before he began speaking again, Robert knew that he neither liked nor trusted this richly dressed merchant who lived so opulently while better men than he had to scramble for survival. The Venetian clothed himself in the finest of woolen robes and his feet were encased in soft, tooled leather. His hands had never known callouses and his old skin was stretched tight over the fat of good living, while Robert, though hard and muscled from outdoor living, suffered periodically from the same debilitating dysentery his father had known, a malaise brought on by the evil food and poor sanitation of camp life. He would ride and fight, be wounded or perhaps killed outright, risk all he had or ever hoped to gain in the service of his suzerain, yet who would always be assured of a profit thereby? Not the knight who conquered the land, but the merchant who exploited it. It was enough to turn a man's stomach.

"Yes, there has been great suffering in this city, and many have known the blackest despair. We have had to absorb over fifteen thousand refugees, you know. I myself took in as many as my house could hold. And without complaint, mind you, for the sake of Christian charity, yet it has worked a great hardship upon every man, no matter what his station. The tales we have been told would move even the hardest heart to tears. Many of our people were lost during the two days and nights when the fire spread unchecked. A wind came up and fanned the flames, you see, so that many knew not where to run to escape them. The kinsman of whom I spoke has not been heard of since the outbreak of the blaze. We searched as best we could and made inquiries of the Greeks, but he and his whole household, even the children and every servant but one, disappeared without a trace. We had not even the comfort of giving their poor bodies Christian burial. That is the greatest blow of all, not to know the manner or the place of their dying. Our only comfort is the knowledge that they are safe in the bosom of the Lord, and with that we must be content."

Signor Matteo talked on, his words tumbling over one another in an almost incoherent babble until Robert's head began to ache with the strain. He nodded from time to time, but he heard little of what the merchant said. His ears were listening for the sound of approaching footsteps, and when at last he heard a soft knocking at the door he sprang eagerly from his seat, only half conscious that Signor Matteo's voice had trailed off into silence.

But it was Theodora, not Anne, who advanced into the room with hands outstretched in welcome. Robert peered into the darkness behind her, but she had come alone, and the touch of her hands on his was dry and lifeless. She kissed him on the cheek, a tender, motherly gesture that surprised him and made him vaguely uneasy. Always before she had treated him with a very distant respect, rather like an old and privileged retainer whose liberties stopped short of intimacy.

"Have you told him yet?" she asked Signor Matteo, continuing to hold Robert's hands in hers.

"I had not the courage, Theodora."

Robert stared at Theodora, then at the door through which she had come, now being softly closed by the same old man who had tried to keep him from entering this house. Anne was not coming. She was not even expected, else why the closed door? Some unknown fear screamed briefly in his brain before he managed to push it back. "If she is ill, let me go to her at once," he said, trying to pull his hands from the old woman's strong grip.

"Robert, sit down," said Theodora firmly. "You shall know it all, though I would rather have died than be the bearer of such news." Her eyes filled with tears as she let loose his hands. With a terrible sense of foreboding Robert sank back in his chair and stared numbly at her. "Robert, this is a house of mourning. Anne, our beloved Anne, is no longer with us."

"No longer with you? How could she leave? Where has she gone?"

"We have not seen her since several days before the great fire, Robert."

"But Galata did not burn. You are all safe. She was not to leave this house. She made me a promise."

"Robert, we tried to stop her, but she was restless and discontented without you. She wanted to visit the great cathedrals of the city and offer prayers for your safe return in the Venetian chapel there. We begged her not to go, but she wouldn't listen. So finally we arranged that she should spend a few days in the house of Matteo's kinsman. The city was quiet. We did not dream that she would come to harm. No one could have foreseen the attack on the mosque or that another fire would be set. She left this house laughing and happy, Robert, and that is how you must remember her."

He sat as if dead himself while Theodora rubbed his ice-cold hands and glanced anxiously at Signor Matteo, who had moved from in front of the crackling fire into a side pool of darkness. The orange light flickered over Robert's set face, picking out the high cheekbones and the muscles that stood out in knots in his throat and along the line of his jaw. Still he said nothing, but the crackle of the fire drew his eyes and the dark pupils widened as he saw the full horror of Anne's death.

"To die by burning." His voice seemed to come from a great distance.

"We do not know that for certain, Robert. Do not allow yourself even to think of such a thing. Many died in their beds from the smoke, never knowing that they were passing from this life until it was done."

"She died in the flames," he continued. "And I was not here to save her or to share her death."

"This way lies madness, Robert." Theodora picked up the wine cup and held it to his lips. "Drink," she said sternly, "all of it." The wine trickled from the corners of his mouth and he choked on it, then he snatched the cup from Theodora's hand and drained it at a single swallow. She took it from him and refilled it, and as she handed it to him again his eyes turned finally from the flames. They bored into her with terrible urgency, but she met his stare unflinchingly and finally they wavered and fell. He seemed to believe the unthinkable.

"The servant who escaped," he said, clearing the thickness from his throat. "Bring him here."

"He can tell you nothing," said Signor Matteo, a bodyless voice from the shadows. "We interrogated him ourselves over and over in those first few days. His mind is addled and he is worse than a child."

"Bring him here," repeated Robert, his hand on his sword, "or I shall find him myself."

Theodora nodded her head and Signor Matteo went to the door, opened it quietly and spoke to someone just outside. Robert watched him closely, and as the man whose face he had glimpsed through the wicket shuffled into the room he strode to the door and slammed it shut. The servant started at the boom of wood striking wood and began to whimper, his hands spasmodically clasping and unclasping the folds of his shirt. A miserable creature, but Robert was far beyond pitying him.

"Giovanni," said Signor Matteo softly, reassuringly, "this knight has questions to ask you and you must answer them as best you can. Will you do that?"

The man grinned a foolish grin and bobbed his head up and down. The thought came maddeningly to Robert's mind that he looked just like the puppets that jesters worked to amuse a crowd of children. He stood where he was, back against the door, hand clasping the hilt of his sword, and rapped out a question. No one would leave this room until all his questions were answered.

"Giovanni!"

The head continued its rhythmic bobbing, but the servant shuffled his feet and faced the strange, angry knight.

"A lady came to stay in the household you served, a lady with black hair and blue eyes, a countrywoman of mine. Do you remember her?"

"I was doorkeeper, my lord. I saw everyone who came and went. It was my duty to bolt and unbolt the door to my master's house. I performed my duty well, always. My master had no complaint of me."

"Do you remember the lady I have just described to you?"

"Lady? There were many ladies. My master had five daughters and many ladies came to the house. Sometimes they gave me a coin or two for my services."

"Giovanni," prompted Theodora, "the lady of whom we speak was a Frenchwoman. She came to the house two days before the fire broke out."

"Everyone was burned in the fire. All the ladies dead and all the gentlemen. The children screamed. My wife was burned too.

She was head cook and she burned in two fires." Great convulsive sobs burst from the man's throat and he swayed on his feet, eyes tightly closed on his memories, until it seemed he would fall on the floor in his agony.

Robert slapped him hard on the face, then shook him until the tongue drooled from his mouth.

"Tell me of the Frenchwoman," he hissed, his face close to the servant's slobbering jaws.

"Wait, Robert. You will get nothing from him like this. He has told us his story and he will repeat it for you, but you must not beat him." Theodora turned the servant around and led him to Signor Matteo's chair, then knelt in front of him. "Tell it again, Giovanni, as you told it to me the first day you came here."

"The lady came to my master's house. She went out with my master's daughters. They went to pray in the churches and they visited the goldsmiths' market." The voice droned on, expressionless, as the story was told like a lesson learned by rote. Theodora's eyes never left Giovanni's, and when he stumbled in his recitation she pressed his hands firmly until he could continue. "She was a beautiful lady and kind. I remember her well because she always spoke softly to me. We all slept through the first night of the fire. It was far away and no one brought the alarm. In the morning my master said we must leave the city while there was still time. All the ladies wore their best jewels, but concealed beneath their clothes. They wore plain dark cloaks so no one would be tempted to set upon and rob us. We left the house all together at Tierce. My master said we would hire a boat in the harbor by the Boucoleon Palace. The fire was north and east of us and we thought we could skirt it easily. But the wind began to blow and the flames swept through Mesé Street, cutting us off from the harbor. We turned to go back the way we had come, but we could not go quickly because of the small children we carried. We returned to my master's house, which was not yet burning, and we thought that if we hid in the stone cellars with wet rugs piled over the entrance we would be safe. We set to work with buckets, even the children, but my master took me aside and told me I must run through the burning streets and somehow reach a tiny cove where his eldest sons often went to fish. Their boat was hidden there, if none had stolen it. I did not want to go, but he said they would be safe enough and that I was to bring the boat up the shore as close to our quarter as possible. When the fire burned itself out I was to return and lead them to the boat." His voice trailed off and after a moment Theodora picked up the recitation.

"You went to the cove, but the boat was not there. Then you attempted to return to your master's house, but the entire quarter was ablaze and the streets were full of burning timbers."

"Theodora, I want to hear it from his own lips," interrupted Robert harshly.

"The boat was not there," continued Giovanni in the same rotelike manner. "I tried to go back, but the streets were blocked. I tried to lift the burning timbers that fell across my path, but I could not. My arms were burned." He pushed back the sleeves of his tunic, exposing the scarred and withered flesh of his arms as though challenging Robert to doubt the truth of what he said. "I don't remember anything else. Someone led me out with a crowd of other refugees, a friend of my master's who recognized me. I was brought here, to this house. Mistress Theodora treated my burns and would not let me die. Ever since I have kept the door for Master Matteo. I never leave this house."

"Sir knight," said Signor Matteo, laying a restraining hand on Robert's arm, "he has told his horrible tale many times. We have pressed him over and over for more details, but what he says is true, he can remember nothing more. Let him go now. He is an old man and deserves to spend the rest of this night in the peace of his own bed."

"I will bring you a sleeping draught, Giovanni," Theodora said as she guided the servant to the door. He still mumbled under his breath and shook his head from side to side like a blown horse before it sinks to its knees. Robert moved aside to let him pass.

Theodora sighed deeply. "There is only a little more, Robert, and then we shall be done with it."

Matteo Pareto took up the grim tale.

"For many weeks after the fire no foreigner was permitted to enter the city. If it had not been for the presence of your army here the Greeks would have massacred us in our beds. But your priests and monks, especially the Cistercians, went daily to the gates and pleaded to be allowed in to nurse any Westerner who had escaped the flames and recite the prayers for the dead over the bodies of those who had not. They were told that all who had not fled had perished, and this was true. A deputation visited the abbeys and the hospitals and found only Greeks in them. I do not know what threats were used, but finally we were allowed to send people in to search the rubble. By that time it was too late to recover the bodies of our loved ones, for the Greeks, greatly fearing disease, had scoured the city and buried all the fire's victims in a common grave. My eldest son, after great difficulty, found the ruins of my kinsman's house. Heavy beams had fallen across the entrance to his cellars and for a day and a night he and his servants worked to clear them away. We hoped, you see, to find the family still alive underground, for Giovanni had told us that the cellars were used as storehouses and that there was food and wine there more than sufficient for their needs. They broke through at last, but the cellars were empty. My son said the air in them was fresh and breathable from many small open places between the stones, and there was a large pile of pillows and rugs heaped on the floor. Somehow they were cut off from the cellars. Perhaps they delayed too long, trying to save the house. No one will ever know. My son continued to search even after it was apparent no one had survived, and in what was once the garden, lying on a stone bench, he found this."

On Signor Matteo's palm lay a small circlet of twisted black metal. Someone had rubbed the soot from one side of it, and the firelight caught the dull gleam of gold and a spark of blue light.

"I gave this ring to the Lady Anne myself," said Signor Matteo, handing the tiny object to Robert. "God did not give me any daughters, but when your lady came to grace my house it was as though He had at last relented. Forgive me, but I loved her too."

The ring was burning into the flesh of Robert's palm with a cold fire more painful than any he had ever known.

"She must have taken it from her finger and laid it on the stone bench for you to find," said Theodora softly.

"She said she would be waiting for me in the garden."

"That was all we found, Robert. She died with the others, perhaps in her last moments comforting a frightened child." Theodora stared at the ring for a moment as if to summon up the spirit of its owner. "Keep it, Robert. None but loving, sorrowful hands have touched it since it left her finger." Theodora took the piece of black velvet Signor Matteo held out to her and wrapped the ring securely in it. A tiny smudge of soot remained on Robert's outstretched, empty palm. Gently she placed the precious velvet in his hand, then closed the fingers over it.

"Masses have been said for her soul and the souls of all our loved ones and there will be prayers in perpetuity. It has all been seen to. Nothing more remains to be done." Signor Matteo's shoulders sagged under the weight of his sorrow, as with an apologetic reference to the bodily weaknesses of old age he sank deep into his chair, the very picture of a mournful patriarch whose grief for his people is beyond endurance.

It was time, Theodora judged, to call Robert back to the life he must go on living. "Did Aleaumes return with you today?" she asked.

"Aleaumes?" For a moment Robert did not seem to recognize the name, but as Theodora quickly bent to assist his fumbling fingers and the soft velvet with its hard, bitter core fell into the blazoned purse at his belt he came to himself again. "He asked me to deliver a message to Nicholas. He sends his compliments and will wait on him as soon as possible. He said to tell him there is much he would discuss with one he regards as his teacher."

"That will not be possible," said Theodora sharply. "Nicholas is dying. He lies in his bed unable to speak and recognizes no one. There is no point in Aleaumes' coming. Tell him, though, that before he fell into this sleep, Nicholas spoke often of him with great tenderness."

"I will tell him," Robert said, adding mechanically, "the whole world is dead or dying." He lifted a goblet from the table, drank, set it down, then strode from the room, leaving the door open behind him. He pushed aside the sleepy boy who tried to open the outer door, viciously wrenching it open himself. They heard his footsteps on the cobbles of the street, the soft rasp of the bolt being made secure and the soft, padding footsteps of the boy.

"Go to bed," Theodora said to the pinched white face that peered inquiringly in at them. "And shut the door."

"He did not even thank us for the ring," Signor Matteo said, idly toying with the jewels on his own plump fingers.

"He thinks we have destroyed his whole life here tonight. Did you expect him to be grateful for the one crumb we could toss him?"

"I suppose not. He took it very hard. Will he let it lie, do you think?"

"There is nothing else he can do. Too much time has passed since the fire. The Greeks are rebuilding all over that quarter and most of the debris has been cleared away. The Greek to whom you sold your kinsman's plot of land already has a fine house under construction. And no crusading soldier will be welcomed into the city, not now, with Alexius triumphant and Murtzuphles' faction so strong at court."

"She made it very difficult for us, nevertheless. How is Nicholas, really?"

"I spoke the truth when I said he was dying. His mind is still alert, but speaking tires him."

"I never dared ask him what he thought of the lady's scheme."

Theodora laughed. "He is a survivor, as much a realist as you and I or even Anne herself. Long ago he said that Robert and Aleaumes of Clari would always be the victims of circumstance. Briefly he tried to educate Aleaumes, but even then without much hope that he would be successful. He liked the clerk and Robert too, but Anne is the one who will shape the future to her own design. She is like the French Empress; she will become more Byzantine than the Byzantines."

"Yet she could not simply leave her knight. She had to concoct this story."

"She means never to see him again. And after all, she could hardly have a love-crazed suitor attempting to break into the Blachernae Palace to snatch her away. The Empress would never stand for it. Agnes-Anna has begun to speak of arranging a wealthy marriage for her favorite lady. The situation is very delicate."

"I pity the poor young man."

"That is the wine talking, Matteo. You've never pitied anyone in your life. The only people in this city who feel anything for him tonight are Nicholas and I. But he will live and return to his own country, and the memory of this lost love will relieve the boredom of his old age. He should never have left France. None of them should. We have all of us done him a great favor, though he will never know it."

"You will be lonely when Nicholas is gone, Theodora."

"He has grown tired of this world, Matteo. He doesn't fear death, nor do I fear to deliver him to it. But the passing will be easier knowing that I am provided for."

"Can you be certain of her?"

"I am the keeper of a very precious secret. And I don't ask much. Just a place at court in her service."

"When the Franks leave in March you will have no further hold over her."

"She needed my herbs in the past and she values my skill too highly to disdain any services I may render her in the future. We get on well enough together, the great lady Anne and I. You need have no worries on my account. She is loyal enough to those who serve her interests. You and your house will not be forgotten either."

"It never hurts to have a friend at court." Signor Matteo could very easily imagine the preferential treatment and small favors he could expect to receive, the court gossip and secret trade agreements to which he would be privy long before his competitors, and the steady profits such information would guarantee. But it was growing late, and pleasant though such thoughts were, they lay far in the future. Tomorrow he would have other things to cope with. "Still, Theodora," he said, rising to bank the fire for the night, "I really do feel sorry for that young man."

VI

The winter dragged on, a cold, dull season for the crusaders, most of whom spent their days yearning for spring and the time the fleet would again set sail; their nights they passed in drinking, dicing and whoring.

A few small payments had been made to the men who had marched with Alexius, but these soon ceased, so that within a month of their return many of the knights were as impoverished as they had been the previous summer. Among the common soldiers hardly a man had two coins to rub against each other, and the discontent that had always plagued this army surfaced again in almost continual bickering and frequent outbursts of street fighting.

Alexius no longer visited the Galata encampment to enliven the long afternoons with gifts of wine and demands that the barons share his chessboard or ivory, gem-studded dice. They missed the sight of the red-haired Emperor and his solemn-faced suite, and wondered uneasily at his sudden indifference. His warm regard for the men who had placed him on the throne was grown as cold as the wind that swept down on them from the frozen northern plains.

The Marquis of Montferrat waited impatiently for an invitation from the palace, and as the weeks passed and no word came, he met frequently with the Doge to discuss their protégé's alarmingly independent conduct.

"The days when we could manipulate him to our will are over," predicted the Doge. "He is as weak as ever and will always be easily led, but Murtzuphles plays the ropes now, and his influence grows greater with every passing day."

"He cannot be allowed to ignore our presence or forget the sums he owes us."

"He has not forgotten them, and we can be certain that he trembles every time he looks across the Horn. But he is being advised to put us off with excuses in the hope that when spring arrives our own men will revolt and force us to set sail whether the debt has been discharged or not. Murtzuphles is a canny devil and his spies are everywhere. He knows your army was twice divided and that the division has never been fully forgotten."

"My army," said Montferrat bitterly.

"The Venetians have never for a single moment wavered in their loyalty to me." Dandolo could afford to be smug, for what he said was indisputably so.

"It will be my army yet," said Montferrat. "The game is far from finished."

"What will you do?"

"I have waited long enough. Tomorrow morning I ride to the Blachernae Palace. My escort will be impressive enough to make even those barbaric Warings take notice, but I will see Alexius alone and remind him very forcefully of his obligations. He will not dare refuse to receive me."

"No, he will not dare that final insult," agreed Dandolo. "His people work night and day, but there are still many sections of the wall that would crumble under a first assault."

"I will have him back in the palm of my hand by nightfall," promised Montferrat.

"I don't think it will be that easy, my friend. Murtzuphles will be whispering in his ear again before your escort has cleared the palace grounds."

Montferrat did reach the Emperor the next day, but his request for a private audience was summarily denied and he was forced to wait his turn to approach the throne amid a crowd of Greek petitioners. Wedged in between a black-garbed bishop and a jewel-encrusted minor prince, both of whom ostentatiously tried to keep their long skirts from touching the crude Westerner's mail-clad legs, Montferrat kept his temper in check and concentrated his attention on the godlike figures on the dais. It was nearly impossible to discern the relative influence of the advisers grouped around the thrones, for neither Isaac nor his son so much as moved a muscle as the petitions were presented and the flowery speeches droned on. Only later would they be discussed and matters of policy decided, and no one would know whose voice really spoke from the throne.

Isaac was painfully thin and obviously failing. Not even his rich robes could conceal the fact that he was little more than a heap of bones held upright by sheer willpower. Alexius was stronger, healthier, more the ruling monarch by mere contrast.

Seated on a smaller throne slightly below her husband's was the Empress, Margaret-Maria, sister of the King of Hungary. She was only a few years older than her stepson Alexius, and had given Isaac two children of her own. Prince Manuel would be about ten years old by now, Montferrat reflected, remembering that there had been some unsubstantiated rumors that Isaac had once intended to name him his heir. Alexius had been born before his father's successful coup and thus, strictly speaking, could not be said to have been born to the purple. Montferrat wondered if Margaret-Maria ever pictured herself regent during what would be a long minority. After Isaac's death only Alexius would stand between her son and the throne, and one life was easily snuffed out. Was he imagining a special coldness between Alexius and his stepmother? A more than casual interest on the part of the Empress in the documents being presented not for her consideration, but for her stepson's? Her control over the features of her face was as complete as that of the two Emperors, but lights came and went in her eyes that betrayed the busy brain behind them.

Only one other lady in the room was seated, and Montferrat quickly recognized her from Louis of Blois's description. It was the one they called the French Empress, the French King's sister. The Count had told him that he had paid many visits to his kinswoman, and that although she had no liking for the Franks in general she had treated him politely and with increasing warmth. Montferrat was not fooled. If it did not come to war, if he was obliged to lead the army to the Holy Land as he had promised, Blois might very well fall conveniently ill and have to be left behind. Whatever happened, the regard of an ex-

Empress would stand him in good stead. Nothing but the most polite and banal of conversations could have passed between the two, however, for he was positive that Louis knew no Greek and it was a well-known fact that the Empress no longer spoke French. At least he would not have to worry about plots hatched behind his back by those two.

He heard his name called out and the command to approach the throne. A flicker of movement near the French Empress caught his eye and he glanced quickly in her direction as he bent the knee in homage to Isaac and Alexius. One of the Empress's ladies had drawn her veil around the lower part of her face, and it was the movement of her hand in that otherwise motionless group that had caught Montferrat's attention. They were all gazing steadily at him as he knelt on the cold marble floor, but from one pair of eyes he sensed a peculiar intensity. Blue eyes were not unusual in the noble families, which had often intermarried with fairer Westerners, but though he caught only the quickest glimpse of these, he was suddenly certain that he had seen this lady once before, a very long time ago. There was no time now to search his memory, but he had never in his life forgotten anything of importance. In the days and weeks to come he knew he would remember.

After that first wholly unsatisfactory audience Montferrat went every day to the Blachernae Palace, and as he and his escort rode out the crusaders cheered him on with many obscene suggestions as to what Alexius could do with his tedious protocol. They knew Montferrat was pressing the demand for payment, intruding himself into the Emperor's presence in spite of the small insults so galling to a man of his character and high station in life, and they admired the tenacity with which he pursued their interests.

Eventually he wore Alexius down, as he had always known he would, and their last interview took place in the Emperor's private chambers. For over an hour they shouted at one another, and the Greek servants, some in the private pay of Murtzuphles, others paid by the French Empress and Isaac's queen, huddled outside the room with ears pressed close against the door. The harsh names the Marquis dared to call God's anointed shocked them. Felon, defaulter, dishonorable pup of a weakling sire were among the most innocuous. And in turn Alexius had hurled terrible charges at Montferrat, accusing him of treachery to his own men and disloyalty to his sovereign, Philip of Swabia.

"You swore to Philip that you would restore me to my throne and uphold my rights against all comers," he had at one point shouted so loudly that every word reached the spies in the corridor. "Yet now I believe that from the very first you coveted this throne for yourself. You would have had me killed had you not feared Philip's wrath. But you will never sit on this throne, Montferrat. My people are loyal to me now and it is you who will be destroyed if you remain overlong in my kingdom. We will drive you from this land just as we did your stinking traitor brother."

Montferrat had left the palace in undignified haste, Alexius's mocking, hysterical laughter ringing in his ears.

"I should have strangled him while I had the chance," he told the bemused Doge. "It's war now, and either I or that sniveling whoreson will be dead at the end of it."

"One more attempt at reconciliation must be made, a public one this time, with duly appointed ambassadors whose skills are well known to the whole army."

"It will be wasted effort. Alexius has already thrown down the gauntlet."

"I agree with you. But the fault must lie clearly with him and with those who counsel him, else your men will fight only half-heartedly if at all. The insult to our ambassadors must be so great that even the meanest soldier in the ranks will vow to avenge it personally."

The members of the embassy were quickly chosen by a hastily assembled parliament. Villehardouin was the ranking member, but it was Conon of Béthune, he of the silver tongue, who would speak. If he could not sway the Emperor to honor their just demands no one could. Miles the Brabant was the third crusader chosen, and the instructions he received gave the lie to the others' hope for peace. He was every soldier's hero, and his past exploits in many wars had become almost legendary with frequent retelling and constant embellishment. He had a genius for strategy and a foreknowledge of how his enemy would dispose his troops that was always uncannily correct. During the ride to the palace, as they passed beneath the wall and through the streets, his trained eye and special gifts would spy out and assess the exact state of Greek preparedness.

The Doge chose three Venetians to represent his interests, trusted members of his council who would report every word spoken and every nuance of expression that could possibly give a clue to the true state of affairs at the Greek court.

The envoys were richly dressed, and at Miles the Brabant's suggestion, mounted on the swiftest horses the army could supply. "We may have to make a run for it," had been the Brabant's laconic comment. When the Blachernae gate swung open to admit them each man unconsciously laid a hand on his sword, for the way to the palace was guarded by the Warings and crowds of hostile Byzantines watched them pass in silence. "You were right to insist we go armed, Miles," said Villehardouin as they dismounted. "We shall be lucky to escape from here with our skins intact."

Montferrat had prepared them for the sight that met their eyes in the enormous chamber where Isaac and Alexius sat their twin thrones. "Otherwise," said Conon of Béthune afterward, "we might have stood gaping and gawking like country rustics."

"It was like being in some sort of heathen temple," added the scornful Brabant. "The Emperors and their suite were so encrusted with jewels that they could not lift a finger for the weight of their finery. We spared not a single glance for the marble pillars and the gold that gleamed even from the lintels of the door, but marched straight to the dais to present our case. There were mosaics on all the walls depicting strange beasts of antiquity and the exploits of past Emperors, but I only caught a glimpse of them as we left. Judging by what we saw in that one chamber alone, there will be loot enough to make every soldier as rich as a king."

"It will have to be won before it can be divided," said Montferrat, "but at the moment I am not much interested in discussing it."

"Alexius could easily pay what he owes," insisted the Brabant stubbornly. "The peacock has only to shed a few of his fine tail feathers or let us do it for him."

"Conon of Béthune spoke well," interrupted Villehardouin, "forgetting none of the points we had agreed upon."

"I reminded Isaac of the convenants his son had sworn with us, and of his own agreement to their terms," explained Conon of Béthune seriously. "Then I called upon both Emperors, as men of honor, to fulfill their pledges, and upon their barons and noble princes to bear witness to it. But they sat in silence staring blackly at me; it was as if I had spoken of matters entirely new and unknown to them."

"After that we had no choice but to issue the *défi*." Villehardouin's face wore the distressed look of the seasoned diplomat accustomed to delicate maneuverings who is unexpectedly forced to deal with a power that has no intention of conducting negotiations.

"We are men of honor, I told them," continued Conon of Béthune, "and the custom of our country demands that we give you warning of our intentions. If the covenants are honored, all will be well between us. But if they are not, from this day forward we hold you neither as lord nor friend, and will exact our just due by all means in our power. As far as I can remember those were my exact words."

Villehardouin nodded, confirming that Conon of Béthune's recollection of his speech rang true. "The Greeks were very angry and the one they call Murtzuphles said that no one had ever before dared to defy the Emperor of Constantinople in his own audience chamber. The Warings surrounded us and bore us from the hall to where our horses waited. They had orders to see to our safety, else I fear we should have been set upon and murdered on the steps of the throne itself."

"They took an uncomfortably long time opening the gate," said Miles the Brabant. "The crowds were in an ugly mood, shouting defiances and cursing us from all sides. As soon as we were outside the wall we put spurs to our horses. I've never liked having archers at my back. Their fingers slip too easily."

"So," said Montferrat, leaning back in his chair, "it is done. We are at war with Alexius at last."

"Say rather with the ambitious and unscrupulous men who surround him," corrected Villehardouin. "Let us maintain a state of siege throughout the winter and by spring he will be ready to come to terms with us. He is a young man who fears everything and everyone, seeing treachery in every face. By March he will have weakened again and will be desperate to see the last of us. He will pay eventually. And I for one will bless the day we leave these waters behind us forever."

Montferrat was looking at him with a strange mixture of contempt and amusement. "It will not be as easy as you suppose, my lord Marshal," he said. "You still do not know your Greeks very well."

"They are reinforcing the walls against a new assault," said Miles the Brabant thoughtfully. "I saw enormous piles of cut timbers placed at the foot of every tower. I think they mean to build wooden towers atop the stone to such a height that the ships' ladders will be useless."

"Then we shall simply extend the ramps," said the Doge. "It is a simple task and one to which I will set my men immediately."

"They are taking precautions against fire, also. I saw wagons filled, I think, with hides, but I could not be certain because they were all covered over. It is a logical assumption though, for even those poor soldiers know that wooden towers are death-traps unless they are covered with wet and hairless skins."

"What else did you see?" asked Montferrat.

"That was all, my lord. They practically pushed us bodily from the city. There was no time for leisurely reconnoitering." Miles the Brabant laughed harshly at his own joke. "But I saw many weapons that looked new-made, and there was a certain feeling about the place that I have felt in other cities that were determined to resist a siege. Something or someone has unified these people and put new backbone into them. They may turn out to be a worthy enemy after all."

Miles the Brabant had correctly judged the new solidarity that the people of Constantinople were feeling that winter. At least there was universal agreement on several important decisions. There would be no further attempt to buy off the crusaders, the army would stand and fight at the walls to the last man if necessary, and the projected submission to Rome was utterly and finally rejected.

For a few weeks Alexius strutted about his palace uttering

dire threats against his former friends and meeting regularly
with his council, whose main concern lay in finding a way to destroy the ships that lay at anchor in the Golden Horn. But the
meetings began to bore him, for his advisers were cautious, longwinded men who listened politely to the young Emperor's outrageously impractical suggestions, then returned to their own in-
terminable debates.

"What use is it if they will not listen to me?" he complained to
Isaac. "I have already told them over and over again what must
be done."

"Even an emperor must learn the art of governing," Isaac patiently reminded his son. He himself had almost given up the
task as his health became ever more precarious. Nowadays he
spent all his time surrounded by priests and astrologers, all of
whom confidently forecast a complete and easy victory over the
Franks come spring and the season for war. "Tell me your plan
again, Alexius. My memory is not what it once was."

His father was deceptively mild-mannered these days, yet
Alexius knew that he would tolerate no rash display of disobe-
dience or outburst of temper from his son. In his own mind
Isaac considered himself much more than just co-Emperor, and
there was still young Manuel and his ambitious Hungarian witch
of a mother lurking in the background.

"My plan is simple and completely foolproof. In fact it is
based on an old maneuver that the Doge himself once used.
There are some very large merchant ships sitting empty and
abandoned in our northern harbors. Their owners dare not
reclaim them and the Venetians think them not worth capturing.
We fill these ships with dry logs and wood shavings, wet them
down with resin and other flammable liquids, then wait until a
dark night when the wind blows from our side of the Horn. We
fix their sails so as to bring them into the midst of the Frankish
fleet, set them alight, then let the wind do the rest. The burning
ships will be among the others within minutes, and the Venetians will be destroyed before they can even raise their anchors.
Without their navy these men are virtually our prisoners. And
the knowledge that they cannot sail away at a time of their own
choosing will destroy whatever morale is left among them."

"Would it not rather have the opposite effect?" questioned

Isaac, attempting to concentrate his attention on a type of problem he had long since ceased dealing with. "Would they not fight us all the harder knowing there was no possibility of escape?"

"Father, I do not flatter myself when I say that I believe my knowledge of these men exceeds your own. I spent much time in their midst, and not only in the company of their barons and commanders. I know the feelings of the knights and common soldiers. They want only one thing, to reach the Holy Land, and many among them still feel that Montferrat acted treacherously in bringing them to Constantinople. They will take the destruction of their fleet as a sign that God is displeased with them and will demand that they be allowed to march overland to Syria. Even the barons themselves are divided over the question. So much pressure will be brought to bear on Montferrat that he will have no choice. He will have to lead them where they want to go or risk losing them entirely. If necessary the army will march off and leave its commander sitting shamed and alone in the palace he now occupies. Montferrat knows what his fate would be should he allow himself to fall into our hands. He will go. Have no fear of that."

"What do you want me to do?"

"Go to the council. Speak to them, persuade them to adopt my plan. Let them think that you too conceived the idea of fire ships independently of me. They will listen to you."

"I wonder. In my prison I had much time to think, Alexius, and of necessity a sightless man's thoughts turn inward. This life is now a burden to me, and I would willingly give it up if the power over life and death did not lie in God's Hands alone. Lately I have begun visiting your sister in her quiet convent; she alone of all our family has known peace and true contentment and she has thanked me many times for allowing her to withdraw from the world and its cares. Had I been Emperor when she asked it of me I would have been obliged to refuse and she would never have made her vows. I would have had to send her, as I sent Irene, to some far-off court and an unknown husband. Irene suffered greatly. It grieves me now that my children should have had to serve my ambition. It is a sin for which I daily seek to atone."

"Irene is happy now, Father. She blesses you. Were it not for her I would still be wandering the courts of Europe, and that would be a greater sin than the one you speak of." What was the old man thinking of? His mind was wandering, turning soft and foolishly sentimental. It was royalty's duty to make advantageous matches with foreign powers. No one gave a second thought to the wishes of the princesses involved, not even the children themselves. If Isaac had no better control over himself than this, the council would never listen to him.

"Would you not also, Alexius, be happier serving God in one of His holy monasteries, after all that has been done to you, after all the evil you have seen in the world?"

"It is my duty to combat that evil by remaining in the world, Father, a duty that was laid upon me by God Himself at the moment of my coronation." Never, even in his most despairing moments, had Alexius considered taking the vows of religion. The thought of living out his life in a monastery was so abhorrent, so outrageously monstrous, that he gagged on it. "My duties are clear, Father, and I willingly embrace them. But if it is your will that the House of Angelus give a monk to God, my brother Manuel is a quiet, studious boy, and though I would miss his presence at court, I would agree to his taking the vows if it were pleasing to you."

"Manuel." Isaac's voice was soft and loving as he pronounced the name of his younger son. This child was the joy of his heart and the favored one of his five legitimate offspring. He would have made a great and noble emperor, for his character was steady and already well formed. His young manhood would not be deformed by the lusts and weaknesses shared by so many of the men of his blood. There was something very different about the young prince that promised much for the future, but whether he or any of them would have any future at all was what must now concern the father. "He is not of an age to know his own mind yet. Nor would I force him to it."

Isaac could feel Alexius's disappointment. It was like a palpable ooze flowing from the ambitious prince's inner being, an ooze that had the rancid smell of unprincipled selfishness. It was truly amazing how the remaining senses of the body became the more acute when one of them was destroyed. "I will go to the council and speak on your behalf," Isaac said abruptly. "It is a good plan and I think the chances of success are high. But it must be put into action without delay. Many of the army's provisions have doubtless been stored on board their ships the better to safeguard them from their own hungry people. If they face starvation through the long, cold winter, rebellion will break out the sooner and they may not wait for spring to make their retreat."

Though he gave no sign of it, Alexius was amazed at his father's ability to add still another dimension to the argument he would give the council. He himself had been able to think no further than the destruction of the ships. He thought of Montferrat's huge frame growing gaunt and weak and of the hunger pains that would torment him, and smiled at the picture his imagination conjured up. After this one service Isaac could be left in peace with his priests and soothsayers. He would have earned it.

The council was not fooled. They knew that somehow Alexius had roused his father from his lethargy and persuaded him to champion the proposal that had already been rejected on several occasions. Yet as Isaac spoke, outlining the proposal in far greater detail than Alexius had been capable of, the men who listened to him felt a growing excitement that soon had them interrupting one another in a discussion more vigorous and hope-filled than any the council chamber had known for months. Murtzuphles alone remained inflexibly opposed. If the plan failed, there would be no second chance. Never again would the Venetians be so careless in guarding their ships as they now were. Hostilities would be fully opened long before the repairs and improvements on the wall were completed, and who knew but that the crusaders might break with tradition and attempt an assault in midwinter? And as if that were not enough there was always the question of Rome. There was still a chance that the Pope would bestir himself and order a withdrawal from Constantinople on pain of excommunication. Whether the crusaders would obey his command or not was a moot point, but it was a possibility that deserved careful consideration. Up to now Constantinople was the beleaguered, the wronged party in the dispute, but if the Greeks attacked, it put the crusaders in the position of men who fought in righteous self-defense. When the vote was taken, only Murtzuphles held out for a continuance of the state of siege, but his arguments now seemed to smack of cowardice.

The Venetian lookouts soon began reporting an unusual amount of activity in some of the harbors along the city side of the Golden Horn. It was impossible at such a distance to tell what was being done, and after a few days the activity ceased and the harbors were as deserted as they had been when the Venetians had first sailed into the Horn.

"There are six or seven old merchant tubs at anchor," reported one Venetian captain. "It seems the Greeks had the idea of turning them into ships of war, but have given up the effort."

"Are they seaworthy?" asked the Doge.

"Barely so. They lie very low in the water and I would venture to say they are so full of leaks that their crews would spend all their time bailing them out should they try to put to sea. A few of them belong to Venetian traders living here in Galata. Their owners say they are not worth reclaiming. Even the sails are patched and old according to the men who once sailed them, and would rip apart in the first wind of a storm. The Greeks have not tried to raise them, so it would seem they too now consider them fit only for salvage."

"Double the watch on all our ships until further notice," commanded the Doge. "Have you forgotten that even the leakiest vessel can be used to good advantage against a fleet at anchor?"

"Fire ships?"

"You yourself said they lie low in the water. How much lower than before?"

"I do not know, my lord." The captain was shamefaced now, embarrassed before this man who thought of everything. "We paid no attention to them until the Greeks did."

"The watch is to be particularly alert anytime the wind blows across the Horn from Constantinople."

"Yes, my lord. I will see to it myself."

Advent came and went, and Christmas too, but though the wind often blew strong across the Horn and the Venetians con-

tinued to stand double watches, no fire ships broke the gloom of
the cold winter nights. At the end of December the Doge re-
scinded his order, for many of the men who had stood the open
decks in the wet, freezing chill of that month had fallen ill with
fatal chest ailments. They tossed and muttered in their fevers,
and though the best leeches attended them, they reported that
all their skill was useless against the humors that filled the lungs
so that their patients choked to death on them.

It pained the Doge to walk among his sick and dying men,
but it was a duty he imposed on himself and one he would relin-
quish to no one else. Although not even the dying reproached
him for the orders which had caused them so much suffering, he
was no longer as certain as he had once been that those orders
had been necessary.

He hardly slept anymore, both for the pain and stiffness of his
joints that made even the slightest of movements an agony, and
for wondering what was being planned in the Emperor's council
chamber. If he were Alexius or Isaac, he would not hesitate to
send fire ships across the Horn. It was a gamble, but the only
one that held any real chance of destroying the fleet that was a
greater danger than all the army's battalions put together. From
past experience he knew that the Greeks did not like to take
such monumental risks, and he began to believe that they had
decided to sit tight behind their walls.

Tonight, the first night that the watches had been reduced, he
lay awake as usual in his bed while a clerk read to him in a
droning, sleepy voice. One of his captains arrived to make the
midnight report that had become customary, and stood blowing
on his fingers while the Doge interrogated him.

"From what direction is the wind blowing?"

"From across the Horn, my lord. But there is no sign of any
activity on the far shore."

"None at all?"

"Nothing, my lord. Even the torches in the towers are fewer in
number than usual."

"Can you see the harbors?"

"No, my lord. Usually we can make out the silhouettes of a
few vessels, but there is no moon tonight."

"Why are there fewer torches in the towers than usual?"

"My lord, the number varies night to night. We think that when it is unusually cold, the guards keep watch from behind hides strung across the openings. The wind increased about an hour ago and is very bitter now. There may be snow before morning."

"Is there a pattern here?"

"No, my lord. As I have said, some nights there is a great deal of illumination so that we can even see the watch moving about. Other nights we can make out nothing. But there is no pattern to it unless it be that on mild nights the Emperor's builders work in secret on the inner wall."

"Which of our ships lies farthest from this shore?"

"The *Regina Coeli*, my lord. The keenest eyes watch from its decks."

"I have no eyes, captain, but my other senses serve me well. Age has not diminished my hearing nor affected my brain. I will go back with you to the *Regina Coeli*."

"My lord, the cold is severe and my men perform their duty well."

"I am not criticizing you, captain, and my presence is not to be taken as a rebuke. But sleep comes hard in old age and perhaps an hour in the open air will benefit me."

Wrapped in furs from head to foot by his solicitous body servants, the Doge sat motionless in the prow of a small boat that wove its way surely among the ships of the fleet. The transports were gathered together close to the Galata shore, ringed in a protective arc by the Venetian galleys. From each vessel they approached, a low-voiced challenge rang out across the water, and the watch paced the deck from stern to bow, following with unseen eyes the progress of the small craft.

"I congratulate you, captain," said the Doge quietly.

"Not even a fish could swim amongst us unnoticed," came the proud reply.

They reached the *Regina Coeli* and climbed aboard its deck. The captain came to greet the Doge and urge him to warm himself in the cabin, but though the tip of Dandolo's hooked nose was frozen beyond feeling, he declined the offer and asked to be led immediately to the bow of the galley where the watch stood his silent vigil. All the galleys pointed outward from the fleet they guarded and the captain assured him that none had been allowed to swing inward with the current.

"Not a sound is to be made aboard this vessel," commanded the Doge as he stood beside the watch while his two captains hovered behind. The wind was indeed blowing strongly from across the Horn, so that the waves slapped against the ship's wooden sides, the masts and shipped oars groaned and creaked against its pressure and even the furled and tightly wrapped sails added their small sounds to the rhythmic night music of the sea.

For almost an hour the Doge stood there, his sightless eyes fixed on the opposite shore while his ears strained to catch the slightest noise. He stood like a mystic in a God-given trance; not a muscle moved and he seemed to be scarcely breathing. The watch did not dare to stamp his feet or rub his frozen hands in such august company, and even the two captains remained motionless where they stood.

At last the Doge raised his hand, a warning gesture. "Listen," he whispered. But try though they might, his three companions could hear nothing but the ordinary shipboard sounds. The captains glanced at one another. Did they dare insist that their commander retire to the cabin? If he remained much longer on this open deck he would surely catch the lung fever. Sensing their distress, the Doge waved his white-gloved hand impatiently, a ghostly blur in the darkness. "Listen," he repeated urgently.

And then finally they heard what his keen ears had picked up minutes before. It sounded like muffled footsteps, over there, just outside the city's closest gate. Not a great many men, but unmistakably the dull, imprecise sound of cautious movement.

"They have wrapped their feet in rags," said the Doge.

"Refugees fleeing the city?" questioned one of the captains.

"Soldiers," said the Doge. "Some of them have disobeyed orders and continue to wear their weapons. I can hear them move in their leather scabbards."

"Look, my lord," said the watch suddenly, and there was excitement and the beginning of fear in his whisper.

"What is it? Quickly!" demanded Dandolo.

"The gate opened for a moment, just a crack, but I caught a glimpse of light, as though from many torches."

"Raise anchor," snapped out Dandolo decisively. "Rouse the crew, each rower to his oar. Signal the other ships. But quietly, else they will know they have lost the advantage of surprise."

Even as he gave the order, he heard the protesting creak as the city gate opened on its metal hinges, and the gasp from the watch told him that his premonition had been right.

"What do you see?"

"My lord, men carrying torches, perhaps thirty of them, running to the harbor. They've reached the ships. My lord, the ships are in full sail. They throw the torches on board." The man's voice faltered as a great sob rose in his throat.

"The ships are ablaze," continued the Doge.

"Fire ships," breathed the watch, all the horror of generations of sea-bred men in his cry. Pulling himself together, conscious that he was his master's eyes, he continued to describe the holocaust he had hoped never to see. "They are cutting loose the anchor ropes with axes. I can see the sweat on their faces, my lord. It is brighter than day."

"Or the fires of hell. We shall not burn in them, my lad," said the Doge reassuringly.

The Venetian galleys moved out one by one to meet the fire ships, which were bearing down on them with desperate accuracy. The wind was against them, but the rowers, chained to their benches, knew that if their ships were overtaken they would burn alive until the cold waters of the Horn put a merciful end to their sufferings. They hardly felt the whips lashing their backs as they struggled to match their stroke to the fast beat of the overseer's drum.

"There was no time to regain my ship," said the captain who had earlier assured the Doge that Constantinople lay serene and sleeping.

"Your officers have their orders, do they not?"

"Yes, my lord. But a captain's place is on his own deck."

"Or with his admiral." The Doge's tone was purposefully intimate. "Do not reproach yourself, my friend. Your men will do their duty bravely and well, and together we two will bear witness to it. What is happening now?"

"The grappling hooks are out. The fire ships will cross over the main stream of the current before we can reach it, but it will slow them down. There are only seven of them, but the transports are beginning to move and scatter in case one breaks through our line. We'll pierce the sails with crossbolts and arrows, and tow them back to where the current flows the swiftest. Their own flames will do the rest."

"I can already feel the heat on my face."

"They are very close, my lord. You must take shelter in the cabin."

"Captain's orders?"

"Captain's orders, my lord."

"Even an admiral must yield occasionally." The Doge chuckled, confident that the extra warning his sharp ears had been able to give would prove the decisive factor in the night's engagement. "Your arm, captain, if you please. I will sample some of our friend's excellent wine and keep well out of his way."

A spontaneous cheer went up as the Doge moved slowly amidships. In just a few minutes his amazing feat had become common knowledge, and the sailors, who had always held him in great veneration, now felt fully protected by the godlike aura of the blind old man who had, some said, smelled out fire before the first flint was struck in the walled city that lay leagues away.

The last Greek fire ship did not sink below the waves until daylight, and in the intervening hours between the first alarm and the final victory the noise and confusion on both shores was greater than the clamor of a pitched battle.

When the first Venetian galley towed the lead fire ship into the current and cut it loose to burn harmlessly far away from the crowded port area, a howl of rage and disappointment burst like thunder through the wind. All of Constantinople seemed to have been watching from the dark walls of the city, and as though by sheer force of numbers alone they would prevail against their enemies, soldiers and townsmen streamed through the gates to scream and leap in frustrated rage on the firelit shore.

Dozens of tiny boats, some carrying only two or three men, were rowed out into the Horn in the wake of the beleaguered fire ships. They clustered like flies as close as they dared to the busy Venetian galleys, shooting arrows and hurling rocks onto the decks. But the water was rough and their aim was poor.

First one, then another of the small craft capsized, and the screams of drowning men were added to the unholy din, for the Venetians would spare no time to rescue the floundering bodies that dotted the surface of the Horn. It was a brave, foolhardy attempt, doomed to failure; the flotilla that regained the shore had been diminished by half its original number and had accomplished nothing.

On the Galata shore the battalions were swiftly assembled and marched out onto the plain where Alexius III had once threatened them. No one knew where the Greek army was, or even whether the fire ships had been but the opening blow of a major attack. The troops watched the desperate maneuvers in the Horn and cheered as each fire ship was encircled by galleys, then secured by grappling hooks. They watched awestruck as Venetian sailors leaped onto the burning ships, disdaining the flames that threatened to engulf them, made fast the heavy tow ropes, then seemed to fly, dark silhouettes against brilliant orange, back to the safety of their own decks. Six times the maneuver was repeated. The glow of the flames grew less as each fire ship went down, until finally it was replaced by the soft light of dawn. Only one of the Frankish ships was lost, a clumsy merchantman so heavily loaded it was unable to avoid the fire ship that crashed into it. Its crew was rescued and it, too, was towed out to burn harmlessly and sink to a watery grave with its attacker.

By the time the sun had fully risen the wind had died down and only the black smoke lingering above the Horn gave evidence that a decisive naval battle had taken place. The Greeks had disappeared inside their walls, and the army stood alone and intact on the empty plain. Back they marched to their quarters in Galata and the Jewry, a subdued but bitterly angry force. The Greeks had once more proved themselves a craven, treacherous race of cowards. They had been properly, honorably given the *défi*, yet the only answer to the challenge had been the sneak attack of the fire ships. It was an unbearable state of affairs. The Greeks must be made to fight; only the spilling of blood would satisfy the army now.

VII

It was very strange, Alexius thought. Not one among his advisers, not even Murtzuphles, had thrown it in his face that his grand scheme had failed so miserably.

The council met in the early hours of the morning following the debacle, their drawn and tired faces bearing mute witness to the long vigil they had kept throughout the night. But though Alexius expected to be blamed for the disaster, and had even dragged Isaac from his bed to accompany him to the meeting, both Emperors were greeted with grave respect and the loss of the last-ditch fleet barely mentioned. The discussion returned to the work, almost completed now, of strengthening the seaward walls. Alexius, who had come prepared to bluster and threaten, did not know what to make of it. Privately, Murtzuphles assured him that his popularity and the loyalty of his people were greater than ever, for though the plan had not succeeded, it had proved that the young Emperor was a man to conceive bold strategy, a man born to lead his people to eventual victory. He, Murtzuphles, in company with his Emperor, would devise and implement the next phase of the war. Isaac was so terribly ill that both agreed he should not be disturbed in future, and if Alexius wished to spend more time with his dying father, Murtzuphles would be happy to report personally the gist of the council meetings.

Alexius had no desire to spend any more time than was strictly necessary in Isaac's rooms, but he was grateful for the excuse that would enable him to avoid the council chamber and the tedious debates, which often put him to sleep. He had worked hard for his fire ships; he deserved a rest and some pleasant distraction.

He had developed a taste for gambling while in the crusaders' camp and he indulged it now in the long hours of the January nights. He had his favorites, young noblemen of about his own age who gathered in his private apartments and played the Emperor's games, taking care that his losses should never be overwhelming. Alexius was not good at gambling; he was often so stupefied with wine that he could barely toss the dice and certainly could not make out the pattern he had rolled. But there were always sycophants to praise and flatter him, to assure him that he had won again or to encourage him to another toss when he lost.

When the gaming palled they turned to other distractions. Since the Emperor obviously could not visit a brothel, the most skillful, most expensive whores of the city came to him. He had a small adjoining chamber set aside for their convenience, where the ladies could sit chatting, eating sweetmeats and drinking wine until their services were called for. The whores of Constantinople, like the city itself, were a cosmopolitan mixture of many races and cultures, and the devices and deviations they used to revive a man's flagging interest or to overcome his wine weakness were far beyond the imaginations of any of the whores Alexius had enjoyed during his short stay in the West. They were not in the least reluctant to display their skills in front of an appreciative audience, especially since all were paid even if only one or two actually exercised their remarkable professional talents.

Only the approach of dawn put an end to these nightly revels, for Alexius still possessed an element of caution which demanded that the whores be smuggled out of the palace before daylight. His people loved him, but he knew the love would be severely tested if they learned that while they worked and prayed and lived in constant fear, their Emperor disported himself in sinful pleasures and gave no thought to their precarious future.

In spite of Alexius's precautions everyone soon knew what was going on in the Blachernae Palace, for no whore has ever lain with a king and not boasted of it afterward. The lights in the

Emperor's apartments, burning through the night, and the sounds of revelry that occasionally reached the nearby streets, confirmed the rumors. The latest scion of the House of Angelus was proving himself a worthy successor to his father and his uncle. Isaac, of course, was almost a saint now, but he too had been a wild man in his younger days.

One afternoon in late January Murtzuphles came to Alexius's apartments, apologizing profusely for disturbing his prince while he still lay abed. The council was meeting in two days' time to hear a final report from the engineers, whose efforts had been truly magnificent. Would the Emperor deign to attend the meeting? It would be a great honor to his loyal workmen. And perhaps a general audience could be held following the council meeting, at which the engineers could be suitably rewarded and a pronouncement that would hearten the entire city could be given from the throne. The suggestion had come originally from Isaac.

"My father no doubt thinks it is past time I return to the business of ruling," responded Alexius tartly. "But perhaps he is right. You have all worked well and faithfully, but now that your tasks are completed you will once more need my direction. I will be at the meeting and will receive in audience afterward. I leave the details to you."

Murtzuphles backed from the room, and slowly, with aching head and sore muscles, Alexius left his bed. He gave orders that no one should come to his chambers in the evenings until further notice and went to steam himself in the hot waters of the baths.

It took almost the full two days before he began to feel sharp and alert again, but it had been well worth it, he reflected, as he soaked in the baths and submitted himself to the pummeling of his favorite masseur. He had been tired, tense, unable to think clearly in the days immediately following the loss of his fire ships. The body had clamored to be served, and now, though he noticed with dismay the slight bulge of an old man's belly, it was satiated and at peace. Now he could turn his formidable intellect to the continuing dilemma of the crusaders and their insulting threats.

Murtzuphles had assured him that the walls were once again impregnable and the city amply provisioned for a long siege.

But why, reasoned Alexius to himself, why submit his people to such a hardship? Why could he not do what other emperors had done? Simply pay off the Franks and watch them sail away to their insane rendezvous with the Saracens. The more he thought about it the more logical it seemed. There were still hundreds of gold- and jewel-encrusted altar vessels and icons in Constantinople's monasteries, convents and churches. They could be easily broken apart and melted down. There would be more than enough gold to pay the cursed debt he had so blithely agreed to. The people would mourn their loss and the Church would resist giving them up, but when it was explained to them that it was the only sensible thing to do, they would agree. And he had the weight of tradition on his side, too.

Gleefully he decided not to confide his new plan to anyone, not even to Murtzuphles. After the engineers' report had been read and applauded, after the men had been dismissed, when only his councillors remained in the chamber, he would announce that he had found a way to save the city from further destruction. He could almost see the surprise and admiration on their faces now. He would be remembered in history as the greatest emperor Constantinople had ever known, and in the throne room a new mosaic would be created, a mosaic that would fill a whole wall and cause future visitors to the city to gape openmouthed at his exploits. His councillors would stand behind him in the audience chamber when he announced his new decision publicly, and afterward he would instruct the finest artists in the city to lay aside their other work until the opus celebrating Alexius IV was completed.

Rested, refreshed, gorgeously dressed and bejeweled, ridiculously optimistic, Alexius met with his council. He listened attentively to the engineers, praised them extravagantly and assured them of their Emperor's undying gratitude. The councillors looked at one another in amazement. Was this splendid, authoritative figure the same prince whose sordid other life Murtzuphles had described to them in disgusting detail so many times in the last weeks? The same prince they had almost come to believe had forfeited the right to the scarlet buskins that had been worn in honor and dignity by a long line of emperors? Was this the callow, unfeeling, tainted Emperor to whose immediate overthrow they had almost committed themselves? Murtzuphles was the most fanatic patriot among them. Was he also serving an overweening ambition that would lay them open to the anger of their own people? When an ignoble emperor fell, everyone rejoiced. But Constantinople had finally accepted Alexius. Conspirators who misjudged the temper of their people often suffered far worse fates than their victims. They stirred uneasily in their comfortable chairs, mesmerized by the calm beauty and sense of power emanating from Alexius IV.

"In a few moments I will publicly proclaim a decree that by tonight will be known throughout the city," Alexius was saying. "It may at first be unpopular, but it is in the best interests of the people of this city and the entire kingdom as well. It is an unalterable decree, my absolute wish, and I am confident that it will be obeyed with perfect fidelity and loving hearts." He had their complete attention now, and the dazed expressions that had puzzled him for a moment had been replaced by an alertness that seemed almost wariness. "My people have suffered greatly, yet because of what I do today their suffering will at last be ended. My uncle's treachery incurred the just wrath of Western Christendom and brought a foreign army to assault this peace-loving kingdom, to kill and maim its guiltless, oppressed citizens. A large part of my capital has been destroyed in two fires; more homes, churches, monasteries, public buildings and priceless statuary will be crushed to rubble by the mangonels and catapults of the invaders. We may even see our streets in flames again. I cannot allow this to happen, nor in our glorious past has any other emperor permitted such an abomination to take place. We honor tradition, we Greeks, and adherence to the wisdom of tradition has preserved our culture intact for generations. I will not break with tradition nor ignore the sage example of the emperors who have preceded me. This afternoon the order goes out. Every icon in the churches, every chalice, every gold altar vessel is to be brought to the Mint. There they will be melted down into coins that will bear my image, until there is gold enough to pay the debt the invaders claim." The councillors sat stunned, and hurriedly he continued. "It is, in a sense, a lawful debt, though we of course do not consider it so. I view it as just another payment to barbarians whom it is beneath us to fight.

And there is ample precedent, as I have said. The Franks will disappear from our shores, glutted as befits barbarians, and in time we will replace the sacred vessels we were obliged to sacrifice. God Himself has given us this treasure to confound the armies of Rome. If we do not use it, Rome will overwhelm us and our Church will be no more."

No one protested, no one argued, no hot debate broke out. Several councillors sat with bent heads, their faces hidden in their hands. The others merely nodded sadly. Alexius had the impression that they were nodding, not in his direction, but at Murtzuphles, who sat at his right hand. Perhaps they waited for the chief councillor to signal his approval too.

"We are agreed then?" questioned Murtzuphles, his eyes sweeping the men gathered around the long table. No one spoke. He nodded, the decision made, and turned deferentially to Alexius. "You will announce this publicly from the throne?"

"At the end of the audience, after the other matters have been dealt with. Do you advise otherwise?"

"No, sire. On the contrary, I think it well the people hear from your own lips the course you have decided upon. They must know where you stand in this matter. I am sure the rest of the council agrees with me."

Victory was sweet, thought Alexius as he progressed in solemn procession to the audience hall. Almost as sweet as a woman's body. Perhaps after his duties were fulfilled he might summon a few attendants to celebrate his triumph with him. He longed to describe to their delight how the pompous ones had fallen.

"I crave Your Majesty's pardon if I am intruding or keeping you from your bed. The hour is late, I know."

"Not at all, madam."

"I would not have disturbed you had the matter not been urgent."

"I often work at night, when the rest of the palace lies sleeping. The throne is not all pageantry and glory. Though few know it, an emperor works harder than any of his subjects."

"How true, Your Majesty."

Would she never get on with it? It was nearly midnight and yet the witless woman babbled on. Wife she might have been to two emperors, but her title was mere courtesy now. She presumed too much, this French Agnes-Anna.

"What is it that so disturbs you, madam?"

"An act of charity, sire, that I fear some will call treason. You know that my love and loyalty have never faltered since the day I came here as a child."

"You became a Greek when you married, madam, and your life has been an example other princesses would do well to emulate." More Byzantine than the Byzantines, people said of her. He could well believe it.

"When the French first came amongst us a kinsman of mine presented himself to me, a nephew, Louis, Count of Blois and Chartres. At first I rebuffed him, as I thought Your Majesty would wish me to do. But then when the Franks seemed to be loyally serving Greek interests, before the fire, when they marched into Thrace at your command, I thought better of my actions. It seemed to me that I could best serve the kingdom by wooing this man's favor. He is one of their chief commanders and I thought his goodwill valuable."

"I know him well," interrupted Alexius. "He is devious, ambitious, without the moral scruples of a snake."

"As are all the French," agreed Agnes-Anna. "Not excepting their king, my brother, and now this woman."

"I fear I am not following you, madam." If she lingered much longer his companions would be snoring in their own apartments and he would have to postpone the planned festivities. He wondered if the whores had arrived yet, but no sound came from the adjoining privy chamber.

"So that we could converse together more easily and in the hope that my nephew would reveal something which might be of value to Your Majesty, I took into my household a young French noblewoman to serve me as waiting woman and as tutor, for I had forgotten the barbaric tongue of my childhood. She served me well at first, and in gratitude I gave her many rich gifts. But I fear I have nursed a viper in my bosom."

"How so, madam?"

"She now claims that I promised to arrange a marriage for her to a member of one of our most noble houses. That is ridiculous, sire, as you must surely know. No Greek prince would so demean himself as to make an alliance with a woman who sprang from nowhere and possesses nothing but the gifts I myself gave her. She began to press me with this demand as I prepared for bed this evening, and finally, sire, my patience at an end, I told her that there had never been any possibility of such a marriage and that if she did not cease harassing me I would have her locked in a convent for the rest of her days. Sire, she has been the calmest of my women, cold to the point of unfeeling, but as soon as the word convent was spoken her control vanished and like a beast she went berserk, completely hysterical. She screamed and shouted and actually struck me." The French Empress touched her cheek as if the blow still smarted. "Then she tried to run from my apartments, screaming that she would go back to Galata if she had to swim the Horn to do it. Naturally she was restrained by my guards, who were forced to bind her hands and feet and even to stop her mouth with a gag. The obscenities, the abuses that poured forth were appalling."

"Have her strangled, madam."

"In my anger I almost gave that very order, sire. But caution stopped me. She is completely crazed now, but in the quiet of a convent she will soon regain her senses. She knows much about the Frankish army and even claims that Montferrat himself is no stranger to her. It may be that she has information to give that will be of value in Your Majesty's negotiations."

"Do you approve what I plan to do, Agnes-Anna?" Alexius asked suddenly.

"Your Majesty is wiser than any of his councillors," came the prompt reply.

"Strangle the woman and be rid of her. I cannot see that she will be of any use to us."

"I persuaded her to renounce Rome and be baptized in our faith, Your Majesty. She took the name Anna in my honor. I feel responsibility for her soul, which will surely be damned if she dies in her present state. I believe she will come to accept being a nun, and such an action would lie easier on my conscience."

"You are not yet as Greek as you think you are, madam," said Alexius, chuckling at the French Empress's sudden attack of scruples. "Is the order for her confinement prepared?"

"I brought it with me in the hope that Your Majesty would

sign it tonight. She can be in the mad cells of the Convent of the Seven Sorrows within the hour."

Hardly glancing at the document, Alexius scratched his signature, attached his personal seal and handed it back to the grateful Empress. It was the last act of his reign.

He was in bed, asleep, when Murtzuphles and the captain of the loyal Waring Guard entered the royal bedchamber shortly after midnight. Startled at the noisy intrusion and the flare of torches, he half bounded from bed, then sank back in relief at the sight of the only two men he had recently come to trust, the fair-skinned, serious Waring captain and the black-browed, dark-complected Murtzuphles.

"You gave me a fright," he said, laughing weakly. "What is it? Have the Franks launched an attack?"

"My lord, you must come with us," said the Waring captain. The room was filling quickly with the familiar blond giants of the Emperor's bodyguard. Some watched the door and the corridor outside; others came to range themselves around the bed where Alexius lay, so that his vision was entirely blocked by their heavily muscled bodies. No one laid a hand on him, but suddenly he knew why they had come, and the knowledge was like steel fingers gripping his neck, choking off breath and life. He clasped the covers to him, trying to raise them over his eyes, whimpering like a child in the grip of a terrifying and all-too-familiar nightmare.

"Alexius Angelus, you are Emperor no longer," boomed out Murtzuphles' voice, as formal as if he read from a document devised in council. "You have been lawfully tried and found guilty of conspiring to betray your kingdom and its people to the enemy, of crimes against the Church and against Nature itself. You will be imprisoned forthwith and your fate decided by law and the Will of God. Resign yourself and place your soul and body in His care."

"My eyes, don't let them put out my eyes," babbled Alexius, his words muffled and indistinct beneath the covers he clutched to him like a shield. "I'll pay you anything, anything. My eyes, my eyes."

"Seize him," said Murtzuphles. Contempt for so base and

weak an object as this red-haired youth hardened his voice and the words themselves were an implacable harbinger of death.

Naked and screaming, they dragged him from the imperial bed. He fought them with all the primitive fear of an animal caught in a trap, kicking, biting, scratching, howling his hatred and desolation until the room rang with his screams. They rolled him in a heavy rug, the Warings performing this duty as they performed all others, efficiently, unquestioningly, stolidly ignoring the blood that welled from bites and scratches on faces and forearms. They hoisted the rug to their shoulders, where it moved and twisted like some enormous snake, and as they bore it downward to the prison in the bowels of the palace, a familiar, loathsome stench hung in the air as they passed. When the rug was unrolled Alexius lay unconscious in his own filth. Unceremoniously they dumped his naked, befouled body into the damp, freezing cell from which only death could release him. He would awaken in darkness blacker than the night and if he were lucky he would soon croon insanely, not even feeling the sharp-toothed rats that hungered for his flesh.

Murtzuphles stood in the disordered imperial bedchamber, his eyes raking over the broken tables and chairs, the ripped bedcovers and the pools of wine rapidly spreading over the tiles, shreds of fine crystal being carried along like tiny boats in a dark sea. The Warings were all around him, immensely tall, silent men, alert to every sound in the adjoining apartments and the empty corridors. Alexius's body servant cowered almost unnoticed in the darkest corner of the room, praying that somehow it would be forgotten that he had been a witness to his master's downfall.

"You," said Murtzuphles suddenly, his sharp finger pointed at the man's chest. "Have this chamber cleaned and made fit for an Emperor." Then he turned abruptly on his heel and, trailed by the loyal Warings, walked to the council chamber where his advisers were even now squabbling over the exact wording of the proclamation that named him Emperor.

Ten days later a very worried man stood trembling in the imperial bedchamber to which he had been summoned in the middle of the night. Murtzuphles lay comfortably reclining in the great bed, official papers and documents scattered all about him. The room was brightly lit, for it was said that the new Emperor had difficulty sleeping in the dark and kept his personal demons at bay with candles that had to be replaced every few hours. He was devoting himself to the details of governing with a frenzy that would have killed many a lesser being.

"So he will not die," said Murtzuphles conversationally.

"Sire, we have three times introduced enough poison into his food to kill ten men, but he vomits it up and no harm is done."

"How long have you been in charge of the imperial dungeon?"

"Fifteen years, Your Majesty. And in all that time I have never seen a like case. My apothecary is in great despair. He is a skilled man and his brews have never failed before."

"I do not tolerate failure in those who would serve me."

"Is it Your Majesty's wish that we try again?"

"What use would it be, if, as you say, he vomits up the poison as soon as he tastes it?"

The man hung his head, dreading the order that he knew must come next. Alexius's disposal should properly have been left to the imperial executioners, but it had been given out that the former emperor was dying a slow but natural death, a victim of the same illness that had carried off Isaac four days ago, a melancholia that disrupted the humors and was the despair of the physicians. So great was Murtzuphles' passion for secrecy that no one knew for certain where Alexius lay. The Warings kept guard before an empty chamber which no one was permitted to enter for fear of hastening Alexius's decline. No Waring had ever broken their private code of silence; only Murtzuphles, the wretched prison commander and the bewildered apothecary knew for certain that Alexius lay in a cell so vile that even the rats had begun to desert it.

"He will have to be strangled then," said the Emperor. "But there must be no marks about his throat."

"Your Majesty, no one can enter his cell. He has the strength of a madman. If you would permit me to employ one or two of my executioners and a few trusted guards to hold him down, it could be accomplished in a few moments. But alone, Your Majesty, I fear it is I who would be strangled."

Murtzuphles glared at the man in silence. This one might hold his tongue, but what of the others? He had already planned a splendid double funeral for Isaac and his unfortunate son. There must be no suspicion of foul play, else his people would for all time call him a murderer. Wearily he pushed aside the piles of documents awaiting his attention. A Waring brought him a dark chamber robe, and as he put it on he spoke softly, reassuringly to the now thoroughly frightened man standing uncertainly at the foot of the great bed.

"Dismiss your guards from the corridors. They are to remain in the guardroom with the door tightly closed and barred until the captain of the Warings instructs them to return to their duties. No explanation is to be given, now or ever."

"They will obey without question, Your Majesty."

"Good. Remember, the corridors must be empty and safe from prying eyes."

"It will be done."

Almost as an afterthought, Murtzuphles added, "Summon your apothecary to join us at the door to the prisoner's cell. We may need his services when it is done."

The man left the imperial bedchamber, almost running in his haste to reach the familiar depths he seldom left. The Warings would do it then. It was just as well. Executioners, even the finest of them, had a distressing tendency to go mad at the very height of their hard-won skills. And their ravings were always listened to with great attention by the populace.

Ten Warings accompanied Murtzuphles through the palace and down into the dungeons, their leather-clad feet as noiseless as the Emperor's own, a ghostly patrol that struck fear into the heart of the French Empress and delight into the cool brain of the newly widowed Margaret-Maria. Empresses had their secret peepholes hidden everywhere or they did not long survive at this court. Agnes-Anna was contemplating a long, safe retreat to her own palace, for events were moving too swiftly for her, but Margaret-Maria, knowing that not even Murtzuphles would dare lay hands on her innocent ten-year-old son Manuel, rejoiced to see her stepson's murderer going so determinedly to his work.

The dungeon corridors narrowed as they wound down to the lowest tier of cells, so that finally only two could march abreast. An inch of black, foul-smelling water covered the stone floor, icy cold and repulsively slimy, but every second torch had been extinguished by the overcautious prison commander, and the tiny creatures that slithered in the darkness and were crushed underfoot were unidentifiable.

"There is only one prisoner on this level," said the commander significantly.

"But sound must echo to the floor above," commented Murtzuphles thoughtfully. A Waring detached himself from the Emperor's side and strode to the end of the corridor. The heavy iron door that led to freedom was quietly shut, and just as quietly the well-oiled bolt slipped into its fastenings. The Waring did not rejoin the group that stood in the deeper silence. He spread his legs in a wrestler's stance and hefted his heavy ax from hand to hand. No one could possibly get by him in one piece.

"It has been explained to you what is to be done here?"

The apothecary nodded, bowing low before the Emperor who had counted on his skills. "There will be a blueness of the skin, and the eyes and tongue will protrude. The tongue will also turn black. I have means to remedy the disfigurements." It was best to adopt a strictly professional tone, to make no apologetic reference to the poisons that had accomplished nothing. That had been the advice of his friend, who had reassured him that the Emperor understood and had already forgiven their failure.

The prison commander inserted a heavy key into the iron lock of Alexius's cell, and as the other keys on his ring jangled together, the creature within began to howl, long, high-pitched screams that reverberated down the corridor, beating against the distant Waring whose body seemed to absorb and defeat even sound itself.

Six Warings poured into the cell, sliding and falling in the muck as the gaunt, slippery body of Alexius thrashed and twisted in their grip. Two Warings had moved to stand behind their captain, whose eyes never for an instant left the faces of the prison commander and the apothecary.

Alexius nearly burst through into the corridor, but Murtzuphles blocked the doorway. As the greasy, red-stubbled face almost touched his own, the Emperor reached out and caught the neck in a grip the prisoner could not break. Warings pulled at his arms and legs so that he was immobile in their grasp, and there in the doorway of the cell, Murtzuphles throttled him to death.

For a long moment Alexius's face hung suspended in black space, his eyes staring lifelessly into those of his murderer. When the body ceased to twitch, Murtzuphles let it fall to crumple face up on the floor. It was as the apothecary had predicted; the marks of his death were there for anyone to read. Almost absentmindedly Murtzuphles nudged the absurdly flaccid genitals of his victim. Only one of Isaac's sons remained alive, but he was a boy yet and it would be many years before his seed could be planted. Castration was not uncommon; perhaps the boy could be made a monk guaranteed to remain faithful to the vow of chastity.

A great weariness came over the Emperor and he shivered in the chill he had not felt before.

"In the morning he must be found to have died peacefully in his sleep, in the chamber he has occupied for the past ten days. Is your skill great enough for this task, master apothecary?"

"It is a matter of a few hours only, my lord."

"Good. Your friend will remain with you and bring me word when he is fit to look upon."

"My guards, Your Majesty, and my duties here below?" The prison commander had not expected this order. It made him vaguely uneasy.

"The Warings will return them to their posts as previously arranged. I will reward you personally for this night's service."

"The service is its own reward," murmured the apothecary obsequiously, wondering if his dyes and ointments would ever bleach out the ten purple marks that stood out obscenely on the body even in this poor light. Perhaps a high jeweled collar could be fastened around the throat when the body lay in state.

It was still dark outside when the apothecary straightened up from his cramped position over Alexius's body and began replacing his ointments in the carved wooden box of his profession. The bed had been ringed with tall candles which burned steadily in the dead air of the closed chamber. As the prison commander stepped into their bright light to inspect the apothecary's work he marveled at the transformation his friend had wrought. The body was clean and sweet-smelling, though a heavy foulness hung in the air about it. The face on the pillow was as composed and tranquil as that of a sleeping child. Even the unnatural whiteness of the skin exactly imitated the pallor of a death that had followed a long, wasting illness.

"Marvelous. I don't know how you did it, but the Emperor is sure to be pleased."

"A few wooden pegs to hold the tongue in place, a little judicious bloodletting here and there, some paints and unguents," confided the apothecary almost jauntily, moving back from the bed to survey his masterpiece. "The important thing in cases like this is to move quickly."

"The eyes," continued the prison commander, leaning down to peer into the dead man's face. "How did you do that?"

"I must have some professional secrets even from you, my friend. It was difficult, but in this cold weather there is no danger that they will begin to protrude again as long as the Emperor does not delay the burial longer than a day."

"Alexius and Isaac will lie in their tombs before nightfall."

"Almost indecent haste for an emperor and his son."

"The father has been dead for four days, and the mourning has gone on long enough, even for an emperor. The people will be touched by the thought that they will be entombed together and share the same obsequies. There will be little talk, if any."

Moving slowly from candle to candle, the apothecary deposited a small amount of white powder in each flame, and soon a heavy cloud of incense overlay the nauseous death smells that had caused the prison commander to hold a scented handkerchief to his nose throughout the long process of transformation. Relieved that he could breathe freely again, he paced around the chamber, looking for signs of the apothecary's work that sharp eyes would spy out and whisper over. Many official witnesses would be summoned to this chamber in the morning to gaze at the body and certify that the ex-Emperor had died peacefully in his sleep. It would not do if one of them were to stumble over a forgotten instrument or vial.

Satisfied that every trace of the night's work had been removed, he knocked softly twice, then twice again, on the chamber door. He heard one of the guards outside move off quietly down the corridor and knew that Murtzuphles would be entering that door in a very few minutes. The apothecary was standing near the small table on which his box rested, gazing almost lovingly at the body he had worked over, and the prison commander, hearing returning footsteps, moved to stand beside his friend. Though both men were utterly exhausted, they were strangely unaware of their fatigue. An exhilaration possessed them at having been a part of an adventure that they would remember all their lives. And when people spoke sadly of the young man who had so grieved over his people's distress that his grief had caused his death, they would nod their heads sagely in agreement, delighting in the secret knowledge to which only they and an emperor were privy. The Warings did not count. They were more statues from the past come to life than men.

"Exquisite," exclaimed Murtzuphles from the threshold, where he had halted in amazement at the sad beauty of the scene before him. "Death is doubly tragic when it strikes down a youth in his prime," he continued, approaching the bed and slowly circling it, unable to take his eyes from the figure that lay there. Not a speck of grime remained on the body, not even under the newly manicured fingernails of the corpse, fingernails which bore no resemblance now to the claws which had ripped at the Warings so brutally and so uselessly. Alexius's arms were crossed over his breast just as a thoughtful priest might have arranged them in the first moments after death. There was even the hint of a smile on his lips, and the bright red hair, artistically arranged and curled, glowed like a saint's halo in the candlelight.

"I am very pleased, very pleased indeed," said Murtzuphles. "Is there anything further to be done?"

"No, Your Majesty. I have dressed him in the garments he is to be buried in so that there is no need for any other hands to touch him."

"None shall, I assure you. The Warings will place him in his coffin after the witnesses have seen the body. As his loyal bodyguard, it is their prerogative."

"I might warn Your Majesty against the effects of too much heat," began the apothecary hesitantly.

"The candles will be extinguished when we leave here, and the chamber kept as cold as the grave." The Emperor almost laughed at the simile. "The witnesses will not be tempted to linger in such a chill." He smiled conspiratorially at the prison commander and the apothecary, cast a last, lingering look at dead Alexius, and gave the signal knock on the door. "One of my guards will carry your box for you, master apothecary. You must be very tired after this long night's work."

The apothecary, bending to lift the heavy case, straightened in surprise at the Emperor's thoughtfulness. Was there ever such a master as this? He caught the eye of the prison commander. Such a mark of favor promised a great reward in the not-too-distant future. Both men bowed low as the Emperor passed through the open door. He paused briefly to whisper a command to the captain of the Waring Guard. It was several seconds before the echo of his words made any sense to them. Strangle them? Surely there was no one else whose death the Emperor needed. But there was, and the Warings were very quick, very quiet, very efficient. This time it was the captain of the Waring Guard who sprinkled white powder in the candle flames to banish the smell of fear and violent death.

The bodies were carried from the room, weighted with stones and cast into the Horn. The apothecary's wooden box was emptied of its powders, broken up and used to fuel the guardroom fire. The sharp instruments became useless, unidentifiable lumps of metal, and by the time the cooks began stirring in the predawn stillness of their kitchens, the dark rooms of the imperial apartments had grown quiet and cold again. Even Murtzuphles finally slept.

VIII

By the time the news of Murtzuphles' coup reached the crusaders' camp the ugly suspicion of murder had taken on the certainty of truth. The Greeks themselves believed it and someone among them, perhaps a high noble whose house had managed to remain steadfastly aloof from the corruption of the court, had a letter shot into the Galata camp. The archer who had somehow crept unnoticed to the fringes of the camp was never found, but the arrow and the document it had carried were displayed for all to see.

The bishops, priests and monks of the army were particularly enraged by the murder and its consequences. The Greeks were little better than openly defiant heretics, for the earlier agreement to bring their Church back into obedience to Rome was now exposed as a devil's trick to buy time to strengthen their unholy determination. Murtzuphles' coronation was invalid, they thundered in sermon after sermon, for a murderer could not sit among God's anointed. The war was just. The war was lawful. It was also absolutely inevitable. Even those who had secretly nursed the hope that Alexius would weaken and decide to buy them off knew that not a single ship would sail to the Holy Land until Constantinople had fallen and delivered up its new Emperor for execution.

It was February and still bitterly cold. By mid-March, surely not later than early April, they would move. In the meantime groups of foragers went further afield each day, but the dried stores they stole from the few farmers who still remained on their lands were pitifully small. Near-starvation had been the only constant in the crusaders' lives since their arrival in Constantinople, and in the cold darkness of winter a man felt the hunger even more. There was plenty of flour to be baked into small round cakes so hard you could crack a tooth on one, but an egg, a skinny hen or a good mouthful of wine were luxuries that only the very rich could afford to purchase.

Several monasteries had been converted into hospitals, but not even the desperately ill and dying ate any better than the well. So many had died that winter. Their bodies lay stacked like cordwood in temporary tombs until, for fear of disease, orders were given to light huge fires that for a few hours at least thawed out the frozen ground enough to permit hasty mass burials. The rats that scurried busily in the dark prospered and grew fat; even the knowledge of how that sleek plumpness was acquired did not stop the enterprising rat catchers from doing a brisk business. Skinned and roasted, one could imagine that one was eating hare—old, sharp-tasting hare such as was often trapped in the hills of faraway France. It kept them alive and that was all that mattered now.

Aleaumes had moved permanently into one of the monastery hospitals a few days after Robert, unconscious and nearly dead, was brought there by the watch that patrolled the Galata streets. He nursed his brother himself, only leaving his side during the hours when Robert was sunk in deep, exhausted sleep. Then he helped care for other patients, emptying slop jars, wiping fevered brows, changing the soiled linen of those whose bowels had turned to water, closing the eyes of the dead, carrying off stiffened corpses to make room for new sufferers. The tasks he performed were unspeakably foul ones, but he did them with a casual heartiness that lightened the hospital's grim atmosphere. The monks were grateful for his help, and even those who were jealous of his skill grudgingly admired it.

"The knight ought to have died, Father Abbot," Brother Mark declared. "If I had not been at his side almost constantly in the hours of crisis I would have called it sorcery."

"The brother shared his brews with you, did he not?" asked the abbot.

"Grudgingly," admitted the monk. "He said a woman skilled in herbs gave them to him, but he would tell me neither her name nor where to find her. I cannot believe a woman could possess such knowledge."

"Nor I," agreed the abbot. "But the knight appeared to me to be suffering also from some deep malaise of the spirit. I would have said that the will to live had gone out of him. Perhaps only a brother could have eased the soul's agony and tempered it. The medicines may have been secondary in this case."

"I wish I knew for certain," Brother Mark sighed. "Four more will die before Vespers."

"God's Will be done, Brother."

As he reentered the ward, Brother Mark saw that Aleaumes was sitting by his brother's bed, holding a cup to Robert's lips. There were secrets in that cup that the monk would have given anything to possess—if they were not devil's work, that is. He approached the bed, his nostrils twitching to identify the herbs and powders that gave off such a pungent odor. The clerk was a strange man, half knight, half religious. He seemed to occupy no safe niche in the social order of the army, moving easily and as one of them among the soldiers, equally familiar with the monks among whom he had lived for the past three months. Brother Mark gave a sigh for such freedom, then reproached himself sternly. It was a criticism of his vows to yearn for freedom. He decided to pass the night on his knees in prayerful vigil. Long experience in the religious life had taught him that the body was an enemy against whom a good monk must fight unceasingly.

"That one hovers over me constantly," Aleaumes said cheerfully to Robert, watching Brother Mark veer off from them and plod over to another bed. "He wonders if I'm in league with the Devil. Theodora would laugh at that."

Robert winced at the name. He was still too weak to walk unsupported by his brother's arm, but his mind and memory were strong and seemingly unaffected by the months of fever and delirium. He could not block out a single minute of the terrible hour he had spent with Theodora, Signor Matteo and the grief-demented servant she had called Giovanni. The pain of it had lessened when he had been certain he was dying, in those few lucid moments when he had opened his eyes and seen the priest working over his soul. But when Aleaumes snatched death away from him it had returned with all its original intensity. It was always with him now, like the pain of a cancer that grew unwanted in a man's body until the agony of it was unbearable and the victim cried out for the blessed relief of oblivion.

"I wish you had let me die, Aleaumes."

"God did not let you die, Robert. I had nothing to do with it."

"You know what I mean. I was already a dead man when they brought me here, and glad of it."

"The dead cannot be brought back to life, no matter what Brother Mark may believe. Theodora's herbs merely stopped the flux temporarily, long enough for your mind and body to heal themselves. If you had really wanted to die, you would have, in spite of the herbs. Theodora said she has seen it happen often. Something inside a man snaps, he lies down, and never gets up again."

"I don't want to hear about what Theodora says or thinks. I don't want to talk about her at all, ever again."

"She said you wouldn't," Aleaumes continued tranquilly. "She also said that until you could speak freely about Anne, weep openly and unashamedly, and remember her as others do your cure would be incomplete. She said that mourning heals the heart and that unless you can forget you will go mad."

"I will never forget," Robert said bitterly.

"I think she meant that you must forget the manner of her death, not Anne herself. You did not see her die, so you lie here torturing yourself with images of a horror that she may well have been spared. And you'll never know, Robert. She's dead. It's best to let her go."

Almost he thought that he had reached him, that his words had had the desired effect. Robert's face contorted and his body shook with spasms that followed so closely one upon the other that he seemed to be in the grip of a giant hand that tossed him about for its careless pleasure. But the tears did not flow, and gradually an iron tightness held him still.

"I beg you, as a brother, Aleaumes, never to speak of her again. Neither you nor Theodora can understand the kind of love Anne and I shared, and I will not have that old woman's lips profaning it."

"You're safe from Theodora at least, Robert. She's dead. She died in her sleep two days ago. Signor Matteo says that her heart was weak and failed her, but I don't think he even believes that himself. Something happened a few weeks ago that deeply troubled her. She said that someone had failed her, and she wondered what Nicholas would have advised her to do about it. I didn't pay much attention at the time, since she seemed comfortable and secure enough in Signor Matteo's house. But when I saw her last she asked me more questions than usual about your health and whether there was any new sign of weakness of the bowels. She said that your death would have weighed on her conscience, but that now you were well again she was free. I asked her what she meant, but she just smiled and did not answer me. I think she meant she was free to die."

"Free to roast in hell, if she took her own life."

"They didn't really believe in heaven and hell, those two. Nor much of anything else. They kept up the pretense, but Nicholas hinted to me as much several times. He used to talk about perfect freedom of mind and soul. He said it could be attained only when we had cast out the last vestige of fear from our lives. I warned him that such talk smacked of heresy and he said no, that it was philosophy and that young men could never understand the thoughts that troubled old men in the night, nor where their true comfort was to be found. He died, you know, a few days after you were brought here. I shall miss them both."

"Aleaumes, I'm tired. The drink always makes me sleepy."

"I'll come back when you awaken, Robert," Aleaumes said, straightening his brother's meager covers as gently and solicitously as a woman. "Brother Mark is signaling to me. I fear another soul has slipped away from him. He is a good man, but too rigid in his thinking. I've noticed here how often one sees fear in a monk's eyes. They meditate too often on hell and not enough on life."

Robert's eyes were already closed. The drink, whatever it was, soothed him, lulled him. His body seemed to drift away, leaving his mind to wander at will through strange fantasies and waking dreams. It was not unlike the effect of wine, except that Robert had felt an urgent craving for the drink that he had never known for wine or the double beer of Picardy. He had mentioned this once to Aleaumes who, he was sure, had immediately consulted Theodora. Gradually, almost without his fully realizing it, the drink had grown weaker. Now it merely relaxed him and gave him the illusion of strength.

He feigned sleep, to be left alone with his thoughts. For the past few days his mind had been obstinately returning to Picardy, remembering all the events of his childhood; his mother's face, the lush green of the hills in early spring, Gilo sitting by the fire in the late evenings. He saw two small boys sitting at their father's feet and heard again, as if for the first time, the stories of Gilo's years in the Holy Land, of his hopes and dreams for the future of his house.

"You, Aleaumes, my son, will be a bishop someday, a learned, wise and holy man."

"Yes, Father."

"Robert, because he is the elder and my heir, will marry Aelis. Her lands will double his inheritance and from her body will come the new sons of our house. You will found a great family, Robert, one whose name will burn gloriously in the monastery annals. You and your sons will not sink into the oblivion of our ancestors."

"No, Father."

How peaceful, how placid, how happy those days now seemed. It must be the drink, Robert thought. I am not a man who yearns for a quiet backwater in which to hide himself. He tried to think of the assault being planned for spring, the changes Aleaumes had described in the long ramps of the Venetian galleys, the city walls that grew higher each day, the men in whose company he would ride.

"I think he has fallen asleep, my lord." It was Brother Mark's voice.

"Is he well and truly cured, Brother?"

"He will ride again, my lord, within the month."

"That is what I came to hear. I cannot stay long. Tell him when he wakes that I was here and that I rejoice in his good fortune."

"Wait, my lord," Robert called out, struggling to sit up.

"Not too long, my lord," cautioned Brother Mark. "He is still very weak."

"You do not look weak to me, Robert," said Peter of Amiens.

"They fuss over me too much. I get no peace from them, and Aleaumes is the worst," complained Robert.

"What can you expect?" Peter laughed. "We were all prepared to slide your body in between a German and a monk. But you did not die, and the space was taken by a Venetian. The tombs are filled and there's no room left for you. Besides, I think the monks would take it as a personal affront if you were to sicken again. They like their miracles to be beyond reproach."

"I have no intention of dying, not now at any rate, my lord." The words and the ease with which they came to his lips startled Robert. When had he decided that?

"Life must seem doubly sweet in a place like this," said Peter, shuddering as he looked about him at the doomed men lying on all sides. Even the cold could not dissipate the nauseous smells that hung in the air above every bed and every body.

Could a life without Anne ever seem truly sweet again, wondered Robert? "It is indeed, my lord," he answered mechanically.

"We almost caught Murtzuphles," said Peter, determinedly ignoring the sounds of purging that rang hollowly down the long hall. "He slipped through our fingers at the last moment, but we have the imperial standard and the icon he carried into battle. One of the Venetian galleys has been rowing up and down the Horn with them for three days. It drives the Greeks mad to see a Venetian wave their precious standards in their faces."

"How did it happen, my lord?"

"We were very short of food, as usual," Peter said. "So Henry of Flanders persuaded his brother to let him make a night ride to Phile. He took a goodly company with him and they captured the city easily. They stripped it of everything we could use and sent the food and clothing by boat down the Straits to us."

"We had soup with meat in it yesterday," said Robert. "I wondered where it came from."

"He and his men stayed in the city for two days. They claim it took them that long to round up all the horses in the area and load them with more food and the booty they had found. I think they drank the city dry and used up all the women. I know I would have. In the meantime, though, refugees from Phile reached Constantinople. The city was in an uproar so Murtzuphles decided that he himself would lead out a portion of his army, perhaps to demonstrate that this Emperor does not cower behind his walls or refuse to do battle. The Greeks lay in ambush, and as James of Avesnes tells it, allowed almost the entire caravan to pass unmolested. Our people suspected nothing until Murtzurphles and his men attacked the rearguard. The fighting was fierce, but our knights had been strengthened and refreshed by their two days in Phile and they quickly repulsed the Greeks. Henry of Flanders was nearly unhorsed several times as he tried to break through the Emperor's bodyguard. Only the Warings stood firm until Murtzuphles decided to make his escape through a nearby wood. The rest of the Greeks had already broken and run, leaving twenty of their knights dead on the ground. We captured the icon and much else, but the Warings covered the Emperor's retreat and no one could break their line."

"A pity they do not fight on our side," remarked Robert.

"So said we all. But their hatred of us goes back many generations and is bred into them from earliest childhood."

"Is the Emperor back in Constantinople?"

"Sitting snugly in his palace, but not so easily on his throne. No one knew the icon had been captured until the Venetian galley began displaying it before the walls. This is the first time it has ever been lost in battle, we are told, and it is an object the Greeks hold in great reverence. It has almost the holiness of a precious relic to them. Without its protection they are fearful and despairing."

"So should they be," said Brother Mark from behind Peter of Amiens. "They are heretics who must be brought back to Rome. This is a just and lawful war, my lord, and God will grant us the victory."

"No one doubts that, Brother. Not now."

"My patient's face is flushed, my lord. We must guard against a recurrence of his fever."

"I am leaving, Brother. I have stayed overlong as it is."

"It was good of you to come, my lord."

"I expect you to ride beside me when the time comes, Robert."

"I will be there even if they have to strap me to my horse."

Peter of Amiens turned to go, then stood hesitant for a moment. "I was grieved to learn of your loss, Robert," he said quietly, without looking directly at him. Robert said nothing.

"God's Will be done," sighed Peter.

"Amen to that, my lord." Brother Mark fussed about Robert's bed, smelling the dregs in the cup Aleaumes had left there, laying a cold hand on the knight's forehead to check for the heat of fever, assisting his patient to lie down again beneath his covers. Perhaps now he would pick up some hint of the spiritual malaise the abbot had suspected. But he was to be disappointed, for Peter left without another word, and Robert again closed his eyes.

"We shall soon be in the holy season of Lent, sir knight. Now that you are conscious again and your strength returning you must give some thought to your religious duties. Would you like me to send for Father Abbot to hear your confession?"

"In time, Brother Mark," answered Robert feebly, his eyes tightly shut. "Talking still tires me and my mind will not concentrate for long on any one thing. I will send for your abbot when I am ready to confess."

"As you will," said Brother Mark, reluctant to let the subject drop. "But do not delay too long. Many call upon our abbot's wisdom and guidance during Lent and he is sore pressed to counsel all who ask it of him."

Peter of Amiens's parting words hung in Robert's consciousness. God's Will be done, he had said, with true resignation and acceptance in his voice. Robert had heard those words all his life, and he could not even begin to count the many times he had repeated them himself. They were like a seal set upon an action or an event that froze it in time so that it was forever unalterable by man. They were comforting words, even in the worst of times, for they bespoke a Father who made decisions that were beyond His children's understanding. Gilo had said them when racked with a pain Robert could now finally appreciate, and he had been strengthened by them. Aelis had also said them during the long months when her moon flow had been uninterrupted by pregnancy, but with a desperation in her voice that belied resignation. Strange that he should think of Aelis now. Aelis and the child. Anne had never conceived, though he had often hoped she would. A child bound a woman to a man like nothing else could. Had there after all been some imperfection, some uncertainty in their love that had made him yearn to plant a son in her womb? He did not want to believe it, but the odd new periods of introspection to which he had lately been prey would not leave him, and try though he might to distract his thoughts, they had become as probing as a surgeon's instrument and just as pain-giving. He saw Anne as she had looked the first time he had spoken to her, cropped hair and shortened nun's gown unable to mar her beauty. He saw her again in the convent parlor in Amiens, lying naked on the sands of the Isle of St. Nicholas, in the house in Zara where they had played at being husband and wife, riding the hills of Corfu, standing beside Theodora on the deck of their ship, in Signor Matteo's rich house, chaperone at her side.

From being his alone during the earliest days of their journey, he realized now that she had begun reaching out to share herself with many others ever since Zara. She had ridiculed the two old sisters who had first taken her under their wing, avoiding their company as much as seemly. But in Zara she had struck up a friendship with Theodora that had lasted until her death. He was jealous of their companionship, of the hours they had spent together when he was denied her company, of the fact that Theodora had taught her Greek. It had put a barrier between them that she could converse and laugh with strangers in a language he could not understand. Why had she done it? Why had she bothered to learn Italian when everyone in Signor Matteo's house could have spoken to her in French? If she had been a young man, Robert would have remarked the signs of ambition and predicted a glorious future for such an assiduous youth. But she was a woman, a woman who was, moreover, bound to a man by her own admission of love. It had not become her to act as though her future lay not in Robert's hands but in her own will.

He saw her, finally, seated in the shade of the Pareto garden, untouched by the humid August heat, gowned and bejeweled far above her true station. She had been composed, loving, a little distant, as though her thoughts were on something or someone else. Even her promise to meet him on his return in that same lovely spot now seemed to ring false. It was as though she had thought it all out beforehand and come up with a phrase and an image that could not fail to send him away believing in her and trusting her absolutely, as though she had struck a pose approved by the Courts of Love that had nothing in it of real life. She should have wept, should have clung to him, should have acted like any woman would whose lover was leaving her alone in a foreign land with only strangers to comfort her.

She had done none of those things, and it was quite true that the image of her that Robert had carried in his heart during the three months of campaign was very like that of an ethereal, impersonal statue of the Virgin. The image had comforted him, had been like a steady flame burning to light the way home. But I was ambitious, too, he admitted to himself, consumed with bitterness and disillusion. He remembered the gold chalice he had brought back, looted from God's altar, and now he burned with shame to think how callously he had accepted it, how jealously he had hidden it from others' eyes. I am no better than any of them, he thought, yet all I really ever wanted was to do my Christian duty in the Holy Land and return to Clari with my beloved at my side, to have sons with her and grow old together.

Somewhere deep inside his body the cancer lump of hate and despair began to break up. He could feel the pieces of it dissolving as a last truth crept into his mind and lay there, impossible to ignore. Anne would never have gone back to Clari with him, not even if he could have assured her that Aelis was dead and he was free to wed her. She would have laughed at him, mocked him as she had done in the first cruel days after she had joined Signor Matteo's household. My uncle serves the King of Jerusalem, she would have said. Do you really expect me to spend my days on a fief so poor and mean that not even the crassest moneylender craves it? Go back to your mudhole, if you wish, Robert of Clari, but you go alone. I shall dwell in palaces.

Briefly, darkly, as through a veil, he saw the gleam of sapphires on her fair skin, saw the proud head lift, felt the dismissal and disinterest in her eyes. Then the image faded and she was gone. He fumbled beneath his shirt for the lump of blackened gold he had hung about his neck. The leather thong, rotted with the sweat of many fevers, parted easily. What once had been a ring no longer burned in his hand with a demon's fire of its own. I will keep this to remember you by, he whispered, and lay it beneath the altar stone of the place you would have despised. You would have grown to hate me there, at Clari, where my roots go deeper than I knew, and your misery would have poisoned our love. Peter knew it and he was right. God's Will be done.

Aleaumes came to wake him from his sleep for another draught of Theodora's medicine, but seeing Robert's face so peaceful, the lines of pain erased as though they had never been, he left him undisturbed. The medicine could wait. It was healing, natural sleep he needed, and this sleep, Aleaumes knew, was one of the few his brother had known that was not induced by drugs.

Robert's sword hand hung slack and completely relaxed, the fingers just touching the floor. The arm would cramp like that, Aleaumes thought, and awaken him. He placed the hand on Robert's breast, stepping on something hard and rocklike that had fallen beside the bed. He bent to retrieve it, and stood offering a silent prayer of thanks, Anne's ring and the broken leather thong clenched in his fist. Then he placed them in Robert's leather pouch, blazoned with the arms of Clari, and went to tell Brother Mark that it was high time Robert began a program of serious exercise.

PART IV

April, 1204-April, 1205

Should a people who treated one another so cruelly
be deemed worthy of holding their lands, or should
they lose them?

—La Conquête de Constantinople
Geoffroy de Villehardouin

I

Friday, April 9–
Tuesday, April 13, 1204

The long-awaited, meticulously planned spring assault on the sea walls of Constantinople was launched on the morning of Friday, April 9.

No army could have been better prepared than Montferrat's, no ships more skillfully manned than Dandolo's, no city more doomed to fall than Constantinople. And yet by midafternoon the Franks were fleeing back across the Horn while hundreds of dead and dying Westerners, as crushed and broken as the bogged-down siege engines among which they sprawled, lay abandoned on the muddy banks below the city.

The Greeks celebrated their easy victory far into the night. The crusaders, bleeding, numb, bewildered, the proof of God's displeasure all too apparent, wandered their camp, each man asking the other what had gone wrong.

It was sin, thundered the Bishops of Soissons, Troyes and Halberstadt, and the prostitutes were quickly driven from their tents out onto the open plain where they pitched a temporary camp and settled back to rest and wait for fortune to shift once more in their direction.

These women, well attuned to the needs and desires of the soldiers they had pleasured for so long, grasped immediately the import of the changes that were wrought in soul and spirit during the three nights and two days which followed. And being realists with empty purses, they applauded the shrill sermons preached almost hourly, knowing that a man whipped to the point of frenzy fights better than one whose emotions are not touched, fights without admitting the possibility of defeat, fights with such blind fury that he cannot be stopped until he dies or tastes victory.

While the Greeks ate and drank and danced in their secure streets, and rushed to the walls every time the wind freshened, expecting to see the sails of their enemy unfurled and disappearing over the horizon, the Franks fasted and prayed, confessed themselves, received the Sacred Host, and espoused, finally and completely, the new task an unfathomable God had set them.

"There were military mistakes made today," Montferrat admitted to his commanders, "but these can be easily rectified. One vessel targeted against each tower is insufficient. Every siege engine must be permanently mounted on a transport and its various ranges calculated well before the next attack begins."

Dandolo nodded. His sailors were already scurrying over every ship in the fleet, carrying out the instructions he had given as soon as port had been reached.

"I misjudged the effect of the compact we agreed to," the Marquis continued. "When we proclaimed our intention to elect a Latin emperor from amongst ourselves, when we specified how this election would take place, when we published the details of how we will divide this city and its provinces, even when we bound each man to service here for one additional year under pain of excommunication should he attempt to desert, when we did all these things, my lords, we did them for ourselves, and we were satisfied. In our minds the matter was settled and the future made clear."

"They fought halfheartedly," Baldwin said. "I command the largest contingent in this army, men I have trained myself, men who have never before swung an ax carelessly or taken a backward step before the order was given. But I saw more faces glancing over defeated shoulders this afternoon than ever before in my life."

"Do you know why, my lord?" Montferrat asked softly.

Baldwin shook his head.

Montferrat smiled, St. Pol shrugged his shoulders, Dandolo raised disbelieving eyes to heaven. Villehardouin, his lips set tight against an explanation he would not give, waited quietly for the Marquis to answer his own question.

"Jerusalem." Montferrat lingered over each hissing syllable, repeating the word three times, like a blessing or an incantation to evil. "We are in the season of Lent again," he said. "Every morning's Mass reminds us of the Passion to come, our faces are turned to the East, our souls are straining toward Golgotha and the Cross, but you and I, my lord of Flanders, you and I and every other baron who has sat in council with us during the past year knows that our Jerusalem bears a new name."

One of the most admirable of Baldwin's qualities was his basic stupidity, Dandolo reflected, watching the Count's face as he struggled to understand the meaning of what Montferrat had so baldly stated. A child could have grasped its significance before the cousin of the King of France.

Yet Baldwin was neither a child nor as bland an individual as everyone but his Countess supposed him to be.

"Whom shall we elect to rule our kingdom?" he asked.

"That's unimportant now," said Montferrat sharply. "The man whose nature is most suited for command will wear the crown, but it is for the electors, when we have chosen them, to decide that issue."

The reprimand was quick, an insult to the man who asked the question, and Dandolo, knowing the depth of the Marquis's ambition, looked with an inkling of new respect at Baldwin. You're underestimating him, my dear Boniface, he decided, and not crediting a rival with a nascent greed as great as your own is always a grave error.

"Many of the common soldiers and even some of the younger knights persist in honoring the Lion Heart's custom of calling aloud the name of the Holy City each evening," continued Montferrat. "It's a dream, a myth, a shadow before the reality of Constantinople, but we have erred in not naming it such. We must make them understand and welcome the fact that the war we undertook against the unbeliever has now become a war against the heretic. Murtzuphles instead of Saladin, Constantinople in the place of Jerusalem, the vow to serve Christ honored, the intention still pure and unsullied by compromise, the will of God accepted, proved by the testing He has sent us. Do you understand now, my lord of Flanders?"

"I understand," Baldwin replied with as much dignity as he was capable of. "But will the army?"

"That is a task our learned and persuasive prelates will accomplish with ease," Montferrat predicted.

The Bishop of Halberstadt, who had sat silent throughout the brief meeting, nodded his head. "The monks and priests will be set to their duty immediately," he said. "God's Will be done."

Heresy was a worse crime than disbelief, the priests proclaimed, and the Emperor of Constantinople, already a black-souled murderer and a devil who denied the sacredness of kingship, was also an arch-heretic, the one man almost solely responsible for the error in which his people walked. He thumbed his nose with casual obscenity at the chain stretching from Christ to Peter to Pope to laity, and thus denied his countrymen and subjects the wisdom, the mercy, the discipline, the truth and the absolute authority of Rome. He was felon, he was false, he was a perjurer. He would roast in everlasting fire, and the faithful who sent him there would earn God's special blessing.

And what was the sin for which Christ had punished the men who wore His Cross? They were absolved of the weaknesses of the flesh, of lechery, drunkenness and concupiscence, forgiven the sins of pride, covetousness, anger, sloth and the breaking of lawful oaths, but, and the priests lowered their voices and beat their breasts, was a divided heart a fit vessel to receive the full outpouring of the Savior's love?

Simon of Montfort no longer lingered among them to play the dark role of individual conscience, and more than a thousand others, truth seekers, religious fanatics, tired, disillusioned, bitterly honest men, had gone their separate lonely ways, taking with them the memory of what they had once sought in common. The bright image of Jerusalem had grown a little dimmer as each of the city's advocates left the army. It was merely a shadow now, a name called at sunset by a few stubborn voices, a pinprick at the soul, a lever to be used against the barons, an excuse to sail away to travel East or West, in any direction that did not lead to Constantinople.

A man could not serve both Christ and the devil. Christ commanded, Satan tempted. They had taken the cross to serve the one and thwart the other, and there was no doubt in anyone's mind that the Savior of the world still bled in Jerusalem. But God dwelt in eternity, and in His own eternal time He would ordain the rescue of His Holy City. A mortal man lived out his days within a framework sharply limited by the passage of his earthly years, years that were absurdly tiny fragments of reflected eternity. Standing alone before so great a mystery he was lost and helpless, buffeted by the demands of the present, the past and the future, incapable of comprehending what never began and what would never end.

If he were obstinate and stiff-necked, did not bend his will to those whom God inspired to lead him closer to Divinity, he sinned the sin of pride. He set his feeble intelligence, his vacillating will, his weak flesh and weaker heart against the One in whose perfect image he had been created. To cling now to Jerusalem, now that Christ and His bishops had revealed a greater crusade, a more urgent task to be accomplished, was more than merely sinful. It was nearly as heretical an action as the denial of the Pope's supreme authority. Excommunication was the punishment in this world, and as the power to excommunicate came directly from God Himself, the sentence, without a hope of appeal or mitigation, would be carried out in the next.

It had been said at last, first in imagery and oratorical meanderings, then in words so brief and plain that Montferrat's message was as evident as if he himself had grabbed each soldier by the arm and bluntly told him who he was and where he was going. You wanted a holy war, you have been given one, though not in the place of your own choosing. Leave Jerusalem to the Saracens for this next year at least. Conquer Constantinople, help to found a new kingdom from the ashes of the old. God wills it, His bishops urge you to it, and in your heart you know that there is both Divine and worldly wisdom in the act. Leave, and you are excommunicated. Remain and fight, and your rewards will be both temporal and spiritual.

Nothing the preachers said was either completely new or totally surprising. The army had known since Zara that Montferrat was leading them to Constantinople. But it had taken time for opposition to be beaten down, time for feelings to coalesce, time for the hot Jerusalem fever to cool, still more time for cynicism and greed to scab over the tender, wounded places where con-science had been violated. Now the army, all but a very few men, was whole again and healed. The sin of doubt had been punished on Friday afternoon, revealed in all its grimy smallness on Saturday, burned out with the hunger of fasting by Sunday. The True Cross, lying in some heretic church of Constantinople, called out to each cross stitched on tunic, painted on shield, worn on a chain around the neck. And to answer its call was no longer sin, but an act of grace and religious duty.

The army slept well on Sunday night, certain that on the mor-row Constantinople would be pushed to the brink of surrender, might even capitulate. Men who give themselves wholeheartedly to God's work are seldom troubled by nightmares. They dream of beauty, of celestial streets paved with gold, of soft garments, jeweled crowns, silver-stringed musical instruments, the ful-fillment of all their aching wants and the balm of old voids replete with a honey sweeter than any ever tasted in life. Heaven is a perfect earth, and Constantinople, where bands of sightseeing knights and soldiers had walked with gaping mouths, dry tongues and burning fingers, was a very rich city indeed.

By early Monday morning the crusaders' ships had been spread out in a long line that stretched for nearly a league down the Golden Horn.

Dandolo's sleek Venetian galleys had a top-heavy look, their open decks roofed over with stout timbers on top of which a thick layer of grapevines had been secured, the better to absorb the shock of Greek missiles. Hide-covered ladders and tunnels through which the assaulting forces would swarm rose to new heights, dwarfing the masts of the transport vessels. An eerie man-made forest floated on the blue waters that lapped gently against the rocky ground just below the city walls.

The troopships and supply vessels, mangonels and ballistas firmly mounted on their decks, glittered blackly in the thin early sunlight. The engineers who worked these formidable machines of death sat or stood on their framework. Each ship carried its full complement of men and horses, and the decks were so crowded with knights and soldiers that there was scarcely room to move.

The ships lay at anchor now, linked together two by two with ropes the thickness of a man's arm, awaiting the rising of the wind that would carry them across the Horn.

The Greeks moved in a gay, almost festive atmosphere. The city's walls were thronged with crowds of people, handsome, confident men, lovely women with dark flirtatious eyes, children held up by their parents to see the rare and grand sight of a foreign fleet no longer feared by the populace it would soon attack. Friday's victory, so swift and so decisive, had been achieved without the loss of a single Greek life. It was too much to hope that today's encounter would be as bloodless, but though men would fall and widows weep, Constantinople itself would never die.

Murtzuphles had pitched his tents on a high mound near a previously unattacked portion of the city wall. The camp, its imperial standard, the Emperor himself and all the commanders gathered around him were in full view of the Franks, and he in turn could gaze out over the walls at the vessels which threatened them.

He chuckled to himself as he regaled his senior officers with the stories his spies had brought in, of men who prepared for battle by fasting and prayer, of the ruse of the new Jerusalem which, he judged, would soon be exposed for the lie he knew it to be, of a few cowards who had actually managed to commandeer a ship and threatened to sail away with it, of Montferrat pacing his tent for three nights, unable to sleep for the rage and frustration that consumed him. "He feels power slipping from his grasp," the Emperor said, "and soon he shall feel his head parted from his shoulders." There was no reason to believe that this second assault would be any harder to beat off than the first.

They waited for hours in the warm spring sunlight, the ships poised to sail, Constantinople holding its breath to receive them, each sailor and each soldier aware that the faster the speed of the approach and the greater the shock of the initial contact, the higher the chances of quick success and the more difficult the repulse.

At last the wind the Franks had been praying for began to

blow, gently at first, then with a sure, steady force that would last throughout the afternoon. The signal was given, the ships weighed anchor, and to the accompaniment of drums and trumpets they swept majestically across the Horn.

As soon as they came within range, huge rocks so heavy that it took two men to lift them rained down upon the decks, killing many who stood in the open, but landing harmlessly on the grapevine-covered Venetian vessels. The Frankish engineers worked frantically, finding and adjusting their range, pushing aside the heavily armored knights who got in their way. Huge boulders met and shattered in midair, sending their sharp, splintered pieces to splash harmlessly into the sea while others crashed against the towers and the walls. They were sending forth streams of fire also, but the Greeks had covered their new fortifications with wet hides and the fires sputtered and quickly died.

From his high mound Murtzuphles directed the Greek army, sending contingents against the few transports which managed to beach themselves. The men pouring from the ports of these vessels found themselves running into a rain of crossbolts, arrows and skull-crushing rocks. They darted and dodged, finding what shelter they could on the boulder-strewn shore, desperately returning the fire and barely holding their own.

The crusaders' main objective, as it had been on the previous Friday, was to capture the towers that dotted the wall. Once a tower was taken, the Doge insisted, that portion of the wall it guarded would quickly fall, and the towers on which they concentrated their efforts most heavily were those that lay on either side of the city's gates. But the grappling hooks flung out from the decks found no surface to cling to, or if they did, a Greek sprang from nowhere to chop the heavy rope in two before the assault ladders could be lowered. And now the Venetians realized that they had misjudged the new height of the towers; only four or five of their ships carried ladders tall enough to reach them. The drums of the Emperor beat out a triumphant tattoo and the sound of his trumpets carried over the shouts of the besiegers.

The noise was so great that at first no one heard the sharp crack of staved-in wood as two ships, one carrying the Bishop of

Soissons, the other the Bishop of Troyes, crashed against one of the towers in a place where the wall stood far out to sea. It was clearly a miracle vouchsafed by God, most said afterward, while the Venetians sniggered over their wine and named it purest accident and bad navigation that caused those two ships to be caught in waters that boiled against the shore. A Venetian who leaped from the bridge to the tower was hacked to pieces by the defenders. The ships, bound together and totally helpless, were carried back, then forward again by the turbulent waters.

As the ships struck repeatedly against the tower, Andrew of Dureboise managed to scramble through one of the narrow apertures on his hands and knees. He was as surprised to find himself inside the tower, he declared later, as were the Greeks who rushed at him from all sides. He barely had time to regain his feet and draw his sword before the first blows fell. The short swords and axes of the tower's defenders could not match his thrusts, and single-handedly he drove them to the floor below. Another knight joined him, then a whole stream of knights poured into the tower, forcing the Greeks to abandon each story successively until the tower lay wholly in French hands.

The damaged ships were secured to the tower. They crashed back and forth in the current, wrecking themselves timber by timber and threatening to destroy the tower itself. Reluctantly the besiegers cut them loose and watched them drift out to sea and founder. They stood alone in their tower now, and from its height they could see Murtzuphles directing a large party of Greeks to retake it no matter what the cost.

Pierre of Bracieux had seen the *Paradisus* and the *Peregrina* hurled against the tower and had quickly realized that no other maneuver would succeed so well as destruction of the ship that carried him and his men. He gave explicit orders to his sailors, ordered his knights to stand well back from the bow, and in a matter of moments that ship, too, struck with tremendous force against a tower that was as quickly and easily taken as the first had been.

There was a lull then in the battle, one of those moments that stretch into eternity as the Franks waited to see whether those who held the two towers would be able to venture out on the wall to join forces and the Greeks inside the city boiled about, seeking to enter the towers from below.

"They are deathtraps," said Peter of Amiens.

"If we could make a breach in the wall and break through it would draw the Greeks away from the towers. We could crush them between us."

"How, Robert, how?"

"Look, my lord, there, near that gate."

"What is it, Aleaumes?"

"It looks like a smaller gate, a postern. They've removed the wooden door and walled it up with stones, but you can still see the marks where the hinges were. It's been done recently, too. The mortar there is cleaner than anywhere else. It's a weak point in the wall, my lord."

"And perhaps the only one there is," agreed Peter, squinting to make out the stones at which Aleaumes was pointing. "I'll take a party of ten knights and sixty sergeants. Get whatever picks and axes you can find in the stores. We'll go by foot and hug the wall while the Greeks are watching the Venetian galleys."

As unobtrusively as possible their ship nudged closer to shore, turning broadside at the last moment. Shielded by its high wooden side, Peter and his men let themselves down and splashed ashore. Miraculously, no one seemed to notice them as they inched their way along from boulder to boulder, moving ever closer to their objective.

Suddenly they rushed the walled-up postern gate, Aleaumes and some of the sergeants hacking furiously at the weak mortar while the knights held their shields over them. The first blows of picks and axes had awakened the Greeks to their danger and now, from the wall directly above where they worked, boiling pitch and oil poured down, splashing over the shields to burn the skin from exposed hands and arms. Greek fire followed, and enormous stones that dented the shields and caused several men to sink unconscious to the ground. The Greeks screamed at them from above, but no battle cries answered their imprecations, only a frenzied grunting as the mortar was chipped away. Tiny flakes of it powdered their faces, arms and clothing, then pieces the size of small stones flew out at them. The Greeks on the wall redoubled their efforts, pouring down a hell's mixture of burning liquids, boulders and arrows. The knights were now crouched over, their shields strapped to their backs, sides overlapping to repel the torrent that flowed over them. The slender picks broke, one after the other; now the desperate crusaders were using pieces of wood, the daggers from their belts, the stones hurled at them, bare, bloodied fingers.

"This one gives," shouted Aleaumes, wrenching with all his strength at a stone that rocked back and forth in its bed but would not come out. He gripped it tightly, seeking a firm handhold, hunched his shoulders and tightened his muscles until they were like knotted ropes. A moment later the stone was in his hands and through the small opening it had left they could see Greeks running toward them, pulling out swords and brandishing axes as they came.

Before the Greeks had reached the wall the hole was made just large enough for a man to squeeze his body through, but every knight and sergeant in the small band stood as if paralyzed. The spot they had pierced was hardly more than a stone's throw from where Murtzuphles' tent stood. Aleaumes threw himself into the opening, feeling the scrape of stone on his shoulders as he began to worm his way through. Suddenly he felt his legs seized from behind and heard Robert's strangled cry, "No, Aleaumes, you cannot." He kicked out and heard a sickening crunch as his foot struck his brother in the face. The move propelled him through the hole and stones crashed inches from his head as he fought to regain his footing. He pulled his sword and charged the group of fifteen or twenty lightly armored Greeks who had come running from the direction of Murtzuphles' tent. He lunged into their very midst, his sword flashing in the sunlight, and unbelievably, they melted away and fled.

"They flee, they flee," he shouted above the noise of drums and trumpets. "My lords, they run away."

First Peter of Amiens, then Robert and soon the whole party stood within the wall. The Greeks in that area had drawn back and clustered closer to the mound on which Murtzuphles rode his horse back and forth in a restless arc. They seemed undecided whether to advance or fly away to a place of greater safety.

Peter of Amiens's lip curled scornfully as he looked at them, and he laughed aloud as the men on the wall above them deserted their posts and leaped to the ground as far away from the crusaders as they could get.

Murtzuphles wheeled his horse in their direction, seeing them for the first time. He had not believed the garbled report of a group of Franks hacking with knives and swords at the great wall. Now he made as if to charge them and the crusaders closed ranks. He rode to the bottom of the mound, alone and unattended by the Warings, reined his horse in sharply, stared almost uncomprehendingly at the crusaders, then returned to where his tent stood. They could see him giving orders, but the blare of his own trumpeters drowned out his shouts.

Peter's eyes never left the Emperor as he directed twenty of the sergeants toward the great wooden gate a few paces away. Unguarded for the moment, it was their best chance to escape if the Emperor's men descended on them in force. The sergeants lifted down the heavy iron bars and broke the bolts that still held it fast. Slowly the huge wooden door swung inward, and through it came a stream of their own mounted knights and foot soldiers. An alert transport captain had seen the tiny breach in the wall, beached and unloaded his transport. Others had followed him and soon half the army would be swarming into the city.

As soon as he had seen the reinforcements galloping through the gate, thrusting aside the wood which hung at crazy angles from the broken hinges, Peter of Amiens led his men on a wild charge toward Murtzuphles, intent on capturing the Emperor himself. For a few seconds the figure of the last Greek Emperor of Constantinople was outlined against the late afternoon sky. He sat his horse, solemn and majestic at last, while all around him his bodyguard and soldiers swarmed like ants, pushing and trampling one another as they forced their way past him toward the narrow streets that led into the heart of the city. He seemed to recognize Peter of Amiens, for he raised his right hand in grave salute before plunging his horse into the midst of his fleeing army. No one made way for him. The horse reared and flailed its sharp hooves desperately, then, with Murtzuphles' cruel spurs digging into its flanks, trampled down the men who barred its passage. The Emperor disappeared from sight just as Peter and his men reached the royal pavilion.

"He headed for the palace of Boucoleon," he informed Baldwin of Flanders a few moments later. "Shall we follow, my lord?"

"No," ordered the Count as his squire rushed forward to help him dismount. "It's nearly Vespers. We are to camp here tonight and prepare to take the city tomorrow, street by street if necessary. Anyone who ventures into those twisting alleys by night will be cut down in the darkness and never see the face of his assailant." He moved wonderingly toward the Emperor's scarlet tents. "Do you claim these, Peter?"

"No, my lord. They are an emperor's gift to whoever will replace him."

Baldwin stood irresolute for a moment, fully aware that the seigneur of Amiens's words and his own reaction to them were tantamount to an open declaration of candidacy. Montferrat badly wanted to be elected emperor, scarcely troubled to hide his belief that the electors, whoever they were, would hand him the crown with little or no debate, behaved, in fact, as if the choice had already been agreed upon. Yet Baldwin knew that his blood was more royal than the Marquis's, that his name did not bear the taint of suspected treachery that clung to Montferrat's, that by seeming to hang back reluctantly from decisions he had not really cared enough about to question, he had won enormous popularity even among men not under his command. He took a few steps forward, paused, smiled thoughtfully to himself, then marched with an ever-quickening pace up the mound that was not unlike the ascent to a throne. Only Peter, Robert and Aleaumes knew that he had decided to challenge his commander.

The army was to remain where it was that night, the Marquis of Montferrat and his men camped the closest to the main city area, Henry of Flanders and his battalion before the palace of Blachernae, which they dared not enter yet, the others strung out between. It was agreed that if the city would neither surrender nor fight the next day Montferrat's men would set it afire if the wind blew right. Another fire would nearly destroy it entirely, but as long as the treasure-filled palaces, churches and monasteries remained undamaged, and all were built of stone, no one really cared what happened to the humbler sections of Constantinople.

"There is to be no wholesale looting, whatever happens tomorrow," Peter of Amiens was saying. "Each baron and each knight must restrain the men under his command."

"That will be difficult, my lord," said Robert. "We have waited so long and suffered so much at the hands of these people."

"Nevertheless it must be done. My lord of St. Pol has sworn to hang any man who breaks the oath, and no one who rides under his banner doubts that he is a man of his word."

Peter stretched out his hands toward the tiny campfire. His face was grave and troubled, yet because he was a very private man he could not, would not for courtesy's sake, share even with the two men who knew and loved him best the deep foreboding that had come over him tonight.

He had heard the talk around a dozen campfires, seen the glassy, brooding stares with which so many men, knights, sergeants, archers, pike and ax men, looked into the darkness that was Constantinople. Action had dissipated the euphoric sense of mission induced by the fast, the prayers, the promise of absolute salvation in death. Those who had not died had already forgotten their fear, already brushed aside the notion of a new sacred city, already ceased to remember that knowledge of sin had weighed them down three days ago. Men with a dream once, merely hungry, discontented soldiers throughout the winter, crossed anew, but more lightly, they were fast becoming, as the hours of the night wore on, men of empty flesh and blood poised trembling on the brink of the greatest conquest their age had ever known. It was a frightening transformation.

"I must see that the men are bedded down," Peter said tiredly, rising to his feet as though burdened with a weight almost too heavy to carry, "and remind them of my cousin's command. They fought well today. I would not like to see any one of them dangling from a gallows."

Robert and Aleaumes listened in silence, hearing murmured, respectful words of greeting as Peter made his rounds. Little pools of quiet erupting into muffled sardonic laughter told them when he had passed beyond earshot of each of the small groups of men who had sworn to serve him loyally. Even these were finally too far off to be distinguishable from the steady low-pitched rumble that was the night music of the wakeful camp.

"What do you think will happen tomorrow, Robert?" Aleaumes asked.

"Murtzuphles will have to make a stand against us somewhere or lose everything he schemed so hard to get. I cannot imagine him abandoning the city, but if he does it will only be to withdraw for a few weeks or months, just long enough to regroup his forces and recruit new men from the outlying cities and provinces of the realm. If it had not been for you, Aleaumes, we might be lying in Galata again tonight."

"The victory belongs to God, who inspired us to fight . . ."

"Like devils?" Robert smiled. "I may die tomorrow, Aleaumes. Don't play the priest with me tonight."

"We've cheated death many times on this voyage. We'll cheat it again."

"To what purpose? We both know why my lord of Amiens cannot sleep, and why the campfires will continue to burn until morning."

"He became a gloomy man after Zara."

"Zara was the turning point. We should have left with Simon of Montfort or Enguerrand of Boves."

"To return to France or fight in Syria?"

"To keep our oaths."

"We've sworn a new oath now, just as sacred, just as binding as the first. The vow to reach Jerusalem has been dispensed."

"By men with venal hearts and grasping hands."

"You're toying with theology, Robert, and you know too little of the subject to do it well. The character of the priest does not affect the validity of the sacrament he administers. If there is sin, it is his, not ours."

"There is form, but there is also intention and spirit."

"The forms are what tie, and they have been observed. Spirit and intention are conduits of God's mercy. We are bound here for another year. Do your duty and forget the rest."

"I began with duty, Aleaumes, bound hand and foot and heart

and soul by it. Duty brought me here, duty keeps me at Peter's side, duty is all I have left. But how can I not remember all the rest?"

Robert and his brother sat for a few more minutes by the dying fire. Then without a word, without another glance exchanged, they rolled themselves in their blankets. Eyes closed, they rested and waited, but neither of them slept.

Sometime in the early hours before dawn fire broke out in the narrow streets near Montferrat's camp. The wind carried the flames toward the heart of the city, and for the third time its citizens saw the morning sun obscured by clouds of heavy ash. Most of Constantinople's nobles, many of its distinguished prelates and half its merchant class saw the flames rise behind them, for throughout the night families had hastily bundled together their most precious goods and left the city by its southern gates, streaming out over the plains to make their way by foot or mule to distant cities of the Empire.

The exodus had begun moments after the news was whispered from house to house that Murtzuphles, their Emperor, had checked his wild ride to the Boucoleon Palace and fled ignominiously through the Golden Gate, that special portal through which only triumphantly returning emperors had passed before. None knew where he meant to find refuge, but it was clear to all who heard the story that he had irrevocably abandoned his capital. As the streets filled with people more rumors flew. The bishops had met in Santa Sophia and elected a reluctant noble, Theodore Lascaris, to reign over them. His reign lasted only a few hours. By morning he had crossed the Straits in a swift galley to found a new empire in Nicea.

Montferrat was awakened as soon as the fire was discovered. For safety's sake he moved his camp closer to that of Baldwin of Flanders, but men remarked that he showed no surprise at and very little interest in the flames that were clearing a broad swath through the center of the city. Later it was said that he had secretly ordered his Germans to set the torches, but the accusation was never proved.

So much of the city had been destroyed in the earlier fires that this time the flames moved with casual grace from one wooden dwelling to the next, contained and directed by the empty, burned-out stretches on either side of it. No one attempted to quench it, knowing that the task was useless. It would eventually burn itself out, but its progress was so slow that there was ample time to avoid it.

By dawn a thick pall of smoke hung over Constantinople. Shafts of early sunlight glittered and skipped warmly on the waters of the Horn, but when they darted through the dark gray cloud over the city they were as cruelly hot and piercing as the flames that here and there leaped up to greet them.

The crusaders' camp was still and silent, the campfires burned out, the nighttime eating messes cleared up and packed away, the men themselves fully armed, filthy from yesterday's battle, already sweating in their armor. They were waiting for full sunrise, for Montferrat to emerge from his tent and give the order that would decide the fate of the city.

An hour passed, perhaps two, and then at last he appeared, clad all in crimson and silver, sword strapped to his side, spurs tinkling as he walked toward the mound from which he would address them. Every head in the camp turned to follow him, and one by one the barons left their men to walk in his wake, rivulets of power converging on the single central stream whose strong current they would swell with their joining.

But as Montferrat reached the top of the mound, Baldwin stepped from Murtzuphles' tent and raised a hand in greeting. He was dressed in gold and white, a brilliant figure in the gray morning air, dazzlingly bright against the background of scarlet and the dark robes of the monks and priests who waited to bless those below. At the sight of all that shining whiteness the men of Flanders and Hainault raised a cheer for their lord, a cheer that was picked up by thousands of throats, infecting even the Germans and Lombards, who, not knowing whether it was for Montferrat or Baldwin that they cried out, applauded both of them.

Montferrat's face was impassive and distant as the noise rose up around him. Baldwin, blessed with natural grace and handsome features, smiled, nodded his head, caught an eye here and there in the crowd, raised his arms to still them, good-naturedly gave up the attempt to restore quiet and stood at ease, one hand on the hilt of his sword, laughing and accepting the tribute so freely and unexpectedly given.

The men were good-humored now, relaxed and ready to listen, either to Baldwin or Montferrat, it did not seem to matter which. Both men were spectacular, both great and powerful lords, both extraordinary fighters of proven ability, both suddenly acknowledged as worthy of a crown.

But as order was gradually imposed and the shouting died down, neither man moved forward to take precedence over the other. The soldiers glanced uneasily at one another, shifted their feet impatiently, and then, their ears catching the sound of chanting, their nostrils picking up a whiff of incense, they realized that Baldwin, Montferrat and all the others on the mound were staring at something they could not yet see. They craned their necks and whispered excitedly to one another as the chanting grew louder, the tang of incense stronger, the sound of shuffling feet closer and more distinct.

A long procession of bishops and minor clergy, Greeks, Danes, English and other foreigners, entered the enormous square. Berobed in their finest vestments, they were led by a monk carrying aloft a huge golden cross, and the psalm they chanted as they walked was the *De Profundis,* the plea for mercy sung over the dead. "Out of the depths have I cried unto Thee, O Lord: Lord, hear my voice . . . My soul waits on His word: my soul hopes in the Lord."

The army parted to let them through, and when they had reached the foot of the mound all of them except one ancient, stooped bishop fell to their knees.

They had walked barefoot all the way from Santa Sophia, he told Montferrat in a voice that choked with emotion and cracked with age. Murtzuphles had fled during the night, Lascaris too. Only poor people, clergy, monks, nuns and foreigners remained in the city. Murder was already being done in the quarters to which some Latin traders had previously returned at the Emperor's invitation and under his protection. They begged Montferrat to take possession of the city, to restore order, to station his troops on its streets, put out the fire, stop the looting that had begun during the night, protect them all, give them justice at last, and also mercy. In the name of Christ and as spokesman for all who still hoped to live and work and worship in the city they loved, the bishop surrendered Constantinople.

Montferrat did not say a word. His mouth tightened and he half pulled his sword from its scabbard. He turned to look at Baldwin, whose eyes shone, whose lips stretched in an idiotically complacent grin, whose head was already inclining regally, as if he had the power to grant the bishop's request.

Then suddenly someone in the crowd hissed, a single, greedy soldier whose lust for plunder and blood broke through the awe, the surprise, the expectant restraint in which all had been held. One after another his fellows joined in, a valley of vicious, angry serpents stirred up to strike, uncoiling to sink their fangs into the enemy now at their mercy.

The smile faded from Baldwin's face. His features hardened as he saw that Montferrat's quick glance in his direction was one of mockery and calculated challenge. Will they love the man who keeps them from what they covet? he seemed to be asking. I counsel mercy, Baldwin said, but only in the privacy of his own mind. He knew, quite clearly and abruptly, that he would not lead his men today. He would follow them, satisfy them, buy for himself with whatever currency they demanded the crown that lay at his fingertips, the crown he could never hope to wear in France. He stepped closer to Montferrat, loathing the man, loathing himself for what he was about to acquiesce to, but thrusting himself forward in every soldier's sight so that later they would all remember that it was his wish too that they should be set loose.

"I accept the surrender of this city," Montferrat shouted, not deigning to speak directly to the men kneeling before him, "but to its people, for their heresy, their lies, the fire ships and men they sent against us and the deaths they brought us, I grant no terms whatever. Let God have mercy on them and forgive them, for I will not. Constantinople is yours. I give it to you. Do with it what you will."

German knights on horseback surged to the foot of the mound, bringing their commander's huge black war-horse to him. As Montferrat mounted, the destrier reared, pawing the air wildly, and when his hooves struck sparks from the cobblestones, the Marquis unloosed the last restraint. "The city is yours," he proclaimed once more. "Take it. Each man is today his own master."

He galloped through the square, the Germans riding furiously at his heels, sweeping through the broken gate he had entered the day before, pounding furiously down the shore toward the Boucoleon Palace, the cathedral of Santa Sophia and the ecclesiastical mansions that surrounded it.

The army watched him go, then turned back to gauge the temper of the remaining barons. They saw Villehardouin turn wearily away, one hand raised to his eyes in willing sightlessness, noted that St. Pol no longer stood on the mound, that priests and monks were streaming down its sides, cowls over their heads, deaf, dumb and blind to the sins not yet committed but certain one day to be briefly condemned, then swiftly absolved.

Henry of Flanders, who had once advised caution, was whispering to his brother, gesturing excitedly toward the nearby Blachernae Palace. Baldwin nodded his head, clapped his brother on the back and signaled for his knights to mount. He left the mound, pausing once to wave back at the now totally leaderless mob which had such a short time before been an army. "Take it," they thought they heard him shout.

It was the command every soldier had been waiting for, and as their white-and-gold prince turned his back on them to claim an Emperor's palace as his own, they began to run from the square, those nearest the procession of bareheaded clergy hacking their way through the arms and crosses thrust out to stop them.

The priests died quickly, silently, but through the fountains of blood spurting over victim and murderer alike the men who killed them caught the glint of gold-embroidered vestments, the sparkle of episcopal and abbatial rings, the shine of crosses and croziers fashioned out of precious metals, studded with stones as blue as the sea, as clear as crystal water, as green as hope, as deeply red as the hearts which bled so freely. They paused to strip rings from fingers curled against pain and death, ripped off the sacred, bloodied vestments, carried away the crosses and the fragrant gold censers, rolled aside the boneless corpses beneath their feet.

It was a madness that lasted only a few minutes, for the men of God were helpless and swiftly butchered, even more swiftly robbed and abandoned. Before the last soul had sped gratefully to heaven, the square was empty. Murtzuphles' scarlet pavilion, what was left of it, lay crumpled on the ground, its furnishings and gold cups carried off by Baldwin's bodyguard, soldiers who did not bother to spend their strength even on prey as tempting as the ridiculous priests when other riches could be found so easily.

Peter of Amiens, Robert and Aleaumes had pressed themselves against an undamaged portion of the city wall and hung there, their fingers widespread for balance, as the mass of men swept by. Screams of pain and long, drawn-out howls of greed and lust drowned out the crackling of the fire. The sounds came from deeper and deeper in the city as the crusaders ran mindlessly amok in the twisting streets until finally they were a distant roar, as of a pack of demons entombed within their own reverberating hell.

Peter pulled his sword from its scabbard, but it slipped from his numb fingers to clatter noisily on the cobbled street. Robert bent swiftly to retrieve it, pressing it back into Peter's hand, frightened by the haunted look he saw in his suzerain's eyes.

"Are you all right, my lord?"

Peter shook himself like a dog shaking off water and stepped away from the wall. He made no reply, but walked slowly and steadily toward the crushed and mangled bodies of the men who had so foolishly thought to find mercy in quick surrender. He stopped when he reached the body of the bishop who had spoken for them.

"Look, Robert," he said tonelessly. "They sliced his fingers off the better to get at his ring of office." Then he bent to close the lifeless eyes that protruded from the pulp of bone and tissue that had once been a man's face. He moved from body to body, ceremoniously, with the precision and dignity of a monk pacing through an infirmary of dead men, pausing to close staring eyes in skulls that still possessed them. His lips moved; he was reciting from memory the prayers for the dead.

After a moment's hesitation Robert and Aleaumes followed him, the tips of their fingers growing bloodied from the work. They made their way across the square until they stood beneath a narrow stone archway that joined two houses together high above their heads. Peter stopped then, to gaze back at the bodies that littered the ground, absentmindedly wiping his fingers on the sleeve of his shirt.

"We have done all we could here," he said wearily. "The city has been given up for pillage. It will be sacked, looted, violated, possibly destroyed beyond human memory. Its people valued it so cheaply that they would not fight to preserve it, and perhaps for that reason it and they have earned the death that we will bring them." He paused, mutely asking Robert and Aleaumes to assent to yet another judgment born of compromise, violated logic and the pitiful human need to throw off a guilt no mind could healthily accept. They said nothing and would not meet his eyes, each of them mechanically wiping the blood from his hands. The white tunics they wore over their armor were as red as the aprons of those who slaughtered cattle and cut the carcasses up for meat.

"Will you join the Count of St. Pol, my lord?" Robert asked, more to break the silence than because the question held any real meaning.

"I don't know where my cousin loots," Peter said flatly. He looked back at the square again, shuddered convulsively at the sight of a thin dog creeping out on its belly from the darkness of a narrow alley, and turned his head away. A lifetime of training straightened his back, strengthened his shoulders. "St. Pol will hang no one for whatever crimes are committed today," he said. "Everything is permitted, everything sanctioned. But I will have no part in it."

Robert nodded, his fingers seeking the hilt of his sword and the saint's relic embedded there. The oath he swore at that moment was more truly his own than any other he had ever taken.

Aleaumes' hand, too, had moved to caress the tiny remains of earthly sanctity he wore. "Will you return to one of the ships or to Galata?" he asked.

"No vessel would carry us across the Horn," Peter answered. He stared down the empty street that beckoned them. "We may

be able to do some good there," he mused. "Certainly we can do
no greater harm. If an armed man comes against me I will slay
him, but I will harm no woman, abuse no cleric, grant mercy to
any man who asks it and profane no House where Christ is worshiped." He remembered the phrasing of the original oath sworn
by every knight and soldier of the army as perfectly as at the
moment he had agreed to it.

Robert followed Peter and Aleaumes into the twisting streets
that led away from the square. My father left the Holy Land
carrying only a pouch half filled with spices and a curved scimi-
tar taken from the hand of the last Saracen he slew there, he
thought as he walked. But though he came back nearly empty-
handed, his honor remained intact.

Aleaumes turned to look at him, as if the thought had been
spoken speech. The brothers would not break any oath already
sworn to. Both would finish the year of service just begun, but
neither would swear blindly to any new commitment.

The first streets through which they passed as they walked
deeper into Constantinople were devoid of human life, but the
door of every house, of even the meanest wooden shack, hung
crookedly on its hinges. The army had passed through this section like a cloud of swift-flying, ground-skimming locusts, leaving behind it a wreckage of broken furniture, shattered pottery,
and clothing torn apart in the search for coins or jewels hidden
in hems and linings. Cooking fires had been raked out from
under pots that still bubbled and the hot coals spread over dry
wooden floors in an added touch of cruelty. There were corpses
in the streets, and then here and there whole Greek families
peering out from their hiding places or working feverishly to extinguish the flames already licking at the walls of their tiny
wooden homes. They paused in their work to stare at the three
crusaders who approached, falling to their knees with arms
upraised and crossed to show that they, too, were Christians.

Again and again Peter, Aleaumes and Robert made an answering Sign of the Cross, but no Greek called out for help, no Greek
smiled, no Greek did anything but stand as if turned to stone
until they had passed by.

They stayed well away from the main fire, which continued to burn its way through the city. As they approached the first of the great forums they began to encounter bands of crusaders roving haphazardly through the streets, lurching drunkenly under the weight of the gold and silver objects they had looted. Many of them had thrown long Byzantine robes over their armor and they carried on their backs huge sacks which they had fashioned out of the stiffly embroidered garments of the rich. They kept their sword hands free though, to hack mindlessly at the dead and maimed, to run a woman through when they had finished with her, and to fight each other over some particularly desirable object. They were caught up in the swirl of these bands, mocked for their tardiness, then urged goodnaturedly to join in the revelry as they were carried along to the Forum of Theodosius, where two enormous columns stretched skyward.

The crowds swept by the columns, uninterested in the mutilated sculpture that covered them, and as they passed Robert caught a glimpse of ships and scaling ladders and men swarming up the ladders. Someone, perhaps the Greeks themselves, had defaced the columns, but enough of the sculpture remained to cause Robert to cross himself in awe. It was as though a hundred years had passed and some unknown sculptor had immortalized yesterday's assault.

As the crowd entered the Hippodrome it widened its front and Peter was able to force his way out of the press of men. Followed by Robert and Aleaumes, he climbed the stone steps from which the Greeks had watched the Emperor's Games until they reached the topmost row. There he sank exhausted, panting from the climb and the mad run from the Forum of Theodosius. Larger-than-life statues of men and women, bears and lions and beasts of mythology were all around them, their neglected copper surfaces greenish and eerily fleshlike. Others had climbed the steps of the Hippodrome to escape from the madness below, and a small group of foot soldiers nearby were crouched over a dice game, gambling for the gold goblets and jewelry which lay in heaps beside each man. They laughed and swore as the game grew hot, pausing only to empty fine porcelain wine jugs, then hurl them grandly to smash on the stone steps below.

Peter looked at them with disgust. Much of the jewelry was

obviously women's, so covered with blood that the rings and bracelets were stuck together as if with a heavy tar, and one soldier had jammed a delicate circlet of gold far down on his head so that his ears stood out ludicrously beneath it. Feeling Peter's eyes on them, the soldiers turned to stare menacingly, fingering their weapons as if daring the three knights to challenge their right of possession. Peter returned the stares calmly, unafraid of vermin such as these, showing the extent of his disdain in the curl of his lip. The soldiers could not stare him down; they averted their eyes and, muttering loudly, returned to their interrupted game.

"Over there lies the Boucoleon Palace," said Peter, rising to his feet to point toward the easternmost edge of the city. "You can see Santa Sophia's domes."

Robert and Aleaumes stared across the rooftops toward the palace that was in reality an entire city within a city. The fine buildings that made up the sprawling palace seemed to stretch endlessly before them, with here and there a high dome indicating one of the many royal chapels within the complex.

Until trapped by the mob they had walked without conscious direction, each man lost in his own thoughts, each brain functioning separately with the effort to assimilate the shock of what the eye had seen, the ear heard, the heart felt and the soul bemoaned. But they were soldiers too, and once their inundated senses ceased reeling with the heat, the swiftness, the brutality and rage of the rape to which they were witness, the coolness of mind and body that had yesterday cracked the wall returned.

The soldiers had finished their dice game and were now weaving among the statues that overlooked the forum, joining forces to topple each one from its pedestal. The mob below, its attention caught by the crash of marble and clatter of copper, applauded the destruction and began to break apart, spewing forth groups of forty or fifty to join in the fun. Climbing madly, scrambling on hands and knees, they were soon happily annihilating what had taken centuries to create.

"We'll be caught up again if we stay here," Peter said, his eyes turning once more to lovely, magnificent Santa Sophia. "We've come too far to be able to turn back, but I remember a section near Boucoleon where there are many monasteries and convents. It will be hours yet before the mob overruns it."

"Surely the monks and nuns will have fled," Aleaumes said, the horror of a plundered House of God darkening his eyes.

"Who will have brought them warning?" Peter asked. "And there must be some who will have chosen not to leave their altars, even knowing the fate that awaits them."

"Constantinople already has a surfeit of martyrs," Robert said bitterly. He shut his eyes briefly against today's flames and yesterday's memories, then opened them again, sealing off once more the part of him that was like a door with a faulty lock, always threatening to burst open at the slightest breeze or pressure. He was healed of despair, but not of the pain of remembering.

"We'll go there then," Peter said, knowing why his knight's face was suddenly white and pinched. To save a woman, a nun, might be the final balm his sore heart needed.

He began to march down the stone steps of the Hippodrome, Robert and Aleaumes following close behind, broke into a run to cross the game field, then darted through a small gate at the southernmost end of the great amphitheater. They saw no other crusaders in the narrow streets on this side of the Hippodrome, and though the houses were small and defenseless, they had not been broken into. Peter grunted in satisfaction. He had guessed the mob's movement correctly. It would soon spread out over the entire city, but for the moment at least, this back way to the Boucoleon Palace and the Santa Sophia district lay unobstructed.

They trotted through streets which grew broader and more prosperous-looking the farther away they moved from the Hippodrome. Soon there were mansions on either side of them, their gates shut fast, the frightened servants within peering through barred windows at the first crusaders they had seen. It would take more than three armed men to break into any of them, the Greeks whispered to one another, the thick stone walls of this quarter cutting off the noise of the devastation that was being wreaked just north of there. The cannier among them took the opportunity to do a little quiet looting on their own, revenging themselves on the masters who had ordered them to remain behind, slipping out back doors with heavy bundles beneath their arms, making their careful way to the southern land gates through which the remaining population of the city still fled.

"It's not far now," said Peter, pointing toward the palace roof which rose above all the mansions and domed, cross-topped religious foundations surrounding it. They could see the Bouco-leon's massive encircling wall at the far end of the street.

The Convent of the Seven Sorrows, founded by and for an emperor's daughter, was a pleasant place to live, if, that is, one had to choose between it and other, more austerely religious houses. The chapel was as large and richly ornamented as any of the Emperor's own, its altar vessels of pure gold, its icons framed in precious gems, its priest garbed in vestments that were the envy of the Patriarch himself. The library, which contained hundreds of volumes, was housed in a sunny, wood-paneled chamber whose walls breathed exotic forest smells, and the common rooms, where the nuns gathered together for recreation, were hung with silks. Even the chairs on which they sat were softly padded, cushioned with velvet, inlaid with gold and silver as if they were miniature thrones.

The gardens were spacious and well laid out, long, shady, winding alleyways, beds of riotously colorful, profusely blooming flowers, small pavilions here and there, private and secluded, statuary that was faintly pagan in its perfection, recalling the old days of Roman rule that no Byzantine had ever quite forgotten.

The nuns, noblewomen all, performed their religious duties, chatted contentedly with the friends and family who visited frequently, studied, intrigued among themselves, and occasionally managed a discreet affair which, if it did not result in a pregnancy that could not be aborted, was tacitly accepted by a long succession of tolerant, worldly superiors. Their lives were serenely uncomplicated.

The cellars of the Seven Sorrows were vast and solidly built, a long series of airless subterranean chambers used for the storage of wine, grain, discarded furniture and heaps of gold altar plate, vessels still shining and precious, but constantly replaced by newer, finer, more costly gifts from the nuns' families and the convent's imperial patrons. There were other, more secret treasures kept there also, for the convent was both a prison and a temporary repository for noble madwomen prone to fits of melancholia.

The girls and women confined in its luxuriously appointed cells were quite often as sane as the lay sisters who attended them. They were there for dynastic crimes, for refusing to accept marriage to an aging pederast or a fifteen-year-old prince who delighted in the use of whip and prod. But no matter how firm their original resolve, how wildly angry their rebellion, they soon decided, every one of them, that sexual abnormalities could be tolerated, but lack of sun, companionship of their own choosing and freedom could not.

The cell into which Anne was locked, at almost the same moment when Alexius IV disappeared into his rat-infested death hole, was as beautifully furnished, as pleasing to senses too deranged to appreciate beauty, as his was horrifying. Neither had been insane when confined, though one quickly became so. The ex-Emperor's madness vanished only an instant before he died, when his eyes looked into Murtzuphles' pitiless heart and wholesomely sane anger drove him to try to kill before his own life was ended, but Anne began to regain control as soon as she heard the heavy sound of the iron bolt that shut her in and saw the wariness with which the lay sister approached her.

This sister, as tall and strong as all the fifteen whose religious lives were equally divided between the chapel, their own separate sleeping quarters and the women they guarded in rotating shifts, was prepared to be neither indifferent nor unfriendly toward her new charge. She did not know who Anne was, nor upon whose order she had been sent to the Seven Sorrows, and for the moment she was only vaguely curious. In time the prisoner would tell her more than she wished to know. They all did. But in the first few hours of isolation it was what the girl or woman did, not what she said, that counted.

The truly insane were the happiest, the most easily distracted, the hungriest, the thirstiest, the most childlike, the ones who could be coaxed to lie down and sleep, if, as had happened tonight, they had been shifted from one place to another in the dark. They gave up rather quickly, most of them, withdrew into themselves, cunningly aware that no sharp tools were available to them here. What violence they might later display would erupt suddenly, but only when the tortured mind had grasped the fact that the sister who was always with her was her jailor, only when and if that sister's back was turned.

The other ones, the ones whose plight often threatened to touch a sympathetic sister's heart, wept when they entered their cells, wept sometimes for hours, flung themselves against the padded door, screamed through the tiny barred window, paced the floor, cursing the man, almost always a man, it seemed, who had incarcerated them, wept again, and finally, especially if they were very young, gulped down the food and wine laid out for them and turning a ravaged face to the sister who had watched the tantrum declared proudly, "No matter how long they try to keep me here, I won't give in."

Never once in all the years that women had been entering the Seven Sorrows' mad cells had one of them ever gone directly to her bed and stretched herself out on it without a word, a tear, a rush back toward the door, never once lain there for hours staring at the ceiling, silent, self-possessed, not a limb twitching, not a single finger tearing at the silken coverlet beneath her. Such behavior was more frightening than babbling, uncontrollable laughter or frenzied screams and weeping. And when, an hour before dawn, the spell was broken and the prisoner sat up, climbed down from the high bed on legs that shook visibly beneath her skirt, walked to the low table and reached out a trembling hand for the wine that stood there, the sister crossed herself and refilled the cup as soon as it was emptied.

"I've heard of this place," the woman said quietly, "so I know where I am and what lies before me. I know too which actions of mine caused me to be sent here and what I must promise to gain my release. There is very little now I do not know, except only whether the knowledge comes too late. Is there always a sister in attendance?"

"Night and day, lady."

"The same one?"

"That depends."

"On what?"

"On whether it is safe for the sister to close her eyes."

"Whether the woman she guards is truly mad or not, you mean. I am not, so you may rest easy. What is your name?"

"Magdalena."

"Do you know who I am? Anything about me?"

"No, lady."

"I am called Anna in your language, but as I am not a Greek and do not wish to be constantly reminded of the woman who changed my name and gave the order for my imprisonment, I would prefer that you call me Anne. Will you do that?"

"Yes, Lady Anne."

"Shall we be friends, you and I, Sister Magdalena?"

Even a humble lay sister of peasant origin knows that to lie is not always a sin. "You honor me, lady," said Sister Magdalena, "and I shall do my best to deserve your trust."

For several weeks after her confinement Anne was careful never to vary the routine of the actions that made up her day, actions which would have seemed totally meaningless in that place if one did not remember that Sister Magdalena almost certainly reported them to her superior every time she absented herself from the cell to perform her religious duties or eat a meal with her sisters. Other nuns took her place when she was gone, but though Anne courteously asked their names and engaged them in polite, trifling conversations, she pinned her hopes on Magdalena, who had, from the very first, kept her company during most of the day and all of the night, sleeping on a hard straw sack beside her bed.

Sister Magdalena woke her every morning, and together they prayed before a gold-leafed icon of the Virgin, keeping silence until the bread and fruit and heated wine that was their breakfast arrived. While Anne bathed and dressed herself for the day, the lay sister tidied the tiny cell and surreptitiously finished off whatever food Anne had left on her plate. She was a big woman, still young, and always hungry.

They sewed until noon, Sister Magdalena occupied with yard after yard of plain white linen sacking, Anne at first with necessary alterations to the long-ago-discarded gowns left behind by some forgotten, rotund royal lady, then later, when there were no more seams to take in, no more hems to lengthen, with the stitching of fine, delicate, weblike cloths for the convent's altar. It was work she had asked for, so as not to sit with idle hands, she explained seriously. They talked while they sewed, and it was thus from Sister Magdalena that Anne learned of the death of the boy emperor and the name of the man who had succeeded him. She also learned that Constantinople was preparing itself for the assault that would come with the first warm breath of spring.

In the afternoons Anne read aloud from the *Lives of the Saints,* a delight for Sister Magdalena, who could neither read nor write, but whose hungry soul and yearning heart thrilled to the tales of sacrificial love and courage. They ate the evening meal in quiet harmony, then Sister Magdalena left her for an hour or two. When she returned, so subdued and yet uplifted that Anne knew she had spent the time on her knees with her superior, they prayed again, the much longer prayers of night, and then, in Christ's holy silence, they went to bed.

For more than a month, from the end of January until the first week of March, days nicked out on the farthest wooden post of her bed, Anne played the model, somewhat confused, piously obedient prisoner. It takes time to lull a jailor's suspicions.

On the morning of the thirty-eighth day she sighed over her breakfast, left the food and the wine untouched and untasted, threw herself to her knees before the icon, bowed her head in prayer and waited for Sister Magdalena's anxious question.

"Is something troubling you, Lady Anne?"

"Sister," she said, digging her fingers into her eyes to redden them, "I must speak with your abbess." At the sound of whistling indrawn breath behind her she quickly added, "Or if that is not possible, I beg you, at the very least, to carry a message to her from me, a message I will write out so that you need not know what it is I ask."

"But Lady Anne, I must know. It would be my duty to know."

"You will carry it then?" She rose to her feet, crossed the cell swiftly and gracefully, reached out for the first time to clutch at the lay sister's arm, smile pleadingly, trustingly at her, a smile so like that worn at the end by all the girls who had in fact given in that Magdalena, still not knowing why her charge had been sent there, felt sure the letter she wanted to write would be one of humblest submission. It had been obvious from the beginning that she was not one of the mad.

"I will carry it," she said, "and now that I have promised, you must forget your fears and sorrows and eat some of this bread while it's still hot."

"You eat it for me, Sister," Anne replied sweetly. "I feel my release drawing near and I am too happy to eat."

Sister Magdalena munched away contentedly, more certain than ever that this lovely young woman, by far the most likable she had ever been set to guard, would soon be leaving the Seven Sorrows forever. She vaguely wondered what her new charge would be like. A cell did not remain vacant for long. She was strong enough to shoulder whatever burden God saw fit to lay on her, but she sighed nonetheless. Very few ladies came back to sanity or resignation as quickly as this one had done.

"Thank you for receiving me, Lady Abbess." Anne knelt to kiss the ring on the slender, withered hand held out to her. "I hardly dared hope an answer would come this soon."

She sat in the chair toward which the Abbess pointed wordlessly, folded her hands in her lap and kept her eyes fixed on the floor. She had been told, many years ago it seemed, that her eyes held unreligious fire, and as old as this woman before her looked to be, she suspected that she was at least as shrewd a judge of character as the nearly forgotten Dame Joanna.

"I sent your letter on to the Empress as you requested," the Abbess said bluntly, "and this is her reply." She began to read in a rapid, emotionless voice from the parchment lying unrolled on the desk before her. "'And furthermore, as I do not believe this lady's repentance to be sincere, I demand a proof which cannot be refuted. If, in your judgment, Reverend Lady Abbess, she is, by the grace of God, restored to grace and sanity, offer her this choice. I hold a signed warrant for her execution, for the crime of laying violent hands upon my person, but I have never willingly desired the death of any of God's creatures. If she will take the veil, adopt my name as hers in religion, and live a life of prayer in expiation for the lust for worldly vanity that previously deranged her, I will lock away the instrument of death in the deepest vault of my palace. She is to make her decision immediately. The priest who brings this letter to you will witness her vows within the hour or the soldiers accompanying him will take her from your care and deliver her to mine. This is the will and command of Agnes-Anna.'"

"I will take the vows," Anne said promptly. "Even had she forgiven me, invited me to my former place at her side, I would have asked it of you. I am deeply conscious both of my many sins and my unworthiness."

"All is arranged," said the Abbess. Very nearly the same choice had been offered other young women who had sat where Anne was sitting now. Not one had chosen the quick death of the ax or the slower, nearly eternal death of the silk-draped cellar chambers. "The community is assembled in chapel. The priest will hear your confession, and then we will receive you. Afterward the Novice Mistress will take you in charge until you have learned the ways of religion."

Anne rose and kissed the Abbess's ring again, then swiftly touched her lips to the floor.

"What made you do that?" the nun snapped imperiously, suspiciously.

"I don't know, Reverend Mother. I wished to humble myself before God and in your sight. It was an impulse, one I hope has not offended you."

"Sister Magdalena speaks well of you. She is a simple soul, one of those it is hardest to fool with a show of unfelt piety. I accept you here reluctantly, because even an Abbess does not always rule supreme in her own house, but I will remember that the Empress, a very astute woman, believes you to be false. You have one friend here, whom you will see only infrequently, and that by accident, and one impartial judge. All the rest are strangers, though they will call you sister. I will watch you, Anna, and some day, if you are faithful and obedient, hold out to you the olive branch of charity. Until that day you can expect justice, nothing more."

It took thirty-eight days to win over a stupid, stubborn peasant, Anne thought as she followed the Abbess deep into the cloister. She felt the high walls close around her, sensed the inner emptiness even in this most opulent convent, began to smell the thick heat of women's bodies as they drew nearer to the chapel. Thirty-eight days and we are now at the beginning of March. Pray that spring comes late this year, she commanded herself. Pray that the Abbess, being old, is also weak and easily fooled. Let down your guard just once, old woman, and I am gone.

The freedom she had been waiting for came five weeks later, at dawn. The nuns filed silently into chapel as they did every morning, struggling against sleep even as they walked, their skin still warm from the beds they had left, their eyes still aching with the grit of their dreams. But before the first prayer had been intoned, even before the last of them had reached her place, the convent bells began to peal wildly, clanging back and forth and against one another as though they would come tearing loose and plunge through the chapel roof to the floor.

The nuns clutched at one another, dropped beads and books of prayer, screamed aloud into the din of the bells, called out for Lady Abbess to tell them what it meant. Then abruptly, silence. The hand that had set the bells in motion no longer pulled on the ropes.

Lady Abbess entered the chapel, and as she walked toward the altar, the nuns stood as if turned to stone, watching her bow before the Presence, ascend the steps, turn to look down on them.

"The Emperor fled during the night," she said. "The breach that was made in the wall yesterday afternoon let in a flood of Latins, and the man who could have stemmed it has deserted us. Portions of the city are already ablaze and the people are saving themselves as best they can. The bishops are on their way now to arrange the terms of surrender. It is over."

They were too astonished, too frightened to weep. Like children in the grip of a nightmare they looked at her with unseeing eyes, mouths opening and closing on words that refused to be spoken.

"I have considered all night long how best to preserve both our lives and this convent. We will not know the terms of surrender for several more hours yet, but I cannot believe that being Christians the Latins will dare to desecrate our churches and houses of religion. It is gold that they are after, and that makes them dangerous and unpredictable. If they enter here, and some may, the sight of God's bounty, which is not ours, but His, will inflame them. The more they see the more they will believe has been hidden. And so, my dear daughters, while we wait, while we pray, we must also work. The sacristan will strip the altar of all but the simplest, most ordinary hangings and vessels, and all of you, all who possess any strength of limb and firmness of purpose, must carry down to the cellars the precious statues that adorn our corridors, the icons before which you bow in your cells, anything, anything which has the appearance of worldly value."

"It is a judgment on us," said one old nun dully. "We have been too lax, too comfortable, too close to the luxuries we vowed to despise."

"No, Sister," the Abbess snapped. "Everything in this convent was given as a gift to God. We have had no more than the use of these things, and to have refused them would have been to deny a soul the opportunity of sacrifice, to fail in humility and charity. My house is not a lax one, and the Holy Virgin whom we serve will protect us. Is your faith weakened by the first test it has ever had to meet?"

The nun did not reply.

Chattering like squirrels, the sisters left the chapel, each one intent on hiding the things that were most dear to her. The Abbess had been frank but reassuring. The idea of danger to their persons was unthinkable. It was their possessions that the Latins would covet. They were prepared to give up what could not be saved, the beautiful furniture, the pieces of statuary too heavy to move, perhaps even some of the silver plate off which they dined. But for the rest they would imitate the cunning animals who stored up plenty in the far recesses of their burrows against a time of need.

The Novice Mistress was at Anne's side before she could leave the chapel. "You will assist the sacristan," she said firmly. "The outer doors are locked and Mother Abbess holds the key. There will be ample time for what you must do."

"We are close to the Boucoleon Palace, are we not, Mother Mistress?"

"The wall at the end of our garden is built against that of the palace," the Mistress replied, "and the square in front is one through which the Emperor often passed when he did not care to travel with a public show of pomp. Why do you ask?"

"The palace will surely be looted," Anne said, feigning a show of thought. "Are we not in danger if we remain here?"

"Lady Abbess does not think so, nor do I."

"I am a Latin, Mother. I've seen what Montferrat's soldiers are capable of doing. Would it not be wiser to flee, as so many others have done?"

"It would be wiser, Sister, to obey your superiors."

All of Anne's being was focused on two objects, the double wooden door of the chapel, and beyond that, the still stronger, still higher door that sealed in the nuns' private domain and gave on to the square. Both were now locked, both were impossible to penetrate. Yet she was sure that within the next few hours the men of her own country would be battering at those very doors, would, if denied entrance, break them down as easily as if they were made of kindling instead of solid oak. And when that happened, when the first Frank burst through, and God grant he was a knight, she would run to him and cry out the tale of her imprisonment, beg him to save her, place herself under his protection. Who he would be she could not imagine, though names and faces flashed through her brain. In her state of near frenzy she could remember only those names she had once given Montferrat, faces of men whom she had betrayed, men whom she now saw as saviors.

The thought that Robert might be among them was one she refused to dwell upon. If they met again it could not be as lovers. She herself had seen to that. Could any man forgive being deceived and scorned? When he knew himself used, manipulated, lied to, made a fool of, did his love not turn to hate? Could a man continue to love a woman who had played so falsely with him? And if Robert were to see her alive, he would surely realize, in one blinding clash of heart and mind, that hers had been the guiding hand behind the story of her death, hers the voice that had spoken in the dark night of Corfu, hers the will that had led him to Constantinople, hers the greed that had kept him from Jerusalem. She had dishonored him. He loved her still because he thought her dead. Alive and nakedly exposed, the bones of what she was and had done as irrefutably bare and telling as those of a corpse in its grave, would he even remember that he had once loved her?

The first hammerings on the outer door echoed throughout the silent, waiting convent. They boomed into the chapel like thunderclaps, and the clink of the Abbess's keys as she rose from her place to face the intruders was as clear and tinkling as the first drops of a heavy spring rain.

The nuns were on their knees, rank after rank of them, a flock of black crows settled onto the chapel's cold stone floor. Here and there a veil trembled, a shoulder twitched uncontrollably, nerveless fingers rattled the beads they held. The Abbess paused for a last look behind her. If they remained on their knees, kept their eyes firmly fixed on the altar, ignored the men who would march up the center aisle, did not panic, did not scream, did not betray that the garb of religion covered the bodies of women, many of them still comely and firm-fleshed, all would be well. Whatever waited out there was not yet a mob, not yet a mindless, soulless animal. They were still men, still individual men, and the Abbess knew that men could be dealt with.

The hammering grew louder, more insistent. She hurried off to answer it, not hearing, because her ears were old, the deep, ominous rumble of voices that growled in a language she could not understand, not knowing, because she could not, that what was called an army had disintegrated, that the worst among them, the unbelievers, the ungodly, were also the fleetest of foot, the most determined and the most cruelly rapacious, that to soldiers such as these rape, mutilation and murder were almost happily accidental pastimes.

The Abbess died with her hand still on the door she had opened, run through by a man who did not even trouble to look at his victim. Her fingers dragged the key from the lock as she fell, and all those heavy keys, one for every door in the convent, clattered to the floor beside her, sending up a spray of hot red blood.

The men who trod on her body as they surged into the Seven Sorrows were faceless, brutish beings, foot soldiers who usually wielded pikes and axes, men who were accustomed to blindly slashing their way through an enemy's ranks. Under a tight rein of command they were efficient and nearly unstoppable. With no knight to lead them, no commander to enforce discipline, no sergeant to restrain them, their appetite for senseless violence had grown to an insatiable hunger which only total exhaustion would extinguish.

They fanned out along the length of the corridor running in front of the chapel, the stolen swords they were unused to wielding held awkwardly, ungracefully. The corridor itself was dark and empty, its marble floor cold and slick beneath their feet, the gold frieze above the chapel door a beckoning glitter of light.

Slowly they grouped themselves before the chapel door, falling silent as they hesitated, knowing where it led, some last faint vestige of God-fear holding them back—but only for less time than it takes to draw two deep breaths, shake off the childhood memories of awed devotion, laugh aloud and learn that sound dispels confusion and uncertainty.

The unlocked, unbolted chapel door seemed to swing inward of its own accord, its noiseless, well-oiled hinges silent, its smooth sliding an invitation. Were there thirty nuns, forty nuns kneeling there before an altar more stripped and unadorned than any they had ever seen? No flowers, no incense, no gold monstrances, no candle flames quivering in the air, nothing but the women on their knees to say that this was God's House.

A flash of white as one head turned, a shriek of tiny, darting fear, a hand that clutched at black, wool-covered breast, a sob that was more moan than cry, a figure rising to its feet, backing slowly away from them, a head that shook no, two arms reaching out to push away bodies that had not yet advanced, the swirl of a skirt as the nun turned to run. Within seconds they had surrounded them, within moments slashed the old ones to an ugly, disfigured death, waded in among the smoother, unlined faces, fed on the terror and the horror mirrored there, with two or three long strides brought down the few who tried to flee, reduced the living to a manageable number nearly equal their own.

And then they stopped, paused, looked at one another, shrugged their shoulders, laughed the wild beast cough that

could not come from human lungs, rubbed the bulging, throbbing mounds between their legs, reached out to grab a woman,
slap her into submission, tear the hot black robe from flesh
sticky and moist with the dread of dying. Dark hair tumbled out
from under the coifs and veils, hair as blond as gold, hair still
thick and luxuriant, hair streaked here and there with a thread
of silver. And there was flesh, white skin that had never been
browned by the sun, plump, well-shaped arms and legs, thighs
that curved and swelled, breasts that jutted out, hung heavily,
rose sweetly to tips of pink and brown. Arms crossed and
uncrossed, hands moved frantically to conceal what no man had
ever penetrated, flew up to shield a breast that pulsed and
quivered, darted down to deny that between the legs was a
sweet, dark, secret place where a man could pump himself dry
without paying a single coin for the privilege.

There was a nun to play the female thing for each man,
though a few were so badly injured that they died before it was
over, almost before they had time to realize that the nightmare
was a part of waking daylight.

Of all the women in the chapel, only Anne and one other were
spared, a tiny little wizened old virgin who had kept her vows
for more than thirty years. Anne saved them both, falling prone
on the floor before the careless killing began, lying still, eyes
shut, limbs loose and boneless in imitation of death, never moving even when another sister's body fell across hers, willing herself insensible to the smell and feel of the blood that bathed her
face and soaked through her habit like a wave of warm seawater, daring to move only when the old nun stirred from her
faint, urgently squeezing the hand she held in hers. A whisper,
"Don't move," absolute immobility through the screams, the
pleas for mercy, the heavy slaps of flesh on flesh, the grunts and
laughter, the soft whir of sword through bodies used and discarded, the gabble of last prayers, the silence when it ended.

The men left the chapel, hitching up their clothing as they
went, relaxed, a glow of well-being bringing smiles to their lips,
sleepy eyes sharpening, lighting up again as they passed through
the door and remembered that there were other doors to open,
other chambers to investigate, somewhere a store of hidden

treasure to be found. One or two glanced back, out of habit, fearing always the enemy who sneaks up from the rear. But not a single hand was raised behind them, and their fellows laughed and taunted them. They weren't on a battlefield, remember?

Anne and the old nun, whose name was Sophia, listened to the footsteps fading off in the distance, heard the calls from room to room, the crash of statuary, the excited shouts from the cellars below.

"They've found the vaults," Sophia whispered.

"That means they'll soon be gone. Don't speak, don't move. Wait. Pray with your mind, Sister, not with your lips. Close your eyes again."

Sophia did as she was told, not to save her life, but only because she was so numb that obeying was the only natural thing to do. They waited, hidden in the carnage, and soon they heard the tramp of feet and the dragging of bundles too filled with gold to lift, smelled smoke and knew that the library, its precious manuscripts and carved reading stands, its polished furniture and walls, were all ablaze.

"Not yet," Anne said urgently. "They'll run and not look back once the fire takes hold."

And she was right. They ran from the burning library, down the marble corridor, past the chapel door, out through the portal around which were carved the familiar, gently heartbreaking scenes depicting the Virgin's Sorrows, into, across the square, out the other side, away from the Boucoleon Palace where other looters might take what they had worked for, back in the direction from which they had come, sniffing out a lair in which to rest and contemplate their riches. They lurched as they ran, stumbled, fell, cursed, got up again, ran faster, disappeared into the city's winding streets. "They found the wine, too," Sophia said.

"It's safe to go now." Anne closed her ears to the dull, rolling thud of the body she displaced as she stood.

"Where?" Sophia demanded, her eyes following the limbs that moved so briefly, then settled into rag-doll stillness again. "That was my cousin who lay on top of us. Elizabeth. Where can we go?"

"Think, Sister. Do you know a family nearby, a house too small and poor to attract attention, anyone who would recognize you and let us in until this is over?"

"Can't we stay here?" the old nun pleaded. "Not here, not in this place, but somewhere in the monastery, some room inside which we could barricade ourselves?"

"The fire will spread, Sophia, and others may come, others who have been told that our cellars are far from emptied. Those same men perhaps."

"On the next street," Sophia said quietly. "A merchant and his wife. Not rich, but their house is of stone. I sat with them when their daughter died. She was to have entered here. Lady Abbess allowed her the privilege of being buried in the habit. The parents were grateful. They'll shelter us, if they haven't fled."

"Even if the house is empty it will be a better refuge than the streets."

"Couldn't we say a prayer?"

"There isn't time, Sister. We'll pray later, I promise you. But only if we are alive to do so. You must lead the way. I came at night, you know. I saw nothing and remember nothing."

Sister Sophia was thin and fragile, barely able to totter to her feet, wholly incapable of walking unassisted. She shook as if palsied, so that Anne, half carrying her from the chapel, ground her teeth to keep from shouting at her. No one today would unbar a gate or unlock a door to a stranger. If the merchant and his wife were cowering in their little stone house only Sophia's tired old treble would reassure them. Thank God they had a debt to pay.

They moved slowly out into the cloudy sunlight of the square, a warm but dim sunlight, and looking upward, saw that the unnatural clouds above them were billows of smoke, rolling, boiling masses of black and gray that rained down ashes on their heads.

"It's not far," whispered Sophia, gasping for breath. "Is the whole city burning?"

"Not all of it," Anne said grimly. "They won't let the palaces go up. Montferrat wants to rule here, and he cannot rule a wasteland. Hurry, Sister."

There was a fountain in the center of the square. Sophia reached out a hand toward the clean, wet coolness, and Anne, cursing under her breath, stripped the veil from her head and bent to soak it in the water.

A man stood in the doorway of the Seven Sorrows, his arms filled with wax-stoppered stone jugs of wine. He'd labored up the winding staircase from the cellars to bring them to his comrades, lugging them all that way for nothing. He was swaying on his feet, and there were tears in his eyes. They'd gone and left him, never even called his name, taken all the lovely bundles with them, even the one he'd filled so carefully and trustingly left piled with the others in the corridor. There was more below, but also all those stairs, the darkness, the litter of destruction through which he'd have to scrabble for what had been flung aside. The best was gone. Timbers crashed behind him as the library roof fell in. Flames shot upward into empty air. Would he run the risk of being trapped down there?

He took a drink of wine, squinting at a flutter of black by the fountain. His eyes were red-rimmed and bleary. He couldn't quite make out what it was. And then he realized that it was a nun, a nun without her veil on, a nun who was trying to lift something heavy and black from the ground, a nun who was creeping off with gold and silver altar vessels tied up in a bundle almost as big as she was.

He threw down the jugs that were suddenly so unimportant and sprinted across the square, howling as he ran, throwing off the scabbard that tangled up his legs, brandishing the lovely, shiny sword in great swirling circles around his head.

She tried to run away, stumbled over her bundle, dived for his legs as he leaped at her, almost unbalanced him. He was clumsy, and the first downward stroke merely cut off the hands that clutched and clawed at him, nearly grazing his own toes. The second stroke was through the back, a two-handed push that was neat, clean, almost unnoticeable when the sword was withdrawn.

He kicked the body aside, reached to scoop up his newfound treasure, and found himself clutching a veil, staring down at a balding old skull that mocked him obscenely. Dying of fright, the old one, but not dead yet. He slashed at the skull, cracked it nearly in two, spat into the white and red mass of brain, sobbed in weary, drunken frustration.

A few moments later he was gone, following a trail of bloody footsteps down a street he hoped would lead him to where he could reclaim what was rightfully his. Only the sound of splashing water broke the silence of the square.

"There's water up ahead, I can hear a fountain," Peter of Amiens said. His face was grimy with soot, and traces of the blood he had wiped from his fingers had dried and hardened into scaly brown patches on his hands. "I may be leading us in the wrong direction. I thought no Germans would have penetrated to the rear of the palace, but that fellow who ran past us was no Frank."

"I wanted to cut him down as he ran," said Robert angrily. "He was covered in blood, but not from any wound of his own."

"We've seen enough to know what must be happening all over the city, and more than enough to know that we cannot stop it," Peter reminded him. "That man may live to die in battle, and if so, you did right to spare him. The city will have to be held, the countryside reconquered. The army will regroup when this is over and we'll need every man, even fodder like that one. The Greeks will not forget Constantinople. We'll be fighting for our lives again within the year."

They stood just within the perimeter of the square, staring at the stone building whose roof blazed fire, whose wooden doors were a sheet of flame.

"Blessed Lord Christ, receive their souls," Aleaumes said quietly.

"What is it?" Robert asked, his hand on the hilt of his sword, his eyes searching for signs of human movement, darting toward the other streets that led away from the place.

"It's the Convent of the Seven Sorrows," Aleaumes replied, "the most famous monastery in the city, a house where only royal ladies and those of certain noble families were admitted. One of the monks at the hospital told me about it. He said its altar was more beautiful than any he had ever seen."

"Looted and burning," Peter said. "We'll never cleanse ourselves of this."

They turned away from the fountain, away from the two still bodies lying there, seeing the river of blood on the cobblestones, smelling the scent of death.

"I am a priest," Aleaumes said. "I must go back. I must be certain no spark of life lingers, no soul waits for a word of consolation or forgiveness."

Peter and Robert watched him walk back into the square. They saw him kneel, saw him cross himself, turned away again as if even seeing were an intrusion.

The old nun was dead. Aleaumes pulled her veil back up over her shattered head, turned then to the other one, his eyes filmy with tears he would not let fall.

On his knees, bent over to bless the corpse, he saw black hair spilled out on the pavement, long, lustrous black hair that shone with life and prideful care, hair that swept around a wound in which the blood welled, drew back, welled again. Two lovely, long-fingered hands lay just beyond their bloody wrists, two hands as pale and graceful, as gently curled as the stone hands of a statue. And by the hands and the hair he knew who lay before him. He turned her over, saw the lips part, the eyelids flutter weakly.

"Anne," he said, his mouth nearly touching hers. "It's Aleaumes. Can you hear me?"

"Don't tell him, Aleaumes," she whispered. Blue eyes, bluer than the sky, stared into his, clear eyes which quickly dimmed, began to glaze over with the death of sight and self. "Robert must never know. Promise me."

"I promise."

"I'm truly sorry, Aleaumes. Now when it's too late, I'm sorry. Will you give me absolution?"

Before he had finished she was dead. He closed the blue eyes, touching them gently, feeling their warmth, knowing they would soon grow cold and open again.

"You weren't worthy of him," he said aloud, "but you didn't deserve this."

He covered her body with her veil, stood over her in prayer for a few more moments, blessed the air above her, and then walked slowly back to where Peter and Robert waited.

Peter's look was a question.

"One of them was still alive," Aleaumes said. "I gave her absolution as she died. It's over now."

"It's all over," Peter said. "For them, for us, for Jerusalem too. There will never be another crusade. This was the last one, the greatest hope, and now look what we have made of it."

I I

April 13–May 16, 1204

The unchecked looting of Constantinople lasted for three days and nights while the fire continued to burn, completing the work of destruction so joyously begun by the army that rampaged through the city streets. On the morning of the fourth day the Doge at last succeeded in convincing the Frankish leaders that unless they restored order and discipline immediately much that should have gone into their own coffers would be melted in the flames or crushed beneath the careless feet of the common soldiers. There was also considerable danger, he pointed out, that the mob would attack the very palaces in which Montferrat and Baldwin had established themselves and to which they had had carried the most valuable objects found in the many lesser palaces of the city.

The order went out that each man was to bring whatever gold and silver he had found to one of three churches designated as common repositories, churches that would be well guarded by representative troops from each battalion in the army. Nothing was to be held back, on pain of death, for all were to share in the plunder according to each man's rank and position. A mounted knight was promised the equivalent of twenty marks, each sergeant and man in holy orders ten. At first there was a mere trickle of mediocre goods into the central coffers, but after St. Pol had publicly hanged one of his own knights, his shield attached upside down to his body, the piles of rich cloth, jewelry, church vessels and icons grew enormously. There were other hangings to drive the lesson home, but nothing struck such fear into the soldiers' hearts as the sight of the body of an anointed knight rotting in the warm spring air, a feast for carrion birds and night-prowling rats.

The crusaders quartered themselves wherever they could, but so much of the city had been destroyed by fire and the mob that groups of ten or twenty were forced to crowd themselves into houses formerly occupied by a family of five or six. Disease broke out almost immediately. The bodies of the dead had been left to rot in the streets, Constantinople's famous underground water reserves were fouled and undrinkable, human and animal excrement was shoveled into evil-smelling piles at street corners, and the food supply from the surrounding countryside seemed to have been exhausted overnight. Only wine was still in abundant supply, and many a soldier lived on nothing else during his first week as the new conqueror of a great empire.

But gradually, hour by hour and day by day, order was restored and the discipline that had been maintained before the attack was reinstated. Sergeants routed their men out of bed in the morning, picked them up, still drunk, from the gutters into which they had fallen the night before, set them to guard duty, to building ovens in which bread could be baked, ordered them to form burial details and clean-up squads, sent them to forage, to steal or to buy food from farmers still working their land, turned them into herdsmen to drive in the vast numbers of cattle required to fill the thousands of hungry bellies of this huge army.

The smoke of the fire was blown away by the wind, though the smell of it remained. Late April's early-morning rains washed clean the city's marble churches and palaces, and turned the rubble into soggy heaps of ash that steamed in the afternoon sun.

Not all the Greeks had fled. Many had remained to defend and preserve their homes, many more slipped quietly back to furtively assess the situation and decide whether life under the Franks was more tolerable than the shelter of a far-off city's slums or the cold ditch beside a road. Some who had sheltered foreign traders during the days of their persecution now found refuge in Galata with those they had befriended. The threads of life and commerce were picked up, a new, more precarious, far less comfortable way of living worked out. There was no other choice but to start anew or die.

Robert and Aleaumes, more fortunate than most, shared a tiny chamber in the palace that St. Pol had appropriated for himself, which he had invited his cousin to share. Their duties during those first weeks of the occupation were primarily those undertaken at every change of camp, and though they were time-consuming and often frustrating, they were neither arduous nor dangerous. There were disputes about billeting to be arbitrated, lines of supply to be established, sergeants' reports to be listened to and evaluated, inspections made of areas of the city that had been ordered cleared of rubble and made livable again, returning Greeks to question, both about Murtzuphles' whereabouts and their own reasons for coming back to Constantinople. It was assumed that many were spies, and some whose stories did not satisfy their interrogators were ejected from the city or summarily put to death.

For Robert it was a busy time, a needed period of transition. The capture of the city had been the climax of two years of traveling, hardship, disappointed hopes, disillusionment and fighting. Now, from being one who takes and destroys, he had to assume the role of one who builds and consolidates what he has achieved.

The arguments beginning to be heard on every side over which baron was the most likely to be elected emperor confirmed the assumption that the Latin Empire to be founded on the ruins of the Greek would be a permanent one. No one was neutral in the matter of the election. Too much was at stake. Every aspect of the new kingdom would to some degree depend on the character and temperament of the man who ruled it. Almost against his will Robert found himself drawn into these discussions, and though he refused to commit himself fully and openly either to Baldwin or to Montferrat, the two men most frequently mentioned, he did attempt to draw Peter of Amiens out on the subject.

"Of the two I prefer Baldwin," Peter said bluntly, "but it is possible that neither will be elected."

As it was Peter, not Robert, who sat privily with St. Pol in the long spring evenings, he took Peter's comment to mean that

Count Hugh was also looking at Constantinople's unoccupied throne with more than dispassionate interest. And why not? Theoretically any baron of suitable rank and lineage could push his own candidacy. There were surely some who hoped that the presence of two seemingly equal aspirants would force the electors to choose a compromise emperor. It had been done before in papal elections. Why not again?

"It will be Baldwin," Aleaumes predicted. "No one really trusts Montferrat. They may not know Baldwin as well, but they know his good points, and they'll be more than willing to weigh those heavily against the ways in which the Marquis has manipulated them. Montferrat is a strong man, much stronger than Baldwin. Will barons ruling little kingdoms of their own want to bow down before an emperor whose whole energies are focused on controlling them? I think not."

On the ninth of May twelve men met to elect, by secret ballot, the first Latin Emperor of Constantinople. That they were able to meet at all, and in a place of assured security, was a small miracle in itself, for choosing the Frankish electors had proved an almost impossible task.

Ambition had surfaced sluggishly at first, but as if to make up for lost time, every baron who dreamed of coronation quickly formed his own party, gathered his supporters around him, and set about undermining the strength of the only two really viable candidates. Even Louis of Blois, who had lain mortally ill in his ship all winter, raised his weak head and proclaimed that it was strong enough to wear a crown.

The parliament at which the electors were to have been nominated dragged on for days. Accusations were flung out, characters maligned, threats shouted above the din and even a few swords drawn to emphasize that this was a deadly serious business.

The Doge grew more impatient as the rivalry continued, growing more ridiculous with each passing day. He had his favored candidate and knew that the Venetian electors would vote his choice without a murmur of dissent. But almost two weeks dragged by before he felt forced to interfere in the Frankish quarrel. It could no longer be dignified by the name of either debate or parliament.

He made his discreet suggestion to Villehardouin, who more and more frequently of late held himself apart from the arguments of his ambitious colleagues. The Marshal of Champagne had taken up residence in a small, luxurious palace near Santa Sophia, close by the palace the Doge himself occupied. He seldom left his new residence, and when the Doge went to call on him he found Villehardouin pacing the once fine library of the house, dictating to an elderly clerk who scuttled away, obviously relieved at the interruption. A pile of close-written manuscript pages lay neatly stacked on the tall writing desk and Villehardouin laid a protective hand on them as he greeted his visitor.

"I would not have disturbed you, my lord, had the matter not been grave," began Dandolo. He noted with dismay the queerly abstracted look on Villehardouin's face and the unnatural pallor of his skin. The Marshal had always been a man of action, a man who saw reality for what it was and dealt reasonably with it. It disturbed Dandolo to find him now so withdrawn from events that would have enormous significance for years to come.

"I am writing a true account of what we have seen and done," said Villehardouin, "from the moment that Thibaut took the cross to the present."

"An apologia, my lord?" queried Dandolo.

"No apologia is needed," said Villehardouin, slamming his fist down hard on the manuscript. Several pages fluttered to the floor and he bent to pick them up, muttering something the Doge could not quite make out. "Almost from the beginning there have been factions in this army which sought to dissuade us from our duty, men who forsook their oaths and evilly deceived weaker spirits, men who in their self-willed blindness refused to see the light of God's command. I do not seek to justify what we have done; no lawyer's arguments are necessary. I but recount the facts as I was privy to them. Let others judge us harshly if they will. But they shall not judge without knowledge of the truth."

"Even a blind man can see God's Light," said Dandolo quietly.

Villehardouin looked sharply at the old man, distrusting his even tone of voice, the honeyed words that flowed so readily from his lips. He had not dealt harshly with the Doge in what he had written thus far. He had instead made a special effort to point out the absolute fairness of the Venetian demands. He wondered if he had been too fair, if perhaps when the time came to revise his manuscript he might not permit himself the luxury of inserting a personal commentary of his own. Dandolo's face was set in an expression of sincere concern and once again Villehardouin was perplexed by this man. He could and did condemn most vigorously his own countrymen who had deserted the crusade and those who had sought to thwart its direction through intrigue and cabal, but he was never certain just how great a role Dandolo had played in the army's diversion to Constantinople. He had an irritating certainty that there were many things that had been wrongfully concealed from him, and a suspicion that Dandolo and also Montferrat had the answers to questions he did not dare ask.

"It will be years before the work is complete," he said, dismissing it. "I have little leisure in which to work on it."

"And I have come today to ask you to give up what little you have," said Dandolo, mournfully shaking his head. "It is wrong for a man of your abilities to absent himself from the world's travail."

"I have addressed the parliament several times already, if that is what you are referring to," said Villehardouin. "I have stressed the need for unity at this moment, for a fair and open election in which God's inspiration working in each man's heart will decide who is to occupy this Empire's throne. They listen politely to me, then return to their squabbling like cocks in a barnyard. What more can I do?"

"A thought has come to me," said Dandolo slowly, as if only now making up his mind to express it. "Each baron seeks to place his own men amongst the ranks of the electors, and as only six are to be chosen it is impossible for them to reach agreement. Baldwin wants at least four of his supporters chosen, Montferrat, Blois and St. Pol the same. Mathematics and simple logic suggest that there is no solution to such a problem. But what would happen, my dear Marshal, if the electors were chosen solely from the ranks of the clergy? The bishops are fair men, accustomed to asking Divine Guidance in the many decisions they make every day. Might not all parties be willing to place their fate in such trustworthy hands?"

"It depends," answered Villehardouin, interested now in where the Doge was leading him.

"On what?"

Villehardouin's mind had begun to work again in the old familiar channels of compromise, a concession here, a promise there, a workable solution finally reached in which no man clearly triumphed over another. He drew a chair close to the Doge and lowered his voice. "The only two possible candidates are Baldwin and Montferrat. Blois is too ill and St. Pol commands neither the love nor the respect of the entire army."

"You forget that a Venetian might be elected," said Dandolo.

"Only one amongst you has the wisdom and the stature to reign. And I do not think, my lord, that you wish to be Emperor."

The Doge shook his head, delighted that in this game of wits which he would win, the opposition was at least worthy of his efforts. "A few islands, a portion of the city, some favorable trade concessions," he murmured. "We shall ask for very little."

"So we come back again to Baldwin and Montferrat."

"To Baldwin, I think."

"Montferrat will not give up easily," said Villehardouin, playing for time. The Doge's preference had surprised him, since he had seemed so closely linked to Montferrat in the past.

Villehardouin rose and walked to a window, seeing before him not the palace's tranquil garden, but a partial map of Europe. The Holy Roman Empire in the north and west, stretching its tentacles downward into Italy; independent, rich Venice in the center; the new Latin Empire on the east, ruled by a vassal of Philip of Swabia? Impossible, of course. The new emperor must be a man who had no ties of fealty or family with the ruler of the great Germanic Empire. Divide and conquer. The Roman phrase flashed into his mind and he smiled at the simplicity and perfection of it. Baldwin, then, was to be emperor. He had no personal objections. In fact he preferred Baldwin above all the other candidates. By virtue of his long association with the crusade, his personal integrity and the reverence in which the common soldier held him he was the most worthy. He was ambitious, as he had recently proved, but Villehardouin judged that ambition to be an honest one, far removed from the excessive greed and the lust for absolute power that he had lately come to believe dominated Montferrat's every action.

"I cannot, of course, interfere personally," the Doge was saying.

"The bishops will elect Baldwin," said Villehardouin, turning from the sun-filled window. "It remains to me to persuade Montferrat to agree to their designation as electors. He will sense which way the wind is blowing and will object strenuously."

"He walks with the weight of a crown on his head."

"Will he settle for less than an emperor's diadem?"

"He must, and he will. He is a man who is accustomed to profiting from this world's realities. He will be bitter at first, but if the prize is rich enough he will take it. Better a small kingdom of his own than nothing." Dandolo paused, allowing the silence to grow, sensing that Villehardouin was considering each rich city of the Empire, rejecting one after another as too small or too isolated to entice Montferrat's interest. "The kingdom of Salonika might be appropriate. His brother Renier once ruled there. It was a gift to him from the Emperor Manuel, who also gave him his daughter Maria. The young man was, alas, unable to hold either of his acquisitions. Montferrat still burns to succeed where his brothers failed. They are a proud house."

"Salonika is not Baldwin's to give. Much of that territory will go to you and to other barons."

The Doge dismissed Villehardouin's objection with an easy wave of his hand. "It is enough that an understanding be reached between Baldwin and Montferrat that after the coronation an exchange of lands will be arranged that will eventually result in Montferrat's receiving the whole of that kingdom. It will come about naturally, gradually, and as it will appear to be but a part of the new Emperor's plan for the reorganization and pacification of his realm, no one will object."

"I will approach Baldwin first," decided Villehardouin, "then Montferrat. But only after Baldwin has given his sworn word to honor the arrangement. If he were to go back on it we would have civil war before the kingdom is a year old. It will take several days to arrange."

"Do not delay too long," counseled Dandolo. He rose, and as he waited for the servant who guided his steps, he gestured toward Villehardouin's manuscript. His sight was clouded and milky on good days; on bad he could see only grayness. Today, after so satisfying a conversation, he could see almost as clearly as other men. "What will you write, my dear Marshal, of what has been said in this room?"

"Nothing, my lord." Villehardouin seemed startled by the question. "I record only the facts. I will write that Baldwin was elected, that is all."

"And leave posterity to marvel at the simplicity and ease with which such a feat was accomplished." Dandolo chuckled. "You will make a fine historian, my lord Marshal."

"I believe that history must inspire as it teaches," said Villehardouin.

"Oh, yes indeed," replied the Doge. He bowed courteously, and still chuckling at his private joke, allowed himself to be led from the room.

The process of election, once begun, proceeded smoothly. The twelve electors were locked within the chapel set apart for their use, while outside the Doge's palace the barons and knights crowded the streets, keeping silent vigil as they waited to learn who among them would rule. The electors would remain in strictest seclusion until their vote was unanimous. The solemnity of the moment was felt by all; it was not unlike the election of a pope.

The first vote was inconclusive and hardly surprising. Five of the Venetians urged the election of their Doge. This was expected by all as a purely formal gesture of respect, an act in which Nevelon, Bishop of Soissons, and Garnier, Bishop of Troyes, joined. Their first vote thus concealed their true intentions, leaving the four other representatives of the army—John of Noyon, Bishop-elect of Acre but still chancellor to Baldwin; Conrad, Bishop of Halberstadt; Pierre, Bishop of Bethlehem, the Pope's legate; and Pierre, Abbot of Locedio—voting their feudal loyalties. It was obvious now which votes had to be changed.

Pantaleo Barbo, who, acting on instructions from the Doge,

had abstained on the first ballot, rose to address the electors. In a carefully reasoned speech he urged his fellow Venetians to cast their votes for Baldwin on the second ballot. The Count of Flanders commanded the largest single contingent of the army, he pointed out, and went on to praise his obvious virtues and military experience, not forgetting to dwell on the beauty, grace and saintly disposition of his wife, the Countess Mary, who, by her inspiration and love, would bring a truly Christian atmosphere to a formerly decadent court. The Doge, he continued, was not ambitious for the honor they sought to bestow on him. Indeed, he believed that that saintly old man would feel obliged to decline the emperorship should they attempt to force it on him, pleading his extraordinary age and desire to return to his beloved Venice now that the task he had set himself was accomplished. With tears in their eyes the five Venetians voted for Baldwin on the second ballot.

Conrad of Halberstadt was confused by the sudden shift. He had expected hours of deliberation, a more even division of votes, had even prepared a passionate speech by which he would swing the election to Montferrat. The Pope's legate, newly arrived from Syria, knew next to nothing of the army's divisions and troubles. His instructions were to support Baldwin for, like Venice, Rome feared encirclement by the Holy Roman Empire. The Abbot of Locedio looked into his heart and voted for Baldwin, then lapsed into a nervous telling of his beads.

It was hours before the Bishop of Halberstadt acknowledged defeat. If only he could get the ear of the Pope's legate, promise the Holy Father magnificent relics such as the Western World had never seen, reassure him that Montferrat was a true son of the Church, hint at a break between the Marquis and the Holy Roman Empire, anything to sway the man's vote. But such politicking was not to be tolerated.

While the fourth ballot was being tabulated he left his stall and strolled casually toward where the new Bishop of Bethlehem sat. Nevelon of Soissons, who had been chosen spokesman of the group, looked up from the ballots he was counting, said something quietly to the Venetian who was witnessing them, then rapped sharply on the wood of his stall with his heavy episcopal ring. The sound echoed authoritatively in the silence of the chapel, and Conrad, arrested in mid-aisle, knew that eleven pairs of eyes were implacably fixed on him. He drew himself up as if to relieve a cramp in the back, then continued his slow walk, past the Bishop of Bethlehem to the foot of the altar. There he stood for a few moments, his head bent in prayer. The eyes remained fixed unblinkingly on him until he had returned to his stall, where he sank to his knees and covered his face with his hands. He heard the rustle of movement and knew that his moment had passed and that he would be allowed no other. He had not managed to come closer than two feet to the papal legate, whose expression had been uncommitted and even slightly bored. The Abbot of Locedio's eyes had faltered and fallen as Conrad passed him, but on the fifth ballot he again voted for Baldwin.

As the sixth vote was taken, Conrad knew that this time the decision would be unanimous. He wondered if he should make some sort of conciliatory speech, explain that although in conscience he supported Montferrat, he had bowed to the manifest will of the majority of the electors. But he was tired and not looking forward to facing the Marquis and could not rouse himself to make the effort. It would not impress these men anyway.

The Bishop of Soissons rose and with relief in his voice announced that Baldwin, Count of Flanders and Hainault, had been unanimously chosen Emperor. God be praised.

It was nearly midnight, and by delaying for a short time to burn every scrap of parchment on which the votes had been scratched, a mystical symbolism could be attached to the creation of the Latin Kingdom of Constantinople. The electors sat patiently, watching the slow burning of the squares of parchment. All of them knew and appreciated the importance of symbolism and theatricality to the minds and hearts of the laity.

As the church bells rang out the midnight peal, Nevelon led them in procession from the chapel, through the palace and out into the square. The last note still quivered on the night air as he raised his arms above his head, imploring Heaven to look down upon the rejoicing of earth's children. "Thanks be to God, we have an Emperor." His powerful preacher's voice carried over the heads of the crowd and rang majestically down the silent streets. "At the very hour when God deigned to become man, we give him to you. The noble Baldwin, Count of Flanders and Hainault."

The square exploded with sound as Baldwin was brought forward to receive the acclaim and homage of his new subjects. Montferrat was the first to bend the knee, and in recognition of the nobility of his gesture and perhaps also in huge relief that the Marquis was seemingly content to accept the electors' decision, he too was cheered and applauded. No sign of anger or disappointment contorted Montferrat's face as he touched his forehead to Baldwin's hand, then stepped back into the anonymity of the group surrounding him. Conrad of Halberstadt drew a great sigh of relief and felt the knot in his stomach dissolve. Powerful warrior-bishop though he was, he had a healthy respect for the Marquis's temper. But his overlord was displaying a control and resignation that was admirably Christian. Now perhaps they could get on with the business of bringing these heretic Greeks back to the true light of faith. By word or by sword, it hardly mattered which. The bishop began to look forward to the campaign.

Baldwin's coronation took place a week later in the cathedral of Santa Sophia. Greek laborers had been rounded up and set to work under heavy guard to prepare the ancient church for the ceremony. Night and day they toiled—often, the jaundiced guards reported, with tears streaming down their faces. Santa Sophia had been a visible proof of heresy and it had been badly desecrated and almost totally looted by the mob. Animal dung and human excrement had to be laboriously scraped from the floor and walls of the church, and broken bits of once-magnificent marble altars and finely enameled icons carted out in huge basket-loads. Shreds of altar linens and vestments, their gold thread ripped off, the jewels pried from their delicate settings, were thrown carelessly on the heap of rubble. Monks pawed through the piles of loot in the central repositories, choosing the most magnificent altar vessels, the least Byzantine vestments and hangings, to grace the cathedral in which a Latin Mass would at last be sung.

On the day appointed for the coronation every crusader in the city donned his finest robes. Crowds of common soldiers and lesser knights thronged the streets between the Boucoleon Palace and Santa Sophia, wildly cheering the knights who passed in mounted, dignified progress, leading Baldwin to his moment of glory.

Baldwin entered the cathedral a richly dressed knight of Western Christendom, but when he emerged from the small robing room to which his nobles had conducted him, he was to every man's eye an emperor. His legs were encased in vermilion samite hose and he walked in shoes so covered with precious stones that he seemed to move on a wave of flashing brilliance. His coat was cloth of gold, fastened front and back with buttons of pure gold. Over this he wore a long robe solidly encrusted with emeralds, diamonds and stones few had ever seen before. The train of this robe was draped over his left arm, lending a priestly character to his splendor. Finally, a mantle had been placed on his shoulders on which jeweled eagles stared defiantly, their ruby eyes flashing red fire as he walked.

The procession passed within arm's reach of Robert and Aleaumes, and as it swept by, Robert felt his brother's involuntary shudder. Louis of Blois carried the imperial standard, his emaciated body and ashen face proof that death still held him in its grip. The Count's eyes were bright and feverish; there was no point of focus to them, yet Aleaumes shrank back against his brother and ducked his head.

St. Pol carried the Emperor's sword, and behind him marched Montferrat, two bishops at his side, helping him bear the weight of the imperial crown. Then Baldwin himself, one pace ahead of two other bishops. The Emperor's authority came from God, their presence said, and let no man forget it.

Baldwin knelt at the altar while one by one his upper garments were removed. His bare flesh was anointed with holy oils and his robes were replaced with even greater reverence now. The bishops formed a ring around the imperial crown, raised it high above their heads for all to marvel at, blessed it with the Sign of the Cross, then all together placed it on his head. One final touch before he turned to face his subjects. A ruby as large as a man's fist now fastened his mantle, a jewel that had once belonged to the Emperor Manuel I. Baldwin was the first Latin to occupy the throne of Constantinople, but the long-dead Emperor's ruby set the seal of lawful continuity on his accession.

Robert's attention wandered during the Mass that followed the crowning. His eyes moved restlessly over the altar, leaping from the bright candle flames to the glittering vestments of the celebrants, then always back to rest on the motionless figure enthroned before him. His eyes feasted on the magnificence, on the scepter held in one hand, the golden globe surmounted by a cross in the other, the heavy, unbelievable crown above a familiar face grown strangely remote with the exaltation of kingship. The sound of the monks' chanting filled his ears and incense burned his nose with a familiar tingling warmth. Some deep-hid memory was surging through his body, beating its slow way to his brain, and at last he knew what it was. Here in ruined Constantinople, in the midst of an emperor's coronation, he was remembering ceremonies witnessed long ago at the great monastery of Corbie, where the holy feasts of the Church were celebrated with the same incense on other candle-filled altars, where the same chanting uplifted the spirit, and always the miracle of bread turned into the Body of Christ humbled and awed the greatest sinner. Other churches in which he had worshiped passed through his mind's eye as slowly, inexorably, the memory he had unconsciously been fighting took control of his will.

The chapel at Clari was a tiny room, barely large enough to hold the family and the household servants. Its stone walls were bare and damp, its floor unyielding and always wet, its altar covered with a rough linen cloth woven by his grandmother before old age had crippled her fingers. The cross that hung above the altar was of some base metal, the Christ a crudely fashioned figure, and when the priest came to say Mass he was obliged to bring his own altar vessels with him, for Clari possessed no gold of any kind. Yet as a child Robert had thought the place awesome, terrifyingly sacred and strangely comforting. He remembered creeping in to lay a small arm on his mother's shoulders during the long vigils she kept there while Gilo fought and suffered in the Holy Land, and how she had lain prostrate on the floor each time an infant brother or sister had died. He could not now recall how many others there had been, nor even the names the tiny, lifeless creatures had been given.

Wonderingly, as he stared at the Host elevated for his adoration, he felt himself lifted and carried out of magnificent Santa Sophia, transported through gray clouds over lands and seas he could sense but not see. He looked down and saw the roof of Clari's manor house, the fields green with the spring's planting. Somehow everything dissolved, and as though peering through a long tube he saw the interior of the chapel, everything exactly as he had known it in childhood. He saw himself, still a babe, cradled in his mother's arms as she knelt in prayer. But her face was not the young mother's face that had so often delighted him with its smiles and laughter, its quick kisses and comforting words. This mother looked older, more worn and tired even than the woman he had left standing straight and proud as he had galloped from the mounting yard two years ago. And she wore a widow's veil on her head. The babe stirred and cried and he looked into the small face that was his and yet somehow not. She crooned softly to quiet the child, signed its forehead with the cross, and slowly, painfully, got to her feet.

That was all. The vision was swept away like smoke from a fire and he felt Aleaumes' hand tugging at his arm. He bowed his head as Baldwin passed and heard the shouting of the crowd as the Emperor mounted his white horse.

That night, while the new Emperor entertained and feasted in the Boucoleon Palace and every man ate and drank his fill at lesser feasts all over the city, Robert spoke seriously to Aleaumes for the first time about the possibility of going home to Picardy.

III

Summer, 1204–March, 1205

Adrianople, Messinopolis, Christopolis, Blache, Cetros, Salonika, Cetros again, and now back to Blache, where Hugh of St. Pol had persuaded the Emperor Baldwin to rest his troops for a day so that Peter of Amiens might die in the relative comfort of a litter that did not sway and jolt with every step of the two mules between which it was slung.

Robert and Aleaumes kept vigil on either side of Peter's hastily improvised bed, a couch made of cloaks and horse blankets laid on bare, rock-strewn ground beneath a skeleton tree that did little to shade the dying man from the fierce summer sun. They bathed his face and tried to force a little wine between his lips, but he had lapsed into unconsciousness. The slight rising and falling of his chest was the sole sign that he still breathed. He might have been peacefully asleep but for the heat of fever that burned their fingers each time they replaced the tepid cloths draped like burial garments over forehead, legs and arms.

"He is no longer in pain, my lord," Aleaumes said quietly to St. Pol, who had come again, hoping to find his cousin miraculously recovered from the fever that had already claimed more than forty knights on this mad, frantic forced march.

"The crisis will come tonight," Aleaumes continued. "If he lives until morning he will recover."

"I will send a priest to you at midnight," St. Pol replied. "Will you stay with him and send for me if there is any change?"

"Yes, my lord," answered Robert. "I am his man in life and death."

St. Pol nodded thoughtfully, then walked slowly toward Baldwin's tent. Peter had often praised the loyalty of these two brothers, so much so that St. Pol had personally seen to it that Aleaumes was paid a knight's fee for his part in the capture of Constantinople. If Peter died he would invite the elder to join the select group of knights who were his personal attendants—and perhaps find a place for the younger brother also. Loyalty was now a scarce and much-prized commodity among the followers of the new Latin Emperor.

The first hint of the trouble to come had surfaced even before the coronation, when Montferrat had hastily wed Isaac's widow, the ex-Empress Margaret-Maria, acquiring at the same time guardianship of her two children. Deprived of the crown himself, Boniface lost no time in courting the love of his new stepchildren, paying particular attention to the boy Manuel. St. Pol remembered the rumor that had so shocked the crusaders. Isaac, so they had been told, had intended to pass over Alexius in favor of this Manuel. Isaac and the wretched Alexius were long dead, moldering in their tombs, yet St. Pol could not help but wonder how many Greeks still whispered the name of Manuel in the night. Especially now, since open, bloody warfare was about to break out between Baldwin and Montferrat.

He could hear Baldwin's voice long before he reached the Emperor's tent, and he paused to listen and compose his face.

When he had been merely Count of Flanders and Hainault, Baldwin had seldom raised his voice except on the field of battle. He had been the least ruffled of men, the most even-tempered, the most courteous, the army's best-loved battalion commander. And he had not begun to change until after the elaborate ceremony which raised him to a kingship only a little less than divine.

The changes were at first so subtle that few had remarked them, a hasty, ill-chosen word spoken in the flush of anger, a demand made too imperiously, a new attention to the details of ceremony where once he had casually dispensed with formality, a look of suspicion and disbelief on a face formerly open and compellingly trusting, a gradual turning away from old friends and their blunt remarks, a preference for the company of knights who fawned and played the courtier, a loss of the sense of oneness with his troops. He was less approachable than he once had been, less willing to unquestioningly accept decisions made in council, insistent that his own views be given more than equal weight. He was taking his election seriously, not as a man who knows that it came about through haggling and compromise, but as one who, being born to inherit a throne, believes it to be his natural and God-given due.

Power attracts little men, base men who bask in its warmth and delude themselves into thinking that they share it, direct it, uphold it, give it because they accede to it. They stand just outside its sphere, of course, but consider themselves indispensable. And by persuading the man who rules to this action or that other, they feel more kingly than the individual who wears the crown. Those who have reigned long and well know this. But Baldwin, emperor for only a few months, did not.

He lost his temper often nowadays, since that is supposed to be the prerogative of kings, and seeing an emotion which he read as fear and respect on the faces of those at whom he railed, his outbursts became longer, louder, more uncontrolled. Mary would have gently mocked him back to reality and proportion, but though she had reportedly set sail from Flanders to join him, he had had no word of her since the city fell. Immune to the Salonika fever, Baldwin had contracted a worse disease, one that affects the mind more than the body, a sickness shared by only a very few men placed as highly as he. King John of England knew its fury; King Philip of France did not. One was feared, tolerated, intrigued against; the other was prayed for daily in hundreds of tiny churches.

Once the Emperor had been a commander so solicitous for his troops' welfare that it was the marvel of the army. Now Boniface enjoyed that distinction. Baldwin rode headlong through summer's heat leading a column of dead and dying men, and his soldiers whispered that a devil had entered into the body of their lord.

St. Pol stood listening as Baldwin's voice rose and fell. The Emperor's tirade was winding down. A knight stepped from the tent, but as the Count approached he waved him back apologetically.

"Not yet, my lord," he said. "The Emperor is demanding that John of Noyon be brought to him."

"John of Noyon died at Cetros," said St. Pol.

"For the moment he has forgotten that," the knight replied, fear of and loyalty to his suzerain making his voice crack with emotion. "Others are with him and soon he will remember and call for you, my lord. He prizes your counsel above all others now." The man's voice was pleading.

St. Pol ignored the unseemly remark. "I will be with my cousin, who is dying," he said.

The knight crossed himself, but did not dare offer comfort to this great lord so far above him in station. St. Pol walked away, toward the silence in which Peter of Amiens lay.

Murtzuphles had begun it all, and once he did, the events of that summer following Constantinople's capture moved with blinding rapidity. He had never retreated further than a four days' march from the capital city he had lost, and within a few weeks of Baldwin's coronation struck the first blow designed to push his Western rival from the throne. He took and sacked the city of Tzurulum, a city which had peacefully surrendered to Baldwin and flown his banner on its walls. Everyone in Constantinople had agreed that the action could not go unpunished. The time had come to leave the capital and secure the rest of the realm before revolt broke out everywhere. Alexius III held Messinopolis and was growing stronger every day. Two ex-Emperors roaming the countryside made a mockery of Baldwin's kingship.

Henry of Flanders had taken one hundred good knights and set out to find Murtzuphles. But the crafty Greek remained always two or three days ahead of Henry's band. At Adrianople Henry halted. Baldwin would join the chase after he had assured himself of Constantinople's security in his absence. Louis of Blois, slowly recovering from his long and almost fatal illness, would remain behind, as would the Doge. The old man could not be expected to keep up with a fast-moving army.

Baldwin had another reason for leaving him in Constantinople. Ever since the election the Doge had openly displayed his affection for the emperor he had created, supplying him with a wealth of information gathered by a hitherto unsuspected network of Venetian spies. If a man in his cups dared to suggest that Montferrat after all should have been elected emperor, his name and remarks were within the hour whispered privily into Baldwin's ear. Conon of Béthune and Villehardouin might rule the city militarily on Baldwin's own command, but the Doge was the Emperor's guarantee that the heart of his kingdom would remain loyal in spirit as well as fact. Miles the Brabant and Manasses of l'Isle had protested at being left behind; they longed to escape the boredom of occupying a captured city. Baldwin laughed at their entreaties, but did not change his mind.

Adrianople welcomed Baldwin royally, and in the midst of the festivities had come messengers with the unbelievable news that Murtzuphles was no longer to be feared. Over and over they told the story while the Franks relished the details and even acted them out in the palace's great banquet hall.

Here comes the murderer Murtzuphles, wandering the land with two women in tow, Alexius III's wife, the Empress Euphrosyne, and his daughter Eudoxie, whom Murtzuphles had ravished, then married after his precipitous flight from Constantinople. Crusaders harry him until at last he flees to Messinopolis and humbles himself before Alexius. Euphrosyne whispers in her husband's ear and evil Alexius's eyes begin to gleam. He welcomes Murtzuphles as a son and another wedding is celebrated. Eudoxie attempts to protest the regularization of her unwelcome union. Tut, tut, says Alexius to his daughter and sends her off to her husband's tents outside the city. A few days pass until one morning Alexius invites his son-in-law to dine with him and enjoy the baths. Off goes Murtzuphles with only a few attendants. What devil fears another? Murtzuphles strips naked and is about to step into the baths when Alexius beckons to him, hinting at a secret delight kept for his guest in a nearby chamber. Murtzuphles, holding his father-in-law's arm conspiratorially, enters the tiny room, where he is thrown to the floor and his eyes are gouged out. Eudoxie steps from the shadows, crushes the eyeballs underfoot and gracefully thanks her father for avenging her. What father would do any less for a daughter, says Alexius, and off they sweep to dine.

The travesty grew more obscene with each repetition and nat-

urally enough the actors added a sequel in which Alexius himself was captured and subjected to all the gruesome tortures the
inventive Franks could devise. Greek servants, watching the
drunken young knights cavort for their commander's pleasure,
shook their heads as new hopes were born in them. Barbarians,
they whispered to one another, like so many other outlandish
peoples who had sought to devour their civilization. Obviously
their reign would not be a long one.

The lure of Alexius III sitting comfortably in Messinopolis
was too great for Baldwin to resist. Leaving Eustace of Saubruic
in command of a garrison of forty knights and one hundred
mounted sergeants, he led the rest of the army in a quick and
easy march to Messinopolis. But Alexius had fled the city, moving in the direction of Salonika, according to the Greeks Baldwin
interrogated. It was a potentially tricky situation. Salonika
belonged now to Montferrat. Technically Baldwin could not
move onto his vassal's lands without the latter's knowledge and
consent. He decided to await the Marquis at Messinopolis, but
as the days passed with no sign of Montferrat and his troops, his
annoyance at the Marquis's tardiness turned to anger and suspicion.

At last Montferrat arrived, pitched his camp by the river outside the city and sent messengers to Baldwin with a request that
surprised and infuriated the Emperor. The Marquis wished to
go alone to his new kingdom where, he had been told, the people were ready to receive him as their lord with appropriate
gifts and homage. The city and kingdom of Salonika were
among the richest in the world, but if Baldwin let loose his army
in pursuit of Alexius they would be ravaged and despoiled, to
the great detriment of their lawful ruler. Let Baldwin turn his
attention elsewhere for the moment and Montferrat would soon
return to aid him in conquering the rest of his lands, bringing
much-needed supplies and a contingent of Greek soldiers to
swell the ranks of the army.

In spite of his anger Baldwin hesitated. The Marquis's request
was, after all, so reasonable. But, pointed out certain members of
his council, the Marquis would have to travel slowly to Salonika
because of the Empress and the two royal children who accom-

panied him, and Alexius would make good his escape. Look how long it had taken him to arrive in Messinopolis. And there were other considerations. Salonika was so near the Kingdom of Hungary that Montferrat might be tempted to pay greater homage to his new brother-in-law than to his Emperor. He was setting himself up as a king in his own right, and unless he was taught early that Baldwin would tolerate no infringement on his imperial authority, his ambitions would merely increase with time.

Brusquely Baldwin's envoys informed the Marquis that the Emperor would go to Salonika with or without his vassal's consent. Alexius was the prize he must have, and if Montferrat could not understand that, then he and all his followers could go to the devil.

The Marquis took the insult in silence and without further protests. He remained in his tent by the river when Baldwin and his army rode out, and the Emperor's councillors congratulated him on bringing the proud Marquis to heel at last.

It was a triumphal march, unmarred by resistance from any of the castles and cities along the way. One by one they opened their gates to Baldwin, acknowledged him Emperor, did him homage. So many tongue-twisting Greek names. Only one, Blache, easily became La Blanche. His spirits alternately exalted by so swift a conquest and depressed because there was no sign of the wily Alexius, Baldwin at last reached the city of Salonika, one of the most beautiful and wealthy in Christendom—second only to Constantinople, his advisers pointed out. The city surrendered, but not unconditionally. Baldwin's army was not permitted to enter and the Emperor had to agree to respect the Greek customs of the populace. That he should have to accept any conditions at all galled him, but, he reminded himself, agreements made under duress were easily and lawfully broken.

It was on the third day of their encampment that news of the Marquis's treachery reached them, and Baldwin, staring hungrily at the walls of sparkling, beautiful Salonika, made the vow that needlessly cost so many valiant men their lives.

Montferrat had remained at Messinopolis only until Baldwin was at a safe distance, beyond the reach of rumor. Then he had marched his army to the castle of Demotica, accepted its surrender and urged the Greeks of the area to join him in destroying their hated Latin Emperor. He grandly renounced all his lawful claims in favor of his stepson Manuel, whom he promised to make Emperor in Baldwin's place. The Greeks were overjoyed at the thought of the civil war Montferrat was precipitating, and whether or not they supported the young Manuel, whose reign would have to be supervised by a regent for many years to come, they flocked in great numbers to Montferrat's army. The city of Adrianople was currently encircled by Montferrat's troops, though the loyal Eustace of Saubruic had sworn never to surrender it. But every day Montferrat paraded the Empress and her two children before the walls and it was only a question of time before the Greeks within overran the small Frankish garrison and opened their gates to Manuel's stepfather.

It was only early August, but in the short space of four months an emperor had lost both his crown and his eyes and Baldwin and Montferrat, once indifferent allies, had become bitter enemies. The old territorial loyalties of Western Europe were beginning to break down also, as knights from Flanders and France coolly deserted the barons they had followed all the long way from home to join themselves, as blatantly as any mercenary, to the Italian marquis whose star seemed to be rising once more. Many of them were prepared to switch loyalties as often as necessary, quite certain that since the size of the pool of available fighting men would necessarily remain the same, both Baldwin and Montferrat would be playing a game of numbers. No embarrassing questions would be asked.

Within hours of receiving the news, the army had broken camp and begun to retrace its steps, moving at a pace that exhausted men and animals alike, driven on by Baldwin's implacable fury and his solemn vow to personally rend the Marquis limb from limb. A strange fever had taken a few victims even during the brief stay at Salonika, but now, on the road, it swept mercilessly through the ranks until even Baldwin's closest advisers counseled prudence. But he would not stop. The dead were hastily buried along the route, the sick and dying strapped to their horses or carried in improvised litters, their piteous moaning rising above the clatter of harness and the beat of the horses' hooves.

Now, tonight, another man would die, a man whose bravery and honor had surely earned him a better end than this.

Peter regained consciousness briefly, just long enough to recognize the faces of the three men who knelt beside him.

"Serve my cousin of St. Pol as well as you have served me," he said to Robert, the words bubbling in his throat.

"I will, my lord. I swear it."

St. Pol held his cousin's right hand in his. Peter reached out his left to Robert. With his last reserve of strength he brought the two together so that as he died the four hands lay clasped on Peter's chest. They felt his last breath leave his body, and as the lifeless fingers slipped away, Robert placed his hands between St. Pol's and became his man.

"The Emperor requires your presence, my lord," said the knight who had been standing patiently for ten minutes or more in the moonlight.

"From this day forward you will ride beside me," said St. Pol, ignoring the interruption.

"Yes, my lord." Robert withdrew his hands and gently drew Peter's lids down over his staring eyes.

"May he rest in peace," murmured St. Pol, then rose to his feet to attend his emperor.

"I wish he had not asked it of me," Robert said later, when he and Aleaumes had finished preparing the body for burial. "I swore that I would take no new oath, but at the end I could not refuse him."

"What will you do now?" Aleaumes asked.

"My duty," answered Robert dully. "I have no other choice."

The fever seemed to have burned itself out with Peter's death. A few others died as the march continued, but no new cases broke out. Robert rode at St. Pol's side as he had sworn to do, but the Count often seemed unaware of his presence. He was in the grip of an introspective melancholy, and not even Baldwin's delight at coming closer and closer each day to the perfidious Marquis could shake him from it. He spoke seldom, and then in an abstracted monotone that proved his thoughts lay elsewhere.

They were only a few days' ride from Adrianople when envoys from Constantinople intercepted them with letters from Louis of Blois and the Doge. Unwilling to halt his progress, Baldwin refused to dismount, ripping open and scanning the letters while his army streamed by. He glared at Bègues of Fransures, who had ridden night and day to find the Emperor, and the knight returned the look steadfastly and without the slightest trace of fear.

"If Montferrat thinks to save himself by this ridiculous charade," thundered Baldwin, "he is badly mistaken. We will continue to march to Adrianople, where I will mete out to him the punishment he so richly deserves."

"The siege has been raised, my lord. The Marquis has retired to Demotica with the Empress his wife."

"Then I will attack Demotica," said Baldwin, flinging the letters from Constantinople to the ground. The hot wind blew them across the flat plain and the Emperor watched in satisfaction. "So shall the Marquis be swept from my sight," he declared.

"My lord," said Bègues of Fransures wearily, "I am entrusted with oral messages also. My lord of Blois, whose liege man I am, commands me to inform you that neither he nor the Doge nor any other baron will permit you to war against the Marquis of Montferrat. And further, that those of your councillors who fomented ill will between you two are greatly blamed and condemned for their action. Montferrat has agreed to submit his grievances to arbitration. He has placed his case in the hands of the noble Doge of Venice, of Count Louis of Blois, of Conon of Béthune and of the Marshal of Champagne, who persuaded him to lift the siege and earned all our thanks by that action. He accepts as binding the decision of these barons, and they strongly urge you to do likewise."

By the time Bègues of Fransures finished speaking, St. Pol had halted the column and ridden to Baldwin's side. Baldwin turned on him angrily, but St. Pol, his lethargy gone now, urged that the Emperor at least meet with his advisers before sending a hasty and perhaps unwise reply to Constantinople. It would take no more than an hour, he urged, and the men and horses would move more swiftly for the brief rest.

Grudgingly Baldwin gave in. The council met on horseback,

just out of earshot of the worried Bègues of Fransures, who watched apprehensively as fists were shaken in the air while the horses, responsive to their riders' emotions, whinnied and pawed their hooves restlessly. St. Pol alone remained calm in the midst of voices that were raised higher and higher until even Bègues of Fransures could no longer pretend that he did not hear the shouted arguments.

"It is monstrous, my lord, monstrous!"

"It is your right to take vengeance on your enemy. None can deny you it."

"My lord, these men are your vassals, yet they dare to sit in judgment on you. They dare to order you to obey their commands. It is they who deserve harsh judgment."

"They threaten to rebel against their rightful lord. It is plain enough, though they do not say it outright."

"My lord, the Doge is wise and farseeing. If he, too, counsels arbitration it must be for reasons he may wish to reveal only to you." St. Pol was insistent. "Return to Constantinople, but make no promise which binds you to your barons' will. The Marquis sits in Demotica like a rat caught in its burrow. He will not dare to leave it except at your pleasure. He gambled heavily, my lord, but the toss was a false one, and he must know it."

"Let there be a truce then," Baldwin finally said to Bègues of Fransures. "For the moment the Marquis has nothing to fear from me, but I make no promises, agree to nothing, do not submit my imperial will to any man's direction."

Bègues of Fransures sighed with relief. Once Baldwin reached Constantinople more persuasive voices than his would lead him to reconciliation with Montferrat. The survival of the kingdom—all their futures—depended on it.

For three days the barons bombarded Baldwin with their arguments, and as St. Pol had taken the precaution of informing the Doge just which members of Baldwin's council were hot for war, these men found it difficult to gain access to the Emperor. The palace was sealed off to them by the faction urging peace. On the fourth day Baldwin broke. Yes, he now admitted, perhaps he had been ill-advised. But he was quick to add that an error in judgment did not necessarily signify evil intent. The

Doge was careful to preserve the fiction that the Emperor's pride was in no way humbled. Salonika was rich and strategically placed, but it was not the center of power. Baldwin, reigning in Constantinople, would find his arduous task lightened by the presence of a strong ally in Salonika. Montferrat was a reasonable man. Treat him honorably and he would be loyal.

Five envoys were sent to Demotica. Almost too easily Villehardouin persuaded Montferrat to leave his stronghold and return with them to Constantinople. The Emperor was anxious to make peace and to formally invest the Marquis with the promised kingdom of Salonika.

One hundred knights accompanied Montferrat to the capital, their presence resented but overlooked. "There is no quarrel between us," Baldwin privately assured his guest. "Salonika is yours. An Emperor does not break his word. But if you still doubt my intention, I will give you further surety. Villehardouin will hold Demotica in your name until you send him word that you have secured Salonika. And I will send envoys of mine to accompany you, so that your people will know that it is my will that you be obeyed and honored."

Montferrat guessed that it had cost the Emperor an enormous effort to make his speech. It was plain that Baldwin had no real affection for his former commander. As he rode to his promised kingdom, he mused on the changes power wrought in a man's character. The milksop, the easily persuaded one, had become a hungry eagle. In Baldwin's place Montferrat knew that he would have dealt harshly with so rebellious a baron as he had become. Prison or a quick knife thrust in the dark would have settled the quarrel for all time. But Baldwin had not yet learned the tricks of kingship. Montferrat was immensely pleased with himself. His reading of the Emperor's vacillating nature had been correct. And as usual the other barons, even the Doge, had unknowingly played his game. He had Salonika, he had an empress to wife, and he had Manuel. He would pacify Salonika and all the lands surrounding it and he would bide his time.

By the end of September the country between Salonika and Constantinople was as secure as any European duchy. It was a good twelve days' ride between the two cities, but messengers rode back and forth in perfect security, bringing to the capital news of Montferrat's vigorous war against Leon Sgure, a Greek who had allied himself with Alexius III through the ex-Emperor's oft-married daughter Eudoxie. He held Corinth and Nauphlie, but soon Montferrat would lay siege to these two cities and he was confident that the campaign would be brief.

The Emperor sent messages of encouragement, then turned his attention to the division of the rest of his kingdom. The barons and knights were bored in Constantinople, a city that was only slowly being rebuilt from its ashes.

Louis of Blois received the duchy of Nicea, and on All Saints' Day, November 1, Pierre of Bracieux, Payen d'Orléans and one hundred twenty of Louis's best knights left to conquer the Count's new lands.

There was a continual stream of men leaving Constantinople in November; Renier of Trit took one hundred twenty knights to capture Philippolis, another one hundred crossed the Straits with Macaire of Sainte-Menehould to subdue Nicomedia, one hundred twenty more set out with Henry of Flanders for Abydos and many others slipped quietly off to join Boniface.

Even as the conquerors of Constantinople were leaving the city, ships arrived from Syria bearing many who had waited out the war in more comfortable surroundings. Stephen of Perche, who had not been seen since Venice, arrived with a large force of men and was given the duchy of Philadelphia. Renaud of Montmirail, who had deserted from Zara, popped up again like a bad coin to demand his share of the spoils, Thierri of Tenremonde arrived just in time to join Henry of Flanders's expedition.

Robert of Clari received nothing. Nor was he the only knight who found himself landless in the new country he had conquered. The pattern that had held him fast—in a poverty all the more bitter to bear because he belonged, in theory at least, to the ruling warrior caste that lorded it over merchants, artists, craftsmen, minor clergy, free peasants and those bound to the land—was being repeated with no regard for the changes war might have made possible.

The finality of the deception and the theft which had been

practiced on the vast majority of the knights who made up the middle ranks of the army was evident as soon as they returned from Salonika. The three churches in which piles of treasure had lain were empty. The barons and the Doge had divided the caches among themselves, and each man had had his portion inventoried, carted off, and locked up securely in the hidden vaults of the palace he occupied.

Their greed was thorough and well calculated; not a single loose gem escaped them. Groups of angry younger knights visited each church in turn, only to find them swept as bare and clean as an industrious farmwife's kitchen. When they protested, and they did, both individually and together, they were told that they had in fact and in truth been promised nothing but the wages already paid them. Their rage and frustration, intensified by the awful affront to their pride and this callous reminder that they were afforded scarcely more courtesy and thought than the common foot soldier, were quickly spent. They threatened to kill the clerks and minor household officials whom the barons had deputized to deal with them, shook mailed fists in their vapid, full-fleshed faces, brandished swords above their heads, knocked one or two to the ground, bloodied a nose, loosened a few teeth. Nothing more, because they knew themselves defeated.

With nearly empty purses and not even roofs over their heads, for the houses they had appropriated after the city's fall had also been taken away from them, given to Venetians, traders, knights who had stayed behind, even bands of filthy pilgrims who were armed and quite prepared to defend themselves, the newly impoverished knights consoled themselves in the unsavory wine-shops that dotted all the harbor areas. They slept by day, lurched drunkenly around the city in the early evening hours, and by nightfall were once more insensible.

Robert kept himself apart, no longer willing to join any group, any faction, any band that too loudly promised action. He served St. Pol, kept his thoughts to himself, did his drinking privately, and as early fall turned into early winter, ticked off in his mind the name of each young knight who sobered himself up, had his sword polished, his armor refurbished, his garments washed and his hair cut. One by one they returned to duty, collected the fees earned in old, familiar service, left Constantinople to ride under the banners of the wealthy, powerful lords who had cheated them. The system worked even better here than it had in France; there were no equally important lords to challenge those who claimed everything.

The exodus was completed by the end of November. Only the highest-ranking barons and their household knights remained in the city, and only because they so distrusted Baldwin and one another that close daily contact was judged an imperative safeguard against further intrigue and cabal.

Constantinople settled down to endure another winter, but before the first snow fell, before the first good reports reached the Emperor of new castles and cities captured, garrisoned and made secure, Thierri of Loos brought his sovereign a gift that was the envy of every other knight.

By an incredible stroke of luck Thierri and his men had surprised the ex-Emperor Murtzuphles in a narrow ravine. Although blind and nearly powerless, Murtzuphles had managed to gather around him a small band of followers, chiefly former court officials and their ladies who rode with him from town to town, finding, if nothing else, at least beds to sleep in and food to eat. There were still places where he was revered, where his midnight desertion of Constantinople had somehow become a narrowly managed, death-defying escape in the face of overwhelming odds, where the true story of his blinding was unknown.

The party accompanying Murtzuphles was neither capable of fighting nor inclined to do so. One and all they surrendered, even before Thierri had called out to them to lay down the few arms they carried, most of them quite content to return to Constantinople, quite prepared to swear allegiance to the new Emperor and slip unobtrusively back into the sinecures they had once enjoyed. They had done nothing deserving of either death or close imprisonment.

Murtzuphles' fate was, of course, already decided. He had usurped a throne, murdered an anointed king. He was a dead man, only the place and manner of his execution a subject for debate. And they did debate among themselves, Baldwin, Louis of Blois, St. Pol, Villehardouin, rejecting, one after another, the forms of death familiar to them, as well as the exotic variations that were more common in the East than in the civilized West.

The Doge's suggestion was the one finally adopted. "For a high man, high justice," Dandolo proclaimed, and the catchy phrase, so apt, so succinct, so unforgettable, was soon on everyone's lips.

Murtzuphles was taken to one of the two high columns in the Forum of Theodosius, the same columns into which the fall of Constantinople had been carved, and at whose summits hermits had once dwelt. He was led up the winding inner staircase, stripped naked at the top, guided to the edge by two soldiers holding fast to his arms, displayed to the silent, watching crowds below, then given a choice. He could leap or he could be pushed. He chose to leap, defiant, black-browed, angry to the end, a man outlined against the winter sky, a bone-shattered, blood-gushing mass of bubbling brain and ruptured inner organs lying inert and lifeless on the ground.

Someone remarked that among the sculptures on the column from which he had jumped was one that depicted an emperor falling to his death. It had all been foreseen a very long time ago. Only the name of the emperor had been omitted from the prophecy.

Montferrat, fully occupied in far-off Salonika, did not witness Murtzuphles' death. He did, however, send congratulations to Baldwin at having dispatched his enemy in such a satisfying manner, and he sent something else, too: the scarlet buskins and the imperial vestments which neither Murtzuphles nor Baldwin had ever worn. Alexius III and his empress were Montferrat's prisoners. The man who had blinded his own brother, from whom a nephew had fled in terror of his life, who had run away from his capital city long before it fell, who had laughed to see his daughter grind her husband's eyes to jelly, this same pitiless, spineless, decadent, pleasure-addicted man would, in a few months' time, find himself a closely guarded captive in the Marquis's native province in Italy, with only his wife, and she very inept at the task, to distract and amuse him.

Baldwin ordered a great feast to celebrate the death of one emperor and the capture of another, a meal of celebration which he planned to attend in the garments held sacred by every Greek, garments which even the jaded Latins had not dared to touch. The only trapping of Eastern royalty he did not now possess was a Waring bodyguard. Had he been unfortunate enough to have succeeded in employing any one of those grudge-bearing giants his throat would have been slit or his brains axed out long ago. As it was, he surrounded himself with the handsomest, the blondest, the tallest young knights of his retinue, fondly imagining that their loyalty was as deep as that any emperor had ever enjoyed.

But the feast was never held. From Acre arrived a ship of mourning, a ship whose sails had been dyed black. Even before it reached anchorage Baldwin knew that only Mary, his wife, could have commanded such a display of love. She had given birth to a daughter, then set out to join her husband. Her ship had sailed from Marseilles to Acre, where she first learned of Baldwin's election and coronation. The lady's joy was brief, for before the ship could be readied for the last leg of the journey, the August heat of Acre overcame her. She fell ill and died, her husband's name the last to issue from her lips.

The court immediately became a place of mourning. The Emperor received no one, the administration of the kingdom was given into the hands of his councillors and all Constantinople prayed for the lady's soul while wondering which princess would journey from Europe to replace her.

Winter, while not the season for war, is always its true beginning. Old grievances are resurrected in crowded, smoke-filled halls, the summer's harvest of dusky, fermented grain and sun-ripened grape drunk deeply against the cold and the short, empty days whose hours drag and seem sometimes unending. New alliances are contemplated, plans laid, battles fought and won in the bright light of the imagination, manhood reaffirmed in strange, casually warmed beds. It was no different in Constantinople than it had been in France, Flanders, Germany or northern Italy. One stayed close to the den in winter, waiting for spring, grateful for every day that passed without fever and sickness, remembering other, harsher winters, deeper snows, thicker ice, cloudier, darker skies.

Louis of Blois was ill again, his cough deeper than last year, his face more flushed, his fever hotter and his limbs more painful. But this time at least he had a soft bed to lie in, solid ground beneath him, and all the comforts a well-staffed kitchen and decent cellar could offer. He would get well eventually, when the sun came out to dry up the fluids in his chest and balance the heat within with heat from without.

One who would not recover was Hugh of St. Pol, who collapsed during Holy Mass on Christmas Day, feebly protesting, even while he was being carried to his bedchamber, that it was only the long Advent fast that had made him light-headed. But when his heavily embroidered wool robe was removed and the soft linen undergarment drawn over his head, a physician was sent for at once. It was obvious now to everyone who served him that for weeks St. Pol had been walking on legs as swollen and reddened as those of any woman suffering from milk fever.

The physician diagnosed the Count's affliction as gout and applied leeches to the balloonlike legs and feet to draw out the poisonous fluids. He came often throughout January and early February, then daily as that Lenten month wore on, bleeding his patient at the close of every visit, so that St. Pol's legs and arms were soon crisscrossed with scalpel marks and bits of the plaster used to seal off the wounds inflicted by the anxious doctor. He should have improved with this treatment, but he did not. The swelling crept upward through his body, stealing stealthily among the hidden parts no doctor ever sees, to burst out into arms and hands. At last he could not even bend his fingers.

Robert, who slept in a tiny chamber adjoining the Count's, knew that his master was in almost continual pain. He was often unable to sleep for the moans that not even St. Pol's tremendous will could stifle.

"I have a fire in my belly," he told Robert, "that no physician can cure. It will consume me until I am nothing but an empty shell. And perhaps I have deserved this suffering, for I only lately came to be a man who values peace."

Except for the enormously distended hands and feet, the Count's body was shrinking daily as the flesh gathered into itself. His ribs protruded against his yellow skin like the naked structures of the vessels Robert had seen in Venice's shipyards.

Toward the end of February Robert knew that he could delay no longer. St. Pol's hours of lucidity were more and more uncertain. His physician had despaired of saving him and now sought only to ease his sufferings with drugs he had obtained from certain Greek apothecaries, drugs that induced slumber though they did not cure.

It was nearly dawn, and for almost an hour St. Pol had been whispering of France, conjuring up visions of his youth and of campaigns against the English in which he had ridden proudly at his king's side. The pain was surfacing again even as he told Robert of how he had come to take the cross, out of piety and duty, he insisted, with no thought of earthly reward. In a few moments he would be forced to beg for the physician's potion and soon afterward he would slip into the merciful unconsciousness that was now his only refuge from the fear of approaching death.

"My lord," said Robert, choosing his words carefully, speaking slowly and distinctly, "I too find my thoughts fixed on France these days."

"Be patient, Robert. You have been faithful to me and your release will come soon."

"My lord . . ."

"I know what you would say and what you ask of me. I grant your request, Robert, for I can read it in your eyes. When I die you become your own man, bound to no lord of this kingdom." St. Pol reached for the cup that was just beyond his fingertips. Robert held it to his lips as the Count thirstily drained it of its contents. He sank back upon his pillows, waiting for the blessed oblivion to steal over him.

"Are your lands fruitful in Picardy?" he asked.

"It is a small manor, my lord, but with careful management we prosper on it."

"Who administers it in your absence?" The Count was becoming drowsy, his words blurred and difficult to understand. "Tell me about it. Stay with me yet awhile."

"My lady mother keeps the manor," said Robert, drawing St. Pol's covers over the body that alternately shivered with cold and sweated in fever. "I have a son named Peter in honor of my late lord, your cousin." He sat down on the edge of the Count's bed, telling his story softly, soothingly, the tone of his voice more important than the meaning of the words he uttered. "My father rode with Philip Augustus to the Holy Land. He died of a sickness contracted there. But he died happy, knowing that his grandson had been baptized and would live. My lady died giving birth to him. Her name was Aelis and she welcomed death because her life was not the one she would have chosen."

St. Pol's eyes were closed and his breathing was easier. Robert poured himself a cup of the strong wine that eased the Count's pain and stood gazing at the fire. A few more minutes to be sure St. Pol's sleep was deep and he could at last go to bed himself. He thought of the house at Clari and the old woman and tiny child who lived there with none but servants' company, and he felt the hope that sustained Lady Agatha and made her days bearable.

Gilo had returned from his quest broken, ill and poorer than when he had set out. Robert would at least bring with him death gifts from St. Pol: a sum of money almost equal to the entire value of Clari, and two cross-shaped reliquaries, one of silver and gold filigree, the other of crystal, both containing pieces of the True Cross. They had come from one of the chapels of the Boucoleon Palace, but whether the Count had taken them from their altars with his own hands or was merely given them later on Robert did not know. With gold to spend he could at last replace the older, wooden portion of the main manor building with a strong new structure of stone. He had planned it room by room throughout the long winter months of the Count's suffering.

A high tower, it would rise from the land to stand sentinel over his son's inheritance. And he would build other structures too, living quarters that were spacious, warm and private. The Greeks knew how to build for comfort, and though Robert's new home would not be luxurious, he would harry and direct the workmen until his partially Greek house was completed. In years to come companions of this crusade would drift back to France and they would find their way to Clari, to sit and reminisce by the fire, to refight old battles and argue over what had gone wrong. His son would stand at his knee and listen open-eyed to the tales, but after the guests had gone, before the child came to prefer illusion to reality, Robert would tell his version of the expedition. Perhaps he would even dictate it to one of the monks at

Corbie. He was no historian and the tale was a bitter one. Lived there a clerk courageous enough to accuse the princes of this world of treachery, greed and betrayal?

Aleaumes would do it, but Robert had not seen his brother for months. He had gone off to Demotica with St. Pol's men, dressed and armed like a knight, with the Count's promise that his pay would be equal to that of every other knight in the garrison. He had become less and less the clerk after Peter of Amiens's death, and while that might be overlooked in this new land which badly needed fighting men, his bishop in Amiens would never tolerate scandal touching one of his clerks. Robert wondered if, when the time came to choose, Aleaumes might not decide to remain in Constantinople. In Picardy he had nothing to look forward to but the cloister.

St. Pol died in March and was buried in the monastery of St. George of Mangana. Even before the feather-light body had been carried to its last resting-place Baldwin's men came recruiting.

War had broken out again with the arrival of spring, and in only a few weeks the situation had grown nearly hopeless. In every corner of the kingdom the Greeks were revolting against their Latin masters. Johanizza, King of Bulgaria, supplied them with money and troops from his own lands, directing the rebellion from afar. The Emperor needed every man who could wield a sword.

Robert listened, but promised nothing. Even when the enraged Manasses of l'Isle called him coward and traitor, he merely smiled and murmured vaguely that perhaps after the Count's obsequies were completed and his effects properly disposed of, perhaps then he would be at liberty to pledge himself to Baldwin's cause. But for the moment duty bound him to his dead lord. He had a vigil to keep, he reminded Manasses, who had been so desperate that he had pursued St. Pol's household knights into the very chapel in which the Count's body lay. Reluctantly Baldwin's emissary left them in peace, both the living and the dead.

He came again a few days later to announce that the Greeks

in Demotica had massacred the Franks of the garrison on direct orders from the King of Bulgaria. Now, he insisted, St. Pol's men no longer had a choice. Demotica had belonged to the Count; honor demanded that they join Baldwin's army to avenge the wrong done while St. Pol lay dying. Some refugees from Demotica had reached Adrianople, but there, too, the Greeks had risen and only a few survivors had escaped to Tzurulum. Arcadiopolis, a Venetian-held city, had also been attacked. The Greeks had been beaten back, but the Franks had not dared remain there. Tzurulum was swollen with refugees and a major offensive was even now being planned by Baldwin, the Doge and Count Louis.

Manasses of l'Isle had made his point. St. Pol's household knights, few in number and uncertain where their loyalties now lay, packed their gear and moved to quarters set aside for the officers of Baldwin's army. Robert remained with a few clerks in the small, almost deserted palace, supervising the final disposition of St. Pol's papers and personal effects. In the morning he supposed that he, too, would present himself before Baldwin's field commander. There seemed to be no other alternative.

The clerks retired just before midnight. The last document had been cataloged and safely deposited in one of the huge iron boxes that stood stacked in what had once been an audience chamber, and St. Pol's worn everyday garments lay piled in a heap for distribution to the city's poor. The chief clerk had reported that even the kitchen servants had been paid and dismissed. Doubtless the palace would lie open and deserted for a few days until the hordes of homeless Greeks in the city discovered it. After that it would fall gradually into ruin. It was a sad state of affairs, he went on companionably. After the conquest was completed many Latins would doubtless flock to Constantinople, but in the meantime it was a city inhabited by ghosts. The clerk shifted about on his feet, eyeing the wine at Robert's elbow, but the knight did not offer to share it, and presently he excused himself and disappeared into the darkness of the palace.

An hour later Robert heard stealthy, animal-like noises in the corridor outside the room in which he had dozed off. He was stiff from having fallen asleep in his chair, but all his senses came alert as the soft footsteps moved closer. He was on his feet, sword in hand, long before the door opened. The clerk had spoken of Greeks coming to live in squalor in these very rooms, but surely not even one of the half-mad, starving creatures who infested the back alleys of Constantinople had dared to come so soon. The hair on the back of his neck prickled as he stood to one side of the door, waiting to destroy with one swift stroke whatever nighttime apparition breathed so heavily on the other side.

"Robert?" The door was opened only a handbreadth, and the whisper was soft.

"Aleaumes, you fool. I might have killed you." Robert flung the door wide and clasped his brother in his arms. The sword banged against Aleaumes' back as Robert pounded him joyfully.

"You look terrible," he said, stepping back to look at Aleaumes. "Manasses of l'Isle said . . ."

"Manasses of l'Isle is a fool and so is every other Frank in this kingdom," said Aleaumes bitterly. "Is that wine I see over there?"

"The last and the best of the cellars. I'll pour you a cup while you tell me what happened. I thought you were at Tzurulum with the others."

"I was, briefly," said Aleaumes, sinking into a chair and gratefully accepting the cup Robert hastily filled for him. "That's good," he said, draining it at a single gulp.

Robert quickly refilled it, though his hand shook and the wine spilled onto the floor. Aleaumes was thin and haggard, incredibly dirty, and his garments were practically in rags.

"It was a massacre, a rout," he was saying. "They crept into our quarters just before dawn and killed every man there as he slept. I was on guard that night, but we were looking for signs of Johanizza's army, not for an uprising within the castle. We fought them off as best we could, but it was useless. Only a handful of us were able to hack our way out. It was the same story in Adrianople, only worse. Tzurulum is so packed with refugees that people are sleeping in the streets and glad to find a corner or a doorway to curl up in. I left with the messengers William of Blanvel sent to Constantinople. Blanvel is a brave man, but an idiot. He is urging Baldwin to come out against Johanizza and Baldwin is listening to him."

"I know," said Robert.

"Johanizza's army is huge, Robert, according to the rumors we have heard. He has fourteen thousand Cumans alone marching with him, and that's only a fraction of the total. There's no holding any of the cities. As soon as the Greeks spy Johanizza's army they'll rise up. We can't fight enemies without and within."

"St. Pol is dead."

"We heard in Demotica that he was dying. I almost went crazy in Tzurulum until I persuaded Blanvel to let me ride with his messengers. No man is safe alone on the roads."

"How did you manage it?"

"I convinced him that I could persuade St. Pol's knights to join the army Baldwin is raising. He believed me because he's desperate for reinforcements."

"Manasses of l'Isle did the job for you," said Robert. "I'm the only one left here, and he expects me to join the others tomorrow morning."

"Will you?"

"Will you?"

"No. It's all over. And I have no wish to fling my body gloriously on the ax of some unbaptized, bloodthirsty savage." Aleaumes paused before continuing. "Before I came here I went to the harbor. There are five Venetian ships being readied to sail."

"And every day Baldwin sends messengers imploring them to stop the work and remain. They are merchant ships, owned by the captains who sail them. Not even the Doge has had any influence.

"What cargo will they carry?"

"Crusaders and pilgrims, Aleaumes. As many as can be squeezed on board. It will be an uncomfortable voyage."

The brothers looked at one another. "I can pay for two passages with St. Pol's death gift," said Robert quietly.

"I am grateful, brother, more than I can say, and in your debt. If ever . . ."

"I will call upon you some day, Aleaumes, but if you decide

to help me it must be freely. Between brothers there can be no debts." Brusquely he changed the subject. "I was told the sailing could not be managed until mid-April."

"Then for several weeks we must disappear. I have hidden myself before, and in a city far smaller than Constantinople."

"We have no obligation to go with Baldwin, Aleaumes."

"No, but the waiting will be pleasanter if we are not constantly harassed. A man does foolish things when his honor is questioned. You might find yourself in Baldwin's army in spite of yourself."

It was not difficult to disappear in Constantinople that spring. For lack of sufficient soldiers to perform the duty, no regular watch patrolled the streets and the few Greeks Robert and Aleaumes met in their wanderings slipped quickly by them without ever lifting their eyes from the ground.

They found a little house on the outskirts of the city, far away from any area occupied by either Frank or Venetian, in a section so desolate and barren of life that it might have been another country altogether. All but one of the rooms were roofless, and the street on which it stood was blocked for its entire length with charred timbers and debris. It was a place given up for lost, and after several carefully executed forays for food and wine, they settled into their hideout, completely confident that they could remain there totally undisturbed until the ship on which they had taken passage was ready to sail.

For several days they did little but sleep, eat and sleep again, sometimes for twelve to fifteen hours at a stretch. In three years of nearly continuous compaigning neither had known more than a handful of nights during which he had rested well and truly. They were tired, tired to the very marrow of their bones.

On the fourth day they began to talk, sitting hunched over around a tiny fire, each with a jug of wine in easy reach. Aleaumes' first hesitant "Do you remember?" brought forth a host of memories, and first one, then the other would interrupt to question, correct, relive what neither could forget. They were very often drunk, so that the food supply, scarcely touched, lasted far longer than either had expected.

The things that hurt the most were the first spoken of, the first to be tenderly laid away again, pain a little less sharp, image a trifle less vivid, disappointment perhaps accepted and somewhat blunted. Robert did most of the early talking, though he seldom remembered what he had said.

"Not much really," Aleaumes told him. "I was too far gone myself to understand, whatever it was."

They reached a point where the wine no longer made them either sleepy, angry, sad or even maudlin. It merely sharpened their perceptions and drove Aleaumes to ask questions that were harder, almost impossible to answer.

"We should feel guilty that we didn't even try to reach Jerusalem," he said.

"We did try," Robert reminded him, "on Corfu."

"No, we didn't. We played at trying, acted out a charade, did it so badly that someone who should have known nothing of our plans knew everything. I remember that night on the hillside. One word from Peter and we would have left Montferrat and his little princeling. Just one word. But he didn't choose to speak it."

"He left each of us free to vote his own conscience."

"Free, Robert? How free? Did any one of us, knowing we would be dead within hours if left behind without ships on an island whose population had already proved itself hostile, call such a choice freedom? No, we compromised. Until Michaelmas, we said. And we sailed away to safety, glad our little moment of glorious rebellion was over."

"I don't know," Robert said, shaking his head.

"Nor do I," confessed Aleaumes. "I play it through in my mind from beginning to end, from the Isle of St. Nicholas to the streets of Tzurulum, and I can make no sense of any of it. Each league traveled, each tiny step, led us further away from the point at which we aimed."

"Does it matter?" Robert asked. "Can it really matter now?"

"I am a good Christian," Aleaumes said sharply, a trace of the old fire in his voice, "though I have not always been a good clerk. I ought to feel remorse, I have tried to feel it, but I cannot. I'm only sorry that the Empire will not last, that all the hopes and dreams are fading, that there is no bishopric for me here or anywhere. Perhaps I never believed we would reach Jerusalem. Perhaps that has been my sin."

"I wonder how many of us ever wanted to," said Robert quietly.

From talk each man retreated into silence, making decisions he was not yet ready to confide even to a brother.

EPILOGUE

Mid-March–April 18, 1205

The day after Robert and Aleaumes disappeared without a trace from St. Pol's palace, Villehardouin and Manasses of l'Isle were sent to Tzurulum, leaving Baldwin in Constantinople with barely a dozen knights. The Emperor fretted impatiently. Louis of Blois had recalled Payen d'Orléans and Pierre of Bracieux from Nicea, and Macaire of Sainte-Menehould was leading his men in forced marches from Nicomedia. Farthest away was Henry of Flanders, but he, too, had sent word that he would join up with the others as soon as possible. From Montferrat also came a promise of troops, even though his own war was still in progress. The threat from the King of Bulgaria had at last united the Franks.

Villehardouin moved to Arcadiopolis, then to Bulgaropolis, where he found the city deserted. The Greeks had fled to the safety of Adrianople. The Marshal of Champagne settled down to await Baldwin, urging the Emperor not to leave Constantinople until all the reinforcements had arrived.

But by the twenty-fifth of March Baldwin's patience was at an end. One hundred knights had arrived from Nicomedia, and with this small force the Emperor and Louis of Blois set out to rendezvous with Villehardouin.

Four days later they came in sight of Adrianople. The King of Bulgaria's flag flew above the city, and Baldwin ordered an immediate attack. It was easily beaten back and a siege was begun. For three days they anxiously scanned the plains for Henry of Flanders and Payen d'Orléans, and on the morning of the fourth the Doge arrived, doubling their number. He had seen no sign of the others and reported bands of heavily armed Greeks all along the way, too small in number to have challenged him, but obviously primed to join the King of Bulgaria's army. The Doge had known the necessity of traveling swiftly and had brought few supplies. Foragers were sent out led by Louis of Blois, but they returned bloodied and empty-handed. The hungry men were set to work building mangonels and catapults, digging tunnels to undermine the walls. The watch continued.

Easter was celebrated with feverish piety, but three days later scouts brought the news that Johanizza's army was camped only five leagues away. Almost before the scouts had finished their report the Cumans swept down upon them, a force of wild horsemen dressed in sheepskins, controlling their small mounts with their knees as hundreds of arrows poured from their bows.

They swerved before reaching the camp itself and galloped furiously off in the direction from which they had come. Some few of the Franks pursued them, but their heavy armor and huge chargers were no match for such light, mobile cavalry. The Cumans thought to draw them on, but in spite of the jeering, mocking faces of the enemy the knights turned back after a league or so and returned to camp, where they described the strategy to which they had almost fallen victim.

The next morning the Cumans were back, screaming and dancing their horses just beyond range. The Franks had vowed not to be tempted away from their camp, but the provocation was too much. Louis of Blois led his men out in pursuit of the Cumans, who had again turned to run. Two leagues away they wheeled their horses and attacked. Villehardouin and Manasses of l'Isle, guarding the vulnerable city side of the camp, pleaded with Baldwin to remember the battle plans agreed on the night before, but the Emperor shook them off disgustedly and rode to Louis's relief.

The battle lasted throughout the day while the wounded crawled and stumbled into camp with tales of unbelievable horror. Louis had been severely wounded in two places, knocked from his horse and then rescued by John of Friaise, who had pleaded with him to leave the field. He had refused and charged again. Now he was dead, and so was the faithful Friaise.

By Vespers what remained of the Frankish battalions had broken off the fight and was streaming back toward camp. Now Villehardouin and Manasses of l'Isle, threatening their men with swift and certain death if they left their posts, rode out to stop the rout and restore some semblance of order to the retreat. Miraculously they succeeded, and the Franks turned and held off the Cumans until nightfall.

They would have to withdraw before the next attack. Baldwin had been captured, alive, witnesses were certain, but the list of the dead was appalling. Robert of Ronsoi, Renaud of Montmirail, Matthew of Wallincourt, Stephen of Perche, Pierre, Bishop of Bethlehem. On and on it went, but there was no time for mourning, no time even to retrieve the bodies from the field where they had fallen.

Under cover of darkness they moved out, taking the wounded with them, led by the blind Doge toward the seaport of Rodesto. Villehardouin's men, who were not exhausted by combat, kept the rearguard. Rodesto was a three days' march, but it was their only hope.

Before Villehardouin's rearguard could stop him, Count Girard, a Lombard vassal of Montferrat, deserted the column, taking with him Odo of Ham and some twenty-five other knights. He had offered to ride by a more direct route to Constantinople earlier in the night, but Villehardouin had forbidden it. Every man would be needed to help and protect the wounded, and the Marshal of Champagne would leave no one behind to fall into the hands of the Cumans. No help could be expected from the capital anyway, so the offer was a coward's pretext for flight. Now, as he watched the band swing off and disappear into the night, Villehardouin felt himself shake with a killing rage. One day, he vowed, one day all Christendom will know the names of the animals who deserted their own kind and left them weaker than ever while their enemies pursued them. Somehow he would reach Rodesto and not a man would be lost along the way.

At dawn they sighted the towers of Pamphyle, but a sobbing moan of despair burst from the throats of the wounded as the city's gates opened and a party of horsemen thundered toward them in close battle formation. It was Payen d'Orléans and

Pierre of Bracieux, leading the reinforcements Baldwin had not waited for.

They listened in horror to Villehardouin's account of the disaster at Adrianople, swearing to rescue the Emperor from captivity. It was galling, humiliating, unbelievable that so many had died while they had rested themselves just one day's march away.

Villehardouin was almost insensible with fatigue when Pierre of Bracieux proposed an audacious lightning attack that would drive like a wedge into the center of Johanizza's army, where Baldwin presumably rode under heavy guard. But he immediately vetoed the plan, reminding the angry knight that he and he alone, by virtue of his rank, now commanded what was left of Baldwin's army. Johanizza's force numbered in the tens of thousands, and even with Pierre's one hundred knights and one hundred forty mounted sergeants, they were hardly a match for them. The Doge, looking far more fit than any of his much younger companions, agreed.

After a few hours' rest they moved out onto the plain, Payen d'Orléans' men guarding the rear of the column. At Cariopolis they again paused briefly, but Johanizza was only two leagues behind, so at nightfall, without fresh supplies and carrying barely enough water for the wounded, Villehardouin led them on the last leg of their journey.

They rode without stopping throughout that long night and the following day. Miraculously, none of the wounded died on the march. The immense force of the Marshal's will somehow kept them alive. Late Saturday night they reached Rodesto. The Greeks in the city offered no resistance to men who, they sensed, were desperate enough to kill for even a defiant look, and the King of Bulgaria gave up the chase and turned his back on them. For the moment, at least, they were safe.

The Doge commandeered the swiftest ship in the Rodesto harbor, manned it with his most experienced sailors, and ordered them to sail on the night wind to Constantinople. Then he, too, fell into the nightmare-ridden sleep that overcame all who had tasted death and yet escaped from it.

At dawn the seaward vigil began. Villehardouin paced the walls endlessly, exhorting his men not to lose heart. What they were waiting for no one knew. Reinforcements hastily crammed onto transports, or empty ships sailing to evacuate Rodesto and abandon yet another city to the Greeks? Over and over as the day wore on they tried to guess what strategy Conon of Béthune and Miles the Brabant would decide on. News of a disaster spreads swiftly. Perhaps at this very moment Henry of Flanders was skirting Adrianople to rush his army into Constantinople. He knew the country well. It was unthinkable that even Johanizza could entrap and ambush him. Already men were calling Henry the next Latin Emperor of Constantinople. He was, after all, their sole surviving prince. If Baldwin had not already been executed, he soon would be. They prayed that his death would be swift, painless and honorable, shuddering at the certainty that it would not. They crossed themselves and waited for sails to fill the horizon.

The first ship was sighted in late afternoon. It moved ponderously through the water, others lumbering behind, their decks silver and black with heavily armed men. A great shout went up from the walls, cries of welcome, paeans of thanksgiving. Rodesto was not to be abandoned after all! Gleefully Payen d'Orléans and Pierre of Bracieux clapped each other on the back. They would rescue Baldwin, or at the very least avenge him as no man had ever been avenged. Johanizza's Cumans would be swiftly dispatched to their heathen god, and as for the King of Bulgaria, they would drag him back to Constantinople's dungeons.

"My lord, it might be wiser if we did not anchor here. There will be accusations and recriminations that will anger our people once our destination is known."

"The wind has blown us to Rodesto without our desiring it," replied William of Béthune. "Our resolution was not shaken by the entreaties of Peter of Capua and Miles the Brabant and it will remain firm despite Villehardouin's oratory. God has a care even for the blind and foolish sheep of His flock. By His Will we are here and it must be that He commands us to disabuse these sorry survivors of Adrianople of their dreams of revenge and glory. We will put in, but only the commanders will disembark. Everyone else is to remain on board. We sail again at dawn tomorrow."

Villehardouin at first refused to believe what William was telling him.

"We are a company of seven thousand, my lord Marshal, knights, sergeants and pilgrims, and we are returning to our own lands. It is useless to argue the matter."

"But, William, you do not know what losses we suffered at Adrianople and by what mischance we were overcome," pleaded Villehardouin. "The Emperor was captured alive. With your seven thousand there is a chance that we might yet save him. Honor demands that we not abandon him."

William of Béthune cut him off sharply. It was not seemly that a man like the Marshal be reduced to begging. "We heard it all last night when Odo of Ham reached Constantinople, and again this morning before we sailed. Like you, we grieve for Baldwin and for those who died in the field, but we have served our honor and our duty these past years, and now that the time of our commitment is past, it is only just that we be allowed to go. Others may come in our place to hold this kingdom, but we are determined to leave it."

"If you will only allow me to go aboard your ships," Villehardouin went on stubbornly, "there may be some who will remain here once they know the full story."

"Geoffrey, it is useless to argue." William of Béthune had once been the Marshal's close friend and he sought now to speak as a friend. "For hours we delayed our sailing so that Conon, my kinsman, Miles the Brabant and the Pope's legate, Cardinal Peter of Capua, could speak to us. Each of the great lords in Constantinople had his say, each spoke to his own countrymen, yet not a single man could be persuaded to change his mind. There was great weeping and turmoil, but we stood fast. It is a scene I cannot allow to be repeated."

"There are Venetians amongst you, and the ships in which you sail are Venetian. You cannot refuse to allow the Doge to address his men."

"I will not," said the Doge suddenly. He had sat withdrawn and motionless until now, seemingly deaf as well as blind. "You Franks have never understood our Republic nor why my people are so united. They do not serve me, I serve them. Their term of service is over. They are free to leave, and honorably so. Some might remain out of love for me, but I cannot play on their emotions and remain true to the oath I swore to them and to God. I will do nothing to prevent their sailing."

The Doge had been his last hope. Villehardouin's face crumpled and tears of frustration stood in his eyes.

"Geoffrey, this much I can do for you," said William of Béthune, determined that his last sight of the Marshal should not be that of a man defeated and lost. "I myself will speak to all who sail with me. I will make it clear that no one is to be coerced, either to leave or to stay. And from my own purse I will refund the passage fee of any who desire to join you here. More I cannot do."

"When you speak, remind them of the dead who cry out for vengeance," replied Villehardouin hopefully. William, the advocate of Béthune, was an honest man. He knew that the case would be presented fairly and as well as he himself would have pleaded it.

"You will have our answer tomorrow morning."

"I shall pray that it be favorable to our cause."

"We are all in God's Hands, Geoffrey," William reminded him softly, "obedient to His Will."

Villehardouin did not reply.

William of Béthune kept his promise. He went from ship to ship throughout the night, and the speech he made aboard each of the vessels was as attentively listened to as any sermon. But though the crowds of knights and pilgrims remained awake, quietly discussing the tragedy that had befallen Baldwin and the others whom they had followed for so long, not a single man packed his gear and left the ship to which he was assigned.

William spoke last of all on the ship commanded by John of Virsin. After the last pilgrim's question had been answered, he gratefully accepted a cup of wine in the captain's quarters. With John of Virsin sat Peter of Frouville, who, without Villehardouin's knowledge, had left his quarters in Rodesto to secretly board the ship. Both men were liege men of the dead Count of Blois, but it was not of their lord nor of France that they were speaking.

"We were deceived from the beginning," Peter of Frouville

said. "And that old man, the Doge, had a hand in the deception. He, more than anyone else, knew that the Greeks cared not a fig for Prince Alexius and that they would never cease to war against us. Nor will they long support this Johanizza. They use the King of Bulgaria for their own ends while he in his pride believes he uses them."

"Our mistake was to believe that these people would thank us for delivering them from heresy and decadence," said John of Virsin thoughtfully. "Just as we have believed that the Kingdom of Jerusalem fell because its rulers were weak and had become nearly Saracen in their love of luxury."

"Who knows why?" said William. "I am tired and I no longer care."

Out on deck, Robert and Aleaumes stood at the rail, gazing at the dark bulk of Rodesto.

"It is strange," said Robert, "but even while I listened to Béthune I felt no temptation to remain here. My mind wandered so that I scarcely heard what he said. Yet not so long ago I was determined to find a castle of my own in this kingdom."

"You might have become a great lord, Robert, and I a bishop," said Aleaumes.

"When Anne died I seemed to come to myself again. It was as though I had been walking in a dreamworld for a very long time." Robert's voice was flat and toneless, but the bitterness and despair that had made him sicken and yearn for death were no longer part of him. Only Aleaumes had known Anne. Only to him would he ever speak of her at length.

"What will you do with the reliquaries, Robert?"

"They cannot be sold, nor could I have left them in Constantinople, knowing that the city might fall again. I shall give them to the monastery at Corbie."

"I'm glad," said Aleaumes quietly. "At Corbie I shall feast my eyes on them daily."

Robert only nodded his head, somehow not at all surprised at what Aleaumes was telling him. "Will your bishop give his consent?"

"With great alacrity, I should think," replied Aleaumes, chuckling. "He often said I was a disturbing influence among the other clerks. He will be glad to give my soul's welfare into the hands of an abbot."

"Will they allow you to make visits to Clari?" asked Robert.

"After my vows are pronounced," replied Aleaumes, "and when the abbot is sure I am firmly set in the mold. He could hardly refuse so reasonable a request from one who has given his monastery pieces of the True Cross."

"When I am ready I shall ask it of him."

"And what will you ask of me?"

"It is no secret that the Marshal of Champagne intends to write an account of this crusade."

"It will be biased. He will not be able to write otherwise."

"Why should our side of the story never be told?" asked Robert. "Why should our names go unrecorded? Thousands of us suffered and died, not for Jerusalem, as we had been promised, but so that barons and lords already powerful and wealthy beyond our dreams could grow still wealthier. Do you remember how I once assured our father that this crusade would be different? That this time jealousy and pride would not keep us from Jerusalem?"

"I remember. And I remember also that he smiled when you said it."

"He was right, though we did not believe him. We thought our leaders were better men, our cause a purer one, our powers of influence greater than his."

"Who will read your chronicle, Robert, after it is written? The monks would destroy it."

"I will hide it away. Perhaps in the chapel at Clari. When my son is a man I will reveal its location to him and he to his son. When times have changed, when we are all long dead, some future master of Clari may decide that the world is ready to accept the truth of this crusade. Perhaps it will lie there for all eternity. But at least I will have spoken, though none may ever listen."

The ships sailed at dawn. No Venetian came to say a last farewell to the Doge. No messenger was sent to Villehardouin. None was needed. In silence Rodesto watched the sails unfurl as the wind caught them, speeding the vessels across the blue sea to the countries the survivors of Adrianople would never see again. Long before the ships had disappeared over the horizon the men who remained in Rodesto had turned their proud backs on them.

AUTHOR'S NOTE

In writing this story of the Fourth Crusade I have relied most heavily on two eyewitness accounts dictated a few years after the fall of Constantinople in 1204. With the exception of Anne of Nanteuil and the Greek couple, Nicholas and Theodora Tripsychos, all the major characters in the novel, and many of the minor ones, were real people.

Geoffrey of Villehardouin, Marshal of Champagne, was one of the most influential leaders of the crusade, an able and seasoned diplomat whose active participation in all areas of decision making, from the earliest negotiations with the shipbuilders of Venice to the final choice of the first Latin Emperor of Constantinople, is well documented in his own words. Over and over again the army is diverted from its original goal, the recapture of Jerusalem from the infidels, because disloyal and self-serving men betray their vows to Christ. Each defection weakens the crusading force and deprives it of the revenue so desperately needed to pay for the fleet of ships that will carry them to the Holy Land. Lack of money is Villehardouin's original nightmare; compromise and delay are his remedies. Villehardouin did not return to Champagne and his family when the crusade was over. He remained in the East, probably dying at his castle of Messinopolis in 1213 after dictating his account of one of the most momentous events of his age. The story he tells is chiefly one of expediency.

Robert of Clari, surely one of the poorest knights to take the cross, did make the long journey back to his home in Picardy when his term of service ended in 1205. He gave certain holy relics to the monastery of Corbie, then presumably settled down again on his miserably few acres of land. Sometime in the next few years he, too, composed a history of the expedition. His accounts of the battles in which he fought are vivid, his descriptions of the marvels of the East compelling proof of his own

poverty, and the mass of inaccuracies through which he wades
when he tries to reconstruct an overview of the crusade tell us
quite forcefully that he, and indeed most of the men who made
up the lower ranks of the army, were largely ignorant of what
went on in the councils of the great. He set out to recount the
truth of the crusade as he knew it, but his viewpoint is not, and
could not possibly be, that of Villehardouin. Robert of Clari
names himself as the spokesman of the poor knights of the army,
and he is at his most eloquent when he finds the high lords he
and they served guilty of betrayal, treachery and greed. Villehardouin's chronicle was well known throughout the Middle
Ages; Robert of Clari's manuscript was virtually ignored until
the nineteenth century.

The question of the diversions to Zara and then to Constantinople have fascinated generations of historians. To whom
should the burden of primary guilt be assigned in each case?
How much of what happened was merely a series of logical responses to nearly impossible situations, and how much was due
to very careful manipulation behind the scenes? For the characters of Boniface of Montferrat, Philip of Swabia and Enrico
Dandolo, I have weighed the historical evidence, read between
the lines and given my own interpretation of their personalities
and motivations. Their conversations are fictional, their deeds
are not.

Since the focus of the novel is the army of Western Euro-
peans, I have occasionally chosen to portray the Byzantine characters largely through the crusaders' biased and usually inadequate understanding of them. The excellent chronicle of Nicetas
Choniates provides the modern student of history with the
Greek side of the story, but the Latins camped outside the walls
of Constantinople knew little of what was going on within. This
is particularly true as it concerns the murder of Alexius IV. The
crusaders considered Murtzuphles an arch-fiend, and in regard
to the emperor he replaced and ordered killed, I have perhaps
depicted him as such. Alexius *was* deposed and strangled, but
only after Murtzuphles was able to trick the Waring Guard into
leaving their posts, supposedly to defend the young emperor
against the mob of Greeks who were meeting openly in Santa
Sophia to elect a successor.

I have studied and consulted all relevant histories and chronicles of the period, both in French and in English, and for any reader curious to make the acquaintance of the historical Robert of Clari I would recommend the translation of his chronicle by Edgar Holmes McNeal, published in the Records of Civilization series by W. W. Norton & Company, Inc. The introductory material is particularly interesting. Villehardouin's chronicle, translated by Sir Frank Marzials, is available in the Everyman's Library published by Dutton. Both chronicles can be read in a single volume entitled *Historiens et Chroniqueurs du Moyen Age*, published by Librairie Gallimard, Bibliothèque de la Pléiade series.

Probably the most comprehensive account of the crusade is to be found in Ernle Bradford's immensely readable volume, *The Sundered Cross*, Prentice-Hall, Inc. (1967). Both the Greek and the Latin perspectives are fully explored, and the reconstructions of naval tactics, along with detailed descriptions of the Latin fleet and of the city of Constantinople, are masterful.

Finally, there is the problem of the hero of this book. When I began writing *The Seven Hills of Paradise*, I intended to tell the story of one man, Robert of Clari. I very quickly found that he could not exist in a comparative vacuum, and that in order to explain what happened to him I had to delve into the minds of many of the figures he mentions in his chronicle, whom he probably saw only from the far ranks of the battalion in which he served. As these individuals crowded into the narrative, each demanding his own chapter, each justifying himself, each clamoring to receive at least as much attention as the obscure knight none of them considered the slightest bit important, I found that no single person was as overwhelming as the fact of the event itself. They acted and reacted, plotted, schemed, betrayed one another and loudly proclaimed that each had held fast to ideals and vows that were pure and unsullied by thoughts of material gain. All of them lied, of course. They made history, but they were also pawns of the events they precipitated. All of them were caught up in a vast, sweeping historical pageant—only the crusade itself was larger than they—and if there is a central character to this book it must be the accumulation of beliefs and deeds that made them what they were, the hubris that drove them, and their denial that they were driven.

Constantinople was built on seven hills, as was Rome. At the height of its glory it was as fabled a city as its imperial predecessor. To men living in less sophisticated, less wealthy societies, it was as much a dreamworld as their hungriest conceptions of the heavenly Paradise toward which they strove. And as has happened to many another paradise that man has envisioned, it was very nearly destroyed by those who breached its walls.

HOLY ROMAN EMPIRE

KINGDOM OF GERMANY

DANUBE

RHINE

KINGDOM

Bruges
St. Pol
Béthune
Clari
Coucy-le-Château
Soissons
Amiens
Nanteuil
SEINE
Ecri
Neuilly-sur-Marne
Montmorency
Montfort
Bar-le-Duc
Friaise
Troyes
Brienne-le-
Château
Villehardouin
Montbeliard
Blois

KINGDOM
OF
FRANCE

LOIRE

RHÔNE

Milan

Montferrat

PO

VENICE
Venice

DALMATIA

Zara

ADRIATIC SEA

Ravenna

Pisa

STATES
OF THE
CHURCH

CORSICA

Rome

SARDINIA

Amalfi

KINGDOM OF THE
TWO SICILIES

Palermo

SICILY

MEDITERRANEAN

Tunis

DOMINIONS

N

OF

MALTA

THE

Tripoli

ALMOHADS

0   MILES   300

0   KM   300

palacios